THE GOOD GIRL AND THE BAD GUY

"You can't control who you want. It just happens." And didn't she know it? Her whole life, one hot, bad choice of man after another. But Aiden wasn't bad, not really, right? He helped people.

"Do you want me?" His gaze narrowed and she felt the moment stretch tight.

The air in her lungs turned to ice and her body went hot, then cold. Whatever she said, it was going to change things. He had to know she wanted him, but if she said no, would he respect that? Her gut said yes. Whoever Aiden DeHart was, she couldn't help believing he was different. Maybe not entirely good, but honorable. He'd respect her wishes if she said no, and once that barrier was in place, she didn't think it could be torn down.

"Yes," she said with a sigh.

"But you aren't happy about it."

"I promised myself I'd only date good guys from now on." She lifted her hand and traced a small scar on his jaw. It had grown faint with time, but this close, she could make it out. "You aren't a nice guy."

"Good and nice are two different things. I think you'd roll right over a nice guy."

"Maybe." She chuckled. Hadn't Lily said the same thing to her before?

His hand coasted up and down her thigh, but she felt the caress much higher up. The little orgasm, the taste of bliss he'd given her last night, it hadn't sated anything. It had just made her hu

DRIVE

SIDNEY
BRISTOL

ZEBRA BOOKS
KENSINGTON PUBLISHING CORP.
http://www.kensingtonbooks.com

ZEBRA BOOKS are published by

Kensington Publishing Corp.
119 West 40th Street
New York, NY 10018

First Printing: March 2016
ISBN-13: 978-1-4201-3921-1
ISBN-10: 1-4201-3921-5

eISBN-13: 978-1-4201-3922-8
eISBN-10: 1-4201-3922-3

10 9 8 7 6 5 4 3 2 1

Printed in the United States of America

To my very own crew for all their support:
Nicole, Mom, Dad, Shawn, Lea, Reb,
Sophia, Bambi, Rachel, Joe, Matt and all my Divas,
this journey would not have happened without you.

Chapter One

There was a good way to start a week, and there was a bad one. Aiden DeHart figured the jury was still out on this one.

"DeHart, microphones are live. Keep Ross near the car."

"It's a Chevelle, Kathy," he replied to the disembodied woman's voice only he could hear. He hated this, working with the FBI, but they had him by the balls.

"Yeah, whatever. Keep him near the Chevelle." Kathy chuckled.

Aiden tapped the steering wheel of his Chevrolet Chevelle and rolled his eyes at the FBI agent chirping more reminders in his ear. Kathy was a good agent, a little too motherly for his tastes, but a good woman.

He tuned her out and cleared his mind, inhaling the scent of the beach. The simple truth was that every word he said needed to be carefully chosen. Microphones were all over the damn car, which irritated the hell out of him that his classic restore was getting adhesive all over the leather. He wouldn't normally allow it, but if this job led to taking down Michael Evers, it was worth it. The son of a bitch had murdered Aiden's sister and her cop husband to make a point to the Miami-Dade

PD. His brother-in-law had been a good cop. A bit too good, unfortunately, and it had gotten both him and Andrea killed.

"DeHart, we're in place." CJ's voice echoed in Aiden's ear. Great, he had not one, but two Feds in his head.

CJ and his wife, Kathy, were FBI agents undercover in Aiden's garage, and often worked support for him and his crew. He hadn't known FBI agents could be married to another agent in the field, but he had the proof under his roof. Hell, there was likely some extensive study with all sorts of data to justify the work/wed arrangement. He could imagine CJ spouting said data as he got down on one knee. Kathy and CJ were a . . . unique couple. He overlooked their *uniqueness* because they knew their shit.

"Try not to break too many laws," CJ warned. They might be FBI, but the deep cover operation had them bending and breaking laws. Which was why it was Aiden doing this gig instead of his co-owner and best friend, Julian. While Julian was a full-fledged undercover FBI agent, Aiden was a contracted employee, or asset. He could break rules Julian couldn't, though that line had begun to blur as of late.

"No promises there. Going silent." Aiden sucked in a deep breath and blew it out.

It was time.

He emptied his mind of the two people on the other end of the radio, of all the little things he needed to do today and simply—let go. The road stretched out ahead of him, a path to anywhere.

He hit the accelerator and shifted gears. The old muscle car roared to life. He blazed down the well-kept street, mansions sprawling on either side of him. His awareness narrowed to the bend in the road ahead and the gate leading to their target's home.

The humid Miami air rushed through the windows, beating him in the face and carrying with it the cry of seagulls. The scents of freshly cut grass, salt water, and flowers drifted on the wind. Here, there was no Latino hip-hop music breaking up the pristine silence. It was all opulence and wealth.

The gate yawned open to his right. He grabbed the hand brake, turned the wheel, and let the Chevelle drift sideways through the space. The whole car vibrated, tires squealing with the maneuver. A security guard in the gatehouse dropped a magazine out of the window and yelled something, but Aiden was already through and accelerating up the drive. Palm trees lined the quarter mile to the two-story mansion. The drive circled around a fountain. Several sleek sports cars were parked around the bend, like some fancy magazine spread. Those cars might have the flash, but his Chevelle had double the horsepower.

Aiden brought the car around the fountain, breaking and letting the tail end swing around. It made for a jarring, flashy stop.

Flash was what he was going for.

"Fuck, Aiden. Did you have to burn so much rubber?" CJ whispered in his ear.

The agent was a stickler for following the rules, and one of their biggest ones was: stay under the radar. The Feds didn't want to have to cover up their shit if Aiden got in trouble, which was bound to happen on occasion. CJ had proven to be an invaluable member of their team. Between his experience in the field and his wife's quick thinking, they'd saved Aiden's ass more than a few times.

He snorted and climbed out of the car. A trio of men

in suits stood on the stairs leading to the grand double doors. It might have been impressive, except the whole community was one mansion trying to outdo its neighbors. At least a half dozen guys in suits hung around, hands poised on their barely concealed weapons. The whole setup was a little pretentious, but then again, men like Dustin Ross weren't exactly classy folk.

Two years ago, Dustin barely registered on the low-level crime scale. He'd climbed the ladder fast thanks to his greed, and he liked to show it off, unlike his boss, Michael Evers. What Dustin probably didn't know was that Evers ran through guys like Dustin every two years, using them up and spitting them out to save his own ass. Dustin was just the latest in a string of dummies stupid enough to get into bed with the Evers operation.

Aiden pushed his sunglasses up on his head and leaned against his car.

"Aiden DeHart." Dustin shook the hand of one of the men he was standing with before heading down the stairs toward him. "Wasn't expecting you so soon."

"I drive fast. You said you wanted to see me?"

"Yeah, why don't you show me what this baby can do?" Dustin didn't wait for permission. He climbed in the passenger side and settled in.

Well, that was easy.

"Sure. Whatever you say, boss." Aiden sank into the driver's seat while CJ snickered in his ear.

Aiden didn't punch it hard out of the driveway. He did want to hear what the other man had to say, after all. And they needed a clean recording. Dustin suggesting they leave his property—without security—confirmed Aiden's suspicions. Whatever this job was, Dustin didn't want his boss to know about it.

In the grand scheme of things, Michael Evers was the real target. Dustin was just a stepping-stone to taking down the criminal mastermind. Jobs like this should never be personal, and yet here he was. Driving an asshole around one of the ritziest areas of Miami, neither speaking. Which was fine with him. Conversation with Dustin was about as stimulating as watching oil drip out of a car. He took his time, winding through the houses, around the properties and eventually out onto the highway.

"How fast does she go?" Dustin asked.

"One-eighty if I've got the distance." The Chevelle wasn't a race car, though he liked its speed. It could perform, but he didn't like to push the car too much. It was a classic that deserved the respect of the road. He had a few newer, American muscle cars tricked out and outfitted for racing.

"Nice." He cleared his throat. "I really appreciate that job you did for me. The guys were right when they said you were the person to go to if I wanted something done quiet—and right." Dustin peered at him through tinted glasses. For someone with so much money, he still seemed sleazy. Maybe it was the off-the-rack suit with the Rolex watch and store-bought tan.

"Glad I could be of assistance," Aiden drawled. Thanks to a few dings on his record, the FBI had been able to embellish the truth a little. Between their additions and what came naturally due to racing, he had plenty of street cred and the experience to back it up. He doubted old Uncle Sam had intended him to put the skills he'd learned in the service to use chopping cars and pretending to be one of the bad guys.

"That street gang, they don't want to mess with us." Dustin acted like he were the one who'd chopped six cars of the rival gang.

"They're punks. Kids. They don't have any business

playing with the big boys. Just let them drive their toy cars in circles."

Dustin approaching Aiden out of the blue like that had shocked him and sent their entire operation into chaos. While they'd had their heads shoved up Evers's ass, Dustin had begun a little war with one of the street gangs. One Aiden knew all too well because he raced against them regularly.

The Eleventh Street Gang was a group of wannabe gangsters for the most part, except they were getting a handle on their criminal lifestyle and were no longer quite so wannabe. Under the leadership of a new crew leader named Raibel Canales, their drug trade was starting to compete with what Dustin had going on for Evers. Typically Aiden and his partner, Julian, opted out of jobs that touched their racing community, but they'd made an exception this one time. If the Eleventh knew they'd intentionally scrambled a drug deal it could make their street races dicey. Except chopping the cars had also meant sidelining several new, teenage members. Hopefully they got kicked out of the gang lifestyle before they'd begun. It was a long shot, but they'd taken the job.

"I bet you'd teach them a thing or two in this beauty." Dustin stroked the door as if he had any clue what was under the hood.

"If they had a brain cell between the lot of them, maybe."

Dustin laughed. "I like you. You sure you don't want to come work for me? I could make it worth your time."

"Sorry, man. I like being my own boss." Aiden would rather give up his left nut than work for Dustin. He eased off the accelerator and onto the service road. They wanted everything Dustin said on tape without the rustling of the wind. "You wanted to see me about a job? I take it this isn't about cars."

"Yeah. My ex-wife took some things that don't belong to her during our divorce proceedings. I want you to get them back." Dustin tapped the door and tipped his head back, the breeze rustling his hair.

That was it?

"This sounds like a job for the cops." He scowled, trying to remember who Dustin had been married to and when. It wasn't recent.

"Madison Ross," CJ said in a low-pitched voice the rumble of the car almost drowned out. "They've been split for almost three years, divorced for six months. Dustin hadn't been the faithful type. Madison's clean. Seems like he did stuff and kept her out of it. She's filed a restraining order on him, looks like he's sent people after her in the past and they haven't been too successful. She must have been a real slugger, used a baseball bat on one of his thugs. There's a note in her file from the PD that they've been putting pressure on her to turn witness, but she's pushed back, citing fear for her safety. From all the notes, I think either there's someone keeping a close eye on her, or she's got an admirer on the force. We'll check it out. Could be why they need you."

"I bet the detective's got a boner for her. I just found her online. She's a looker. Aiden's type." Kathy and her sleuthing. Between her and their resident geek, Emery, they could uncover anyone's secrets. Except Michael Evers's. He had someone on his side that covered the man's trail like a pro.

"I want the cops as far away from me as I can keep them. Got me?" Dustin turned toward him once more.

"Yeah, I got it. What are you looking for?" This might be an easier job than he anticipated.

"A box of stuff she took from my office. There's an external hard drive I particularly want back." The gig had to be more complex than that, but Dustin wasn't offering up more information.

Call him old-fashioned, but Aiden didn't like the idea of Dustin harassing a woman. He found it hard to believe Dustin's ex-wife would be a complete innocent. Something about the situation wasn't firing all cylinders. There was more to it.

"Aiden, we need him," Kathy whispered. It was as if the woman could hear his thoughts. He wouldn't put that beyond the Feds someday.

"I just want the hard drive," Dustin said. "It's about this big." Dustin held up his hands. Going by his estimates, the drive was about six-by-eight inches. "Gray. It has a label that says *Racing* on it."

How had Madison come by the drive? If it was so important, why had Dustin allowed her to snatch it? And how come he couldn't just get it himself? Who was stopping Dustin? All questions he couldn't ask. To Dustin, he was a resourceful street tough. That was it. Too much interest would show his hand.

"What about your ex?" Aiden gripped the steering wheel harder. If Dustin wanted her roughed up or made to disappear, perhaps Aiden could work with it. Makeup and Photoshop could do wonders in this day and age.

"I don't fucking care about that cunt. Get the drive any way you can, but don't mention me. That's why I'm hiring you. I'll take care of Madison in time. I've got her right where I want her."

Aiden's vision hazed red. Violence toward women was something he couldn't stand. Not even when he'd been deployed. There was a scar on his thigh from where a woman had attacked him. Julian had saved his ass that day.

He cleared his throat and banished the memories. "Sounds simple enough. Do you care how I get it?"

"Nope. I don't care. Just get the job done."

Aiden nodded, though he had no intention of that sort of ending. If Madison was living above the law, she would stay alive and breathing. If not, well, the Feds could be very useful motivators in times of need. He was proof of that.

"How much trouble can one woman be? I'll do a soft meet, something she won't see coming." He was spitballing a plan, hoping CJ and Kathy were already working on the bigger picture.

There were a few ways he could play the situation with this Madison, but he hadn't made up his mind yet which might yield her cooperation. He couldn't get a feel for what kind of woman would marry and stay with a crook like Dustin. He'd have to play this one off the cuff, and that was something he didn't like. After a couple years doing under-the-table deals for the FBI, he'd learned to have contingency plans for his contingency plan.

But first, he needed to get Dustin out of his car and find out a little about this Madison Ross.

Chapter Two

Madison gritted her teeth and forced herself to smile. She rolled past the line of bikers taking up the front row of Stoke's Bar & Grill, staring straight ahead. The latest pop-Latin mix hit played over the loudspeakers, the beat making her itch for some speed. The grill was a red, T-shaped building, with limited dining in the front and the kitchens in the back. Most people who came parked under the metal awnings to take advantage of the sound of the nearby surf and carhop atmosphere. Since old man Stoke was a biker himself, there was an area designated for motorcycles. The paint might have changed, and the building was different, but it was one of the few places that harkened back to Madison's high school days.

"*Oye mami,*" one of the bikers called. She blocked out his voice and clenched her fist.

If Stoke's didn't give so much money to her roller derby league in exchange for one night of carhopping, she'd never stand for the kind of lewd comments the rough motorcycle types liked to throw her way. Then again, she was skating around in crash pads, a black pleated miniskirt, and a bikini top with the league's alligator-on-roller-skates logo over each breast. She got better tips this way, and the league was hurting for cash this season.

"Hey." Lily, her best friend and teammate, screeched to a halt on her toe stops. Her frilly skirt flipped up, exposing her Talk Derby to Me booty shorts underneath. She probably meant to do that. Lily was a tease, but that was because she could afford to be one. With her Greek goddess looks, men were always interested in her curves. It was one reason why on the track she was known as A'thing'a Beauty.

"If those assholes touch me, I'm going to bash them over the head with a baseball bat."

"You say that every time we're here. Besides, your cop buddies wouldn't let that happen." Lily pivoted neatly and rolled with Madison toward the ticket window, wiggling her fingers at the cop car sitting in Madison's section.

"They're not my friends." She refused to look at the two off-duty patrol officers. They weren't bad people. Some of the cops Detective Matt Smith sent to "protect" her were even nice. But that was because they wanted something she couldn't give them. Evidence her ex-husband was a drug dealer.

"I've got a guy in my section, and he's been eyeing you since he got here. I swear he's got a thing for you. I think we should switch."

"What?" Madison almost tripped over the curb. Lily never gave up the section behind the grill. The concrete wasn't busted up and it made for good skating. Besides, the bikers didn't park back there.

"I tried flirting with him, but he didn't pay me any attention." Lily rolled her eyes. It was crazy to think a man wouldn't notice her. She was athletic and curvy, with perfectly sun-kissed olive skin, long, curling hair braided into pigtails, and her makeup never ran because of sweat.

"Who is he?" Madison peered toward the back lot, but had no idea which car was his.

"Orange muscle car, black stripes. Here. Take this to him." Lily handed her a banana split with two spoons. "Don't ask. Just go."

"No." Madison shook her head and pushed the frozen treat back at her. "I don't do bad-boy types. Not anymore, remember? If he doesn't have a pocket protector or a suit, I'm not interested."

Lily rolled her eyes. "Honey, have you looked in the mirror? You don't exactly scream 'nice guy material' anymore. Neither of us do. Besides, it's not like I'm telling you to go marry the guy, just flirt a little. You've got to learn how to do it again. Please?"

Madison glared at her. Roller derby had given her the kick in the pants to get her life together when she'd had nothing. But most of all, she'd found a family, something she hadn't had since high school, which was more depressing than she wanted to think about.

"Fine," Madison grumbled, and took the banana split back.

"Yay!" Lily gave Madison a little push and slapped her bottom.

She peered over her shoulder at her friend, nerves clamoring inside of her. Her? Flirt? She hadn't done that in ages. Wasn't even sure if she knew how to anymore. She'd have to trust that if she got into any kind of awkward exchange, she could count on one of the other derby girls to pull her ass out of the fire. That's what derby sisters were good for, right?

The orange muscle car sat under a long, tin awning, shielding it from the afternoon sun. She couldn't tell anything about the man sitting in the car except he had wide shoulders, the kind of big muscular arms she could dig her nails into.

Those thoughts needed to stop—right now. She hadn't had sex in ages and her hormones were in overdrive. At this point, she'd have fantasies about anything with a pulse. Which was probably why Lily was shoving her at this man, but was she ready? Were there rules for newly divorced women about when they could date? How was she supposed to act? Did she need to tell the guy up front?

"Right, because nothing is sexier than saying, 'Hi, my name is Madison and I'm newly divorced after being separated for three years,'" she muttered to herself. Then again, leading with *Hi, want to give my lady parts a tune-up?* probably wasn't a good idea either.

Time to put her customer service face on and stop thinking about s-e-x.

The driver slowly came into view, one delicious inch of muscular arm at a time until she could see the rest of him. He had one arm hanging out of the open window, with a black-and-gray tattoo peeking from under his shirtsleeve. He had short, sandy brown hair and a strong jaw with generous lips she wanted to see smile for some crazy reason. Sunglasses hid his eyes, but she felt them crawl over her body. Madison smiled at the man and felt her pulse in her throat. Why did she have the sudden urge to trace those inked lines with her tongue?

She'd become something of an ink addict since her divorce, as evidenced by the tattoos she'd accumulated in the last few years. One glance at her customer and she shivered despite the heat.

Hot wasn't a strong enough word for him. *Panty melting* might be more accurate. She was out of her league here. He'd chew her up and spit her inexperienced ass out. Lily could have this one all to herself.

Madison slowed to a stop, careful to not spill the quickly melting ice cream. "Hey, I've got one banana split for you."

His lips curled downward a bit. "I didn't order one."

That voice. It rumbled across her senses, straight to her core, setting off her internal alarms. *Danger!*

"Oh, you didn't? They told me to bring it out here."

Shit. Shit. Shit. This is all Lily's fault!

"Give it here." He gestured for her to bring the ice cream closer while he dug in his pocket. "Two spoons, huh?"

"That's what they gave me." She shrugged and handed it over.

Madison hadn't even noticed the plastic silverware stuck neatly in the sides. Now, if he would just take it so she could skate her happy ass away, she wouldn't complain about the bikers for the rest of the afternoon. She could only assume he was studying her. His gaze was hidden, but she felt it drift across her shoulders, down her breasts and stomach to her legs. She'd toss on a shirt, too, no matter that it was ungodly hot. She was not ready for this kind of attention, even if her body screamed something else.

"You look like you could use a cooldown." He pulled his sunglasses off and she nearly stopped breathing. He had the bluest eyes she'd ever seen. Like the sky on a clear day, or the bluest of ocean lagoons. "Want some?"

Nope. Nothing from you.

"It looks really good." He spooned a bite of the slow-churned vanilla into his mouth. The way his lips wrapped around the spoon was completely fascinating. Where had he learned that? "There's plenty for two."

"Uh, sure." Was that breathy voice really her?

He offered her a spoon and held the treat for her to scoop some. Stoke's might be known for their beer-battered fries, but they made a mean homemade ice cream. It was one of their better-kept secrets. She greedily dipped her bite into the fudge, making sure it was dripping with chocolate.

"You want to sit down?" He gestured to the passenger side of his car.

She froze with the spoon halfway to her mouth. Attractive man, tinted windows, sitting here watching her and now he wanted her to have a seat in his car. *Shit, fuck and damn it.* Why hadn't she seen it before? Hot guys in cool cars didn't pick girls up like this, did they? Not when your last name used to be Ross. All the desire burning in her breast went out in one *poof* of nonexistent smoke. This had to tie back to Dustin.

Madison jabbed the spoon back in the dish and placed her hands on her hips, glaring at Mr. I-Melt-Panties-For-A-Living. How dare he take advantage of her self-imposed celibacy with his hotness? It just wasn't fair.

"Why are you here? And don't tell me it's for the beer fries." She glanced toward the patrol car but—*Shit!*—the cops were gone. Could she get the attention of one of the girls in time? What if he grabbed her and drove off?

He blinked slowly at her, completely unfazed by her question. She clenched her hands to keep from trembling. Once, she wouldn't have recognized the dark edge behind his gaze but she'd learned to identify it.

When would it end? Leaving Dustin was the easy part. She'd opened the front door and walked out. Untangling her life from his was a process of years. If she could go back in time and tell her eighteen-year-old self anything, it would be to never, ever accept Dustin's marriage proposal. He wouldn't give her the white picket fence or the family of her dreams. Dustin ruined everything around him, and he'd destroyed her hopes of happiness.

"Well, this isn't how I saw this going." The man placed the dish on his dash and pushed the driver's side door open. He stood and kept going up. Even with her skates on, giving her a good five extra inches, he was still taller than her. She was not about to let him intimidate her. This was a public place. She was safe, right?

"Really? You thought I'd get in the car and you could drive off with me inside? Then what? You want to knock me around a little, too? Maybe rape me?" God, she was so stupid. An attractive face, some fluttering nerves and she'd let herself be blinded.

"Wow. Wow. Wow." He held up his hands, eyes wide. "Slow down there."

"What does Dustin want now?" She wished she still had the ice cream in her hand. She'd make him wear it.

"Madison, right?" He extended his hand. "I'm Aiden. Hi."

She glanced from his face to his hand and back. Yeah, fat chance she'd willingly touch him. She'd rather have rink rash.

"Okay, no handshake. That's all right." He leaned against the door, all casual and at ease. "I can appreciate cutting straight to the chase. So, look. Dustin says you have something he wants and he's hired me to get it for him."

"Fuck off." She plated her toe stop on the ground and pushed off—except he grabbed her by the wrist, stopping her in her tracks. A jolt of—something—shot up her arm. Her skin tingled where they touched, completely robbing her of thought.

"Hold on there. Can we please have a rational discussion?" he said next to her ear. His breath skated over her neck and she shivered.

She gathered enough pieces of her mind to glare over her shoulder at him and twist her arm out of his grasp. He caught her by the shoulders instead and pulled her back against the hard wall of his chest. Her breath left her lungs, and the last bit of rational thought fled.

"I don't want to help Dustin," he said.

"W-what?" She spun and went up on her toe stops to keep from drifting while she gaped at the man. Had she heard him right? Was her brain that scrambled that she was putting words in his mouth?

"Now, will you please have a seat and eat the sundae with me?" Aiden reached through the open window and pulled the keys out of the ignition. She stared at the ring of keys he extended toward her. "We won't go anywhere. I'll even give you these, how about that?"

The first time Dustin had sent someone after her, she'd broken a broom over the guy's head on the deck of her boat. After she'd finished freaking out she'd realized just how much danger she was in, but she was done letting Dustin boss her around. The second time he sent someone to talk to her, she'd been smart enough to have a baseball bat with her at work, of all places. She'd never anticipated needing to protect herself at a derby event, but Dustin was always finding new lows to sink to. Couldn't Dustin let her go? It wasn't as if the creep had ever loved her.

"I'm serious, Madison. I don't want to help Dustin," Aiden said again.

He was different than the other toughs Dustin had sent after her. They hadn't been much for talk. Besides, Aiden was trying to give her the keys to his car, his body language was nonthreatening and they were in the middle of a crowded parking lot. It wasn't exactly the seat of danger. Perhaps she needed to hear him out so she had a better handle on what she was dealing with.

God, what was wrong with her? She wanted to trust him.

If they were going to talk, it needed to be here. It was a public place, with plenty of witnesses and if things went really bad, she had the derby girls and the Stoke's staff to back her up. It was the best possible way for this to go down.

"I'm only talking to you for a minute, okay?" She snatched the keys, threaded them through her fingers into a makeshift weapon, careful to not touch him.

"Okay. Deal." He smiled at her, which was so out of character for one of Dustin's thugs. It was even kind of cute. He had an almost-dimple on his left cheek that gave him a sort of sweet, lopsided look.

Clearly he had supernatural powers, or she was just that man-starved.

She would stay on her side of the car. She would not agree to anything. And if he made one wrong move, she'd scream to high heaven and throw herself out of the car. She was wearing a helmet, after all. It couldn't be much worse than taking a tumble on the track.

They got in the car, tension stretching tight between them. She twisted to face him, but he appeared more interested in the sundae than her, and for some reason that irritated her even more. He took a bite and offered the rest to her.

"What do you want to talk about?" she asked.

"I want to double-cross your ex."

She glanced around. Was there a camera crew hiding around here? Someone was about to jump out and say she'd been punk'd. Lily had to be in on it, except she had no love for Dustin, either.

"I'm sorry. Can you try that again, please?"

"Dustin works for a man I have issues with. A man I'd like to see bad things happen to, but he's too well protected for me to do anything about it. Now, Dustin wants this hard drive from you because it's important to him and he clearly does not want his boss to know he doesn't have it. I'd like to take this hard drive off your hands and use it as leverage to make Dustin go away and possibly put his boss behind bars."

This was crazy. Bat-shit crazy. Like, bad movie crazy.

"I don't have this hard drive," she blurted. Yes, she did, and now someone else wanted it? Well hell. Another thing she'd tell a younger her—never take anything of Dustin's out of spite. She'd thought she was grabbing a box of crap, and instead, she was sitting on a ticking time bomb. She couldn't give it back to Dustin, not with the cops breathing down her neck. Letting the cops have it was out of the question. Once they had it, Dustin would know and she'd be dead. Her best bet was stashing it far, far away.

"Are you sure?"

She shifted in her seat. The man had the steady stare down to an art, and damn it if her thoughts didn't stray. God, she needed to get laid, by someone safe, sane, and nice, which meant Aiden was not a candidate.

"Think about it—"

"How do I know I can trust you?" Madison knew she was in over her head. She needed help in a bad way. The cops couldn't save her. Maybe a bad boy in a hot car could?

"You don't. That's what trust is, blind faith." He leaned toward her, his gaze heavy-lidded and sensual. He was a bad boy, through and through. It practically oozed off him, and Madison had always had a weakness for the bad boys. But there was something different about him, too. He wasn't Dustin's kind of bad. So what other kinds of bad were there? She'd been good for so long, she didn't know.

She put her back against the car door, smoothing her

hands over her thighs and wiping off the dampness. The man was already giving her sweaty palms! It wasn't fair. He'd taken her by surprise, deflating her confidence and knocking her off her stride. No more. She'd never again let a man get the best of her. But maybe he could help her. She didn't need a white knight, just someone to help her out of a jam.

Madison sucked in a deep breath and gave herself a mental shake. "If I do this for you, what do I get?"

If she'd learned one thing from Dustin, it had been that nothing is free.

"You?" He laughed. "I'm doing you a favor by eliminating this pain in your ass."

Damn him, he was right, but she couldn't let him know that.

"Ah, but I'd be helping you by giving you what you needed."

"Sugar, this isn't the only way to get what I want, but it is the more enjoyable and mutually profitable option." His voice rolled over her skin with sensual appeal.

No, she would not entertain erotic fantasies about a man who was essentially trying to blackmail her. She liked good guys. With jobs and bank accounts under their real names. The kinds of guys who had 401(k)'s and retirement plans.

He leaned in closer, until she could make out the odd, snowflake pattern of blues in his eyes and smell the sundae on his breath.

A mental image unfolded of their bodies entwined, panting for breath, covered in sweat as he rocked into her. Desire burned in her veins, hot and insistent. She'd been with the bad boys, and look where it had gotten her—living on a boat, forced to work the only job she could get just to scrape enough together for night classes.

He said he was doing her a favor. She frowned, liking this even less. "You think I'd owe you something for this. . . ."

"Not that kind of favor." His lips twitched with amusement. He produced a white square of paper and handed it to her. "This is a number you can reach me at. Someone will always answer it. You need anything, Dustin so much as breathes in your direction, let me know. Think about it." He stared into her eyes for a moment, robbing her of the ability to breathe.

"And if I say no?"

He shrugged. "I'll have to cross that bridge later."

"I'll think about it." She took the card and opened her door, nearly tripping over her skates to get away from him.

"I'll be in touch, Madison Ross."

That was it? He walked into her life, threw it into disarray and wanted to leave?

"It's Madison Haughton now. I divorced that asshole." She slammed the door with more force than was necessary and tossed the keys through the window.

Aiden caught the keys and grinned at her. He slid his sunglasses back on.

"I like the sound of that. Madison Haughton."

He wanted to play this game with her? Well, she'd learned a thing or two from her sleazeball ex-husband. And the first thing was to never accept help from a stranger.

Chapter Three

Madison pulled her helmet off and stared at the facade of Classic Rides. She couldn't count the number of times she'd driven past the shop, eyeing the row of rebuilt, restored, or refurbished classic cars in front. She would forever be a fan of the retro, rockabilly style. It embodied everything she'd grown up wanting.

She let the motorcycle helmet rest on the swell in front of her seat. Both the body of her motorcycle and helmet had been painted by one of the roller derby league's referees, so they sported a uniform green-flame pattern. It made the bike easy to pick out and hard to steal. But it also made her conspicuous, something her cop shadow must love. Thankfully she'd ditched them by parking behind the rink and cutting across an empty lot to a side street. By her estimation she had maybe an hour before Detective Smith tried to find her. The trade-off was that if one of her ex's goons wanted to find her, she was a lot more vulnerable without the badges backing her up.

The sun crawled toward the horizon, painting the sky with brilliant shades of orange, yellow, pink, and purple. A picture-perfect Florida snapshot. She couldn't enjoy the riot of colors, not with some guy stalking her, or whatever this Aiden DeHart was doing. It was hard to believe he wanted to help her double-cross her ex-husband. Hell, she didn't want anything to do with Dustin. The less involvement she had, the better chances she'd survive the year and after that, another year. Small goals, but it meant she kept breathing.

A simple solution was to leave Florida altogether. Except it was the last thing she hadn't given up. Maybe it was silly to hold on to the idea of living in the city she'd grown up in, but it was all she had left. Which was why she was here. She'd stuck her head in the sand for far too long. Not anymore. If Aiden stood any chance at all of getting Dustin out of her life, she needed to hear him out.

The idea of meeting Aiden again had her stomach clenching. She didn't know if she should be afraid of the man or not. Those eyes, his body, that car—it was the kind of bad-boy siren's call that turned off her better judgment. Which was exactly why she was here when the shop was closed and everyone was gone. She was not looking to run into Aiden, she just wanted to learn a little more about him. She'd passed it at least a hundred times on her way to derby practice.

She swung her leg off her Honda Rebel and frowned. The lights were off, there was a chain corralling the cars out front, the bay doors were shut, and yet the low gate wasn't barring entry to the parking lot.

Maybe someone had forgotten to close it? That was stupid. Someone could cut the chains, bust some windows, and be gone with all those pretty cars. But, that wasn't her problem. She just wanted to look around. If this man was going to follow her, confront her while she was doing a fund-raiser, well, she wanted to know more about him. The Internet hadn't told her anything, except he was a co-owner of the garage and involved in a wreck some years ago. That was it. No one could have that little of an online footprint. These days people had a Facebook profile for their dog and a Twitter account for their cat. So who was Aiden?

The hours on the front window said they were open until seven, and it was edging past eight. The neon signs in the windows of the businesses up and down the street lit up the night and somewhere nearby a band played a salsa tune. She cupped her hands around her face and peered into the darkened interior. She could make out a counter, a rack of shirts, and some other displays that meant nothing to her—but no people.

What kind of a business were they running here? Henchmen "R" Us? What would make a businessman turn hired muscle? She'd glimpsed enough of Dustin's so-called work to know the type, and Aiden was not the type to be hired out by anyone. He was something else entirely.

"Can I help you?" a voice said behind her.

Madison spun around. What she wouldn't give for her baseball bat right now! She had pepper spray attached to her keys, but for some reason the bat made her feel safer. The way Aiden stared at her, assessing and weighing her presence, she could have been one of his cars. Well, if he wanted a look under her hood it wasn't happening.

He'd showered. She could smell the scent of his soap. He'd changed into a black button-down shirt with LUCKY 13 stitched onto the shoulders in white thread, the sleeves cuffed around his biceps.

"Shit, you scared me." Madison took one step back and her calf hit the outcrop of rock below the window. Aiden was maybe two feet away from her. Where the hell had he come from?

One brow arched and he tilted his head to the side. His gaze traversed her body without a care if she noticed or not. Her nipples tightened and she balled her hands into fists. No, she would not have a "thing" for the man who wanted to manipulate her. She was going to date nice, rule-following types from now on.

"What are you doing here, Madison?" The way he rumbled her name, deep and low in his chest, revved something inside of her.

She licked her lips. This was about being free from Dustin and all the crap he slung her way. For better or worse, Aiden was linked with her ex.

"I, uh, thought we should talk more." Maybe she could get him to talk his way into the truth. "You surprised me earlier. I didn't know what to say or think."

The muscles in his jaw jumped. Did he believe her? She didn't believe herself.

"Look, I just want Dustin to go away, so whatever it takes to make that happen, I want to do it." Preferably her ex-husband would end up handcuffed and in jail, but she doubted that. He'd acquired a new boss since they separated.

"Really?"

"Yeah."

"What changed your mind? You didn't seem that interested earlier."

She pushed her shoulders back. "I'm not saying I'm interested. I'm willing to hear you out. It's not like we had a whole lot of time to talk this afternoon. Like, how exactly did you come to work for Dustin?" Anyone who worked for her ex-husband wasn't a person she wanted in her life, that was for sure.

You listening down there?

Now if she could just get her libido to fall in line.

"We don't talk about that here," Aiden replied.

"Then where do we talk about it?"

"Not here."

"What the fuck is that supposed to mean?"

"You've got a mouth on you."

She stared at him, but couldn't figure him out. What did he want?

He glanced over his shoulder, but there wasn't another soul on the lot or the street in that moment, and she'd given her cop shadow the slip.

"Why the hell do you care?" Madison had always had her daddy's knack with language. It was one of the only things the old sailor had left her with before he split.

"Never said I did."

They were talking in circles. She wasn't getting anywhere with him.

"Got plans?" he asked.

"Uh . . ." She should have been at roller derby practice half an hour ago, but this was more important.

He took a step toward her, invading her space even more. He reached out his hand and plucked a leaf from her hair, holding it out so she could see it before tossing it on the ground. "Are you doing anything right now besides holding me up?"

She licked her lips and blinked at him. "Not right now."

Aiden might be a crook and a criminal—which went against everything she'd promised herself she'd stay away from—but she needed Dustin out of her life so she could really move on.

"I'm curious about something."

"Curiosity killed the cat, you know." Right. She needed to not reply in movie quotes.

"Wouldn't it be a lot safer for you to give the drive back to Dustin?"

"Yes. Yes it would be."

"So you have it."

"I didn't say that."

"You have it. So why haven't you given it to him?" He crossed his arms, which just made his biceps bulge.

Madison sighed. "It's complicated."

"I'm a smart guy."

She studied him for a moment. Did she trust him? Could she? Madison didn't know how much longer she could hold out. "I have it, but the cops and Dustin want it. No matter who I give it to, someone will want me dead or behind bars. I don't like either of those options. I'm not stupid, but that's what people like to believe. Appearances work in my favor."

"What's that supposed to mean?"

"I mean, when people see a tattooed girl like me, they make assumptions. I just let them believe whatever they want to."

"Where is the drive?"

She bit her lip. Could she trust him? Her gut said yes, but then again her gut had also said yes to marrying Dustin—the biggest fuck-up of her life.

"Somewhere," she replied.

Aiden sighed. "You aren't going to tell me?"

"I can't. I hid it from myself."

"Can you get it back?"

"Maybe. If I think it's the smart thing to do."

"If you aren't going to trust me, why are you here?" He spread his arms a little and glanced around at his domain.

"Because . . . because I'm between a rock and a hard place. I want Dustin out of my life, but he's convinced I'm trying to steal from him. Then there's the cops who have me over a barrel. I have to sneak out of my own house just to get a little privacy. And now there's you.

You say you don't want to help Dustin." She shrugged. "So maybe you'll help me."

She tipped her chin up, refusing to be ashamed of her past. Dustin's sins were not hers. When she'd left Dustin, she'd promised herself she'd follow the letter of the law. All the rules. So far, all it had gotten her was a burned car, all her cash stolen, a collection of bruises, and a charge for assault for protecting herself after her ex sent thugs after her.

The cops wanted her to spill the beans on Dustin, except there wasn't anything to spill. Their tactics of refusing help were forcing her into this. Into making a deal with someone who might be as much of a crook as Dustin. But did she have any choice? No.

"I'm between a rock and a hard place here," she said again. She couldn't hold his steady gaze, so she glanced over his shoulder to where her Honda Rebel sat just inside the fence of Classic Rides.

Aiden let out a bark of laughter. "You have no idea."

"Thanks for rubbing it in." She glared at him.

"Why does he hate you so much?"

The question sliced her deeper than she would like to admit. She sucked in a deep breath, hating the pang of hurt in her chest. "Lots of reasons. We were never good together once I grew up a little and remembered I had a spine."

Aiden nodded. One sentence couldn't encompass just how wrong their marriage had been. Looking back, Madison suspected Dustin wanted her to grow into the role of his accomplice, and she'd pushed back. She might have stuck her head in the sand, but deep down she'd known he was bad and giving in to him once meant a lifetime of regret. So she'd played the role of a rich housewife instead. It was safer.

"Come on. We can talk more in the car on our way."

He grabbed her hand and her mouth went dry. He tugged on her arm, and she followed to keep from face-planting on the concrete. Aiden led her around the building to where a tricked-out Dodge Challenger sat idling. The white exterior with the royal-blue racing stripes was cast into shadow by the crazy blue running lights under the car. The headlights shone a dim, lime green, making it look like some alien contraption had just landed.

Aiden opened the door for her.

Her rational mind screamed, *No!*

While everything else purred, *Hell yeah.*

She needed to figure out what his angle was on all of this. He couldn't get away from her in the car, so he'd have to listen. On the other hand, she was at his mercy. She gripped the pepper spray for comfort. If he did anything she didn't like, she'd use it on him.

Aiden leaned on the door, but didn't let go of her hand. She turned to peer up at him. What would he do now?

"Madison?"

"What?"

"You will always be safe with me."

She blinked at him, taking a moment to process his words. Safe? With a bad boy? What kind of line was he feeding her? And yet, her knees were a little weak, her heart doing crazy laps around her chest. Men were trouble, but she wanted to believe that somewhere out there was the kind of man who would say those words to her and mean them.

"You'll have to prove it," she replied.

He chuckled and grasped her chin with his other hand. He filled her vision, lowering his face to hers.

"That sounds like a dare." He pitched his voice low.

"A smart man would realize it was." *Oh my God, shut up!*

There was a very good reason she never, ever took out her mouth guard when she was at a bout. Her mouth just skated away from her.

He slid his hand up to cup her cheek, rubbing the calluses across her skin. Their faces were inches apart. She could smell mint on his breath, the fragrance of his soap wrapped around her senses, and her head swam.

He was going to kiss her.

She shouldn't want him to. He was possibly out to blackmail her, screw her ex-husband, and create a world of problems for her. But maybe, just maybe, she could trust him?

Her brain and libido were butting heads for sure.

"Get in the car now or I'm leaving you here." His voice was barely above a whisper.

"Let go of my hand and I will."

He uncurled his fingers from hers though he didn't give her any space.

Was this a smart idea?

Probably not, but she was here.

Madison lowered herself into the seat while Aiden circled the car to the driver's seat. She'd never seen a car like this one. The dash was—well, she didn't think it rolled out of the factory with all those switches and buttons. There was a silver tank bolted to her floorboard. A hose ran out of the top and into the dash. She eyed the G-Force shoulder straps and reinforced seat belt. Even the seat had been upgraded to something that looked more like a fighter pilot's wraparound padded seat.

She fastened the seat belt and glanced at her driver to find him staring at her. Why did she feel as if she were the bug trapped in the spider's web?

"Last chance to leave." He leaned an elbow on the center console.

"Thanks for the warning." She placed her elbow next to his. "I want answers."

Aiden's gaze narrowed and she swallowed hard. "You like to play with fire, don't you?"

"Sometimes."

"I see." His gaze dropped to her mouth and the muscles around her ribs constricted, making breathing difficult. "Is that what happened with Dustin?"

It was amazing what Dustin's name could accomplish. One moment, Madison was concerned about the state of her panties and how damp they were getting, the next her whole body went numb. She straightened and shrugged.

"A lot of things happened with Dustin."

"Sorry." Aiden shifted in his seat, but his gaze never left her. "I didn't mean to bring up bad memories."

"Everything to do with Dustin is bad. The cops are gunning for him."

Aiden shook his head. "Dustin's a slippery son of a bitch. We play this my way . . . and I can make sure he won't be able to hurt you again." His hand closed over her knee. "Can you trust me?"

The million-dollar question. "I don't know you."

"And you still got in my car?"

"Yeah, well, I don't have the greatest history with rational decisions." *Thanks for the reminder.* She reached for the catch on her seat belt. *Yeah. This is a bad, bad idea.*

He stilled her hands. "Wait. Just—hang with me. I meant what I said, Madison. I will stop him."

God, her ability to gauge people had to be all kinds of screwed up, because she believed him. She shouldn't, but she did. He eased back into his seat and buckled in when she made no further move to escape.

"Do me a favor and don't step on that tank, will ya? I'd rather not get plastered all over the seawall tonight."

He flashed her a smile one second, that funny little dimple winking at her, and the next, the force of the acceleration pushed her back into the padded seat and she scrambled to hold on to the oh-shit handle above her head.

He took the turn out of the lot so fast the tires squealed and she could smell burning rubber. Her heart raced and she sucked down deep breaths of air, perfumed by the smell of man and car exhaust.

"Wait, what about my bike?" The Rebel was her only mode of transportation. How the hell could she have forgotten about it?

"We'll lock the gate. Don't worry. No one will mess with it here."

Why? Either he was the baddest badass on the block or he'd discovered a new lowlife repellant she'd never heard about. Chances were, it was the first. Just her luck.

He let the car roll forward and they passed through the fence surrounding the shop before he shifted into park.

"Be right back."

She twisted in her seat to watch Aiden stretch a metal chain across the drive and lock it. That wouldn't keep out someone wanting to steal a motorcycle.

He crossed to her bike and stood back for a moment. She shifted in her seat, waiting for some reaction. It wasn't the most amazing bike in the world, but it was hers and she loved it. Between that and her boat, they were pretty much the sum of her worldly possessions.

Aiden flipped the kickstand up and rolled the bike toward the garage and around the corner where he'd had his car parked. She could just make out a chain-link enclosure attached to the garage. He unlocked the gate and stashed it there.

She shouldn't feel grateful that he'd just taken her only ride hostage, but she did. It was twisted, but she appreciated the gesture.

Madison straightened in her seat and sighed once more. This was the right decision, wasn't it?

Aiden opened the driver's-side door and a wave of hot air rolled over her. He sank into his seat and strapped in.

"Ready?" he asked.

"For what?"

He flashed her a grin. "Hold on."

The engine revved and he shifted. The car shot forward onto the empty street. She yelped and grabbed hold of the door and center console.

Holy shit—I think I left my bladder back there.

"Don't hold on to that, you'll jack with the NOS." He brushed his fingers over her knuckles, where she gripped the console. She shivered in her seat, the vibrations of the acceleration reaching deep into her body, shutting off her mind.

She hadn't even taken in the myriad of buttons and switches that decorated the panel between them. One glance down and she realized she wasn't holding on to the console at all. Her hand was wrapped around a red metal handle attached to a tank under the armrest. She was quickly learning that nothing in this car was stock, just like the man behind the wheel.

Chapter Four

What was he doing?

Aiden downshifted into a lower gear as they reached a busier street. Madison's knuckles were white where she gripped the car. He could hear her panting for breath over the purr of the engine and it set his teeth on edge.

He should have sent her on her way, but he hadn't been able to. The way her eyes had pleaded with him, the desperation.

He'd bet his Challenger she was innocent.

And he didn't harm innocents. There weren't a lot of limits left to him, but that was one.

There was still a chance this whole thing could be a setup. Madison could be playing him. This whole divorce might be a ruse. But if it were, they had even the police fooled. No, Madison's story was at least partly truthful. She was Dustin's ex, but she might also be the key to learning how to pry open the inner ranks of Michael Evers's organization.

That didn't answer why he had Madison in his car, or why he pushed the Challenger in turns or zipped through traffic. This kind of driving was asking for trouble, but the way her breathing hitched, how she squeaked when he cut it close passing another car or skidded around a turn—it only encouraged him. By the time he reached the highway and headed toward the night's meet-up, the pitch of her noises had changed, dropping an octave. Yeah, fast cars had that kind of effect on some people.

"How exactly did you go from being a housewife to a roller derby girl?" She baited his curiosity like few things did these days unless it was connected to Evers. His life was one, sad refrain—catch the bastard.

Madison chuckled. "Wish fulfillment. In high school I wanted the family I didn't have. When I got divorced, I wanted to be the kind of woman who didn't let life keep her down. Want to take a bet on what I do next?"

Her humor surprised a laugh out of him. She was an interesting woman, that was for sure.

It wasn't long before the lights of Miami faded behind them and the Everglades stretched out on either side. For the couple miles it took to reach the race site, he could pretend he wasn't doing a job. That he was just a guy, driving a fast car with a pretty girl by his side. It was a nice dream, but it wasn't for him.

He exited onto a two-lane road that seemed to go nowhere. Unless you knew where you were going. He took a turn and taillights lit up the darkness. Other speed junkies on the search for a fix.

They'd created a loose association of drivers. Those people in Miami who felt they had what it took under the hood to go fast and drive hard met up for a little friendly competition. At least they pretended it was friendly.

He passed a four-way stop, rounded another turn, and the night came alive with headlights, running lights, and the beat of a dozen different sound systems blaring music. There were a couple of groups dancing, some popping and grinding while others pulled out the smooth, salsa moves. People milled up and down the street, taking a look under the hood of some of the most jacked-up cars in the state.

"What's this?" Madison asked. They passed the outlying vehicles, the people lined up to watch the beginning of the race.

"This is race night." He revved the engine and chuckled when she jumped.

"Okay, smart-ass, I can kind of figure that one out on my own. I mean,"—she waved at the crowds gathering on the shoulder, the people set up for a show and the cars—"is this a thing? What's going on?"

She had no idea the world she'd just stepped into.

"Every couple of weeks we have race night. Rules are simple—you have to have won a race since the last race night and someone has to verify you won. We pick a place, set the track, and see who wins. Simple, really."

A redheaded woman stepped onto the asphalt directly in front of them. She wore a tiny pair of white shorts and a bikini top. She wiggled her fingers at him and smirked.

Roni was a damn fine driver, but you wouldn't know it looking at her. She preferred to distract with her looks, as much as her twin, Tori, preferred to hide them under grease. Another of the guys pulled a few chairs out of the way and Aiden reversed into the vacant spot.

"Who's that?" Madison asked. Her posture had gone tense, rigid.

"A friend," he replied.

He gave the accelerator one last tap to hear the purr before shutting it off. Too bad he'd been too wrapped up with a restoration job the last few weeks to make any of the propositioned races. It would have been interesting to see how Madison reacted when he burned over the finish line. Some women really got into it. Was she the type? He kind of wanted to find out.

Since meeting her that afternoon, he'd rolled around a few ways to tackle this situation. He felt pretty certain coming clean with her was the best choice. The question now was how to continue. There was no denying his attraction to her. He could play that angle, which would be a perfect explanation to Dustin why he was hanging out with his ex-wife.

Aiden stepped out of the Challenger. The damp evening air wrapped around him like a blanket. This far out into the Everglades they might as well be swimming. Without the noise of the cars, they could hear the buzz of cicadas and calls of the birds that lived in the wetlands. It was a beautiful and deadly habitat.

Madison circled the car and met him at the edge of the road. He could feel the gaze of not just his crew on him, but everyone surrounding them. There was no doubt that when Aiden or Julian did something, people paid attention, but this was a little much. He let his gaze travel over those gathered, taking in the position of the major players, the sideline jockeys, the outright gang members, and the other crews who just wanted to drive fast and score quick cash.

Why the hell were they staring?

He turned toward Madison—oh.

Standing in front of his Challenger, dressed like she'd just stepped off the pages of a hot-rod magazine, of course she'd draw the eyes of everyone in a quarter-mile radius. Those long legs were silhouetted by the running lights of his car and the thin fabric of her shirt was practically see-through.

"Come here." He grabbed her arm and pulled her out of the light.

"What? What's wrong with you?" Madison grumbled.

He didn't reply, because what was he going to say? *I don't want everyone looking at you like that.*

"Hey, *mami,*" Julian said. He stopped between them and peered down at Madison. Julian was a big man, of mixed Cuban and Mexican heritage. His face was scarred from an IED explosion and more than a couple fights. He still kept his hair military short, which only accentuated the broken lines of his face and his dark, soulless eyes. Julian was a man with a singular purpose in life. Little else filled him now. He was hardly the same man Aiden remembered from boot camp.

Madison arched one brow and stared up at him, as if she were issuing a challenge. Aiden might find the exchange entertaining—were she tangling with anyone else. Julian though, he wasn't a man to be trifled with.

"Madison, this is Julian. He co-owns the shop with me."

"Nice."

Julian's gaze flicked toward Aiden, but he didn't meet it. Why had he brought her?

She put her hands on her hips and the neckline gaped forward.

Right. How could he forget those curves?

"You still racing tonight?" Aiden asked to get Julian to stop leering at Madison's breasts. If she didn't need Aiden in her life, then she really didn't need Julian's baggage barreling into hers.

Julian's lips curled. "Yeah, heat four."

"Hey, boys." Tori stepped into their cluster, holding two beers. Unlike her sister, Tori wore cargo pants and a tank top, her red hair braided on either side of her head. A grease smudge marked her cheek, which was pretty much the norm. "Oh, sorry, didn't realize you had a third. Hi, I'm Tori." She handed the bottles to them and wiped her hand off on her pants before offering it to Madison.

"Hi." It was almost comical to watch Madison's face, the way it creased. She no doubt recalled Roni's distracting shorts and bikini-top number to Tori's cargos and tank top.

"Hey, Aiden." Roni crossed the street at a jog. Up and down the street people stopped to stare, which was exactly why Roni picked her race-day outfits to show as much skin as possible. Distraction was her favorite tactic.

Madison's gaze bounced from Roni to Tori and back again. The women were identical and even after years of being around them, sometimes Aiden mixed them up on a bad day. You had to know to look for the grease under Tori's nails and the slight scar above Roni's left eyebrow, which she covered with makeup.

"What's up?" he asked.

Roni's mouth curved. She nodded to the side, her gaze never coming close to Madison.

"I'll be back." He handed his beer to Madison and thumbed at Julian. "If he gives you a problem, just hit him with it."

Aiden followed Roni past his car and two others so they were somewhat alone.

"What's going on?" Aiden asked without preamble.

"Eleventh knows we disposed of their stuff. I heard Raibel Canales wants to make an example out of the people who stole from him."

And what did he want to bet that point would be made with a bullet in his head if the Eleventh Street crew leader had his way?

"Fuck." Aiden resisted the urge to glance over his shoulder. Talk about bad timing. "Who told you? What do you want me to do? You pulling out?"

"Hell no." Roni appeared almost offended. "Emery texted Tori earlier about it. Said he hacked one of their phones and went through some text messages. Should we do anything? Try to talk them out of it?" By talk she meant something a little more active. Like hitting the Eleventh before they hit Aiden and his crew. Roni fidgeted with a tiny gold medallion she wore around her neck, one of her Orthodox saints, no doubt.

Emery should have reached out to Aiden first. It wasn't the first time he'd noticed their Walking Brain warning Tori of danger before the rest of them. He'd have to take Emery to task. Later.

"What does Julian say?" Like it or not, Aiden and Julian were a team, co-leaders, though more often than not Julian was the Lone Ranger of their operation.

"I didn't exactly tell him." She winced. "He's just been so—I don't know—'Let's just blow the problem up' recently. I'm not too keen on having to pick up radiator parts off the road to cover our ass because he got C4 happy. Or maybe you don't know how his last Hoover job went?" Hoover was the code word for their FBI gigs. It wasn't a reference to J. Edgar Hoover, the famed director, or even the building named after him that housed the FBI headquarters. No, the Feds were Hoovers because so much of what they did was just a huge time and energy suck.

Their crew had started what was supposed to be a onetime undercover operation to take down Evers. Two years later and they were still on the job.

He grimaced. Kathy and CJ had given him the highlights of Julian's off-the-rails exploits. "Let's get through tonight. Be careful out there. They won't do anything with so many people around. Too many witnesses." Least he hoped so. It wouldn't be the first time a gang lit up a race day, but it hadn't happened in one hell of a long time.

"Who's the chick?" Roni asked.

"Oh—the new client." He barely resisted glancing

over his shoulder to make sure Julian didn't have her on the hood of his car and his tongue down her throat.

"Client? Is that what we're calling it now?" Roni slid her arm through his, leaning against him.

He frowned at her. Roni wasn't exactly the touchy-feely type.

"Want to know a secret?" She pitched her voice lower so he had to lean down to hear her.

"What?" he asked.

"Clients don't get jealous." She smiled and batted her eyelashes at him.

Shit. Was it that obvious to everyone else?

He peeked over his shoulder and locked on the narrowed gaze of Madison, arms crossed and lips tightly compressed. She wasn't enjoying the show.

"It's not like that," he said, shaking his arm loose. At least it wasn't right now. "Go get in your car. I'm going to be scarce tonight. No need to make us a bigger target than we already are."

There was nothing between him and Madison. She was a client. A job. Nothing more.

There was no way he'd do anything with Roni, either. The twins were hot, but he'd been around enough old KGB spies to know better than to get involved with the daughter of one. The Chazov girls were trouble, but loyal. He wanted them on his side, not in his bed.

He stalked toward the cluster of people around Madison and laid his hand against the small of her back. Julian glanced at him, smirking. The bastard knew exactly how Roni had played him.

"Heat's about to start," he said when the conversation lulled.

Julian nodded and his gaze dropped to Madison. "You can watch the start with me, if you'd like."

The hell she would.

Aiden shoved Julian with his free hand. Julian laughed, holding up his hands.

"A'ight." Julian backed away a few steps before pivoting and walking past the starting line. "We need to talk later, bro."

Aiden nodded. Between the Eleventh, the situation with Dustin, and having to work with Madison, there was a lot to discuss. They'd also have to decide how big of a role Julian would play.

"See you around, Madison," Julian said with a wink.

Tori shook her head and went to join her sister, leaving him alone with Madison. He could feel the chill coming off her. He pulled his hand away to avoid frostbite and gestured toward the cars taking position, three abreast.

"You okay?" Aiden nudged her arm.

"Fine."

"Been to a race before?" he asked.

"Nope." Monosyllabic answers. Great.

He could see if there were extra chairs, but he wasn't in the mood to sit and stew. Roni's little Lancer rolled past, Tori jogging along next to the driver's seat, the twins saying something to each other. Though it was Roni who always drove, both twins were devils behind the wheel. He suspected it was their way of preventing conflict between them. They had each other's back no matter how wrong the other might be. He didn't know the entirety of their history, but he could guess by the way they were the first to reach for a wrench or a concealed knife when a new person entered the garage.

"Why are we all the way out here? I thought street races happened in the city or something," Madison blurted.

"Qualifying races do, but these get a little . . . heated.

We pushed to move these out here a few years ago after one of the Eleventh Street guys had a wreck. We can more easily control who is on these roads. Besides, it's more interesting and the cops take a lot longer to arrive."

The three cars nosed up to the line someone had spray-painted, revving their engines. Roni had the inside position on the left side. Exactly where she'd want to be for the first turn. She could take corners tighter than the other vehicles, not so much because of the car, but her skill as a driver.

He glanced down the line. Not an Eleventh driver in sight, at least not one he recognized. Raibel Canales was recruiting pretty heavily, and not just for fast drivers anymore. He was pulling in real thugs, people with a laundry list of felonies. The kind who wouldn't hesitate to pull a trigger if the boss said to.

Damn. Aiden needed to get Madison out of here. She was the most valuable piece of leverage they'd had in a while. But they couldn't split until after the heat started and the road cleared.

Madison uncrossed and recrossed her arms, shifting her weight from foot to foot.

"You said there was an accident. What happened?" Her voice was strained and she lifted up on tiptoes, peering down the street.

Aiden tried to slam the door shut on the memories, but they rolled right over him with the same regret and guilt he'd felt after the accident. He'd told the driver his car was listing to the left, that he shouldn't drive in that heat, but Aiden wasn't Eleventh and his opinion was suspect.

"Guy raced though we told him not to. Something was wrong with his ride. He went into a turn and bumped the back of my car. I had to jerk the wheel to keep from hitting the guy on my left, when I glanced in the rearview all I saw was him flipping over and over again. He hit a car at the intersection that was stopped." He shook his head, trying to forget the sight.

"Oh my God, did they all die?" Madison stared up at him, her jaw dropped.

"No, just the driver. The family in the car he hit was fine. Their car was totaled, but they only had bruises."

And that's when the FBI twisted my arm . . .

Instead of driving off, he'd stopped and called 9-1-1. Racing was dangerous, and if you didn't get into a few wrecks you didn't want to win badly enough, but no one should die for it. He'd known staying on the scene would make him liable, but it was one of those times when doing the right thing was more important. If his sister had still been alive, she'd have told him he did the right thing. And he had. His one fault was driving too fast. It was the other driver who hit him and lost control. He was pretty sure the specialist the prosecution hired to testify that Aiden was at fault had taken a bribe. One to make sure that the blame rested in Aiden's lap. He should have smelled a rat when the FBI showed up and promised to make it all go away if he did one tiny thing for them. Too bad Julian hadn't warned Aiden about how the FBI got their hooks into him, at least not in time.

They'd been back to the States for a hot minute. Not even long enough to wash the dust from their BDUs when Julian called Aiden from the ER, screaming about his baby sister dying.

That was the first time Aiden had heard the name Michael Evers. He hadn't killed Julian's mentally handicapped sister directly, but he'd employed her, using her as a drug mule and sending her into rival territory. Evers was a sick bastard, with a lot of enemies. When Aiden's sister and brother-in-law died for investigating the cold case with too much zeal, Julian had shown up out of the blue when Julian should have been incarcerated for attempted murder on Evers himself. Aiden had later learned about Julian's deal with the FBI and new name. He'd essentially traded his life for revenge, a concept Aiden was all too familiar with now.

The cars revved their engines again and people cheered. Drivers up and down the street revved in answer and for a few moments it was impossible to hear anything except the mechanical hearts roaring.

He leaned down, putting his mouth next to Madison's ear, and pointed at a fairly normal-looking man across the street from them.

"Watch him."

Madison nodded while he counted down in his head.

Five.

The man shifted, checking a watch.

Four.

Roni's car roared.

Three.

The man grabbed a flag in the back of his jeans and held it out parallel to the ground.

Two.

Roni's grip shifted on the wheel and her chin tipped down.

One.

The man shifted his weight to his back leg.

Zero.

The flag dropped and the three cars shot forward, the initial burn of acceleration sending off a wave of heat and exhaust as one body, one force of movement.

He spun, keeping his gaze on the cars, noting how one pulled off the line just a little faster, how Roni hugged the line on her left.

Damn, he knew how this would end, but the kick of adrenaline was a drug. He'd do this until either the cops or the FBI put him away.

"Where'd they go?" Madison peered around him.

"They'll do a loop through the Everglades. It's one big circle." He liked this track. They had an agreement with the few people who lived along the route; they were paid, they didn't complain. It seemed like a good use for the steep entry fee, besides the winner's pot.

"Oh."

People began to mill around. It would take the drivers a few minutes even at top speeds to complete the loop.

He turned to face her, studying the slight frown on her face, the crease on her brow.

"Something wrong?" he asked.

"No," she said too fast.

"You don't like the racing."

Her gaze darted to his face. "I didn't say that."

"You didn't have to."

"It's not that I don't like it—but—people get hurt."

"Not this way they don't."

"Are you sure?"

He paused. No, he couldn't be sure. He couldn't control what the drivers did, if someone ran out in front of them or if something caused freak accidents. Neither could he deny that their past time was completely illegal, and for many that was the draw of it.

"I'm a buzzkill, I know. My coach tells me that enough." She rolled her eyes.

"Roller derby?"

"Yeah."

"How did you get involved in that?" His gaze slid down her body, lingering on those legs.

"Uh, well, I left my husband, filed for divorce, and had a lot of anger to work out. I met a girl at South Beach on roller skates handing out fliers and I figured, why not? I had a whole life to fill up."

"What did you do before the divorce?"

"I kept the house." She shrugged.

"What? Like a housewife?"

"Uh, yeah. The tattoos and roller derby were my way of working through my lifelong dream dying."

"You wanted to be a housewife?"

"Yeah. I wanted what I didn't have. A husband and family, the house, all of that stuff. Dustin saw a young, desperate girl who was perfectly happy to be his puppet in exchange for a home, the picket fence, and the appearance of a perfect family. It didn't last long."

"When did you find out he was a drug dealer?"

"I think I always knew he was bad news, but he bought me stuff I'd never been able to have and he gave me a home. I wanted to believe he was the husband I'd always wanted." She glanced away. "Is this what you wanted to know? All my dirty secrets?"

The facts of Madison's life were a lot different when he saw them through her eyes. Fuck Dustin Ross. He didn't deserve the comforts of a prison. Aiden grabbed Madison's arm and steered her toward his car. He threaded their hands together.

"Come on, we're going."

"But, don't you need to stay to see who wins?"

"Roni wins."

"How do you know that?"

"Because she's the only person in our crew that's in

the race. She'll win." Because that was how things went. His crew wasn't just fast, they drove to win. It was the difference between just having a fast car and knowing what to do with it. They had the heart to win, because everything, the lives of the people they loved, their continued freedom, it all hinged on being the fastest.

Chapter Five

Madison clung to the door handle with one hand. The car zipped around a box truck and accelerated down the highway back toward Miami.

"Well that was a waste," she said above the roar of the engine.

"What?"

"What was the point of going if we were just going to leave?" It was like shopping with Lily. They could spend hours out searching for a new bikini and Lily would still leave with nothing to show for it despite trying on ten perfect ones.

"It was no place to talk."

"Then why even go?"

"I had to." He kept glancing in the rearview mirror. Enough that it made her nervous. Were they being followed? Had something happened? Or had her cop shadow found them? "You hungry?"

"I could be." She'd skated off her burger dinner long ago, but nerves had kept her from eating anything else.

He took an exit that was all too familiar to her. A couple miles later, Aiden pulled the Challenger into the back lot at Stoke's. It was just after the rush and there were only two other cars in the covered row. A couple derby girls still skated back and forth, delivering orders.

"What are we doing here?" she asked, glancing around. On one hand, the grill was her territory. On the other, it was an easy place for both the cops and thugs to find her if they were looking.

"I figured this was neutral territory. Besides, I'm hungry and those beer fries were awesome."

"You'd never been to Stoke's before?" She stared at him aghast.

"No."

"Did you grow up in Miami?"

"Yes."

"And you've never been to Stoke's? I don't think this is going to work out, sorry."

He shook his head, and unless she was mistaken, he was laughing at her. "You really like this place, don't you?"

"I might have spent a lot of time here when I was in high school. This lot was still a grass field and the football guys would start a game while we ate ice cream." She smiled, immersed in the warm, fuzzy feelings of hope for a better future.

"Who were you in high school?" he asked.

"I was a cheerleader."

"No shit?" He gave her a once-over.

"Hey, back then I had a plan, and it involved cute cheerleader outfits and marrying my high school sweetheart." Those were bittersweet memories. For a while, she'd had it all planned out. One breakup and a night of bad choices later, she'd landed an older man who bankrolled her wishes. She sighed. "Look how well that turned out? So, about this thing with Dustin?"

"Yeah?"

"Tell me about it."

"I've told you everything. I want to get the drive from you, and use it as leverage against him."

"Yeah, but how?"

He studied her and for a second, she could feel the scales tipping from side to side while he came to a decision. It appeared she wasn't the only one having to trust someone in this little arrangement.

"Do you know who Michael Evers is?"

"Yes." She blinked slowly. After the split, Madison had gone back to work for Lily's parents at a private airstrip they owned outside of the city, Everglades Air. Planes of all sorts landed, carrying passengers, cargo, and even the occasional animal. She'd worked odd jobs for them in high school over the summers to make money. This time she'd scored the office job. It was mostly administrative work, keeping track of the schedules, signing things in and out. Easy work.

But why would he be asking about their newest client? All she knew was that he was friends with a guy referred to them by another airport.

"Dustin is just a stepping-stone to get to Evers."

"Why?"

"Dustin works for Evers."

Madison's body went hot then cold. This was not good. Not good at all. What was she getting into? The muscles around her ribs constricted and she couldn't breathe. She'd known Dustin had started working for someone else, she just hadn't known who. It had all come to pass after their split, and quite frankly she didn't want to know. Between Dustin's threats and the cops pressuring her for information, the best plan had been to lie low and hope it all blew over.

"He does?" She licked her lips.

Shit, fuck, and damn it.

She'd just put a new shipment on the books yesterday.

Was Aiden telling her the truth? What proof did he have? And did Lily's parents know?

"Hey." Aiden reached across and squeezed her hand. "I'm going to take care of Dustin. You don't have to worry about him."

The concern would be sweet, if she weren't hiding a very important fact from him.

"So, what then?" She needed time to think. Keeping him talking was her only recourse.

"Once I have the drive and I know what's on it I can make a better plan for what to do."

"What if there isn't anything on it?"

Aiden shrugged. "Then I hand it over and tell Dustin our deal is done."

"That's it?" What about their deal?

"There's more than one way to get to him. This is just the most convenient path."

"Why are you doing this? What did Dustin ever do to you?" She could think of a lot of people Dustin had swindled, it wouldn't be hard to find a reason.

Aiden's lips compressed and that dangerous edge to his gaze got sharper. Some questions, it would seem, weren't to be asked. Too bad she didn't care about what he wanted.

"That's personal," he said, and pulled his hand back.

"The fuck it is. You're tromping through my life. I think I deserve to know what the hell is going on."

"Yeah, well too bad."

A derby girl skated toward them, wearing tiny shorts and a tank top with her pads, but no helmet. Cat Scratch was going to get herself hurt. She didn't even have outdoor wheels on her skates. All it would take was a rock in her path to make her face-plant and ruin her rink wheels. Aiden rolled down the driver's-side window just in time for Cat Scratch to slow to a stop and lean through the window.

"Oh, hey, Helena." Cat glanced at Aiden, a sly smile on her lips. "Matt Smith was by earlier looking for you."

Great.

The badges had mobilized faster than she'd anticipated.

Aiden glanced from Cat to Madison and back.

"That's nice. Hey, can I get a burger, beer fries, and water? Thanks." Her luck, Cat would spit in her food out of spite. The woman seemed to think they had some sort of great rivalry or something.

Aiden gave his order and threw in a couple of shakes.

If she brains herself on the concrete, it's her own fault.

"Helena, huh?" Aiden turned toward her and leaned against the door.

"Yeah, roller derby names. She's Cat Scratch, I'm Helena Destroyer. It's a thing."

"Helena Destroyer."

When people called her Helena, Madison felt powerful. Capable. An utter badass on the track. Yet when Aiden said it, she shifted in her seat and found a spot on the dash to stare at.

"Who is Matt Smith?" he asked.

"Nobody."

"It's just a question."

"Yeah, well, it's personal." Her personal pain-in-the-ass detective. One minute Matt was trying to help her, the next he threw her under the bus, all while claiming he was protecting her. She couldn't trust the detective, that much she knew. The last thing she wanted right now was for Matt and Aiden to share the same space.

"Your personal life is my business now. Who is Matt Smith?"

She stared out of the passenger-side window.

"Madison."

Shit, was there no privacy left for her?

She could refuse to answer the question, but sooner or later her shadow would make an appearance. If she was going to work with Aiden, he should probably know.

"He's a detective with Miami PD." There. Let bad boy chew on that for a moment.

"Sheesh, was that so hard? Getting you to talk is like trying to pry open a rust bucket. All I'm doing is helping you, remember that."

Then why did it feel like an inquisition?

"When can you look for the drive?" Aiden asked.

"Um, not tomorrow. I have practice. Maybe Saturday during the day?" When she'd realized what she'd done, she'd boxed up all her things in identical white boxes and called up her friends. All they knew was that Dustin was harassing her. What the girls didn't know was that one of them was hiding something dangerous.

"You sure you can't tonight?"

She glanced at the clock. "It's almost eleven. Some of us have work first thing in the morning, and I won't have access to the boxes this late." And she had a list of things she wanted to look up about Michael Evers now, thanks to Aiden. She had to know the truth.

"Okay, okay." He sipped from his drink. "Tell me more about the derby."

With her mind latched onto Michael Evers and his purported mobster status, it wasn't easy to switch gears and keep the conversation rolling. But if she started clamming up over something like skating, he'd know for certain that she was hiding something.

"What do you want to know?"

"Do you play a position?"

"Yeah, I'm a pivot."

"What's that?"

"It's the lead blocker. Do you really want to talk about this right now?"

"You seem a little tense. I thought a change in conversation might help."

"It's not." She glanced away and caught herself looking for a cop shadow that wasn't there. A shiver stole down her spine. She was so used to having that protection around she now felt vulnerable without it. Was Aiden enough protection?

"I'm sorry. I know this must be rough on you."

"Yeah, rough, that's a word for it." She let her head fall back against the seat.

"Why is Matt Smith looking for you?"

"I changed my mind, let's talk about derby."

"Matt Smith."

"He wants to keep me in his back pocket as a witness against Dustin. I gave the cop watching me tonight the slip. He probably realized it, called Matt, and now Matt is trying to check up on me. Matt really wants to bust Dustin for some reason. Problem is, somehow my idiot ex-husband manages to get someone else to take the fall for him."

Aiden shook his head. "A little history? A year ago the cops were about to take Evers down, but someone covered up the evidence and when he was arrested the whole case evaporated. How long you known Matt?"

"Maybe six months. Why?"

"Matt's mentor was the detective in charge. When the shit hit the fan, someone had to take the blame. I imagine Matt is on a crusade."

It fit. Matt carried a weight around with him. A constant aura of anger that was uncomfortable at times to be around.

"You already knew who Matt was."

"I did."

"Then why ask me?"

"To see if you'd tell me the truth."

Madison gaped at him for a moment, visualizing her fist hitting his pretty face. Lot of good that would do her.

"How do you know all this?" she asked instead.

Aiden stared at her and she held her breath. There were a number of things he wasn't telling her. It wasn't in anything he said or did. It was just a knowing.

"I've got sources," he said.

He didn't trust her enough to tell her. She didn't like it, but she understood it.

Cat Scratch skated toward them with a tray laden with food and drinks. The horrible part of Madison wanted the other woman to fall flat on her face and wear those burgers the rest of the night. Too bad Cat Scratch was actually a good skater.

"What's the deal with her?" Aiden asked.

Madison sighed. "She thinks I beat her out for a spot on the travel team."

"Wait, so you guys aren't on the same team?"

"No." Madison leaned closer, pitching her voice low. The other woman skated nearer, burdened now with their meal. "We're in the same league. Within the league, there are five teams. The best players play on the travel team, too. Cat Scratch and I started playing at the same time. We're kind of rivals, I guess, or at least she sees it that way."

"Here's your order." Cat Scratch leaned in the window, batting her eyelashes at Aiden. "Need anything else?"

A skate in your face.

Madison took the bag Aiden handed across to her.

"Nope. We're good here," he replied without even glancing at her.

"Well, if you need anything, just whistle. You know how to whistle, right?"

Aiden stopped shuffling the drinks around and slowly turned his head toward her. "Yeah. We're good."

"Okay, then. Later." Cat Scratch pivoted and skated away.

"If you need anything, whistle?" Aiden snorted. "Seriously?"

"Yes, yes she did." Why was she this jealous over a man she had no right to and no rational desire to see more of? She was well aware of her irrational lust for him, which was stupid and crazy. It would be better to toss him over the boundary line to Cat Scratch, and yet the idea made Madison want to claw the other woman to pieces.

"Does shit like that actually work?" He turned to face her, his expression baffled.

"For some people." She shrugged. "Oh please, like you don't have a couple lines you use on women." Hello, bitterness. Madison needed to get away from him so she could screw her head back on straight. Jealousy, lust, bitterness, what was next?

Aiden tipped his head to the side while he chewed. He seemed to consider it for a moment, then leaned an arm on the center console and cleared his throat.

"Hey, baby, want to straddle my NOS tank?"

She stared at him a moment before bursting out laughing. "What the hell is NOS?"

"That and this." He pointed to the tank in the floorboard by her feet, and the one in the console.

"What do they do?"

"Do you want the technical answer or the simple one?"

"Simple."

"They make the car go really, really fast."

"Okay, I get it. And no, thanks." A tank wasn't what she wanted to straddle, unless he was packing something in those jeans of his she'd never seen before.

An engine whined in the distance, growing louder. Aiden's smile faltered and he glanced over his shoulder at the street. Headlights turned into the carhop, one after another after another.

"Fuck." Aiden reached under the seat.

The cars pulled up on either side, in front and behind them in a cluster of flashy paint and bright lights. Music thumped and blared from at least five different sound systems, drowning out the Stoke's speakers.

"Why do you have a gun?" She could feel her throat constricting as the sight of the slick, black gun struck terror in her.

"Reasons," he replied without looking at her.

Squealing tires broke her out of her trance. There was a very real reason Aiden had the gun, and it didn't appear to have anything to do with her or Dustin.

"What's going on?" Madison twisted in her seat, heart pounding. Was this Dustin? Or Aiden's doing?

"Nothing. Play it cool." Aiden assumed a relaxed posture, but she saw the way he clenched his left hand. In his right hand, he held the gun low, next to his leg and out of sight from the other drivers.

"What the hell is going on?" she demanded again.

"Stay in the car. I'll tell you later," he said in a whisper.

She grabbed her burger and shoved a big bite in her mouth. If her last meal was Stoke's, she at least wanted to get her money's worth.

A tall, thin man dressed in jeans and a white tank top got out of the cherry-red car in front of them. He wasn't the kind of guy you'd pass on the street and think anything of. He was—normal. And yet, the calculating way he was staring at Aiden was the same way Dustin had stared at her, back when she didn't ask questions about where the money came from or where he'd been.

"Who is that?" she asked in a whisper.

"That's the Eleventh Street Gang leader, Raibel Canales. He's not exactly a friend." Aiden grabbed one of the paper bags and used it to hide the gun in his hand.

"No shit, Sherlock." Raibel, why did that name sound familiar? Did she want to remember? Probably not, but she couldn't stop the wheels from turning now.

Raibel sauntered toward the driver's-side door and leaned his forearms on the open window.

"*Que bolá, asere?*" Raibel's gaze flicked from Aiden to her.

Madison took back her initial assessment of the man. He wasn't normal at all. The way he stared at her was more like staring into her and wondering what it would be like to turn her inside out. She'd met a few sickos like that who ran in the same circles with Dustin, and they terrified her.

"Helena, right?" Raibel pointed at her.

Madison froze. Fucking fuckity fuck.

"How's Alison? It's been a while since I saw her."

Alison Plunderland was a derby girl with a short fuse, plenty of brawling buddies, and a little black book thicker than the Bible. Madison wasn't close with her, but she'd been to a few of the after-parties where Alison had come in with a long-haired Cuban man at her side. Without the long hair, Raibel's features were sharper, more defined.

"She's good," Madison said for lack of a better answer. The last she'd seen of Alison the girl was turning in her notice for a month off. Or was it two now? She'd come to a few practices with a black eye and limping, but Madison had never found out why and Alison never came back. Looking at Raibel now, she wouldn't be surprised if he were Alison's reason for leaving.

"I should give her a call, see how she's doing."

"What do you want, Canales?" Aiden asked before Madison's mouth could get her into trouble.

"Just checking in on a friend." Raibel shrugged. "That's not allowed?"

"When have we ever been friends?" Aiden draped an arm on the steering wheel and turned his body toward Raibel, partially blocking her view.

"I wasn't talking to you." Raibel cocked his head to the side. "Hey, Helena, want to come take a ride in a real car?"

Oh, hell to the never no.

"What? You can't pick up your own chicks now, Canales?"

Raibel slashed a glare Aiden's way. "That's some talk, coming from you."

"Hey, I can bring my own girl to the party, that's not a problem for me. If you need a date, though, I might be able to help you out. I'm a nice guy." Aiden's smile was more a baring of teeth.

"Your own girl? Yeah? But what about bringing a car? Can you do that?"

Aiden gestured to the dash of the Challenger. "Looks like it. So where's this party happening? Am I invited?"

"Oh, you'll get your invitation, DeHart." Raibel ground his teeth. From the way he stared at Aiden, turning him inside out was just the beginning of what Raibel wanted to do. "I know what you did."

"I'm sorry, what I did? You're going to have to be a little clearer."

Raibel pounded the door with his fist.

"Wow, hey, easy on the paint," Aiden snapped. He leveled the gun at his door, right at the Cuban man.

"I fucking know what you did," Raibel whispered through clenched teeth. He didn't even glance at the gun, not the least bit concerned that he could get a bullet in the groin.

Madison didn't dare breathe. If Aiden had a gun, what were these other guys packing?

"I don't know what you're talking about, sorry," Aiden said.

"You do, and you'll pay." Raibel wagged his finger in Aiden's face. Raibel glanced down at the gun and smirked. "Cute toy."

Madison pressed her back against the door. Being in close confines with these two was not a good idea, and that wasn't even taking into consideration that one of them had a fucking gun. She didn't know which one was scarier, Raibel with his overt, homicidal thoughts, or Aiden, with his thinly veiled ability to kick some ass.

Aiden pulled out a twenty-dollar bill with his left hand. "Here you go, get a burger. The fries are good too."

Raibel crumpled the money into a ball and threw it back in Aiden's face. "*Coño carajo.*"

"You too," Aiden replied.

Raibel turned and stalked back to his car. He flashed some sort of a sign with his fingers twisted around each other and curved. The cars around them revved their engines. Madison pressed her hands over her ears. Raibel peeled out, followed closely by his pack of followers. The scent of burned rubber and exhaust hung thick on the air.

A cluster of derby girls and people stood along the covered eave of the bar as a light rain began to fall. Hopefully it would cleanse the area of whatever Raibel's gang had left behind.

Aiden blew out a breath and tucked the gun under his thigh, as if it were a cell phone or something he wanted to have on hand.

"What was that about? And why do you have a gun?" Madison asked.

"How does he know you?" Aiden turned toward her.

"He dated a derby girl, Alison Plunderland. We were at some parties together. I heard some rumors he hit her, next thing I know she's on leave and I haven't thought about her since."

"He just knows you from parties?"

"Hey, I'm kind of a big deal in our league, okay? Everyone knows me. I'm on the fucking fliers." She gestured toward Stoke's. There were piles of them inside. The day the league had unveiled the flier, she'd nearly shit her pants. A photograph of her shouldering aside a rival jammer had been digitized and made into the season's poster. It was a point of pride, a sign of how far she'd come that she could wear the Skating Gator and compete for her league.

"Why the gun?"

"How do you think I'm supposed to protect you?" His stare was hard, unyielding.

Crap. He thought he was going to have to shoot someone to keep her safe? Her stomach twisted around into knots. This was bad. Really, really bad.

"Shit." Aiden scrubbed a hand over his face. "We need to get out of here."

He started the car and accelerated out of the parking lot hard enough to press her into the seats. Things had just gotten a lot more complicated.

Chapter Six

A string of curses ran on repeat in Aiden's head.

His play of leaving the races to avoid starting anything with the Eleventh had just gone up in smoke. And not just smoke, but with fireworks. He didn't know what Raibel Canales was capable of, but he had a few good guesses. New gangs like theirs needed a leader who could show force and get things rolling. Raibel had taken over maybe six months ago and the little crew was becoming a true gang. Raibel would kill someone before much longer. It was just the cycle of street life.

Aiden had never liked Raibel much. There was no depth of humanity in the man. It was one thing for Raibel to have Aiden in his sights, but Madison was another matter.

"Hey. Hey!" Madison leaned across the console. "You said you were going to tell me what was going on."

"Hold on for a minute," he snapped.

It was a fifteen-minute drive back to Classic Rides. Somehow, Madison kept her trap shut the whole drive back. He couldn't eat. Too many things were spinning out of control. He hadn't even begun to figure out what Julian was doing, and now he had not only Dustin on one side, but the Eleventh on the other. He needed to get things under control, or at least a little ahead of the game.

He pulled into the drive at the garage and paused, surveying the lot. The security system would pick up anyone trespassing and relay it back to their Walking Brain of an IT guy, Emery, but computers and cameras weren't infallible. Everything was quiet. One small mercy, at least.

Aiden tucked the gun in his waistband before letting down the chain barring entry to the shop and left it there. He didn't plan to be around long. The night was growing old, and there was still a hell of a lot to do.

"Now are you going to tell me?" Madison asked when he got back in the car.

"You are a dog with a fucking bone, aren't you?" He drove the car up next to the shop and shifted into park. "This isn't the first job I've taken from Dustin. A month and a half ago he brings me in through a mutual contact to do a job for him. Quiet-like. Seems the Eleventh Street Gang has started stepping on their territory."

"Territory? Seriously?"

"In case you are unaware, your husband—"

"Ex-husband."

"Your ex-husband deals a lot of coke. Eleventh is getting shipments from someone, and selling to your ex's customers. He didn't like it, but he was also told to take care of the problem without causing a big thing." He shouldn't tell her, but she needed to know exactly what she was dealing with here. Thank goodness she had a cop detail. It would give her some measure of protection.

"And you did it?"

Aiden nodded. "It's economics. Someone like Dustin has the cash to bankroll a shipment of coke. The Eleventh? They're working on credit. So I stole it and burned the take. Now, the Eleventh is in debt to their suppliers, they can't fulfill their demand, so that puts Dustin back on top, without anyone getting killed."

"Except? There's a but in there."

"But, somehow the Eleventh found out what I did, and they're pissed. I don't think Canales knows for sure, but it won't be long before he doesn't care if it's the truth or not, he'll just want to kill me." He shouldn't tell Madison any of this. Outside of his organization, only the mutual contact knew of his involvement. And yet, she was part of it now.

Madison gasped. "Shouldn't you go to the police or something?"

He laughed. That was cute. Real cute. "And what would I tell them?"

She stared at him, mouth hanging open.

"Sorry, officer, I don't have any drugs or evidence why this guy wants me dead, he just does. Trust me, okay?" He shook his head. "That's not going to go over well."

He didn't blame her disbelief. How did he explain the delicate nature of being undercover? On one hand, he had to do the job. On the other, he had to keep up appearances. The Hoovers didn't mind that he'd disposed of the product because it meant the DEA had one less leg to stand on when it came to who called the shots on their operation. And that wasn't even counting the cops, who were butt hurt about being told to back off. If they knew the undercover FBI operation was run out of his garage, they should send Evers a notice as well.

Besides, his crew was capable of handling someone like Raibel. It would just be a lot more convenient if Aiden weren't trying to sell himself as Dustin's go-to guy for outside jobs at the same time.

"What are you going to do?" Madison asked.

"Figure it out later. Canales isn't stupid. He knows he can't come at me unless he can take my whole crew on and he's not ready to open that can." If it came down to it, CJ could tip off the DEA and have the Eleventh raided simultaneously, but Aiden wanted to avoid that. The less federal activity going on, the easier his job was.

"Why?"

"Don't worry about it." He cut the engine and opened his door.

"The hell I'm not worrying about it. Aiden, you pulled a gun on a man at a place I go to all the time. Big fucking deal." She unbuckled and twisted to face him, her face creased by a frown he didn't like.

"Look, Canales is a thug. A smart thug, but still a thug. It doesn't make sense for him to start something with me. If he were a dumb thug I'd be worried, but Canales knows the numbers. It will cost him more money and get the cops interested if he does anything to me or my crew. Until the benefits outweigh the cost, he's just going to make threats." Besides, the younger drivers were nervous around him thanks to the rumors. And Aiden seriously doubted Canales had another driver willing to pull a trigger.

"What about me?"

"As far as Canales is concerned, you're mine."

"Is that so?" She arched a brow at him. Damn, he wanted to kiss that little frown.

"It is. You're safe. Come on, let's get your bike out."

He stretched and he stood from the car, glancing around the lot instinctively. When he'd opened the garage, the last thing he'd expected was to turn it into a front for an FBI investigation. But here he was, on another case. This time, though, he'd finally get to take a piece out of Evers's hide.

* * *

Madison wasn't sure what to make of Aiden. What kind of a man brushed off threats from the leader of a gang while taking on her ex? He was either crazy—or capable. She got the distinct feeling he'd done this sort of thing before. He was helping her. And sure, he might spin it so that he was doing her a favor, but she'd been around bad men before, and Aiden DeHart had none of their stink on his tanned skin. She'd bet money—if she had any—that he'd helped more than a few people.

What kind of a man did that? What kind of training did he have? What life experiences had shaped him into—whatever he was? She wanted to peel back his layers and figure him out.

"You're up past your bedtime," Aiden finally replied. He handed her a bottle of water from the office mini-fridge and gestured to one of the spare chairs.

"I haven't had a fucking bedtime since I was a kid." She sank into one of the empty office chairs. Bedtime with Aiden, now there was a thought.

"Maybe that's what's wrong. You stayed up too late and learned all those bad words."

She tossed her head back and laughed. "I didn't have to stay up late to hear them."

Aiden leaned against the desk and studied her. He hadn't bothered with the overhead lights, just a dim corner lamp. It wasn't quite a romantic glow, but she wasn't in the market for romance. The way he looked at her now, it wasn't like before, when she'd felt exposed, maybe even in his crosshairs. It was like he was seeing her for the first time.

"Who'd you hear it from, then?"

She shifted in her seat. "My dad, at least until he left."

"He taught you all those words?"

"He was a sailor. I'm pretty sure he invented some of them."

Aiden nodded. "Yeah, those navy boys have a certain way with words."

Those navy boys? She tilted her head to the side, taking him in once more. He wasn't the only one who could tell a thing or two about a person just by looking at them.

"You were in the military, weren't you?"

He stilled and there was a deadly air about him, as if in a second he might explode in a flurry of action. His arms flexed, gripping the edge of the desk. Aiden reached across with his right hand and pulled up the sleeve of his shirt, exposing his left bicep. Some truly talented artist had inked the iconic Iwo Jima Memorial onto his arm, set against two pillars of smoke and arching over it all, the words WE WILL NEVER FORGET. There was so much detail to it; she almost wanted to brush the sand from the soldiers' boots out of respect.

It wasn't the kind of tattoo a person could just go into a shop and pick off a wall. She'd spent enough time around the local shops to recognize a custom piece when she saw it.

He'd thought about this tattoo. It meant something to him, more than the momentary jab of emotion pricking her heart. For him, this was something he'd survived. His service alone didn't mean Aiden was a good type of man, but it was hard to not fling her trust at his feet.

Perhaps he wasn't a bad boy at all. Just a badass one.

She licked her lips, aware she was staring. "How long did you serve for?"

"Eight years. That was more than enough for me."

"Thank you."

"For what?"

"For serving."

He laughed, but it was a bitter sound. "Don't thank me for what I did. We did what we thought we had to do."

She knew nothing of how the military worked. Her father had left before her teenage years and with him anything she might have gleaned about the navy.

"Is that where you learned how to do this stuff?" she asked.

"This stuff?"

"Helping people."

"You ask too many questions."

She shrugged. "I learned too late that not asking them was a bad idea."

"How do you completely miss that your husband is a dope dealer?"

She flinched, because his words stung. She deserved that.

"I saw what I wanted to see. I was young, I was stupid, and I was afraid that if I asked what was going on, I'd know the truth. It was easy to live with it at first. I had things and money. Whatever I wanted. But I learned too late the price having stuff cost me. I think I always knew Dustin wasn't a good guy, but I wanted someone in my life so badly I was willing to ignore all the warning signs. Once I started to suspect something"—she shook her head and wrapped her arms around herself—"then I was scared that if I rocked the boat I'd get kicked to the curb."

"But isn't that what happened?"

"The hell it isn't." She glared at him. "I left him. He didn't kick me out. Dustin didn't give one shit about what happened to me, so long as I kept the house and answered the phone."

"But you knew what he was doing."

"No, I knew he was screwing around on me. I suspected there was something else. I thought it was gambling, that maybe he was doing drugs, but I had no idea he was *dealing* until right before I split. I started looking in his pockets, checking his phone and that's when I figured it out. Was I stupid? Yes. Yes, I was stupid and I did what I thought I had to at the time. Would you like to keep rehashing this? We can talk about it again and again and again if you want, but it's not going to change what I'm saying. Yes, I married a criminal. Yes, I willingly remained ignorant of what he was doing. And yes, I left him. Any more questions?" She was practically yelling at him, but her give-a-shit reserve was empty. If he wanted to keep questioning her and doubting her, well, he could do it without her present.

Aiden shook his head. "You're a defensive little thing, aren't you?"

If he was on roller skates, she'd hip-check him onto his ass and feel good about it. Instead, she imagined him flying up, going parallel to the ground, and slamming down. She shoved to her feet and clenched her fists. It would be so satisfying to punch him.

"Fuck you," she spat.

Madison stalked to the other side of the office. One bad thing about roller derby was the way it encouraged the girls to embrace their anger, use it, except once you started wielding the wicked emotion you had the wolf by the ears. Let go of it and it would bite you.

"You shouldn't go around offering things like that," he said in a lazy drawl, except there was nothing lackadaisical about the man.

"You are not funny." She turned to face him, digging her nails into her palm. Heat rolled across her body. So she had a thing for him? Any girl drawing breath would swoon at those blue eyes.

"The guys think I'm hilarious." The deadpan delivery was almost comical.

"Well, good for them." It was time to leave, except he stood between her and the door. "You got a bathroom around here?" If she couldn't leave, she'd retreat.

"Sure." He pointed at the door behind her. The pane of glass shone out into the dark garage. "Through there, to the left."

Madison jerked the door open and the scent of rubber, oil, and grease assaulted her senses. The classic restore shop had always made her curious, and she'd often wanted a closer look at the cars she could never afford to own.

The bathroom was a small, cramped space with barely enough room for the toilet and sink, but it was clean. She shut the door, closing out Aiden and the mess he'd thrown her life into. How could one person stir up so much stuff? He was dealing with Dustin, her, and a street gang. He didn't seem like the man to share his secrets, but she thought it was safe to assume he had more going on than what she knew about.

At some point tonight the pendulum had swung in his favor.

Madison actually trusted him. She was still uncomfortable with the idea, especially after seeing him pull a gun as calmly as he had. But didn't that just mean he had what it took to protect her?

There was no one good reason why she should trust him, and yet she did.

She'd have to keep her trust close and not let him know, because trusting him to handle Dustin and trusting him to handle her were two different things. Not that he'd flirted with her, but there was a certain something between them she was beginning to suspect wasn't just her.

Madison washed her hands, staring at the girl she'd become. She liked herself now. It was the one thing she wouldn't trade, the thing Dustin couldn't take from her after she'd left him. The last couple of years she'd lived with Dustin, she'd been a shell of a person. Hating herself and everyone around her for allowing her to fall in the pit she'd dug for herself. But she'd suited up and climbed her way out of there, and no one could put her back in that hole.

"What do I do about him?" she whispered at her reflection.

Aiden wanted to solve her problems with Dustin by making him go away. It was a lovely idea. Man drives in, his car shining in the sunshine, decks her ex, the cops arrest him, and they drive off into the sand for a celebratory dip in the ocean. When things went down she doubted it would be that neat. For starters, she couldn't deny that she was attracted to Aiden, and trusting him made that attraction dangerous.

Her impending divorce had kept her away from entangling her heart because she had a silly set of values to honor the commitment she'd made—even if Dustin didn't. There'd been a couple of men she'd fallen for—at least in her head—but never acted on. She hadn't changed much where her attractions lay. Aiden was dangerous to her heart, even if she knew it was a bad idea. She doubted there were few things that mattered more to him than cars and whatever personal vendetta he had against Michael Evers. She'd have to check his license plate to make sure it didn't read DANGER.

God, she had no ability to judge the bad guys if everything Aiden said were true.

Her phone vibrated. She pulled it out and glanced at

the screen with a text from Lily. There were half a dozen missed calls from Matt, but she'd long since set his special ringtone to silent.

What r u doing? Cat said you were @ Stokes again w a guy. Spill!

Madison cringed. She hadn't wanted to tell Lily about why Aiden had seemed so fixated on her. If anything, Lily would get protective and then Madison would never get to the bottom of what Aiden wanted. She owed Lily a hell of a lot for sticking with her through the Dustin years, pulling her out of the depression funk and everything else.

Met up w guy from earlier. Not going anywhere. Headed home.

It was the truth. She could fantasize about whatever he had under that shirt, his arms around her, and those eyes, but it was a bout she couldn't skate. Trusting him was one thing, falling into bed with him was another. While many of the derby girls bragged about their sexual escapades, that wasn't for Madison. One-night stands, flings, and no strings weren't in her repertoire, no matter how much Lily pushed it on her. When she found the right guy, it would change her life. But it wouldn't be Aiden.

Madison opened the door and peered around the garage. There were at least four cars in the bays in various states of repair. One was on a lift, with no tires, the body stripped of paint and missing half its windows. Another seemed to glimmer under the emergency light. It looked ready to drive off the lot. The other two had their hoods up and an assortment of parts ready for assembly.

She picked her way toward the blue car, ready to take her anywhere. She didn't know the first thing about cars, but it looked pretty and maybe even fast. The seats were white, the windows and grille trimmed in chrome. A shining jaguar leapt at her from the front of the car.

"1950's Mk9 Jaguar."

Madison flinched and glanced over her shoulder at Aiden. He stood in the open doorway to the office.

"Is it yours? Or are you working on it for someone?"

"Nah, it belongs to a guy out in Coral Springs. He brings it over here every six months or so and leaves it overnight so we can look it over." Aiden crossed the garage to stand next to her.

"It's beautiful."

"He's kept her in good condition. Bought her off a lot when he was in his late twenties. The guy's got to be almost a hundred now, but don't tell him that." Aiden smiled, an unguarded expression she didn't think he was aware of. Damn that dimple. She wanted to lick it. Something about the old man stirred a memory in him. Looked like the badass was human after all.

"What does a car like this go for?"

"You in the market?"

"In my dreams."

"This car, because of the condition and everything, fifty grand, maybe forty if the economy tanks."

Holy crap.

Madison almost took a step away from the car. She couldn't afford to even sit in it at that rate.

"Do you want to drive it?" Aiden asked.

She gaped at him. "Are you serious?"

He shrugged. "You couldn't drive his, but there's one

out back. It's not in as good condition, but it will be when I've got the time to scrounge up the parts for it."

"Okay." She'd take a busted-up car if that was all she could get.

Aiden led her to the back of the garage. He paused to disarm the security system before stepping out into a fenced off yard. Several badly abused classic cars sat in a line. They looked like they'd been salvaged from a junkyard.

He led her to the last on the row. The paint had chipped away to reveal a second coat under the obscure, dark color. The roof had cracked and a tarp now covered the back half of the car. The windshield looked more like a spiderweb.

"You're real funny." She crossed her arms and tried to swallow her disappointment. That's what she got for trusting a man, wasn't it? Broken dreams and shattered hope. But she couldn't pin those faults on him. Not for a poorly timed joke.

Aiden grinned at her. "I am, aren't I? Go on, sit behind the wheel."

"Is there even a wheel in there?"

"There is, it just doesn't turn anything. I think I left it lying on the seat. Well, it's more like a bucket with some foam over it."

"You are a jerk." And despite her disappointment, she laughed.

"So, it's not much right now, but eventually it will be."

It was hard to imagine the car in road condition, but what did she know about restoring cars?

"I need to get home." She sighed, tucking away her dreams of a starlit cruise down US-1. "Where's my bike?"

"Already? Night's young."

"Yeah, well, remember—some of us have to get up early for work."

"I wouldn't know anything about that." He gestured toward the garage.

She fell in line beside him and they walked toward the side of the garage. There were several stacks of crates, a few barrels, and tucked up against the side of the building, her green Rebel. It wasn't the nicest bike on the road or the fastest, but it was hers.

"Do you still have my number?" Aiden asked.

"The one you gave me earlier?"

"Take this one too."

She dug her phone out of her pocket and plugged in the second number he gave her.

"How do I know which to call?" she asked.

"If you're in trouble—the first one."

"And the second?"

"Anything else."

What did that mean? His features were once again shrouded in shadow and she had no idea what to make of him. He pissed her off and made her hot, all at once. She had issues. Serious issues.

"What about the street gang?" she asked.

"I'll take care of them."

"You have enough hands to juggle all that?"

"I'll make it work."

All on his own?

Dealing with Dustin was too much. The rest of it made his workload sound impossible, unless he was some kind of cop or superhero under the garage alter ego.

Aiden took a step closer. "Don't worry about your ex. He's not going to hurt you."

She nodded. Dustin might be the least of her worries.

"Hey." He tapped her chin, his thumb sliding across her jaw. "I mean it."

Not all injuries were external.

Oh, God. Oh, God. Oh, God. "Okay," she replied.

She hadn't let a man take her out or touch her since Dustin. This wasn't a date, but it was the closest thing to one she'd been on since high school. She didn't know if she wanted to bolt or lean in closer.

Was it wrong she thought she might be in more danger from him?

Aiden bent his head, slowly. Hesitating. Giving her a chance to turn away, or maybe he wasn't certain. She wasn't. Madison held her breath until his lips brushed hers. As if by not moving she'd given him permission, his hold became tighter, possessive. He pressed his mouth to hers harder, parting his lips, inviting her to play.

She placed her hands over his chest and opened for him. His tongue darted between her lips, teasing hers. Desire coursed through her veins, waking up those parts of her body long dormant. She grasped the front of his shirt and kissed him back. Aiden dropped a hand to her hip. He pressed so close she stumbled back against the chain-link fence. Their lips parted for the span of a second.

Madison wanted him. Would a little taste be such a bad thing?

He didn't wait for her implied permission a second time. He sealed his mouth over hers, kissing her. He was just as swept up in this thing as her. Heat pooled between her legs. She wanted him closer, so she could feel all of him against her. His hands squeezed her ass, coasted up her back and into her hair. She hooked one thigh over his and rocked against him.

Fuck, yes.

Rational thought fled. All that mattered was how good he made her feel. Years of ignoring her nature, the things she wanted, were behind her. Right now, her need for him was paramount.

Tremors of pleasure shook her and she held on tight.

The cravings, yearning for another body redoubled, driving out her better sense until all that mattered was the press of a thick thigh between hers.

The muscles in her abdomen fluttered and she gasped. She didn't want to think about the last time she'd felt like this.

Aiden rocked against her once more and she moaned. He did it again and she dug her nails into his shoulder and squeezed her eyes shut. Once more and a burst of white light erupted behind her eyelids, pleasure rocketed through her, stealing her breath and robbing her of the last bit of her senses. The release was sudden, brilliant, and shocked her back to reality.

Madison was humping a man she barely knew, in a dark alley.

Aiden stilled his motions, as if sensing her change, and lifted his face from hers. She couldn't make out more than the glint of light on his eyes or the shadows across his nose and mouth.

"I . . . I think I need to go," she managed to say without too much trembling.

"You sure about that?" Was that an offer in his tone?

"Yes." She licked her lips, tasting mint on them.

Aiden straightened, bringing her with him, and putting out a hand to steady the bike. She stepped away from him and straightened her clothes, ignoring the way her hands shook.

"Here, I'll roll this out for you."

He unlocked a small gate and wheeled the bike out into the open space next to the garage. She just watched him, not sure what to think or feel, until he held out the helmet to her.

Right. She was getting her ass out of here.

She crossed the distance between them, her knees wobbling a little, and took the helmet. She buckled it on.

"I want to hear from you tomorrow," he said.

"Miss me already?" she popped off before she could think better of it.

"I need to know if you have the drive or not." He took her keys from her hand, rolling the small, pink pepper spray bottle between his fingers.

"I told you, I won't have time to look for it."

"Make time. Keep this close. You know how to use it?"

"Yup." She snatched the keys back before he could give her a lesson she wouldn't hear, not with lust pounding in her veins.

She took the bike, pushing his hands out of the way and swung her leg over it so she fit into the seat. Her legs were weak, rubbery, as if she'd skated fifty dashes or done a dozen drills. How long had it been since she'd orgasmed under anyone else's power except her own? A long, long time.

"Madison." Aiden grabbed her arm. "I need to know you're safe."

"What? Can't trust me?" She shoved her key in the ignition and turned. The Rebel chugged to life, the vibrations shaking up her body and through her core. Her sensitized body shuddered and she sucked in a deep breath.

The security light illuminated his face now and the deep frown lines bracketing his mouth. Clearly he didn't like her answer.

"I'll call you when I call you." Madison pulled her arm from his grasp and squeezed the accelerator. The bike rolled forward, picking up speed.

She needed space from Aiden DeHart, and to figure out just how badly she'd screwed up.

Chapter Seven

Aiden watched the red splash of color that was Madison's taillights disappear around a turn.

What the hell had just happened?

He shook his head and pressed the dial button on his phone. It rang once.

"Yeah, boss?" a man drawled on the other end.

"Emery, is it on?"

"I told you it was. I've got her right here, heading east. Did you download that app I sent you?"

"Yeah."

"Well, open it and track her yourself."

"Let me guess, I'm interrupting your game?"

"Nah, I'm working on Tori's laptop."

"About Tori—next time, keep me in the loop when shit's going down."

"She said she was about to see you. Thought it might be better if she told you."

"You're talking to Tori an awful lot lately."

Silence.

Yeah, that was what Aiden thought.

"We need to meet. Everyone. Later," he said, giving Emery a pass.

"Julian's already headed here."

"Hey, any idea how's he doing?"

Emery sighed. "That is a complicated question."

Meaning, Aiden would have to catch up with Emery when he wasn't potentially being overheard. People—even their own crew—underestimated the tech.

"Okay." Aiden cleared his throat. "I'm going to check out the GPS and go there. We've got trouble."

"No shit."

Aiden hung up the phone and locked the garage gate once more. He hopped the low fence to the side street. A beat-up, older model sedan was stashed behind a Dumpster. He removed a key from a magnetic box under the fender and climbed in. They always kept a couple cars parked around the block in case they needed to blend in. Like now.

The app worked just like Emery promised. Once he selected the number assigned to the tracking device it showed a real-time map of Madison's location. He dropped his phone into a dash mount and started the car, driving it on a slightly different course than the one Madison had taken.

He needed to know, to be sure she was telling him the truth—and that Dustin had only him on the job. It wouldn't be the first time Aiden had seen someone hire several different people for a gig and only pay the one who produced results. He also wanted to assure himself that the Eleventh wouldn't harass her. He'd told her they wouldn't, and a couple months ago he could have said that without a drop of doubt, but that was before they'd stolen the Eleventh's drug shipment. Money and drugs changed people, and Madison wouldn't pay for his actions.

The streets were nearly empty, and if any of the cars he passed were hiding thugs, he couldn't tell. It left him plenty of time to recall the way Madison's breath had hitched, the way she'd shuddered against him. He hadn't realized what was happening until she clawed at his shoulders. He could still feel the press of her nails in his skin.

She'd orgasmed in his arms. And he wanted her to do it again, which was a dangerous thing.

A woman like Madison didn't need a man like him.

It was all the more reason to find the drive and make a plan for how to use it against Michael Evers. Dustin they could take down as a by-product of the mission.

He followed Madison all the way out to the marina. It wasn't one of the nicer ones; there wasn't security or even cameras from the looks of it. He turned his lights off and eased past some hedges.

Anyone could be waiting for her. And in fact, someone was.

He held his breath and watched.

Madison was already off her bike. A man in slacks and a polo stood in the halo of light from the one and only security light. He had cop written all over him.

Detective Smith?

Aiden hadn't had time to look up the detective himself, but he understood the bigger picture now. Matt Smith was young. A golden boy of the force, no doubt. Aiden suspected Matt wanted more than a closed case from Madison.

She edged away, toward a dock, her body language stiff. The detective followed, trailing her all the way out to a thirty-foot sailboat. Aiden forced his grip on the steering wheel to relax. Madison didn't belong to him. And yet, when she jumped aboard her boat and disappeared below deck, leaving the good detective hanging, Aiden smiled.

Lights flickered on in the lower deck and he saw her pass by one of the portholes.

His gut told him she wasn't working for Dustin. Sure, it would be easy for Dustin to stash her out here, but what would be the point? What would he gain? Especially with the cops circling her like this.

Aiden's phone vibrated in his pocket. He peered at the screen. Julian's name flashed several times.

"What?" Aiden asked. He watched the boat for more movement.

"Where are you?"

"Working."

"Yeah, well, when are you getting to The Shop?"

The Shop was their secondary garage, where their dealings weren't always legal, but with the blessings of the FBI it didn't matter, if they got the job done.

"Soon."

"Okay. Pick up a pizza. I'm starving."

"Order your own damn pizza." Aiden hung up before Julian could pull some nonsense about *that one time, in Sangin. . . .* Aiden hated that story.

He wanted to stay put, to watch over Madison and ensure she'd sleep peacefully through the night, but they needed to make a plan. One that would keep Madison safe beyond tonight. Besides, he wouldn't be surprised if Detective Matt Smith called in a courtesy patrol, just for her. He'd have to have the marina under constant watch to keep her safe, which meant Aiden needed Emery paying special attention to this place. There was nothing safe or secure about her boat residence. So why hadn't Dustin tried to grab her from here?

Tomorrow he'd have to send Emery out to her boat and sweep it for bugs or other surveillance equipment. For now, he did a quick sweep of the immediate area on foot, careful to avoid the detective dragging his feet about leaving, then drove the rest of the marina, but all was quiet.

It took him nearly a half hour to traverse Miami to The Shop. He was the last to arrive. Their full crew was assembled in the open garage, sitting on chairs or the workbenches, even a stack of tires, minus CJ and Kathy who were conspicuously absent. They had a nine-person crew, including their FBI handlers who had proven themselves to the team, and they came from all walks of life, and most of them had strayed off the straight and narrow to land them on this crew, but not all.

Roni and Tori's only crime was being born to a former KGB agent. Their contract employment with the FBI ensured they were protected, and the FBI got to pick their brains.

John "Wayne" was a resourceful bastard from the backwater swamps of Louisiana. He was a decorated war hero, former cop, and the best sniper Aiden had ever seen.

Gabriel was a friend of Julian's from after their time in the service. Aiden wasn't privy to the man's past, but he'd bet a set of tires Gabriel had a history of working for the FBI.

Emery was a by-the-book FBI agent now, but he could fight something dirty. There was a lot under the cool exterior even Aiden didn't know, and he was probably the person on the crew who knew Emery best.

And then there was Julian—and Aiden. The friends that tied it all together. They'd met in the service, been tossed into a unit that didn't exist on the record, and executed dozens of missions before hanging up their boots for the quiet life. Or so they'd thought.

They were a mixed bag, but they were his family. The people he could count on. The ones who had his back.

"'Bout time you showed up," Julian yelled between bites, stuffing his face with pizza.

"I would like to know how the Eleventh found out." He pitched his voice so it cut above the chatter.

Dustin Ross had hired Aiden to discourage the Eleventh Street Gang from competing against Dustin's foot soldiers hawking product on the streets. Aiden's plan for not only satisfying the job, but also sending a message to the young drivers, was to boost the cars carrying the goods, scrap them, and destroy the drugs. It had gone off without a hitch. Or at least they'd thought.

If Aiden weren't so tired, it might have been comical to watch the way everyone found somewhere else to look besides at him.

Emery cleared his throat and wiped his face with a napkin. He hadn't shaved recently and his usual pearl snap shirt had a couple buttons unsnapped. Emery might be their Walking Brain, but the man was built like a tank. In a pinch, he'd make good backup in the field, but there was no arguing his best work was behind a computer screen. "I don't know how they figured out it was us, but I can tell you how they found what's left of the cars."

"I told you we should have chopped and sold them." Julian glared at him. They didn't often outright disagree on what their crew would do, but every so often they butted heads. Aiden didn't like to. They shared equal ownership in this business, and neither of them was the type to back down easily.

"How did they do it, Emery?" Aiden ignored Julian and kept his gaze on the Walking Brain.

"Shit." John tossed his trash into a bin and rolled his eyes.

"They changed the pressure gauges out on the NOS tanks you dumped. We theorize the Eleventh used that make and model because they had no serial numbers, but the pressure gauges did. Really tiny numbers, too.

Cops pulled them out of the ocean and looked up the owners for illegal dumping."

"What the fuck?" Julian roared. Their team did a neat flip on cars when they had to.

Aiden held up his hand. "I want to know how they connected it to us."

"I don't think they have proof," John said. "Maybe someone said they saw one of us hanging around their cars, but they were all snockered when we boosted them."

"I don't care. I want to know how they connected us. Canales and his crew boxed us in after we left tonight."

"How'd she take that?" Roni snickered and flicked something at her sister.

With the exception of Julian who had been on a mission, everyone knew Madison's history. After Aiden's meet with Dustin, they'd had a planning meeting for how to approach her. At the time, she'd been a name and a face. A mark. Nothing more than a job. But after a few hours in her company, he didn't want to lay bare her story for everyone.

Aiden helped himself to a slice of pizza.

"Good. Except she knows Canales."

"I told you she was a bad apple," Tori said, shaking her head.

"She doesn't know him under good terms. Seems he dated one of her roller derby friends and beat her up pretty badly. Can we find out more on a girl who calls herself Alison Plunderland?"

"Alison—what?" Julian stared.

"You missed a lot while you were—where was it again?" There was no holding the irritation back anymore.

"I was on a job." Julian glared at him from across the workbench that was serving as their table.

"Doing what exactly? While we were working on this? This being the job we were all brought in for."

The vein on the left side of Julian's head began to throb, growing more prominent. Aiden knew the terms of Julian's job meant he was at the beck and call of his superiors, who aimed him at something and turned him loose. Aiden hated what they were doing to Julian, how each job seemed to be pushing him toward a cliff. It wasn't worth it.

"The agreement was we did this shit together. Your FBI friends need to remember I don't work for them, and I can walk away," Aiden said. He stared back at Julian, feeling all the toxic rage rolling off him. Someday very soon Julian was going to do something so over the line the Feds wouldn't turn a blind eye anymore.

Unlike Julian, who was at the mercy of the FBI, Aiden was a contracted employee with a specific mission. The FBI couldn't jerk him around like they did Julian.

Once, a long time ago, Aiden had signed on for revenge, but he'd learned from watching the way revenge ate at Julian that it was a toxic thing. Now, Aiden just wanted to see the job done. It was his responsibility because he'd said he'd do it, but when that was done, his time with the FBI was also over.

The room grew very still. Aiden had never spoken those words out loud. The Hoovers liked to believe Aiden worked for them, but the truth was, if it boiled down to paperwork, he was a contracted employee with the ability to terminate his contract whenever he wanted. Except then he lost their protection, and he'd done so many below-the-board jobs for them he probably needed their shielding.

"The fuck you would," Julian growled.

It was tempting to put all of this behind him. Just—walk away. But the few times he'd been ready to pack a bag and fill his gas tank, the images of his sister and her husband on their wedding day, so happy and in love, were the brakes that kept him parked. He'd made peace with their memory, but the weight of responsibility still sat firmly in his lap.

"We need you on this case." Aiden stabbed the table with his finger.

"What's going on?" CJ's voice boomed in the garage.

Aiden turned toward the couple. "Nice of you to join us."

"Nice of you to have dinner already prepared." Kathy flashed him a smile and reached in front of him to help herself to a slice. She'd changed from the jeans and Classic Rides shirt into slacks and a T-shirt. Kathy could be anyone's mother dressed as she was.

"We were just discussing the Eleventh and segueing into Madison," Aiden replied.

"There's literally nothing on her." Kathy turned toward Emery. Between the two of them, there wasn't a technical toy they couldn't dismantle, hack, or build. Not to mention their digital sleuthing skills could uncover just about anything. "Did you find anything?"

"She's got a few social media accounts, but they were all created after she left Ross. All she does is talk about roller derby. She had an e-mail when she was married. I got into it, but there's only junk mail. Not an e-mail from her mom, an e-card, nothing. I think he kept her pretty well cut off from everything," Emery said.

"The girl is like, Miss Roller Derby USA or something. Those hips of hers are dangerous. I watched some YouTube clips. She's a mean one on the track." Kathy glanced at Aiden. "You should go watch her. Hell, I'd go watch her and I don't care for sports."

Madison's hips. Aiden didn't want to hear anyone else talking about those.

"Did you find anything else?" Aiden dropped his half-eaten slice of pizza back into the box. It was hard to feign disinterest when he wanted to know more about the woman who'd come apart in his arms.

"Not a lot. I pulled her financials." CJ set a manila folder on the workbench. "She's got a savings account, but it's all coming from her paycheck, which is legit. Looks like she's trying to put herself through school at the community college. She's got two years under her belt, and if I had to guess, she's studying accounting. There's nothing suspicious about where her money is coming from, and it's not like she's spending more than she makes."

"What about the cops? There's a Detective Matt Smith looking into her." Aiden glanced at John. "You know him?"

"What? You think all cops know each other?" John snorted. "I never worked Miami."

"Cops would stonewall me if I asked them for help." CJ shook his head. The local police had become particularly unhelpful once the Hoovers asked them to back off.

"Okay, then someone needs to get close to Matt Smith." Aiden glanced at the twins, who stared back at him with identical *Who me?* expressions. "Come on. He's a guy. It'll be like winning at go-karts to get information out of him."

Roni rolled her eyes. "All right. Fine. We'll work on him, but no promises."

Tori just glared. The girls kept a low profile. Flirting with a cop was asking a lot of them, but with so many cars on the track, they had to have everyone in the pit.

"What else do we know about this chick?" Julian asked, finally showing some interest.

CJ glanced at his folder once more. "She works at

Everglades Air, a private airstrip outside of the city, which is owned by her high school best friend's parents, she lives in a sailboat and the slip is paid out until the end of next year, her car was stolen and burned out, she owns a motorcycle and has no speeding or parking tickets, though there is a dropped charge against her for assault."

"And you can't get the detective's notes on her?" Julian asked.

Aiden shook his head. "Not after that mess last year. If Smith knows anything, he's probably being smart about it and not putting it in her official record." He scrubbed the side of his face. "What are we doing then? Sitting on Madison until she gives us something we don't even know how to use?"

"Evers wants it, so we want it," Julian replied.

Great. Aiden wanted to end this thing, and Julian would be satisfied to live the rest of his life taking the bastard's toys. Would it ever end?

"Can we guess what's on the drive?" Aiden hadn't seen records of Michael Evers placing a single bet. Dustin was no stranger to the tracks in the city. There were at least a dozen different kinds of racetracks in Miami.

"He told you it was labeled 'Racing.'" Kathy shrugged. "It could be anything. Bank records, an admission of guilt, exchanges with the Colombians, who knows?"

Aiden didn't like not knowing, or the flimsy nature of their nonexistent plan. They were still idling at the starting line while everyone else was burning rubber around the first turn. There was a lot to make up for, but how? How did they get ahead of Michael and Dustin?

"Okay. Gabriel and John, can you see if any of your street contacts know anything about the Eleventh?"

"I want Emery to help me dig into Madison's past," CJ said.

"And we're on cop duty." Roni rolled her eyes.

"Then I guess it's you and me on this chick, bro." Julian smiled at him, but there was nothing pleasant about it.

"Great." Aiden glanced at CJ. "Anything else we should know?"

CJ shifted his weight from foot to foot. He was a built man, with salt-and-pepper hair. "We're getting pressure to produce results."

Aiden shrugged. "What else is new?"

"He means, if we can't get something done, they're going to pull us and put different field agents in our places," Kathy said.

"The fuck they will." Julian snarled. "That is not the agreement we made."

CJ wheeled on him. "It's been three years, Julian. When we started this, they thought a year, tops, to get the kind of evidence we needed to bring Evers down. I saw the report you made, and you said yourself it would be an easy thing—except it hasn't been. The man has someone covering his tracks so well we can't get a read on him. We're relying on an external hard drive that a woman we don't know if we can trust *might* have. That's not the kind of firm results you promised them. So before you go snapping my head off, remember that I catch the shit before it hits you."

"Whatever, I'm out of here." Julian stalked toward one of the exits. No one stopped him as he slammed it shut after him.

The FBI had changed Julian. The fighting had become a constant way of life in dealing with him.

He glanced at CJ. "I'll handle this. Everyone, go get some sleep. We have a lot of ground to cover."

Aiden followed Julian, stepping out onto the sidewalk. Julian leaned against his GT-R, tapping a package of cigarettes on his palm.

"When did this happen?" He nodded at the smokes, another disturbing sign of the depths to which Julian was falling.

"It's not happening. I had them for Mexico."

"Was that where you were?"

"Don't get on my case. It's my job."

Aiden withheld a sigh. "I don't give a rat's ass who made you do what. You just disappeared. That's not how this is supposed to go down."

"What? You're playing mamma now?"

"Why are you picking a fight? I'm tired, you're being a dick, and there's enough shit going around that everything stinks."

"I didn't pick a fight," Julian snapped.

Aiden stood next to the car. While Julian might lean on it, that didn't mean anyone else could.

"What happened in Mexico?" Aiden didn't want to know. He'd long since learned it was better for him if he didn't, but something had happened there that had Julian stirred up.

Julian stared down the street. It was the kind of stare that wasn't seeing the physical stuff, but memories. The ones that haunted your sleep and waking hours.

"It was kids and old people," Julian said, pitching his voice low.

Aiden didn't reply. What could he say?

"They sent me down there to work with a DEA undercover. All the suits are in a buzz and want a piece of what's going down. The border's still pretty hot, and the drug cartel has been pissing people off. I'm not sure why, but a coyote was getting a truckload of people across the border at an illegal crossing point and the cartel massacred them. Whole truck, full of kids and people's grandpas."

"Fuck." Aiden scrubbed his face with his hand. They'd

seen some atrocities serving overseas and seen some of the worst humanity had to offer. And yet, sometimes the worst was in your own backyard. "What did you do?"

"Suits wanted to pull us out, rethink the whole thing, talk about their dicks. Whatever."

Aiden had a bad feeling about this. Hadn't Roni told him Julian had gone C4 happy?

"The DEA guy and I decide to slip across the border while everyone else is packing up. We knew where the cartel boys had their headquarters, so we lit it up. Made sure there was nothing left of them." Julian shrugged. He acted like eliminating an entire arm of the border drug cartel was what you did after changing your oil.

How many had died? What about the innocents caught in the blast? Death was a car they'd learned to handle in the wake of the terrorist attacks of 9/11. What had begun as something to do with their lives after high school had turned into a mission. One that had honed them to kill and move on. But Aiden had never quite gotten on well with the moving-on part. No matter how horrible the person they had to kill—they were still a person. With family, a life, maybe a job and loved ones who would mourn them. Mexico was still so poor in many areas that the only way to make money was the drug trade. How could he fault someone for doing the only thing they could to put food on the table for their children? He didn't agree with it, but he also understood it.

Julian couldn't be completely untouched by what he'd done. The FBI needed someone to end a job, so they sent in Julian. The closing act.

"I'd like to just get in my car and go. Drive away from all of this." Aiden tipped his head back and gazed up at the stars.

"They'd find you. Bring you back."

Aiden glanced at his best friend. Or at least the man who looked like his best friend. This person was a stranger sometimes. Had he tried to leave them at some point? It wouldn't surprise Aiden, considering all they asked of Julian. They'd seen and done enough during their service to leave scars on their souls.

"If we can finish this, we could be done," Aiden said. He didn't see how an external drive and the ex-wife of a boss would bring down Evers, but maybe they were just the wedge in the door.

"Don't kid yourself. This'll never be done." Julian's laughter was rusty, bitter.

"Hey, man, why don't we get out of here? Go back to my place and grab a beer? I still have that fight taped."

"Yeah, okay. I could go for a beer."

Aiden wasn't too keen on spending time with Julian in this state, but keeping him close was better than turning him loose on the streets. Who knew what the ghosts would have him do?

Chapter Eight

Madison stared out of the hangar, the cool sea breeze bringing with it the scent of salt and rain. Out in the distance, dark clouds gathered over the water. The tropical storm all the pilots were worried about was not picking up speed to become a hurricane, but it was sure messing up their flight plans. Between the tropical storm south of them and spring downpours up north, almost all of the flights in and out of Everglades Air today were canceled.

The mechanics hadn't even bothered to come in. The only people here besides her were security and the guys in the tower.

She'd come into work hoping for a day of rerouted flights to keep her mind busy, and instead, all she could do was replay those last minutes with Aiden over and over and over again. Why hadn't she stopped herself? Couldn't she have pushed him away and kept a little piece of her self-respect? Leave it to her to completely muck up a situation.

Her phone vibrated and she cringed. Since it was during work hours, she couldn't ignore it. She peered at the screen and Aiden's number flashed across it. Again.

He'd already called her twice, once from each number he'd given her, but she hadn't answered. She knew she couldn't avoid him, but how did she act after last night?

Only one way to find out.

She sighed and clicked the green answer button.

"Hey."

"Sleep late?" The low pitch of his voice brought the memories into sharp focus in her mind. The way his stubble had scraped her cheek, the tight grip on her body, the way he'd had her bent over the bike.

"Uh, no. Been working."

"Everything okay?"

"Yeah. Shouldn't it be?"

"Yes, but I wanted to make sure."

"Well now you know." She turned and her hair whipped around into her face.

"Are you outside?"

"Yup. It's an airstrip. We do our business outside."

"Someone's sassy in the morning."

She pressed her lips together. Her morning habits were going to stay an off-limits topic.

The silence dragged on to become awkward.

Madison paced a couple of feet and turned around.

Should she bring up last night? Apologize for the wet spot?

God, could her life get any more embarrassing?

"Okay, well, let me know what happens," she said.

"Are you trying to get rid of me?"

Yes.

"No."

"Any chance you could get off early and meet up with me?"

She seriously doubted he just wanted to hang out. This was about the drive. Business.

"Mm, maybe. It's pretty slow today, but don't bet on it."

"Make time. I'm not going to be able to stall Dustin forever."

"I know, I know. Got to go, plane's coming in, bye." She ended the call and stared at the dial pad. Her and her stupid crush. Should she trust him already? When she thought about it, there was no reason to trust him—except he'd been completely honest and straightforward with her. But that didn't mean he wasn't hiding something, did it?

Madison walked out of the hangar and to her office, a little addition on one side of the main building for administrative purposes. When she'd first worked at the strip, she'd been a janitor, did some security and whatever else needed to be done. Over the years and her different employments, she'd worked her way up. She stepped into her office and closed the door behind her.

If her job didn't need her, maybe she could figure out which of the many locations she'd stashed her things when the divorce turned ugly.

There were a few places the boxes could be. She needed to make a list and then a few calls. The entire task took no more than twenty minutes. Three storage units and two friends, none of whom were answering.

The office line rang and she grabbed it.

"Everglades Air. How may I help you?"

"Madison, it's Nathaniel."

"Hey, I was just about to call you." She smiled, a reaction not many had to their boss, but Lily's parents had become her family.

"I just talked to the boys in the tower and nothing else is coming in or out today. The rain's mostly going to miss us, but it's hitting everyone else. Why don't you go on and get out of there? I don't like the idea of you on that bike if the weather report got it wrong and we get some of that storm."

"You don't have to do that." And yet it was just like him to worry about her as if he were her own father. She was lucky.

"No, no, I know, but I'd rather you be home safe. Or, you could come over here for dinner. Unless you and Lily have practice tonight?"

"Not tonight. We don't practice the night before a bout."

"Oh, that's right, that's right."

"Are you coming tomorrow?"

"Wouldn't miss it. My wife had shirts made for us." He grumbled about it, but Madison doubted there was any ill will behind it.

"Great, I'll see you guys tomorrow then."

"Not tonight?"

"I've got some school stuff I'd like to get ahead on while I've got the time. The summer semester's going to start soon and between classes and practice, I'm not going to have a lot of time to get the reading done, so why not get a jump on it now?"

"Think you could talk some of this sense into Lily?" He chuckled. Lily was naturally bright, but not inclined to go back to school. Her grand plan involved doing hair and painting, not exactly jobs her business-oriented parents understood.

"I'm not even going to try to go there."

"All right, all right. Get on the road, okay?"

"Thanks."

She hung up the phone and stared at it for a moment. The weather radar had Miami clear until well into the afternoon.

Did she go searching on her own? Or call for backup?

If she didn't tell Aiden she was looking for the drive he might become suspicious. She wanted him to trust her for some crazy, stupid reason. Maybe knowing he trusted her would make her feel better about trusting him.

She took a deep breath and hit dial on Aiden's number, the second one he'd given her. It rang and rang. She bounced on the balls of her feet and stared out of the window.

It was going to go to voice mail.

"Hey," Aiden said. The sound of a radio and the garage filtered through behind him. Duh. Of course he was at work.

"Oh, hey." She sat down, suddenly at a loss for words.

"Madison. Everything okay? What's wrong?" His tone completely changed, dropping to that deadly pitch.

"Nothing, sorry, I just got off work. Unexpectedly. The rain's messed with flights. So . . . yeah."

"Do you know where Flagler Dog Track is?"

"The Magic City Casino?"

"That's the one."

"Why not just meet at Classic Rides?" It was a strange place to meet, but it wasn't like her life had been normal since she'd left her mother's house.

"If one of the Eleventh guys is watching the garage I don't want them to see you. You're more mobile on the bike, but also vulnerable. Cops following you?"

"No, they don't check up on me during work since we have security here."

Thoughts of the Eleventh had worried her, but honestly, she could only handle so much. The Eleventh might be the straw that broke her.

"I'm taking care of the Eleventh. Don't worry about it." A door closed in the background and the sound of the tap turned on.

He sounded so sure of himself, like he knew what he

was doing. Only a crazy person could trust him. Maybe she'd hit her head a few too many times in practice, because she did. When Aiden said he'd take care of it, she didn't doubt him.

"What time?" She glanced down at her jeans and tank top. If she'd thought she was going to see Aiden before she went home, she'd have dressed cuter.

"Ten minutes ago."

"I'm on the road."

And damn it if butterflies weren't kicking up a storm in her stomach.

Madison peered up at the sky and bit her lip. The clear morning had turned gray and was beginning to rain in earnest. She stood under the awning at the once-sparkling casino and stared out at the parking lot. For some reason, despite all the people around her, she felt vulnerable. Unprotected. Her cop shadows had no idea where she was, and what if Aiden was right? What if the Eleventh, or worse, Dustin, followed her?

"Come on," a deep voice said behind her. A hand pressed against the small of her back, propelling her out from under the covered drive in front of the casino.

She glanced up at Aiden. His eyes were obscured by sunglasses and his lips were tightly compressed. It was crazy how relieved she was to see him, but she was not going to admit that to him.

"Hello to you, too. What gives? I've been waiting for twenty minutes." She veered toward her bike, but Aiden grabbed her hand and pulled her in the other direction. "My bike's over there." She'd parked next to a light pole so it was easy to find.

"We'll come back for it later, just move."

"What the hell?" she grumbled, but something about

the way he spoke or the way he carried himself made her excuse his lack of an answer. For now.

She had to quicken her step to keep up with him. The orange car he'd driven the first time they'd met sat a few rows back. He pushed her a little harder.

"What's the rush?" she asked again, glancing around.

"Just get in the car."

He stayed with her all the way to the passenger-side door and unlocked it for her. She'd have called him a gentleman except he didn't stick around to close her door, and she didn't think he was doing it to be polite.

"What's going on?" she asked.

He sank into the driver's seat and twisted to peer through the back window. "I'm being followed. That's why I didn't come straight to you. I had to see what they'd do."

"What? How do you know that?" She turned, but couldn't see anything through the rain-splattered glass.

He had been right. And—he'd used her as bait?

"There's a Shelby Mustang I saw earlier today at a light near the shop. Now it's parked two rows back."

"How do you know it's the same one and not a different car?"

"Because it has blue-on-blue stripes. That's not stock. It's a custom paint job and it stands out." He clicked his seat belt into place and tugged. "Buckle up and hold on."

The engine roared to life with a vengeance that shook the whole car.

Madison scrambled to grab the nylon strap. She shoved the clip into the buckle as the car shot backward, throwing her forward into the belt. It locked, holding her safely in place, but the inertia whipped her head around. Tires squealed and she smelled burning rubber one second before the acceleration of the vehicle shoved her into the plush seat.

Her heart pounded in her throat and she couldn't suck down enough oxygen.

The car skidded and fishtailed. Aiden steered them around a turn and gunned the engine. From the corner of her eye, she caught a glimpse of blue.

"Take a damn breath already and stop squealing," Aiden said.

Madison clamped her lips together. If she was making any noise at all, it was his fault.

He turned hard and cut off a pickup truck, but in a matter of seconds the irate driver was eating their exhaust.

"Who was that?" she demanded.

"Who do you think?"

"How am I supposed to know?"

"It was the Eleventh." He kept glancing in the rearview mirror.

At the next intersection, he turned, and turned again on the first side street they came across. They pulled into the parking lot of a nondescript building with no sign out front to denote what type of business it was. He shifted into park, pulled his cell phone out of his pocket, and tapped the screen a few times before holding it to his ear. Every few moments he'd twist this way and that, looking up and down the street.

"Hey. Something's up. Eleventh is tailing me," he said to whoever was on the other end of the line. "Uh-huh . . . Okay . . . That's not good . . . Keep me posted."

"What's not good? What about my bike? Were you just going to let them shoot me?"

"What? No." He frowned at her. "We'll get your bike later. It's raining too hard for you to ride that thing now. The tires are practically bald. You need new ones."

"Thanks, Captain Obvious. When I can afford new ones, I'll get them." She glared at him, but he was just stating the truth. Another paycheck and she'd have the summer semester covered, then she could concentrate on new tires.

"And your lawyer did what?"

She laughed. "What lawyer? Dustin scared away the few I could afford. I got nothing from the divorce."

Madison stared out of the window. Well that was a mood killer. For several moments neither of them said a word. The only sounds were the idling of the engine and the rain hitting the car. It was kind of soothing, actually. She'd always liked the rain.

A warm hand closed around hers. "We're going to get him."

She turned her head to face him. "I'll believe it when I see it. Sorry."

"I get it." He swiped his thumb back and forth across the back of her hand, each movement sending tendrils of awareness curling through her body.

There was no doubt that Aiden believed it when he said he'd take Dustin down. But one man against Dustin, his boss, and all their thugs? The cops couldn't even protect her from Dustin. How could Aiden do what a whole police force couldn't?

"What's this?" He pointed at her left arm, one of the last expanses of clean flesh on her arms.

"That would be a perfect outline of A'thing'a Beauty's shoulder. She got me in practice last week real good and it's started to turn pretty colors."

He shook his head. "I'm going to have to see this sometime."

"I'll save you a seat in the crash zone."

"Crash zone?"

"It's one of those things better left experienced." She grinned and one side of his mouth kicked up. That little dimple winked at her and, man, if it didn't twist her stomach into knots.

"Well, guess I'm coming to your next game."

"Bout."

He shrugged. "Bout."

Was it her imagination, or was he closer now than he'd been a few moments ago? It was hard to look at anything except his eyes, but she did like the pleasant twist of his lips.

She could feel his breath across her mouth, and he turned his hand under hers so that his palm was splayed over her thigh.

"This is not how this is supposed to go. I'm not supposed to want you. At all." His gaze flicked from her eyes to her mouth and back again.

"You can't control who you want. It just happens." And didn't she know it? Her whole life, one hot, bad choice of man after another. But Aiden wasn't bad, not really, right? He helped people.

"Do you want me?" His gaze narrowed and she felt the moment stretch tight.

The air in her lungs turned to ice and her body went hot, then cold. Whatever she said, it was going to change things. He had to know she wanted him, but if she said no, would he respect that? Her gut said yes. Whoever Aiden DeHart was, she couldn't help believing he was different. Maybe not entirely good, but honorable. He'd respect her wishes if she said no, and once that barrier was in place, she didn't think it could be torn down.

"Yes," she said with a sigh.

"But you aren't happy about it."

"I promised myself I'd only date good guys from now on." She lifted her hand and traced a small scar on his jaw. It had grown faint with time, but this close, she could make it out. "You aren't a nice guy."

"Good and nice are two different things. I think you'd roll right over a nice guy."

"Maybe." She chuckled. Hadn't Lily said the same thing to her before?

His hand coasted up and down her thigh, but she felt the caress much higher up. The little orgasm, the taste of bliss he'd given her last night, it hadn't sated anything. It had just made her hungrier for more.

Aiden leaned as he had last night, slowly, giving her every opportunity to turn away. Well wasn't that sweet? She cupped her hand around the back of his neck and pulled him closer. Their mouths met in a hard press of skin. Her teeth bit into the inside of her lip, but the pain only made the feel of his lips sharper, more pronounced.

His fingers slid between her legs and he squeezed. She gasped, needing air, and he deepened the kiss, breathing her in and tasting her. For a moment, she was swept up in his touch, the acceptance of this kiss, this chemistry, this crazy mess swirling around them and she surrendered to it. He thrust his tongue into her mouth and she groaned. The sound was loud in the confined space. She shoved her fingers through his short hair, relishing the feel of it against her palm.

Aiden's hand grazed her breast and she gasped, arching slightly. His mouth stilled against hers, as if her reaction had surprised him. If he had any idea how long it had been since someone touched her outside of derby practice, it wouldn't be quite such a shock.

She kept her eyes closed, unable to look at him. He shifted and cupped her breast. His lips grazed hers and she could hear his breathing along with the pounding of her heart. He lifted her breast, swiping his thumb over her nipple. The thin lace did little to inhibit the feel of his firm touch.

"We don't have time for this right now." His voice was

deeper, the frustration real. Well at least she wasn't alone in this.

Aiden cupped her face and crushed his mouth against hers, kissing her hard and fast. Her body thrummed with arousal. He sat back in his seat, staring at her with brows drawn down. He might not like the attraction, but she wasn't alone in it. At least he wanted her as much as she wanted him.

Chapter Nine

Aiden pulled out onto US-1, watching his rearview mirror closely.

"Will you tell me what's going on?" Madison asked.

She hadn't spoken since he'd backed off earlier in the parking lot. A little fancy driving and they were free to cruise for a bit. He did his best thinking behind the wheel of a car, so a little joy ride wasn't a bad thing.

"Canales is encouraging his boys to harass me. It should be harmless, but we can't risk them interfering with what we have going on."

"Harass you? That's harmless? I'd hate to see what you do to someone who actually threatens you."

"The gun was to warn him to back off. For the record, I'm always armed."

"Now?"

"Yes."

She stared at him.

"Where?" she ásked.

"There's one under my seat and another in the glove box."

"Holy hell." She drew her legs up, as if the gun by itself might hurt her.

"Canales hasn't got any proof it was me." Though he was beginning to think Canales wasn't interested in proof, just retaliation.

"How do you know that?"

"I just do." He glanced in his rearview. A silver Scion sports car zipped between an ice truck and a minivan, changing lanes like the Devil himself were riding his bumper. "Shit."

"What?" Madison twisted in her seat.

"Company." Aiden slid a little lower and felt under the seat and flicked the leather strap holding his Glock in place. He prayed he wouldn't need it, but neither would he hesitate to use it.

"Who is it?"

"Two of Canales's boys."

A second, lime-green STI with a spoiler that stuck up like a fin swerved through traffic, following the silver car closely. Did he try to outrun the two cars, or did he play it cool? The road stretched ahead of them with little opportunity to outmaneuver the other two, not to mention the slick conditions would make any fancy driving more difficult. He eased off the accelerator and slid into the right lane. The two cars broke free from the pack of vehicles and zoomed up behind him, one in either of the other two lanes.

"What's going on?" Madison asked, her voice pitched high.

"Play it cool." Inside, he was ready to throw a wrench at these idiots. It was one thing to race, to want to smell the rubber burn, but it was something else entirely to do it on a busy street with pedestrian traffic at every intersection. Hadn't the Eleventh learned anything?

The two cars drew up alongside him. The silver Scion had its windows down. Aiden recognized the driver. He was one of the Eleventh's fastest and cockiest drivers.

He was young, maybe midtwenties, with short hair and a lanky, Cuban build.

All three cars eased to a stop at a red light. The road ahead of them broke free from the urban sprawl, and for about the span of a half mile, cut through a stretch of lowland with little to no other traffic. Belatedly, Aiden realized just where they were. The short distance was prime sprinting ground for short races. But those were usually at night, when the streets were empty.

The silver Scion revved his engine and Aiden sighed. Well, at least they weren't trying to shoot holes in his Chevelle. The windshield wipers squeaked over the glass. The rain was letting up.

"Hold on and don't scream." He found the sweet spot on the accelerator, that point where the engine purred, waiting to be let loose on the open road, but didn't quite burn her tires.

Madison gripped the door and braced her feet on the floorboard, as if preparing herself for a wreck.

Aiden ticked down the seconds, watching the light for the cross traffic, waiting for it to turn yellow. The green STI squealed, fishtailing at a standstill, while the silver Scion wheezed. Julian might like the foreign makes, but to Aiden they all sounded nasal and high-pitched.

The cross-traffic light blinked to yellow.

Aiden pressed his accelerator a bit more and the car began to vibrate.

Madison gasped, but whatever else she might have said or done faded into nothing.

It was Aiden, his car, and the road.

He could see the other two cars in his peripheral vision, but his focus narrowed on the lights.

The cross-traffic light flipped to red.

He locked his gaze on the light above his lane and shifted.

The light blinked green.

His Chevelle shot forward, the good ol' American-made engine roared, but his start wasn't fast enough. The green STI swerved in front of him while the silver Scion bolted forward, taking the lead.

Aiden gritted his teeth and took the center lane. The STI moved with him, cutting it so close Aiden lost sight of the car's license plate. He shifted once more and jerked the car to the left. The STI lurched into the left lane, while Aiden pulled back into the center and slammed his foot on the accelerator. Too late, the green driver realized his error as Aiden cruised past.

The Scion driver hung not too far ahead of Aiden, waiting for his turn.

Adrenaline pumped through Aiden's veins. The next light was in sight, less than a quarter mile to go. He drew even with the silver car, the STI hanging at his bumper. There was no way any of them could punch it to their top speeds and not barrel through the intersection.

He could shift and push it—but was it worth it?

Aiden took a deep breath and eased off the accelerator. The Scion driver matched him, and together the three braked at the light, engines hot.

Madison sucked down lungfuls of air.

He glanced at her. Her eyes were wide, her lips parted. Was that fear? Or excitement?

"Who won?" she asked.

"No one won anything."

The light changed to green and the Scion turned right, while Aiden and the STI continued along US-1. At the first opportunity, Aiden turned off the road and into a gas station.

"I feel like a broken record here, but what the hell are you doing?" Madison asked.

He held up a finger and pointed at the squad car that flew by. "Cops like to hang a few blocks over sometimes. We used to race this strip, then the police started showing up as soon as we did. I bet someone around here called the cops. Works in our favor."

"Wow." She stared at the cruiser, watching it close in on the green car.

Thunder nearly shook the car. Overhead, lightning zigzagged through the sky. A new wave of heavy rain began pelting the Florida coast.

"What about the silver car?" she asked.

"He's long gone." Aiden shifted into park and turned toward Madison. She was a problem, a complication he didn't need and yet he had to face the uncomfortable reality that he wanted her. She hadn't rejected him when he'd gone in for a kiss, but she also seemed to be caught up in the same web of attraction as him.

Madison licked her lips, and damn him if he didn't track that movement, remembering the feel of her tongue tangling with his.

"I want to be straight with you," he said.

"You mean you aren't normally straight?"

He shook his head and she chuckled. Damn, she had a mouth on her. And he liked it. With Madison, he didn't have to sugarcoat things or tone down who he was. She just took it in stride. He dug that.

"Sorry, sometimes stuff just pops out of my mouth. You scream heterosexual," she said.

"Thanks, I think?" The momentary tension was broken. He relaxed by degrees.

"You're welcome. Now what are we doing?"

"We're going to work together, for how long, I don't know." Aiden had approached Madison with the truth, so it was the only way to proceed, even if he felt like a monster truck barreling through this. "I never intended . . . what I mean is we're clearly attracted to each other. I don't want you to think I'm playing you."

"You would do that?" Her eyes grew round and her jaw dropped.

"People use all sorts of means to get what they want. I'm telling you that's not what this is." Why did she look so innocent in her shock? After what Madison had lived through, nothing should surprise her, and yet he'd clearly just opened her eyes to a new kind of deception.

She sat back in her seat. "That never occurred to me."

"Maybe not right now, but at some point you'd have thought about it. You're a smart girl."

"Could have fooled me." She sighed, her shoulders slumping.

"I just told you I can't help myself around you and you're—disappointed?"

Madison's mouth opened and closed. She shook her head and her cheeks grew pink. "That's not what I meant."

He reached across and took her hand—because he wanted to and hell, he needed to touch her, to see some of that spunk back in her gaze. She peeked at him from the corner of her eye, and he could see a glimmer of the girl she'd once been. The cute cheerleader who'd just wanted what she'd never had. He rubbed his thumb across her pulse and the corners of her mouth curled up in a slight smile. She was the reason he did this job. Madison and others like her he helped extract from sticky situations. He'd let go of the idea of revenge as best he could. His sister wouldn't want him to get caught up in it like Julian had.

There'd been a time in his life when he'd expected

to return to the States, get a job and turn it into a career with cars, and somewhere along the way, he'd meet a girl. Probably one a lot like Madison with sass, someone who'd brighten his days until the horrors he'd seen were a distant memory. He'd always wanted a family, kids who would play with the nieces and nephews his sister would have. But that was in the past. It wasn't the future for him now.

"I can't offer you anything except that I will make sure Dustin is never a problem for you again. What happens between us—I can't promise anything. Dates, normal stuff, I can't do that." Aiden wanted Evers put away, he wasn't stupid enough to think it was a slam-dunk case. This was a long-haul war they were waging, and Madison could be a casualty—but not if he got her out of it and far away from him.

Her smile faded though she continued to study him. For several moments she didn't speak, which bothered him. She was a mouthy, chatty thing. Her silence irritated his nerves.

"I'm not sure what made you think I was looking for more, but I'm not. I just got divorced. I'm not interested in relationships. Not now, at least."

It was a reasonable reply, and yet he didn't like it. She deserved more.

"The only thing I am in the market for is some fun, but since you clearly don't know what that word means, well"—she shrugged—"you don't have to worry about that."

The way she purred the word *fun,* he knew exactly what she meant.

"Maybe you should show me?" Toying with her and the lust making his dick throb was not his brightest idea, but bottling it up would be worse.

"Me? Oh, I don't know if you can handle it." She placed her hand against her chest and batted her eyelashes. It was outrageous, a little silly, and yet he wanted to pounce on her, devour her, and spend the rest of the rainy day showing her exactly how much *fun* he could be.

Aiden leaned across the car. He should turn this part of the gig over to the twins or maybe one of the other guys. And yet, it wasn't about to happen. He was keeping Madison all to himself.

Madison held her ground though he could see the way her hand trembled and her throat flexed as she swallowed. He invaded her space until he could smell the tropical scent that clung to her skin.

"Try me," he said. And he hoped she did.

Madison strolled down the aisle between the storage units, forcing herself to concentrate on the numbers—and not the man keeping stride with her, holding the umbrella over her. Her hands hadn't stopped shaking since their chat in the car. What had gotten into her? Her mouth had always been an issue, but around Aiden it got away from her. She still didn't quite know what agreement they'd come to.

He brushed his hand along the small of her back and she sucked in a breath.

"Twelve-twelve?" He pointed at the metal rolling door ahead of them.

"That's it." She marched forward and knelt to unlock the door.

"Here, give me that. You'll get wet." Aiden shoved the umbrella at her and took the key before she could voice a protest.

She stared at his broad shoulders while he worked

the lock. It was one thing to be attracted to him—she couldn't help that. It was another thing to lean on him, to accept his help and even feel some gratitude that he was there. She didn't know if she liked coming to rely on him.

Aiden got the lock off the door and rolled it up, holding it for her to step inside. He clicked on the flashlight he'd brought from the car and shone the beam around the long, narrow locker. There was furniture piled up on top of blocks, wrapped in plastic. A bunch of crates were neatly lined up on shelves.

"Where do we start?" he asked.

She gestured toward the messy stack of boxes and a few plastic bags piled together. "This is my stuff. Everything else is a friend's."

Madison took a deep breath and lifted the first box from the pile.

"How is it you've had something of Dustin's for three years and he just now realized it?" Aiden asked.

"Well, uh, about six months ago, all my things were in one storage unit, but Dustin argued it was his. I had about two hours to get everything out of it before it became his property, so my girlfriends all came over and we divided everything up between their cars and they stashed stuff where they could. Closets, sheds, attics, garages, and a few of them already had stuff in storage units. I'd ridden with one of the girls to grab some burgers for everyone. While I was gone, Dustin's goons showed up and had everyone kicked out of the unit and trashed everything else. I was pissed, so I went to the house we used to live at. He was moving out at the time, and we had a fight. He told me off and stormed out, so I grabbed some of his boxes to trash them."

"But you kept them instead?"

She sighed. "Yeah, they got mixed up in everything

else and by the time I realized what I had, I couldn't exactly hand it over. I reboxed everything so I wouldn't know what was in each box and randomly gave them to my friends to hide for me. It's stupid, but I kind of feel guilty about it. I guess all he's proven is that I still have a conscience."

"That's not a bad thing." He stared into the top box without seeing its contents. "You don't want to lose it. Trust me."

Madison watched him, the distant, hard expression, the way his lips compressed into a thin line. What had he lost?

"Who are they?" Aiden lifted a picture frame out of the box. Three teenage girls with ponytails and bows in their hair smiled back.

She opened her mouth and closed it. The picture had sat on her dresser for years before she'd boxed it up. She'd probably passed it a thousand times without much thought, and yet, the eyes of the girl on the right speared her.

"That's my sister and her two best friends." She swallowed around the lump in her throat. "Well, they were her friends then. I haven't seen her in . . . shit. Ten years."

"Ten years? Why?" Aiden flipped through the rest of the box and set it aside, stowing the picture away with the rest.

"My mother didn't exactly approve of her eighteen-year-old daughter marrying a man thirteen years older. She kicked me out the night I told her Dustin and I were getting married. God, that's the last time I saw her. When I came by a few days later to get my stuff it was just my little sisters. They cried and Amanda gave me her teddy bear, she was barely ten and still slept with it.

Emily, the one in the picture, she barely spoke to me." Madison tipped her head back and stared at the ceiling, willing the unshed tears to dry up.

The memories opened up, fresh and full of punch. The look in her mother's eye when she'd proudly displayed her engagement ring had made Madison's joy wither, but she'd been so determined to be happy. "Mom was so angry. Dad left not long after Amanda was born, and Mom did everything to raise us. Looking back, I think she thought she'd failed me because it was pretty obvious I was only after Dustin's money and what I thought was a better life. Mom raised me better than that. Now, I've lost that life and them."

She moved a few things around in the box without really seeing them.

Great, just unload on the guy, why don't you? Want to handle the rest of my problems too?

Madison took a deep breath and packed her mistakes back into a closet in the back of her mind. She'd deal with it eventually. When she'd made something of herself. Got a degree. Then she'd find her family and make things right—if they'd have anything to do with her.

"It's hard being cut off from family," Aiden said quietly, sifting through another box.

She went very still, afraid to breathe for fear he'd stop.

"I haven't spoken to mine in years. They blame me for—things. About the only person who acknowledges me is my grandmother, but she doesn't give a shit what anyone thinks." He smiled, and she had to wonder what the old woman was like. Did she have his eyes? Would he smile for her?

"Why don't they talk to you?" She set her box aside and pulled her knees up to her chest.

Aiden stepped back, hands on his hips, and surveyed

the small pile of boxes they'd gone through. They were all her things, personal mementos, keepsakes of a life she'd left behind. The silence stretched on for a few moments.

He wasn't going to tell her.

She couldn't blame him. They didn't know each other. Not really.

Madison stood and plopped her box back on the stack. She straightened the boxes, resisting the urge to grab the picture of Amanda. It wasn't like she had any place to put it.

"My sister was murdered and my family blames me for it."

She turned toward him, his words on repeat while she processed their meaning. Murdered? As in kicked the bucket? Dead?

"You didn't kill her." Madison didn't believe for an instant he was involved. She had no doubt Aiden was capable of doling out death, but not to his sister.

"No, but I'm the one who asked her husband for help with something I shouldn't have." His expression was shuttered. It didn't take a rocket scientist to know he wouldn't share more.

"That . . . that sucks."

"Yeah." He nodded. "It's probably better this way."

Aiden wore responsibility like she wore crash pads. It protected him, insulating him from the things he was missing out on. All for what? This thing with Michael Evers?

"Because of what you do?"

Aiden glanced at her, his gaze narrowing.

She straightened her spine and stared right back at him. "I might not be a suspicious person, but I'm not blind. You're doing something dangerous. You can't date. Your family's better off away from you. What's going on?"

He sighed heavily and for a moment she glimpsed his pain.

"It's better if you don't know," he said.

"Probably. But I'm involved."

"Yeah, well, you shouldn't be."

Her heart hurt for him.

"That's why you do this, isn't it? You're helping people. I'm not the first, am I?"

His silence was all the answer she needed. She couldn't guess at the life Aiden lived, but it seemed pretty lonely.

Chapter Ten

Aiden eased the car to a stop at the curb in front of a large, two-story bungalow. The red shutters were freshly painted and the grass just cut. It was the picture of everything he didn't have.

Madison hadn't talked much since leaving the storage unit, which he was grateful for. Why had he told her about Andrea? It was a stupid moment of peering into life's rearview mirror. All because he'd watched Madison relive the entire experience of losing her family. She had an expressive face, and in that moment, he hadn't been able to shut off his own memories from hosing him down.

"I can go in if you want to wait out here." Madison popped her seat belt.

"Of course I'm coming with you."

"You can trust me, you know? I will give the stuff to you when I find it."

He stared at her. Did he trust her? Despite her lack of self-preservation skills, he did. She wasn't like Dustin. There wasn't anything dishonest about her.

"Okay, come in if you want. Just a warning, Sindercella's

grandmother is kind of a trip." She slid out of the car and stepped onto the sidewalk.

He got out of the car and walked around to meet her. "Sindercella?"

"I don't know her real name." Madison shrugged.

"Is that common?"

"For derby girls? Yeah. Once you pick your name your real one hardly matters."

He shook his head as she rang the doorbell. His pocket began to vibrate, the one with his burner phone reserved especially for Dustin.

Shit.

"I need to take this. Back in a minute, okay?"

He backtracked to the car, answering the phone and watching as Madison stepped into the bungalow.

"What?" he said.

"Do you have it?" Dustin asked.

"Not yet."

Dustin blew out a breath, the sound rattling through the phone.

"What am I paying you for?" Dustin spat.

Inwardly, Aiden groaned. Dustin was going to play it this way? Someone had to be leaning on him hard, probably Evers. What was on that drive?

"You're paying me to do what I do best. Getting the job done quietly and with no mess. If you'd like to send your goon squad over to do it instead, be my guest. I'm wasting time with this bitch making nice. You could have told me she has a police escort everywhere." Aiden glanced over his shoulder, half expecting to see Madison trying to listen in, but she wasn't there. He felt a tiny pang of guilt for how he was talking about her, but in the long run his tactics might save her life.

"They let you close to her?"

"Yeah, but I don't like this. You screwed with me."

"You're resourceful. I need this drive soon. You don't understand, no one knows I don't have it." Dustin pitched his voice low.

Was that so? It made sense why Dustin was pulling in someone who had no connection to his organization.

"Think you're going to get it?" Dustin asked.

"Hell yes I'll get it. That's what you're paying me for, remember?"

"Fine. Yes. But I need it. Sooner than what we talked about."

Aiden grimaced. "How soon?"

"Sunday soon."

"I'll get the job done."

"Good. Good. Later."

Aiden shoved the burner back into his pocket and glanced at the house once more. Today had not gone according to plan from the beginning, but instead of being irritated at skipping out on a whole day at the shop, he didn't mind having spent it with Madison.

She made him laugh and her easy chatter about her life gave some semblance of normalcy to what they were doing. Despite what they were doing, being with her made him feel—normal. Like a guy with his girl. It wouldn't last. He wasn't about to kid himself, but it just drove home how far from normal his life had become. The stuff with Dustin, that was his new normal.

It was for the best his family was out of his life, but Madison's? That was something that could be fixed.

He punched in Emery's number and hit dial.

"What's up?" Emery drawled.

"Hey, I want you to find out where Madison's mother and sisters are now. Surface-level stuff, address, occupation, any red flags or notable events."

There was a moment of silence before Emery responded. "Do we think they're involved?"

Aiden could already hear Emery tapping away at his computer.

"No, this isn't related. It's for Madison. When this is all over she's going to need someone in her life." Someone who wasn't him.

"I'm on it. Anything else?"

"Nah, I did just have a little run-in with two Eleventh drivers, but I have a feeling that's the way things are going to be for a while."

"I'll let Julian know."

"No, leave him out of this. Tell Tori and Roni, maybe, but not Julian."

"Whatever you say. Mamma Haughton's information is incoming. Hey, we finally got Ross's financials today and there's some stuff we need to talk about."

"Like?"

"Like the fact that the guy is broke. Unless he's got some hidden accounts somewhere, Dustin Ross has almost no money."

"How's he making deals?"

"Could be he's keeping all the cash on hand, but that's dangerous." Cash could be stolen, which was why banks and offshore accounts were necessity.

"Find out how he's paying for stuff."

Aiden hung up and glanced at the text about Madison's mother. He tried to never think too much about Emery's role in what they did. It was more than tech support. He had to anticipate their needs, listen for chatter, and be proactive. Which meant Emery spent a lot of time digging around in their lives and what was going on in Miami. What that man knew could destroy them all if he wanted to. But he was circumspect. He'd found Madison's family in a matter of seconds, and the only people who'd know he did it would be Emery and Aiden.

It was growing late in the afternoon, and a glance at the weather report showed storms heading their way.

He wasn't positive Dustin hadn't set someone else after Madison, too. There was always the danger that she'd go back to her slip and be ambushed.

There was no denying he wanted to keep Madison close. He wanted to protect her, to keep her safe. Which was exactly why he needed to cut down how much time they spent together. He was man enough to admit she had some crazy attraction for him, and he wasn't sure he'd stop the next time with just kissing her.

Aiden made up his mind. He'd deposit her back onto her bike, follow her to the slip after changing cars once more, and send one of the twins out to be her security detail. Probably Tori so he'd have Emery's eyes on the girls as well. He wasn't sure what was going on with their tech or Tori, but Emery seemed to pay close attention to the mechanic. Once Madison was settled, he could pay Dustin a visit and get a little more information. If he was lucky, he could still get in a full night's rest.

He strode up the walk and knocked on the door.

An elderly Asian woman whisked it open. She wore a bright purple velour tracksuit and her glasses were studded with rhinestones.

"Come in, come in. Are you single?"

He stepped over the threshold and paused, glancing from the grandma to Madison, sitting on a sofa with several boxes stacked around her.

"*Sobo!* You'll scare men off asking them that. Don't! Do you ever want me to get married?" A young woman stomped out of the kitchen at the back of the house, waving a spatula at the elderly woman. He assumed this was Sindercella. She had the indeterminable ageless grace of Asian women, but he'd still peg her for midtwenties. The pigtails and thigh-high rainbow socks didn't help.

"You won't get married if you don't ask," her grandmother retorted.

"You're killing me, *Sobo*." Sindercella rolled her eyes and threw her arms up in the air, but she couldn't smother her grin fast enough.

"Come sit down." The grandma gave his ass a firm squeeze. "Helena, this one is ripe. You should keep him."

Aiden tensed, but put one foot in front of the other. Madison's eyes bulged and she slapped her hand over her mouth. He quickly took a seat next to her before *Sobo* got both her hands on him.

"Not one word," he growled at Madison, and grabbed the topmost box.

Madison studied Aiden's profile in the waning light as he navigated the car back to the main drag. Despite *Sobo*'s eccentric personality, he'd warmed to her over the course of digging through boxes and a light dinner.

"Okay, so what's their deal?" he asked after a few moments of silence. He seemed more relaxed than she'd ever seen him.

"Sindercella and *Sobo*?"

"Yeah. What's *sobo* mean?"

"'Grandma' in Japanese. Sindercella came out to her family last year. She's bisexual. They kicked her out. *Sobo*, who insists everyone call her *Sobo* by the way, said it was stupid, that they moved to America for a new way of life, so Sindercella's lived with her since. I get the idea *Sobo* doesn't see the rest of the family much as a sign of disapproval, and there's a lot of tension over it. But they're happy together. I think *Sobo* likes looking after Sindercella because she's so independent. They're pretty similar. I think *Sobo* always wanted to go to college and now that Sindercella's putting herself through classes, she's happy as a clam. I stayed with them off and on a couple of times. It's a trip."

"Grandmothers." He shook his head and she knew he had to be thinking about his own grandmother. What was she like? Did she have Aiden's eyes?

"Do you see yours often?" she asked, knowing it might not be a topic he'd allow.

Aiden was quiet for a moment and his smile slowly faded. He wasn't going to answer her.

She rested her head against the seat and closed her eyes. The car was a smooth ride, but the way the engine vibrated tickled her skin, almost as if it sought to keep a connection with her.

"I see her the last Sunday of every month. I drive up to a cabin in the middle of nowhere and we have lunch, then spend the afternoon fishing and cook whatever we catch for dinner."

"Fishing, huh? I didn't peg you for the type." She smiled, cherishing the gift he'd given her.

"Really? What type am I?"

"The bad-boy, car type. I'm not sure I can picture you with a fishing pole. Hell, I've never been fishing."

"Don't knock it. It's a relaxing experience, but I'm not sure you'd be much good with that mouth."

"Hey, I like my fucking mouth." Okay, so she had some issues with the way she talked, what else was new?

He glanced at her and in the dim light it wasn't hard to mistake the heat in his gaze. Was her language all he thought about when it came to her mouth? She hadn't performed oral on a man since . . . well, she couldn't quite remember, but for Aiden? She could be a quick student.

Last night had taken her by surprise. What would she

do if he kissed her again and they weren't interrupted by a car chase? He'd admitted his attraction wasn't fabricated, that it wasn't part of a ploy to ease her into acquiescence. But was that his plan? To seduce her, tell her it wasn't fake, and still have her fall for him?

She discarded the idea immediately. He'd been truthful with her from the beginning. There was no reason to not take him at his word.

So what would she do?

Her pulse jumped and her body thrummed with lust. Her nipples tightened, chafing at the silky fabric of her bra. The car's vibrations, once pleasant, now seemed to be especially designed to heighten her sensitivity. She clenched her thighs together, and still felt the car's movement in her clit.

She'd fuck him. She knew, given the opportunity, she'd do it. The trick would be to keep her heart to herself. She had no idea how she'd manage that.

Madison was a serial monogamist. It was what kept her from cheating on Dustin. It was what had made her fall fast and hard in high school for her sweetheart and stick with him, and it wasn't any different now.

Aiden wasn't a bad guy, but neither was he nice. He was something in the middle, dangerous, with a heroic streak, and damn it if she didn't want to fall victim to his temptations. He'd show her what a real man could do to a woman. It wouldn't be a fast coupling, and he'd leave marks below the skin.

The car turned into the parking lot of Magic City Casino and Flagler Dog Track. There were more cars now, and the track lights lit up the night sky. The twinkling marquee glittered against the mist, like a diamond blanket, hiding the shabby exterior.

He pulled around the front and slowly rolled by the light pole she'd left her bike next to.

It wasn't there.

Dread sliced through the aroused fog.

"Where's my bike?" She sat up, peering through the cars.

Aiden sighed and pulled out his cell phone. He flipped through the pages of apps and brought up something that looked like a mapping program. He set it into a cradle mounted on the dash.

"What's that?"

"It's a tracking device I put on your bike."

"You what?" She gaped at him, not knowing what to think. Was this her heroic bad boy?

"Look, if you got into trouble, if I couldn't find you, or if you were really working with Dustin, I needed a way of finding out."

"I left Dustin. How many times can I tell you that?"

"I know, I know. I put the tracker on there before we hashed the hell out of that." He eased back onto the street, following the red path. He smacked the steering wheel with the palm of his hand. "What if one of his idiots chased you somewhere? What if you needed help and just got a connecting call to me before it was cut off? I did what I thought was best for your protection."

She held her tongue, anger and panic at the loss of her bike warring for her attention. So much for trust. He couldn't have asked her? A simple, reasonable explanation would have won her over.

How was she going to get to work and school if the bike was gone? Who was behind this?

She peered at the phone screen while he took a left turn. A red dot blinked to the left of the yellow circle that was the car.

"Fuck."

Aiden turned into a dark, deserted parking lot. His headlights reflected off the green, glittery paint of part of the body. A wheel was propped up against the side of the boarded-up building.

Madison's breath froze in her lungs.

Her bike.

It wasn't a fast bike, or really impressive, but it had been hers. The means to a better life, an education, freedom, that bike carried her hopes and dreams.

She pushed her door open, ignoring Aiden's stern "Wait."

She tromped through a puddle, one hand clapped over her mouth and water splashing her ankles. In a way, the bike was her future. It wasn't like she had a neighbor she could hitch a ride with, and she'd need every last penny to pay for the summer semester.

The custom paint job was chipped and now had black spray paint marring the surface. The bike itself was in several pieces.

There was no fixing this.

"Madison," Aiden growled, and grasped her by her shoulders, the heat of his body warming her back. There was a gun in his hand aimed at the shadows.

She hugged her arms around herself. Desperation and loss threatened to drown her. She glanced around them, looking for the threat, but one didn't materialize.

"Go back to the car." He gently turned her and pushed her back to the Chevelle.

"Is someone out there?" she asked, keeping her voice low.

"I don't know."

"Who did this?" She wheeled around, but he caught her once more by her shoulders. The gun pressed into her shoulder, an ever present reminder that they were still in danger.

"I don't know." He tightened his grip on her. "Madison, stop. I'll figure out who did this, but it would not be a good idea to call the police and tell them we found the bike. What we need to do is have you report it as missing. Let the cops find it. Insurance will take care of the rest."

She cringed. Sure, the bike was insured, but it wasn't worth much. Not enough to get her another set of wheels. She needed to call her boss, let them know she was out indefinitely until she could get a new ride. Maybe summer school was out of the question until she rebounded from this, but then that would put her plans behind schedule, and she couldn't double up on classes in the fall. She might have to take an absence from derby.

Aiden steered her to the car and helped her into her seat. He went back to the pieces of her bike, tucking the gun into his waistband. The seat torn up and the body dented and busted. He knelt next to it and tugged a bandanna that had hung from his back pocket. He pulled something out from under what had been the fender and wrapped it in the cloth.

The tracking device. Right. He wouldn't want someone finding that.

He strode back to the car, his features blank and unreadable as ever.

Aiden said he cared about what happened to her. Did he really?

The headlights reflected off her helmet lodged in some bushes. An eleven was painted on it.

Aiden stepped into the beam of light, blocking the eleven from view. Could she trust him to fix this, too? She wanted to believe in him.

Chapter Eleven

Aiden dropped into the car, dread rolling in his gut. The Eleventh was getting bolder. He couldn't ignore the threat they posed to his team—much less Madison. He closed the door and turned toward her. The sight of tears trickling down her cheek felt like a sucker punch.

Madison wasn't the kind of woman who cried. She was bold and ballsy.

"Hey. Hey." He reached across and brushed the moisture from her cheek.

She flinched away from him, as if she hadn't been aware of his presence, and wrapped her arms around herself.

This was his fault. He'd make it right, but first he needed to take care of her.

He leaned an arm on the back of her seat, hating how she hunched over, drawing in on herself.

She continued to stare at her bike and drew in a deep breath. "I need to call work, let them know I can't come in. I'll have to find something cheap to replace it. I think I've got a couple grand for school I can use. Someone will have to give me a ride to the bout tomorrow and—"

"Madison. Look at me, please."

Her frown deepened. She had a right to be pissed at him. It was only because of him that Canales had her in his sights at all. He watched her eyes dry and that stubborn, determined glint lit up once more. She tossed her hair over her shoulder and turned toward him, her jaw thrust forward and her lips tightly compressed.

He could handle her anger. The tears, though, those made him want to make everything better with no care to what else had to happen.

Aiden rested his hand on her knee, her body heat soaking through the denim.

"I'm going to take care of this. Canales isn't going to bother you again. Let's go back to the track and call in the missing bike. They can do the rest." It was time to get the Hoovers in on this. If the Eleventh posed a danger to her and their operation, they could send in the DEA to hit them hard and take the threat out.

"And what am I supposed to do? How am I going to get home? What about work? And getting to and from practice? I have a fucking bout tomorrow. What am I supposed to do about that?" Her voice broke and he could see the sheen of fresh tears in her eyes.

Not the tears, anything but the tears.

"I'm going to take care of it." He didn't know how, but it wasn't like he was hurting for cars. He'd think of something for her.

Her brows drew down and he could see the distrust taking root. It shouldn't bother him, it wasn't like he needed her trust to do his job, but it rankled him.

"Give me a chance to make it right, okay?" He squeezed her knee, but her wall of anger didn't seem to be coming down anytime soon.

Aiden slipped the gun out from his waistband and tucked it under his thigh. If the Eleventh was stepping up their game, it was time to pay them some attention. He sat back into his seat and shifted into drive. They needed to go back to the track, Emery would have to do his thing and magic away any footage of them on the trail of her bike. It was another complication he didn't need.

He wouldn't be leaving her side. Not unless he could be assured the Eleventh wouldn't go after her. The bike was a thing of opportunity. He could understand that, even if she didn't. Canales was escalating, going from threats to damage of property—Aiden didn't think it would take much for him to go after a person. While he could handle himself, Madison wouldn't stand a chance.

They pulled into the parking lot of Flagler Dog Track. He stuck to the back of the lot and shifted into park.

"Report the bike missing. We can stick around for a bit if they want to talk to you." He wouldn't like being involved in an official report, but it couldn't be helped.

Madison pulled her phone out of her pocket with a long-suffering sigh and tapped the screen.

He took the opportunity to text Emery the barest details and see about any footage. If they caught the Eleventh busting her bike it would be a nice way to wrap things up with them for now. He also warned CJ they had trouble. It would take time to mobilize the DEA, and he wanted to get the ball rolling.

"Hi, Matt, it's Madison." Her voice was different.

Aiden brought up his e-mail, but couldn't help listening to her conversation.

"Sorry to bother you, but you said to call if I needed anything." She sighed and paused. "I know, thanks, I appreciate that. I was out at Flagler Dog Track, I thought I'd hand out fliers for tomorrow's bout . . . Oh, you're coming? I'll be sure to look for you." She cringed, a knee-jerk reaction she couldn't cover up. "My bike is missing. I have no idea where it is and no one here seems to remember it either."

Detective Matt Smith would be at tomorrow's bout, huh? It was probably time to tell the good detective to shove off. Madison was his, and he didn't share.

He flipped back to his text messages and fired one off to Roni, who'd said she would attempt to make contact with the cop today. He'd been so wrapped up in Madison he hadn't asked for an update.

A new text rolled to the top from Gabriel, the shop's mechanic and jack-of-all-trades.

Got the parts in today.

Aiden had to pause to think about what parts he was talking about before remembering the old Mustang they'd picked up at an auction for pennies.

Great. Let's set aside a few days next week to work on that. I need a favor. Can you find Madison some wheels?

"Okay, thanks, Matt. Let me know if you find out anything." She sighed and hung up.

His phone chimed with another text.

Two wheels or four? Engine or no?

He snorted before replying.

Either, engine a must, dumbass.

"What did he have to say?" Aiden asked.

"Nothing much. We'll look into it. Matt has been the

guy they send out whenever something happens with Dustin, so I figured I'd save the cops the work and just call him directly." She shrugged and dropped the phone into her lap.

"I'm getting one of the guys to look for a new set of wheels for you." He turned once more toward her, wanting to ease her mind.

"You don't have to do that."

Of course she'd say that.

"Maybe I do, maybe I don't, but I am. Should know something tomorrow."

She took a deep breath and glanced toward the bright lights of the casino.

"Hey." He grabbed her hand and squeezed. "It's going to be okay."

"How can you be so certain?"

He wasn't, but she needed him to be.

"Tonight was a matter of wrong place, wrong time. I'll make it right. We just need to get the drive, and I can do the rest from there."

"How do you do it all?"

I've got a team of FBI agents and people who might be considered criminals if they weren't working for the good of Miami in my back pocket.

"I know people. I learned a lot in the military. It becomes a useful combination."

Madison had to know he wasn't telling her everything, and she didn't seem to mind. The strain eased from her face and her fingers twined with his, accepting the comfort and maybe his help.

"What now?" she asked.

"I wait for a call from a guy, and after that, we figure it out from there."

"Should I ask who you're waiting to hear from?"

"Probably not." The truth was, she'd only glimpsed

two sides of him. Despite their afternoon, he'd barely told her anything about him.

She stared at him for a moment. "Okay. I won't ask any questions."

Was this a mark of trust? He wasn't sure he liked it. The Madison he was growing to know was hardly what he'd expected. He wanted to bundle her up, keep her safe, and yet he knew if he tried she'd probably brain him with a softball bat.

"You sure that's a good idea?" he asked.

"No, but I don't have any options. I have to trust you."

"You could always tell me to fuck off."

"I could, but you might actually do it. Then where would I be? Walking home in the rain."

"I'd at least call you a cab."

"How generous."

"I want you to know that I mean it when I say that things are going to turn out okay for you." He needed her to know he wasn't yanking her chain, that he was serious.

"I know. Maybe I'm stupid for trusting you, but I do."

"You aren't stupid."

"I've done a lot of stupid things."

"We all have. I'd wager some of my boneheaded decisions were worse than yours."

"This is starting to sound like a who-has-the-bigger-dick contest."

"I'd win that one."

"I bet you would." She tossed her head back and laughed. The sound of her laughter did something to him. He wanted to hear her laugh like that all the time, easy and uncomplicated. His grandmother would like her, even with her sailor's tongue.

"Here's what I'm thinking. Let me drive you back to

your place. I'd like to take a look around, make sure you're safe. Ask Matt to step up the watch on the boat tonight. After that, why don't we figure out how to get you around tomorrow? Then we turn in for the night. Okay?"

Her throat flexed as she swallowed.

"Okay," she replied. "Matt already said he's going to have someone at the marina."

Aiden clenched his teeth. On one hand, that task was already done; on the other, he didn't like the detective being this involved in her life.

"Does that sound good to you, or would you prefer we do something else?"

"No, that's good. And Matt didn't say anything about meeting me here, so we can go."

Her tears were gone and the tightness in his chest eased. Plus, it didn't appear as though she were too keen on seeing the detective.

Aiden reached across and cupped the back of her head, pulling her over for a quick kiss—because he wanted to. He pressed his lips to hers, intending for it to be nothing more than a momentary touch, but her hand tangled in the front of his shirt and she clutched the side of his face. She kissed him, drawing his lower lip between hers, sucking it and gently raking her teeth across the morsel. He groaned and slid his hand up into her hair, anchoring his hold and tilting her mouth just right.

Aiden wouldn't be leaving her with the twins tonight. He wouldn't be leaving her at all, at least not until she was free and clear of Dustin.

"You know where my boat is because you followed me, didn't you?"

Aiden steered the Chevelle into an out-of-the-way spot at the marina and shifted into park. They hadn't spoken much since leaving the dog track.

He turned toward her, a dozen answers flitting through his mind.

"It's okay. I guess, in a weird way, it's nice knowing someone who has my back knows where to find me. I don't exactly tell a lot of people where I live." She tipped her chin up and pushed her hair back. A security lamp cast her in a pool of light. Her cop guards weren't here yet, so it was just the two of them.

"Like I told you, I had to be sure you were exactly who you said you were."

"I'm done being hurt about it. Thanks for the ride home." She reached for the door and he cut the engine.

"You shouldn't be alone right now. Dustin's getting panicked. I don't want to leave you on your own, especially now that Canales is gunning for you, too." The cops were a start, but he wouldn't feel comfortable unless he were on the job himself.

"And you didn't think to mention this earlier?" She sat back in her seat, frowning at him.

"Earlier I didn't know things were getting this messy."

She opened her mouth, closed it, and glanced away.

"I'd say we could go back to my place, but Canales knows where I live and you have free security." There was a very small bunk at the shop, but it wouldn't do for both of them, and he didn't think Madison would be comfortable there. Her boat was the best thing.

"What about a hotel? The boat's not that big." She chewed her lip.

"If you'd prefer. We'll have to go somewhere that will take cash, no cards or IDs, just in case."

"Forget it. This is probably easiest. But I told you—it's going to be cramped in there."

He wouldn't bother telling her about the places he'd had to sleep while deployed. The missions he and Julian had to go on hadn't come with accommodations. Besides, he didn't need much.

He got out of the car and popped the trunk. The jobs he took often wound up putting him in odd positions overnight, so he'd learned to have a bag packed—just in case he also wound up with his car while stranded. It had happened a few times. Madison waited for him while he locked the car. There was an anxious strain to her features, manifesting in lines around her mouth and furrows on her brow.

What was wrong with the boat? Knowing Dustin, the only reason he'd let her escape the divorce with it was because it needed a lot of work. The mental image of her plugging holes with shirts and bailing water was enough to make him want to jump back in his car and go give Dustin a piece of what he had coming to him.

Madison led the way down the docks and to her slip. It was on the outskirts of the marina, and the wood seemed a little warped and worn with age; the other vessels alongside hers had seen better times.

"Do you sail?" he asked. They neared the white-and-blue sailboat.

"What? Me? No idea how." She laughed.

"Then why did you get it?"

"Clearly you've never been divorced."

"Never been married." He'd never had the opportunity; between his time in the service and getting caught up in the FBI, there hadn't been the chance to meet anyone, much less get hitched.

"Well, when they divided up the assets this was what I got. I can't sell it without putting a new motor in it. A sailboat. A motor in a sailboat. I don't get it, but whatever. I'm pretty sure Dustin stole it from someone." She sighed and stepped onto the deck.

Headlights broke up the dark parking lot. He peered at the car until he saw the glint off the rack of lights on top. The cops. Right on time. Madison waved to the car, but didn't give it much mind. He didn't mention how lucky she was that the cops were so interested in her. If it weren't for them, would she be on the bottom of the ocean by now?

He hesitated on the dock. "Permission to come aboard?"

She paused, glancing over her shoulder and smiling for the first time in a while. "Permission granted, soldier."

He made the step between land and the boat, pausing as the deck rolled under him. The gentle lapping of waves against the vessels and the distant crash of waves was soothing, in a way. It was a good defensive position, too. He'd feel better about it if the engine worked and they could drop anchor away from land, but he wasn't much of a sailor.

Madison descended a steep set of stairs and unlocked a door into the cabin. He hung back, surveying the deck and giving her a moment to herself. In the last two days he'd foisted a lot of change and action onto her, and though she'd been hesitant at first, she seemed onboard with their plans now.

At a glance, the boat appeared in decent condition. A little wear was evident in the details and the paint needed a new coat, but it appeared to be a solid vessel. He'd bet that it came to Dustin by way of a drug deal gone wrong, and he'd taken the boat as payment. If he looked hard enough, he could probably find hidden compartments fashioned in out-of-the-way holes where a smuggler would hide his stash. Perhaps once Madison went to sleep he'd do a sweep of it just to make sure all the product was gone and there wasn't a bug onboard. He wouldn't stress her out unduly without the need.

"You can come in now," Madison called from below deck.

He took the stairs two at a time and ducked under the low door.

Shit.

She hadn't been lying when she said it was cramped. Not to mention—it wasn't made with anyone over six foot in mind. His hair brushed the ceiling when he straightened. From where he stood, he could reach into the bathroom for a tissue and into the kitchen to the stove. There was a half circle banquet table on one side and a door slightly ajar where he could see a small bedroom beyond. It was clean, well kept, but even then, living in the boat full-time there was only so much space. A line of textbooks was crammed two deep onto a small shelf next to the door and several binders were on the dining table along with a laptop.

"You won't hurt my feelings if you don't want to stay here." Madison leaned against the kitchenette, a bottle of water in hand.

"Babe, I've slept in worse conditions." What he didn't like was the idea that she'd packed her entire life up into the space of maybe three hundred square feet, and only half of that was livable.

When this was over with, he'd make sure they reallocated funds from Dustin to her. If nothing else, to get her a set of wheels and a better place to live, maybe finish out her school. It would be justice of a sort to make sure her ex provided everything she needed.

"Are you hungry? I've got some fish one of the guys gave me that I've got to cook. Besides, that Japanese food just doesn't stick to me."

"I wouldn't say no to some food. Mind if I sit?" He gestured to the table.

"Not at all." She hurriedly packed her laptop away and relocated the binders to her bed. "Sit."

Aiden sank onto the cushions, folding himself into the small space. He leaned back and admired the view while Madison knelt to grab the smallest baking sheet he'd ever seen from a cabinet. If he put aside the derby and rough times, he could see her as the housewife she'd wanted to be. Someday, she'd make a great mother, fun, stern, and just the right amount of discipline. His chest ached and he knew he had no business mulling over these thoughts. His life was the FBI and leading a pretend life, but what he wouldn't trade for it to be different.

Chapter Twelve

Madison placed her empty plate on the deck and pulled her knees up to her chest. Her slip might not be the nicest, but from the prow, she had a great view of the ocean. There were boats in the distance going to and fro, while the marina was quiet. The storm had blown off, leaving behind clear skies and drying up her deck furniture.

She glanced sideways at Aiden. They'd come up to the deck to eat with a bit more elbow room. Since she never took the boat out, she'd picked up an outdoor bed, complete with waterproof marine cushions, and placed it on the prow for a secondary living space. Usually it was just her, her books, and laptop out here. She'd never thought she'd bring a man here. What must he think seeing her like this?

Out of habit, she checked to see if the cop car was still in sight. The interior dome light illuminated two officers, both with their heads down, probably engrossed with their phones or something else. They never quite made her feel safe. Sure, they were there to protect her, but they didn't really care about her. How long had it been since she'd had an easy sleep? She was always unsettled, except for now. Aiden was there.

"Who is Emery?" She hadn't asked many questions since the incident with her bike shocked her, but she'd had some time to regroup.

The muscle at Aiden's jaw twitched. Was he aware of the tell?

"He's a guy I work with from time to time."

It wasn't a real answer, just like she didn't know the real Aiden. Sure, she was attracted to him, and they'd had a moment of mutual vulnerability earlier, but he was still a stranger to her.

He would always be a stranger to her.

The terms of their—arrangement—were for a short time, only. When they found the drive, he would be out of her life.

She continued to watch him slowly eat the fish and pilaf she'd whipped up with her small pantry. There was no denying she liked him. Sure, he was still panty-dropping hot, but Aiden was more real to her now than he'd been this morning. In time, she could see herself falling into unrequited love with him.

When she was a kid, she'd thought the right man would change her life. Now, she knew that the role of a man only enhanced what she already had. Aiden's life was dangerous and everything she'd said she wouldn't go back to. Her resolve where he was concerned was still solid—whatever happened between them was temporary.

"Staring like that's starting to put me on edge," Aiden said between bites.

"Sorry." She ducked her head and pulled the blanket she'd brought with her across her lap.

"What are you studying?"

"Accounting."

He glanced at her, brows slightly raised.

"What's that face for?"

Aiden shrugged. "Nothing, I just figured you'd do something more—I don't know. Exciting."

"Exciting degrees cost a lot of money. Everyone needs their beans counted."

"What are you going to do when you graduate?"

"Probably take a job with my friend's parents. They own a couple of businesses. The dad does all the books on his own. He's hinted that it would be nice to have someone to help out."

"Couldn't you help without the degree?"

"I do. I organize all the books for Everglades Air and hand them over to him. It's been a good experience. Besides, they'll pay me better than any entry-level job I could get otherwise. I know I'm overpaid now. It's their way of helping me out. I've been best friends with their daughter since high school."

"You're something else." Aiden shook his head and placed his plate on top of hers.

"What's that supposed to mean?"

He reclined, turning toward her and resting on his elbow.

"Anyone else in your shoes would have let Dustin win, but you keep building yourself up. I said it before, and I'll say it again." He glanced toward her, his blue eyes slicing deep, until her heart seemed to quiver for his touch. "You are not what I expected, Madison Haughton."

Warmth bubbled up in her chest that had nothing to do with the way he stared at her. It was—pride. Hell yes, she'd worked hard and she'd keep going until she'd built the life she wanted. Hopefully, she'd find someone to share it with along the way, but she'd learned her lessons about falling for the wrong guy.

Aiden might be the right type, but he wasn't for her. There wasn't room in his life for something without a motor or in need of a tune-up. But there wasn't room in hers for a man, either. He might promise to make Dustin go away, but until that happened and she graduated—there wasn't time to devote to a romantic relationship. But would it hurt her to have a little fun on the side?

They continued to study each other openly. The warmth in her chest moved lower and she shifted.

One minute, they could carry on a perfectly normal conversation—albeit the topic matter wasn't typical—and the next her body hummed with desire. It was as if he flipped some switch in her and made her body wake up in ways she hadn't allowed herself to pay attention to in years.

She missed sex. The connection. Even the weight of a body pressing her into the mattress.

"Cold still?" Aiden's voice was barely above a whisper.

"What?"

"You're shivering."

She ran her hands up and down her arms. The air was cooler, but her shivers weren't from the weather.

"Come here."

Aiden tugged her down to lie next to him and pulled the blanket over himself. He wrapped his arm around her and brought her against his chest. His warmth seeped into her skin, down to her bones, mingling with the low pulse of arousal humming through her veins.

"Is this a good idea?" She didn't know what she wanted him to say. Yes or no, they couldn't keep toeing this line with each other without someone getting burned.

Again, the muscle at his jaw twitched. "I was honest

with you earlier. I'm attracted to you. If that bothers you, tell me to back off and I will."

She opened her mouth and closed it. What did she say to that?

"Are you aware you have a tic?" she asked.

"A tic?" His brows drew down into a line. She didn't blame him for being confused, but she couldn't address the way he made her body sit up and take notice.

"Yeah, the muscle here, it jumps when you're concentrating, or maybe you're irritated?" She brushed her fingers along his jaw.

Aiden sighed and captured her hand. He pressed a quick kiss to her fingers before placing it against him. "What I do—it's . . ."

"You don't have to tell me. I know it's secret."

He blew out a breath. "You're right. I can't tell you."

"But let me guess, sometimes it wears you down?"

He stared at her, and in that moment, his gaze said more than his words ever could. There was more going on that she didn't understand. He was one of the good guys. And the burden of what he did for people like her, it took its toll. So who gave back to him? Who helped him? She would never know his life's story or what role she was playing in a bigger drama with Michael Evers, but right now she was here. With him.

"Let's not talk about it, okay?" She mustered a smile and slid her hand around his chest, to rest on his back.

Aiden seemed to breathe a little easier. She needed to figure out how to tell him about Michael's connection to the airport, but that thought slipped further and further from her mind.

"Kiss me?" she asked before she could think better of it.

He didn't jump on the request like she expected.

Instead, he cupped her cheek, his gaze shuttered and unreadable as he leaned toward her.

"I can't offer you anything," he said.

"I know. I'm not asking for anything except a kiss." She covered his hand with hers. "Whatever happens—happens. No expectations. Deal?"

"You deserve better than that."

"I know, and so do you, but neither of us have time for more. I've got school, derby, and work. You've got your shop, racing and—whatever it is you do." She couldn't tell if it was the roar of the waves or the rush of her blood pounding past her ears, but it threatened to drown his quiet voice out. Could he feel her pulse racing? Did he know what he did to her? Sure, she had a weakness for his type, but this was more than a simple attraction. She liked him. Respected him.

He studied her for a moment longer, his gaze holding her captive. Something about the blues of his eyes, the way the whole world seemed to fall away and his entire focus centered on her, felt as though it knitted them together. The rest of the world didn't matter in this second in time.

What did he see when he looked at her? Was it the same for him?

Aiden leaned toward her. Madison's gaze dropped to his lips. He tilted his head. She sighed the moment their mouths touched and slid her hand up to his shoulder, holding on to him while he pressed her onto her back.

He suckled her lower lip, drawing the bit of flesh between his teeth and teasing her. She gasped as she experienced the first full-body throb of arousal. He covered her mouth with his and flicked his tongue against hers. She mimicked him, teasing him as he teased her. Her nipples constricted into tight points and she found herself arching toward him, but he held himself away from her.

Madison pulled on his shoulders, wanting to feel more of him. He pressed his knee between her legs, settling some of his weight on her. She hooked her knee over his thigh. He'd made her come on a kiss once already. What else could he do? There was no denying her celibacy had left her primed and ready for any sexual experience. Aiden would be different. She knew it. It was in the way he touched her, the long looks, the slow approaches.

He planted his hands on either side of her shoulders and shifted until his weight settled on top of her, his legs between hers and their bodies aligned. She couldn't see his face, but she felt his gaze and smiled.

Whatever happened—happened.

She might not be able to keep her end of the bargain and remain emotionally untangled, but she could sure as hell enjoy the moment. Tomorrow, she'd sort herself out. Tonight, she'd take whatever came.

Aiden swooped down, kissing her again. She wrapped her arms around his shoulders, pressing their bodies together harder, until she could feel the pulse of his heart against her own. He rocked against her and she gasped, the seam of her jeans rubbing her just right. She groaned and arched her hips, uncaring what he thought of her for last night's little light show.

He slid his hand between them until he cupped her mound and moved his palm in little circles. She sucked in a deep breath, eyes tightly closed as fissures of pleasure snaked through her body.

"Damn," he muttered against her neck. "I can't get the picture of you coming last night out of my head. Do you know how fucking hot that was?"

Hot?

Not the word she'd have chosen, but if he wanted to be turned on by her lack of control—that was fine by her.

She groaned an incoherent reply as he palmed her breast with one hand. How far was this going? Her panties were wet, her body aroused, and she was already undressing him with her mind. What did he look like naked?

Madison slid her hands over him, realizing she hadn't quite acquainted herself with him. She mapped his chest with her fingers, tracing the hard lines and ridges of muscle while he kissed her neck and chest. His thumb would swipe across her breast every so often, sending an electrical current through her body.

She grabbed handfuls of his black T-shirt and pulled it up until the fabric bunched under his arms. She tugged and pulled but he was completely unmoved by her, too focused on the trail of kisses he was paving across her chest and shoulders. There was nothing frenzied or rushed about the attention he lavished on her. In all of her sexual experiences, she'd never felt like the focal point. Aiden treated her like the center of his world. Like his own gratification didn't matter. She didn't know how to respond, what to do. Not that he gave her any choice. She was his sensual prisoner, held captive by the way he plied her with kisses.

Aiden sat up, taking the blanket with him and robbing her of his heat. She wrapped her arms around herself, shivering as the cool night air skated over her skin. He pulled his T-shirt off and tossed it on the deck, while his gaze remained locked on hers. There was intent there; of what kind, she wasn't sure, but he was a man on a mission. He hiked the blanket up over his shoulders. With that secure, he grabbed the hem of her shirt and tugged it up.

Heat crawled up her neck when he brushed the hem of her tank top, as if he were asking permission. She held her breath while he slid his hand under the fabric. She let him remove her shirt, though she curled her arms over her chest the moment the garment was off.

He pushed her hands aside and lowered himself once more to cover her body. This time he let more of his weight settle on her, keeping her pinned below him. Aiden kissed her while his right hand traveled down her body until he could grip her hip. He squeezed and flexed his hips, grinding against her. She looped her arms around his shoulders, flattening her palms against his back and reveling in the ripple of his muscles.

Aiden moved lower, leaving her panting. He kissed a trail down her throat. She closed her eyes and breathed deeply of the salt-infused air, concentrating on the sensation of his stubble scraping her chest, his lips as they dipped between the swells of her breasts.

"I've been thinking about you nonstop since Stoke's." He placed his palm over her right breast and squeezed.

She would have squirmed if she could move.

He bent and placed his mouth on the cup of her bra, just over her nipple. Despite the material, she could feel his hot breath. She shoved her fingers through the short strands of his hair and arched her back. He tugged the cup down and she froze. He pressed an open-mouthed kiss to her breast. His tongue swirled around the hard nipple while he massaged her other breast.

Holy shit, she chanted to herself.

Her muscles were warm, supple, and losing strength under his attention.

Aiden lifted his head and she hissed as the cool air teased her heated flesh. He grinned at her, and she knew he was up to something. Before she could puzzle it out, he drew the blanket up over his head and scooted farther down her body.

She picked her head up and peered at the man-shaped lump under the blanket. What the hell? Was this a game of peekaboo now?

He grabbed the waistband of her jeans and tabbed them open while her brain screeched to a halt. What the hell was he doing?

Aiden's breath fanned over her stomach a moment before she felt his lips just below her navel. She sucked in a breath and lay back against the cushion-mattress, clutching the blanket to her chest. He kissed lower, down to her panties. He hooked something, maybe his thumbs, into the waistband and drew them down.

Plenty of the other derby girls talked about their significant others going down on them. Blow jobs she could do, albeit rarely, but never in her life had the act been reciprocated. Did she touch him? Or keep her hands to herself? Was that what he was about to do? Her heart felt as though it had become a racehorse in the sprint of its life.

She gulped and lifted her bottom up enough for him to work the fabric down her thighs. The stars seemed brighter above, or was that just the moon? Crazy things happened around a full moon.

Aiden stripped her of her jeans and panties, shoving them off onto the deck while he remained hidden beneath the blanket.

She flattened her hands on the mattress on either side of her and forced herself to take a deep breath. Aiden pulled the blanket down and peeked up at her, his expression perplexed.

"What's wrong?" he asked.

"N-nothing."

"It's going to feel better if you can relax."

"Easy for you to say," she replied before she could think better of it.

Aiden held her gaze while he gently kissed her inner thigh. The intensity in his gaze alone held her arrested in the moment.

"Babe, I want you to feel as good and sexy as you look. I'm going to go slow and savor everything about you—unless you want me to stop. Now, if that means I need to spend a while showing you how to relax, I can do that." There was nothing calming about the way he looked at her. She was the prey he'd captured, the thing he intended to ravage and eat up. "Okay?"

"O-okay." She hadn't stuttered in forever, but he made her feel small, vulnerable, desired, and a dozen other contradictory emotions she couldn't quite process all at once.

At least she'd shaved, but there were a hundred other things to be self-conscious about. Unlike the current trend among her female friends, she wasn't quite comfortable shaving herself bare. A little hair down there made her feel a little ladylike. It was supposed to be there after all.

"Would you be comfortable if you put your legs over my shoulders?"

Madison had no idea, but she figured he'd done this a time or two, so she did as he requested. She could glimpse the top of his head under the blanket. This was so not sexy. Why did people do this? Was sex just not enough anymore? And yet, she couldn't find her voice to suggest he just stick it in.

He touched her mound, stroking the patch of neatly trimmed hair.

She didn't know if she wanted him to hurry up, or for a whale to knock the boat over. Either would be good for her, because this drawn-out moment where she couldn't breathe was going to suffocate her.

His fingers slid over her mound and down her slit. She gasped, her oxygen-deprived lungs burning while he parted her labia.

Oh God. Oh God. Oh God.

"You're wet."

Yup. Constant state at the moment.

Aiden didn't seem to expect an answer. His hand came to rest on her inner thigh, inches from her pussy. He kissed her other leg, starting with his face nearly in the cleft of her leg, and going toward her knee. He did the same to her other leg, while her breathing hitched and she stared at the stars, her senses too overloaded to process what he was doing beyond the feel of it. This time, he retraced the path but deviated, rising to press kisses to the place where her leg and hip met, across her mound and the pubic area—never touching any of her more sensitive areas.

Was this his plan? To tease and torment her?

She sucked down another deep breath, telling herself to relax, settle back, and enjoy his touch, but she couldn't shake her nerves. Sure, his attentions felt good, but was she doing something wrong? Did he think she was attractive? Did she have a funny-looking labia? It was an outrageous idea, but then again, she'd never had to wonder what anyone except her doctor thought about that particular bit of her anatomy.

Aiden squeezed her ass with both hands, bringing her back to the moment. With him. She glanced down at him and found him looking up at her. He smiled—a genuine smile—with a hint of mischievousness and that little dimple that made her so hot. Her heart leapt into her throat and she found it hard to breathe. Did he know he was smiling? Or how devastating he looked when he did that? She—melted. There was no other word for it. How could she second-guess what she looked like or if she was doing the wrong thing when he seemed so—into it?

He dipped his head, his gaze still on her, and she felt the flat of his tongue against her labia, licking her slit and up over her clit. She gasped and her head dropped back to the cushioned deck, suddenly too heavy to hold up anymore. He kissed her leg and mound once more, as if giving her time to adjust and warm up to what he was doing.

It hit her then, just how patient and considerate he was being. She'd pretty much told him he could have whatever he wanted—no strings attached—and instead of sating his lust, he was focused on her. She blew out a breath, and with it all the tension left her body. Her muscles were supple, relaxed, and more than anything else, she trusted him to show her the pleasures she hadn't known before. If nothing else, she would remember this moment for that alone.

Maybe he sensed the change in her body, because Aiden's next touch was not gentle. He spread her labia with purpose. She had a moment to fist her hands in the blanket before he licked her once more, this time without anything between them. Madison gasped and arched her back, her nipples contracted into such tight points they throbbed within the cups. She curled her leg up over his back, urging him closer without conscious thought.

She felt more than heard him chuckle against her inner thigh. Her foot was now flat against his back, her knee hiked up in the air. Well, if it felt good, wasn't that the whole point?

His hands shifted, reminding her he still had her at her most vulnerable position—and she found she didn't care. He planted his lips against her vagina, kissing her most intimate place. She curled her toes as the coil of lust tightened in her abdomen, warmth making her skin hot. He did it again, and it just undid her.

"Oh-oh, Aiden," she muttered before she could stop herself.

"Hm? What is it?" She felt the vibrations against her mound.

His voice had dropped to a lower pitch. Was he turned on too?

"N-nothing."

"Tell me. What feels good? When I kiss you?" He pressed his lips just above her clit. The hard nubbin throbbed, completely untouched in all of his attentions thus far.

"Yes," she said on a groan.

"What about when I do this?" He licked the length of her slit once more, slowly and pressing the flat of his tongue against her. She held her breath, wondering if he'd penetrate her or not—but he didn't.

"Oh, yes."

"Not as bad as you thought it would be?"

"No."

"Good." He released her labia and kissed her knee. "Tell me what feels good. I can make it feel better."

Better? Was he serious? It was pretty fan-freaking-tastic already.

He pressed another kiss to her mound. She picked her head up and glanced down at him, wanting to see him. Once more, he was already looking up at her, his lower face hidden from view. He pressed another kiss to her mound.

Had any man ever spent so much time simply kissing her? She didn't think so. At least not the way he kissed her, as if she were something to be savored.

Aiden's gaze narrowed. She felt a single, thick finger

press against her entrance. She dropped her head back and let her gaze go unfocused, staring up at the blanket of diamonds above. He worked his finger into her slowly, pressing against one side and then the other of her vagina, rubbing all the sensitive areas.

She wanted to touch him, to feel him, too.

Madison slid one hand down, until she could touch his hair.

His digit thrust once more into her—and he curled it, stroking her inner wall. She gasped and her spine came up off the deck. Her breath stuttered out of her lungs. Her skin seemed to grow too tight, her body too warm.

"Oh my God, do that," she said in a rush.

He paused, kissing the area just above her clit and curled his finger once more. She groaned and cupped her breasts, irritated he hadn't removed that, too. It was too much work to get the constricting garment off, so she shoved her hands up under the cups and rolled the peaks between her fingers. The tide of her arousal was rising, threatening to rob her of her senses.

Aiden removed his finger, but before she could voice a protest, he licked her slit once more while his thumb gently feathered the lightest touch over her clit.

"Fuck, yes."

He licked up and over her clit—finally. She wrapped her legs around him, squeezing him closer. He thrust his finger into her, while he rubbed his tongue up and down on the erect nub. Her hips seemed to move of their own accord and she reached down, threading her fingers through the short strands of his hair. She meant to just touch him, to increase the connection, but it felt good when she urged him to press just a bit harder.

She could hear herself moaning, the sound of it echoing off the water, but she couldn't find it in her to care. The desire coiled tightly in her abdomen released. Warmth flooded her body. Her orgasm crashed into her with such sharp pleasure she cried out and tightened her hold in Aiden's hair, stilling his motions. Her body clamped down on his finger and her muscles rippled with release. It felt as though it went on and on. She saw stars behind her eyelids and her body was so warm and supple the next moment as the sensation subsided.

Aiden didn't move while she lay there, panting.

Did she say thank you? That seemed a little weak in comparison to what he'd just done to her.

He kissed her mound once more and extracted his finger. He shifted and her legs fell away. He brought the blanket up to cover her. She was too weak to do more than turn her head toward him. He knelt by her side, shirtless and sporting a boner even his jeans couldn't hide.

Aiden bent and pressed his lips to her brow.

"I'll be right back," he said.

She grunted something in reply. His footsteps faded as he walked toward the stern and thumped down the stairs.

Madison felt—amazing. She didn't know if sex had ever been like that before. Probably not. High school boys just didn't know as much as Aiden did and after that—well, she wasn't thinking about that. Not now. Just Aiden.

Thinking his name must have summoned the man. Aiden was once more next to her. He brought pillows and a bottle of water. Once he'd helped her situate on the pillow, he insisted on holding the bottle while she drank. It was sweet, if a little presumptuous. Or maybe he knew better. Her body wasn't exactly the consistency of human right now.

Without comment, he slid under the blanket and cuddled her close.

Was this real? Was he human? Did men really behave like this?

If they didn't, and this was a dream, she wanted to stay asleep.

She closed her eyes, inhaling the brine and faint scent of his cologne.

"So, feel good?" He sounded rather pleased with himself.

Madison pried one eye open and glanced up at him. She couldn't even find fault with him. He knew what he'd done and he deserved all the praise.

"I do. That was—amazing. Thank you."

"No need to thank me, babe, just trust me." He kissed her mouth, slow and sensual. Though she'd just come something intense, warmth curled deep in her belly.

She placed her hand on his chest, loving the feel of his skin against hers.

There was no way she could keep her heart to herself. Already, she could feel the hard exoskeleton she'd fostered cracking open, the organ growing, expanding as it started to beat for another person. She would fall for him, but she would also have to keep her end of the bargain. This could only be as friends—nothing more.

Madison pushed her emotions away and slid her hand down his chest until she covered the erection straining the front of Aiden's jeans.

"Do you trust me?" she purred.

Chapter Thirteen

Aiden stared at Madison, his tongue sticking to the top of his mouth. She palmed his dick and his whole body tensed. It was damn uncomfortable in his jeans, especially with her hot little hand on him.

"What do you say?" Her gaze was heavy-lidded and her pupils had grown until she seemed to be eating him up with her eyes.

"I do trust you." He wrapped his hand around her wrist and pulled her busy fingers away from his erection. Somewhere along the road, he had grown to trust her. He couldn't say when, but he did, and that alone was unusual. Everyone lied or cheated, maybe even killed, for the right price.

He slid his hand down to her thigh and nudged her legs apart with his knee. She hooked her knee over his hip and tucked her chin down, staring up at him through her lashes. Her heat seared him through his jeans, but he wasn't about to pounce on her so soon after her orgasm. Madison might look like a hard-bodied pinup sex goddess on wheels, but it was camouflage. There was no mistaking her hesitance earlier, which only further proved just how real she'd been with him from the start.

"Comfortable?" he asked.

She snuggled closer, her head pillowed on his arm. If he wanted to, he could bury his face in her hair and inhale the fragrance he was coming to associate with her.

"I'll take that as a yes." He smoothed a hand over her hair and kissed the crown of her head. It wasn't the gesture of a casual lover. Tangling with Madison was not in his best interests. She was a woman who would want—and deserve—far better than he could give her. But he was only human, still subject to the urges of the flesh. And right now his body wanted one thing—to be inside of her.

She placed a hand to his chest, her fingers spread wide so he couldn't see her face, but he didn't need to. He'd already committed it to memory.

A Japanese-styled phoenix perched on her shoulder, poised as if about to dive down her arm, while the tail feathers fanned across Madison's back.

"Why the phoenix?" he asked. People chose tattoos for a variety of reasons. His were to remember, while some wanted to forget.

Madison picked her head up and met his gaze.

"I'd think it's obvious. Rebirth." She extended her left arm, twisting it. It was almost entirely encased in bright colors, except for a few places around her wrist where it was just black lines on flesh. "We chose each flower and all the elements to tell the rebirth story in its prime. The lotus flowers at my wrist will finish it."

He threaded his fingers with hers and brought them to his lips.

Fuck it.

Madison deserved pleasure, and he'd give it to her. Damn the rest.

He kissed the back of her hand, her wrist, the first lines of the tattoo and up her forearm to her shoulder.

Her chest stopped moving and he held perfectly still. He'd already begun to learn what it took to ease her into lovemaking, and he liked how responsive she was once she let go of her inhibitions.

Aiden nuzzled her neck, waiting. She tipped her head to the side and he zeroed in on that spot, the place where neck met shoulder. He pressed an open-mouthed kiss to the spot and she gasped, sucking down lungfuls of air. A little moan escaped her lips and he smiled. Her hands grasped his shoulders while her head dropped back on the pillow. He had a suspicion no one had ever taken their time, wringing every drop of pleasure from her body.

He shifted, rolling her until he was once more on top of her, the blanket spread out over them, a thin shield against the rest of the world. They weren't in much danger of being spotted unless some late-night boater came in off the water, but Madison might not realize that. Besides, there was something liberating about the perception of being out on the open water.

Her hips rocked up against him and he pressed his face against her shoulder for a moment.

Damn, she knew how to move. Their bodies aligned perfectly. She was just the right height, too.

Aiden inhaled her scent and willed his throbbing dick to pipe down. There was more of her he hadn't yet tasted or touched.

Her hands roved over his shoulders and chest until they framed his face, pulling him up and sealing her lips over his. She clung to him, pressing their mouths together until he felt the brush of her teeth against his lips. He liked a little roughness from time to time, and he'd be willing to bet Madison knew how to play dirty.

He tore his mouth from hers, working his way swiftly down her neck. She arched her back, as if she knew where he was going—that or her breasts were feeling neglected. He released the catch on her bra with a twist of his fingers.

"Practice much?" She grinned at him.

"Once or twice." He didn't want to think about anyone else—except her. "Had to make sure I got it right for you."

"How considerate." She crossed her arms over her chest, hiding them, but she surprised him by drawing the garment up and tossing it away.

Madison was now completely naked. He lifted up, taking a moment to admire her. She was soft in places, and toned in others. Tattoos dotted her body, creating a story he couldn't fully appreciate. Yet.

"Babe, in case I don't get a chance to say this later, you're beautiful."

She chuckled and rolled her eyes.

Aiden captured her chin between his fingers and lowered his weight once more onto her, pinning her to the mattress.

"I'm not just saying that because you're naked. I wouldn't be this hard for just any hot piece of ass." How did he put the sense of normalcy she gave him into words? What could he say to make her understand that she really was special to him?

Her eyes widened and she swallowed hard. Maybe it was his tone, or perhaps she got the clue. Whatever this was, however short-lived, it was special.

"Sorry, it's just—thank you."

He bent his head and kissed her mouth, savoring the taste of her. Her hands traveled down his back until her fingertips could push under the band of his underwear. He wanted to let her strip him, he hadn't fulfilled his mission yet.

Aiden scooted down her body until he could push

her breasts together, plumping the round mounds. She had a good handful, not too big for his tastes, and still small enough they wouldn't be in the way when she skated.

"What are you—?"

"Sh, I'm getting acquainted with them," he said.

"What?" She lifted her head and blinked at him.

"They were sad I didn't spend more time with them earlier." He managed to say it with a straight face. Madison let her head drop back onto the pillow without further comment.

He studied her dusky nipples. Her chest rose and fell with her accelerated breathing. The peaks were already constricted, another sign of her arousal, one that made him feel a little satisfaction.

Aiden licked one breast, then the other. Her breathing hitched, and she let out a quiet, high-pitched moan. She tried to shift under him. Her thighs squeezed, hugging him closer.

He sucked her right nipple, flicking his tongue over the tight bud while she continued to buck and shift mindlessly under him. Her hands clutched at his shoulders and the back of his head, pressing him closer.

If at all possible, her evident arousal only turned him on more. He liked knowing that each lick and suck drove her inhibitions further away from mind. There was no doubt she was here—with him—in this moment.

Madison wiggled her arms between them, plumping her breasts while she reached for the waistband of his jeans. He grabbed her wrists, hauling her arms up above her head and got in her face.

"Aiden," she whimpered, silencing the command on his lips. Her voice was full of pure passion, desire, everything he wanted to show her. "Aiden, don't make me beg."

He released her hands and kissed her, allowing her to clutch his face and deepen the kiss. Her tongue thrust into his mouth and her legs held him in place while she undulated against him.

If he had his way, this proud woman would never beg for a thing.

Aiden pushed up, tearing his mouth from hers.

Madison blinked up at him and brought an arm across her chest to cover herself, her brow creased in such a manner that she looked pained. He slid the blanket off his shoulders and covered her.

"You never beg, understand me?" He pressed his mouth to hers in a hard, punishing kiss. The moment her fingers grazed his flesh he straightened.

He was a man of control. Without it, his people could die. Innocents around them would be casualties. He couldn't afford to relax that hold on himself, and yet, since he'd met Madison, she'd done nothing but distract and throw him off balance in the most delicious ways possible. Did she realize what she did to him? If she had any idea, she didn't show it.

Aiden tabbed open his jeans and toed off his boots, ignoring the laces in favor of getting naked faster. One boot clattered to the deck, followed by the other. He paused to toss his wallet on the deck before hooking his thumbs in his jeans and underwear. Her eyes grew slightly larger when he tugged the clothing down over his hips and hissed as he freed his erection. He kicked out of the denim and stared down at her.

Madison's hair was spread over the pillows. He could make out almost every detail of her face, her hands clutching the blanket and even her toes sticking out the end. She was beautiful, and she was a survivor, and she was his—for tonight, or however long it took to set her free.

"I have a condom." He swiped his wallet up and flipped through its contents looking for the packet.

"I had a checkup a few weeks ago before the season started. I don't have anything."

"Me either." He pulled the condom from his wallet and knelt on the mattress. He couldn't remember the last woman he'd bedded, didn't want to.

She rolled to her side, head propped in her hand. If she wanted to watch, who was he to stop her?

He tore open the packet and held the end of the condom while he rolled it on slower than he might otherwise. She bit her lip watching the progress of his hands. He had to stifle a groan at that. Every soft sigh and needy moan had already done a number on his control. Christ, if this went on much longer, he didn't know what he'd do.

"I'm going to fuck you," he said far rougher than he intended.

Madison's eyes widened and she licked her lips, but there was no protest.

He crawled toward her and she pulled the blanket back, giving him a glimpse of her breast, down to her stomach and that little cluster of curls. Something about the neatly trimmed hair had made him a little crazy earlier.

Aiden slid under the blanket, drawing it over their bodies as she hooked a leg over his thigh. He rolled with her, until he had her under him once more. He kissed her, bracketing her shoulders with his hands and moving against her. He couldn't remember the last time—if ever—a woman had made him this crazy with lust.

He rocked into her, loving the way her breasts pressed against him, how she moved with him.

He rose to his knees between her thighs and grasped his dick with one hand. He touched her folds and found them damp. She gasped and arched into the touch, lifting her hips in a lust-crazed plea. He placed the head of his cock against her entrance and glanced up her body. Her gaze snagged his, and the thrumming in his veins redoubled. He thrust and her lids dropped, groaning.

He gripped her thighs and eased deeper into her pussy, glancing down to glimpse their joined flesh.

Aiden withdrew and thrust again, sinking deep inside of her. He lowered to his elbows, hovering above her while she gasped. Her face creased, eyes squeezed shut and her mouth open. He watched her, holding still while her body adjusted to him. Her gasps turned to little moans. She began to shift, her hands coming to rest on his back.

He bent, kissing her brow, the tip of her nose, and the corner of her mouth. She turned toward him and he sealed his lips over hers. She cupped the back of his head and hooked her leg higher over his thigh.

He levered up a bit and flexed his hips, grinding them together. Her eyes widened and he felt her inner muscles clamp down on him, hugging him tight. He withdrew slowly, all the way until only the head of his cock remained within her, and slid back in. She groaned, the pitch of her mewls taking on a new, pleasurable note. Her body was soft under his, yielding to the intrusion with ease.

Aiden rocked into her before withdrawing once more. He set a steady rhythm, in and out, adjusting the tilt of her hips until she clawed at his shoulders. Her panting increased in pitch and her eyes stared at him, without seeing him.

He would make sure she came.

Madison tossed her head back, her groan rising as the breath left her and her pussy tightened around him.

He slowed his rhythm, but gave her no respite, fucking her through her orgasm until she whimpered. She pushed at his shoulder and he stopped. Was two orgasms too much? Was that her limit?

She inhaled deeply, her breasts lifting to graze his chest. Her eyes slid open and she smiled up at him.

"Sorry, I couldn't breathe there at the end."

He would have chuckled if he weren't so hard.

Her brows drew down. "You didn't—come?"

"No." What did he do?

"Oh." Once more she smiled sheepishly. She stretched her arms toward him, twining them around his neck. "What can I do? Tell me."

He opened and closed his mouth.

"What if . . . want me on top?" she asked.

Madison riding him, her perky breasts bouncing, her hair caught in the breeze and the moonlight shining down on her like some water goddess? Hell yes!

He rolled them so fast she squealed and laughed, clutching his shoulders. She sprawled over his chest. She pushed up, unmindful of her nudity. He covered her breasts with his hands. Those were for his eyes only.

She placed her hands on his chest, leaning forward so her hair fell over her shoulder. Her smile was more carefree and easy than he'd seen it yet. She rose and fell, her gaze centered on him. He squeezed her breasts, giving himself over finally to the myriad of sensations.

He wrapped his hands in her hair, pulling her down roughly until he could crush their mouths together and thrust up into her over and over again. The base of his spine began to tingle. He thrust his tongue into her as he came, wrapping his arms around her, rocking against her.

She collapsed on his chest, her breath hot against his

neck, her hair tangling in his eyelashes, tickling his nose. He wouldn't trade this for anything.

He tugged the blanket up over them and closed his eyes.

Being with Madison warmed a part of him that had lain dormant. She gave him a sense of normalcy, despite how unusual their meeting was. Moments like these, they could be anyone, anywhere. Just two people, losing themselves in lust for each other.

It wouldn't always be like this. That was their reality.

What was it about her that tied him in knots? He hadn't exactly lived the life of a monk, but he wasn't new to the theory of friends with benefits. Everyone had their needs. Fucking Madison should have scratched that itch—if she'd been anyone else. No, he was the fool to think rocking the boat a bit would work this attraction out of his system.

He couldn't offer her more than freedom from Dustin's shadow, but maybe once this mess was cleared up, they could take a weekend. A couple of days without the shop, racing, or the Hoovers to enjoy each other in the most carnal ways.

"I cannot believe you are a Cowboys fan."

Madison tossed her head back and laughed. Her microwave special sausage and biscuit crumbled in her fingers, hitting the table, but she didn't care. Since last night on the deck, Aiden hadn't mentioned Dustin, their deal, or anything remotely connected. It was as if they'd flipped a switch and stepped into a different, happier time. With the exception of the cops on guard and Aiden taking a security stroll before bed, it had been like living in a dream.

"Hey, it's one of the few things my daddy left me with.

Besides, they're America's team." She picked up the broken pieces of her breakfast and popped them in her mouth.

"If they were America's team they'd actually win." He glanced at her from across the table and paused. "What?"

"Nothing." She ducked her head, concentrating on the leftover crumbs. He was so different than what she'd expected him to be. Especially now. She might not know the secret, dangerous stuff about him, but she'd learned that he could laugh, make jokes and they could talk about so many things. It wasn't hard to think about a future where they tried exhausting all the topics, but that was a line of thought that led to disappointment. This magical moment would be over soon.

"What?" he asked again.

She sighed and rolled her eyes. His determination in all things was either remarkable or annoying.

"Nothing, really, you're just cute when you get all worked up."

"I don't think the Cowboys are an accurate representation of America." He set his second biscuit down and steepled his fingers.

Oh boy, he must really have lots of thoughts on this topic. Not only did he have opinions, but a wealth of knowledge about the most random topics. She folded her hands in her lap, prepared to listen to what would be no doubt another interesting look into the man.

"We've got so much going for us as Americans. We're innovative, we've got all the freedoms to explore and create, not to mention the opportunity. Here, we don't have to worry about digging wells, we worry about finding different ways to change a tire, grow an apple. We don't have the same problems as the rest of the world.

We've done so many wonderful and amazing things. Like the Tin Lizzie."

"The what?"

"The Model T?"

"Oh." Cars. She should have known.

"What Henry Ford did changed the world. His assembly line production made a car that wasn't just for the wealthy. He wanted to make something the common person could buy. Did you know he changed his assembly line because three of his workers—uneducated men—said they had an idea? He didn't shut them up. He took what they said and not only changed how cars were produced for the common man but the assembly line. Cars revolutionized the class system. It made a new way for people to live and provide for their families. Take that and look at a dozen—a hundred—other things we've done."

She could care less about old cars and whatever he was talking about. It was the fervor in which he spoke, the conviction that captured her.

He leaned back in his seat and glanced away, but she doubted it was her kitchenette he was seeing. "I've been to some seriously fucked up places, and it makes me appreciate what we have here. The freedoms, the education, even our government—at least they aren't beheading people for choosing to think differently. If we don't like the president we can say so."

"The Chevelle and the Challenger—they're American cars, aren't they?" Maybe it was a stupid question, but she didn't know a thing about automobiles.

"Yes, ma'am. That's all I drive. Nothing against foreign makes, but when I drive . . ." He leaned toward her, elbows on the table, gaze trained on her. "When I drive, it's like I'm somewhere else. A car is pure energy at that point, it's all in how you direct it. Call me a kook, but I want to know that when I go to that place where it's just me, the car, and the road, I want to know that the energy behind it isn't kids on penny wages or factories in shit conditions. I want to know where every piece comes from."

"I get it." She smiled, and found that she'd leaned toward him while he spoke, chin propped on her hand. Unlike him, she'd barely ever been outside of Florida. She could only imagine what life was like in other countries much less another city, how seeing the conditions he described changed a person.

Aiden's smartphone chimed and he glanced at the screen, that inner light that had begun to glow last night snuffed out in the blink of an eye.

It was time to return to the real world.

In the span of a second, she could sense the fun, easygoing, and opinionated man who'd shared her bed leave and the deadly man of secrets return. She sighed and swept the crumbs off the table and into her hand. If last night and this morning was all she could have, she'd have to cherish it.

"What time do you need to be at work?" he asked.

"Ten."

"I thought the airport opened earlier than that."

"It does, usually, but because of the storm we're starting late today." Too bad they hadn't slept in. Her eyes had popped open at seven. Aiden had already been awake, drawing lazy patterns on her arm. Saying good morning was better than good night with him. "Ugh. And I need to find a ride."

"I'll take you." He tapped the screen of his phone, scrolling through what appeared to be a lengthy text message.

Aiden stood and stretched, the muscles of his chest rippling. She'd mapped the width and breadth of his chest with her mouth this morning, and just the memory made her body go warm.

"I'm going to need my shirt back," he said.

"You sure about that?" She glanced down at herself, clothed only in his T-shirt.

"I am."

"Trying to dress me?"

"Babe, I'm only interested in undressing you."

She smiled and ducked her head, feeling goofy and giddy and dangerously close to wanting more than a single night with this man. It was a recipe for heartache, and she was already gathering the ingredients.

Chapter Fourteen

Madison glanced at Aiden, but his eyes were firmly on the road leading to the airstrip, the Everglades stretching out on either side of them.

It seemed so surreal that she was actually going to work, especially after everything that had transpired since yesterday. Right now, it felt like a week or a month had passed in the span of maybe twenty hours.

"I'm going to see about getting you some wheels today," Aiden said.

She stared at him. He was going to what?

"What time is your bout tonight?"

"Seven. Why are you going to do that?"

"Go to your bout?" He glanced at her then, brows drawn down.

"You don't have to replace my bike."

"You need reliable transportation."

"Yeah, but that's not your responsibility."

Aiden eased the car to a stop on the empty two-lane road and turned toward her. "Consider it a loan until you get something. Look at it from my side. I want to make sure you're safe—that includes having transportation to get away, or get to me so I can protect you."

"And know where I'm at?" She had no doubt that he'd have a tracking device on whatever he loaned her. He wanted to know everything about her, but when it came to her knowing what was going on—nothing. It hadn't bothered her much yesterday, but since last night, it felt as though she'd gotten the short end of the stick. He might be everything she'd ever wanted in a partner, but she wouldn't know. She had no one to blame but herself.

He pressed his lips tightly together, until they were just a thin line.

She sighed. "I get why you need to, I might even agree with it—but that doesn't mean I have to like it."

"I understand. You've fought really hard to be independent and I know this must rub you the wrong way, but I only want to help."

She couldn't deny that his words softened her attitude a little. It bothered her that she needed—yes, needed—him to take care of that for her because she couldn't. She just didn't have the resources, and that wasn't his fault. Being irritated at him for that was on her, not him.

"We good?" he asked after a moment.

"Yeah." She smiled even though the jumbled mix of emotions in her chest weren't remotely happy.

"Good." He continued to stare at her, not moving.

She clasped her hands together in her lap.

"Hey." Aiden reached across the space and cupped her cheek. "It's okay to not be okay with everything. I'd be surprised if you were."

"I'm good," she insisted.

"Sometimes you're a really great liar."

"No, I have a good poker face. I'm a shitty liar."

"Do you want to call in and not go to work?"

"I can't, there's a lot of shuffling around to do today. And it would look really bad if I called in to work and still played tonight. Lily's parents—my bosses—will be there."

"Okay, well, be careful. You see anything out of the ordinary, call me?"

"I will." She smiled and warmth curled through her chest. Sure, he was doing his job—whatever that was—but she liked to think he actually cared. It was a nice lie to tell herself, especially while he was touching her, and his face so near her own.

Aiden leaned in closer and kissed her gently, a simple press of lips that made her sigh. His phone rang the moment she let herself sink into the caress, but it wasn't her who groaned.

He straightened and grabbed his cell phone from the cradle mounted to the dash.

"Aiden." He shifted into gear and they were once more flying down the road. "Yes, Mr. York, we can fit you in next week. Do you have the shop number? Call that and talk to one of the girls, they can tell you what day is best. Also, make sure to give them the make, model, and year, so we can go ahead and look for some parts."

She closed her eyes and listened to Aiden's side of the conversation without understanding much of it. Before she knew it, they were pulling through the security gate at the airport.

"What time do you need to be picked up?" Aiden asked.

"Lily's going to come by and get me." She gathered her things, shoving them in the huge bag of her gear she'd hauled with them.

"Oh." Aiden blinked a few times. He didn't seem to like her answer.

"You're still coming to the bout though?" It wasn't a

good idea to foster her attraction to Aiden, but she couldn't help herself. It would be nice to have him there.

"Yeah. I imagine some of the guys will come too."

"Cool. Get there early and bring chairs. Also, beer."

"Chairs and beer?"

"Trust me." Madison pushed her door open and stood, stretching. She grabbed her derby bag from the backseat and hauled it out after her.

Act cool.

Madison strolled toward the office, but she hadn't gone five feet before Aiden honked the horn. She jumped and turned toward him, glaring while her heart pounded three times too fast.

He leaned an arm out of the window. "Not going to say good-bye?"

She opened her mouth, but thought better of it.

In for a wheel, in for a skate, right?

Madison sauntered toward the car and let her bag drop on the asphalt next to the driver's-side door. She reached in, grasping his face with both hands, and planted a big one on him. He leaned toward her, but it was Madison who teased his lips with her tongue, seeking entrance. He opened for her and she thrust into his mouth, flicking her tongue against his. He answered by stroking her and nipping her lower lip, just enough that she sucked in a breath and her toes curled. He reached up, cupping the back of her head, pressing closer and robbing her of breath.

Aiden released her and sat back in the seat while she braced her hands on the car.

"That was not good-bye." His voice was low, rough, as it had been last night.

"See you later?" She grinned and scooped up her

bag. If she didn't get in the office now, she was likely to crawl into that car and never leave.

Madison was in trouble.

Real trouble.

And it wasn't from Dustin. Her ex could only hurt her on the outside and those marks healed. Aiden was the real danger to her. Somewhere along the road she'd let him inside of her, and not just her body, but her heart. Crazy and irrational, yes. But it's not like she could control it.

Aiden idled in front of the office until she'd unlocked the door and stepped inside. Her cheeks burned, but she kept her head up high. There were at least a dozen employees who had to have seen that little display, and every one of them would drop by, wanting more information.

She peeked out of the window. Aiden revved the Chevelle and turned toward the road. She watched until the car was out of sight.

Damn, but this was a messy, complicated situation. Where did she even begin?

Madison glanced at the desk, with the logs and everything else to do. But her heart wasn't here. It was blazing down that little road.

The logs. Shit. She hadn't even thought once about talking to him about Michael Evers.

Damn. Shit. And fuck.

She sighed and tossed her gear in the little storage closet before settling in at her desk. Later. Tonight after the game she'd figure out how to tell him, though she didn't expect he'd take the news well.

It didn't take her long to fall into the regular rhythm. There were phone calls to make, e-mails to check, and schedules to arrange. For such a small airport, they stayed busy. And by some small miracle, they were too busy for anyone to bother her about the kiss. Before she knew it, it was lunchtime and her stomach was rumbling.

Usually when she forgot to bring food, she'd jump on her bike and run down to a corner store and grab something, but she'd have to make do with her emergency stash of microwavable noodles. She put the phones through to their answering service and ducked out to the hangar where they had a communal break room. Most of the guys would eat while they worked today, another small blessing, so she was able to tiptoe back to the office before anyone waylaid her for details.

She stepped into the cool haven of her office and stopped short.

A man in an olive-green suit stood studying a framed map showing historic flight paths.

Shit.

He turned toward her, his dark eyes devoid of life despite the friendly smile he pasted on. Michael Evers had always struck her as a little fake, but she'd attributed that to his wealth. This entire time, the man had known about the hardships Dustin put her through, and he'd had the nerve to show up here and smile, pretending to be friendly. What if he was here to kill her? He could be hiding anything under that jacket and she'd never know.

The man was a creep of the first order.

"I was wondering where everyone was." He glanced at her soup.

"Sorry about that." Did he know about Aiden? Was he there for her? What would he do?

"I wanted to talk about the shipment coming in tomorrow."

"Oh." Crap. She'd have to get to her desk, which put Evers between her and the door.

Madison took a deep breath and walked past the

man to her desk. She set her food down on the corner and reached for the computer mouse, bringing up the flight plan.

"What can I help you with?"

"I was just wondering if they could fly in later, say around eight or nine."

"Hm, you know, you're not authorized on that account? There's not going to be enough time to unload and clear the shipment through customs in the morning before the plane is scheduled to leave. There isn't a crew here that late tomorrow."

"I'm just helping a friend. Besides, I could bring my own crew."

Warning bells went off clamoring so hard it was difficult to hear anything else.

What was he bringing in that he didn't want anyone to see?

"Mm, I can't make a call like that. I'll have to call my boss and see what he says." She put on her most winning smile. Her boss would say no so fast it would give her whiplash, but it was better for him to do it than her. She felt like a bug on a pin with the man standing there studying her.

"I was hoping to not bother him. I know he's been busy lately."

"He does know how to stay busy, doesn't he? I'll pass it along and give you a call. How about that?"

"I think I have his number." He tapped his phone a few times then showed her the screen.

Sure enough, it was her boss's cell phone.

"That's it. You don't even need me."

Michael Evers smiled. It was secretive and made her feel as though she were having a staring contest with a snake. She wanted to crawl under her desk and hide. Did he know Dustin wanted something from her? Was he behind it? What about all those awful things Aiden had told her about him?

"Thanks." He turned and strode out of the office, and she could have sworn the temperature rose a couple of degrees.

She slumped in her chair, drawing her knees up to her chest.

Shit. Damn it. And fuck it all.

What did she do?

Madison had never admitted that Evers flew in and out from the airstrip. She needed to tell Aiden, but how? He was going to be unholy pissed at her, and if everything he said was true, he had all the right to be.

She grabbed the mouse and pulled up the full report of everything Michael Evers had flown in and out. There had to be some sort of proof, something that would point to the true nature of what he was transporting. If she was going to incur Aiden's wrath, she wanted to offer him something.

Her phone began to ring, startling her. She grabbed it and flicked the green answer button.

"You scared the shit out of me," Madison grumbled.

"Working hard, or hardly working?"

"Working hard." She relaxed into her chair, glad to hear from Lily.

"So, I got a call earlier that you were dropped off by some hot guy in an orange car. Is that the guy from Stoke's?"

Madison sighed. "Maybe."

"Helena Destroyer—you cannot skimp on the details! His name is Aiden, isn't it? My brother knows him. He told me stories." Lily's voice got quiet and she whispered. "Did you know he was in a street racing accident and he killed people?"

Madison didn't doubt Aiden had killed people. He

breathed deadly, but not racing. He'd told her about the rumors.

"He told me about those rumors."

"So it is him! And you've been spending time with him. You're holding out on me."

"I'm not, Lil, I swear. It's just—been a really stressful couple of days. My bike got stolen and he was nice enough to give me a ride, and it just kind of went from there." If she glossed over the details, it really did sound like they were on a date. Wouldn't that be a nice idea?

"I'm picking you up later, aren't I?"

"Do you mind?"

"It's going to cost you details, woman. The stuff my brother said, it worries me." Lily's voice softened. She'd seen Madison through the lowest point of her life. She owed Lily at least part of the truth.

"Look, remember how you said I needed to have some fun?"

"I said you needed to get laid."

"Yeah, well, fuck you. I'm having fun, but I know it's not a lasting thing."

"You like him. Your voice gets all wispy. It's been a hell of a long time since I heard you talk like that, but I know what it means."

"I do like him. He seems like such a bad guy, but he's really nice."

"No. No, stop there. Listen to yourself. He's a bad guy with a heart of gold? I love you, Helena, but I will knock your ass into next week, so help me."

Madison cringed. When Lily put it that way, Madison really did sound like a head case, but it wasn't like that. Aiden was so much more than a label, despite how he appeared.

"He's coming tonight," Madison blurted.

"What?"

"He's coming tonight. Please—just meet him? If he's bad, I'll take your word and walk away."

"Promise?"

"On my vows as your derby wife."

"Okay, deal."

"Hey, would you mind bringing those boxes I put in your closet? I'm trying to organize everything, and I have no idea where anything is now."

"Sure, I'll grab it before I come get you. See you at five? I got to go. Appointment just showed up."

"Will do."

Madison hung up and stared at the ceiling, suddenly no longer hungry. What was she doing?

She didn't know how upset Aiden would be with her when she told him the truth, but she expected the worst. And if Lily met him and things didn't go well, she'd just promised to give him up. It was not a good start to the day.

Chapter Fifteen

Aiden stood in a field that had become a parking lot across the street from an old roller skating rink. Cars were directed in neat rows by attendants in bright pink shirts, while the line to get in was already wrapping around the building.

"What the hell?" Julian circled the front of his car to join Aiden waiting on the others. The twins, John, and Gabriel had parked a row back.

"Guess derby is a big deal." He hefted the six-pack and lawn chair he'd brought with him.

"Hope we can get in the door," Tori said. She'd cleaned up, changing out of her grease-stained clothing into jeans and a tank top.

"I bet Aiden's *client* gets us in." Roni gave Aiden a sly look he ignored.

"Let's get in line." Aiden strode across the street toward the line that had begun to move swiftly inside.

He hadn't known what to expect with a roller derby game, but it wasn't this. The crowd was a mix of families, young people hauling coolers and cases of beer, elderly couples with lawn chairs and a thermos. There were people from all walks of life.

The inside of the rink was transformed. Banners for energy drinks, apparel, grocery stores, and a gas station hung on the walls. There were a few narrow merch tables for some of the sponsors doing brisk business and a face-painting booth for the kiddos, but by and large the attention was focused on a large oval in the middle of the rink outlined in rope lights.

The track.

The other side of the rink was cordoned off, with player areas blocked from view by curtains and banners. Front and center was a long, rectangular banner with Madison crashing into a girl with a star on her helmet, hip first. She looked—fierce. To either side were other league banners, but his attention kept straying back to the fifteen-foot depiction of his greatest distraction.

"Good evening, ladies and gentlemen, boys and girls, I am your announcer for tonight, Rinkmaster. Please find a seating area, making sure to stay out of the crash zone. The crash zone is marked by the yellow caution tape. If you choose to sit near that, you might get a derby girl in your lap, or a skate to the face. A reminder, please drink responsibly and recycle those cans. The biggest beeramid tonight will win a season pass for themselves and one other lucky person." The announcer continued to chatter, but Aiden's attention drifted.

The curtains parted and a few women stepped into the crash zone between the two player benches. No two were dressed alike, though there did seem to be a certain theme in the colors they wore. The first couple eased onto the track, followed by more. They came in twos and threes, trickling out onto the track, whizzing by bent nearly double.

"We need to sit somewhere." Tori stood on tiptoe, staring at the milling crowds that hadn't even registered to Aiden.

Where was Madison? Helena Destroyer?

Had she made it to the bout?

Or had someone gotten to her first?

He pulled out his phone and flipped to his text messages.

The last text to her was two hours ago.

He tapped out a quick message to ease his mind.

Here. Where r u?

"Shit," Roni muttered, and turned toward him, ducking her head.

"What?" Aiden glanced over her head and his gaze snagged on a tableau he did not like.

Madison stood on the edge of the roped-off players' area with a blond man he recognized. She looked—fantastic. Her uniform consisted of a bright pink tank top in some sports fabric with a pinup girl and the words DEADLY DAME arcing over her breasts, a short, pleated black skirt, and fishnet stockings. Her hair was braided into pigtails and her makeup was dark and dramatic.

Aiden watched the detective place his hand on Madison's back and lean toward her. Her smile widened, but it was stiff and she cringed when he spoke next to her ear. Aiden wanted to punch the prick's teeth out. Officer of the law? Twisting her arm? Hitting on her? Harassing her in public?

Fuck this.

"Aiden, don't go over there." Roni spoke too late.

Aiden stepped through the crowd and over the caution tape into the crash zone. It was the fastest way to get to her. The derby girls zipped by, some coming within inches of him, but he never wavered from his target. Madison's gaze darted around nervously, as if looking for an out.

Well he'd give her one.

Her gaze landed on him and her brows rose.

"Hey, babe. Was looking for you." Aiden pitched his voice over the music and noise from the crowd. The detective straightened and frowned at Aiden when he moved in and draped his arm across Madison's shoulders. "Not answering your phone?"

"Sorry, we had our pre-bout meeting." Madison glanced from Matt to Aiden.

"That's fine." Aiden turned his gaze on the detective, assessing the man like he might be an opponent. Matt Smith was younger than he expected, something of a golden boy appearance. The guy breathed his uniform, no doubt. He couldn't ooze "cop" more if he rolled around in it. "Who is your friend?"

"Uh, this is Matt."

"Name's Aiden."

They shook hands, Matt's gaze narrowing. No doubt the detective had heard things. Aiden worked hard to stay off the police radar, but a good detective would hear rumors.

"Aiden who owns the classic car shop?" Matt asked.

Bingo.

"That's me."

"Nice to meet you." Matt's tone said otherwise.

"You know what? I saved you a place to sit, if you want. You need to take the spot or someone else will." Madison neatly pivoted on her skates to face him.

"Yeah, show me the way. See you around, Matt."

Madison put her helmet on and pushed off, rolling slowly away from Matt. They skirted the growing throng of people setting up lawn chairs outside of the crash zone. About halfway through the turn a tarp was laid out with two coolers on either side.

"Is that enough space for you guys?" Madison pointed to the tarped-off area.

"Plenty." Aiden grabbed Madison's arm, just below her elbow pad. "He bothering you?"

"What? Matt?" She shook her head. "No, he's just being annoying like he always is."

"You sure?" Would she tell him otherwise? Did she really trust him?

Madison paused, studying him.

"I'm sure. I promise. Matt's doing what he thinks is right. I just . . . he's never flirted with me before and it was—weird."

"He's not your type."

"Really?" She placed her hands on her hips.

"Really." Aiden closed the distance between them, leaning down until he could smell her cherry lip balm. "You're attracted to guys like me."

Why was he doing this? It made no sense. He should be pushing her away, not teasing her. And yet, he couldn't help it. Seeing the cop flirt with the woman he'd had under him last night flipped a primitive switch inside of him. She was his.

"We sleep together once and you think you know my type?" Her cheeks grew pinker, and it had nothing to do with her makeup.

"I believe it was three times."

"Shut up." Madison rolled her eyes. "I have to warm up."

She neatly slid through the crowd and onto the track, gliding as if she were born for it.

He shook his head and stepped onto the tarp, motioning for the others to join him.

"That went well, I take it?" Roni plopped down in her chair, slightly behind him. She'd borrowed Gabriel's track jacket and had it zipped up to her chin.

"Now I see why you didn't want my help the other day." Julian set his seat next to Aiden's, probably so Julian could goad him the entire time.

Bringing the crew was a mistake. He should have slipped in the back, watched the crowd, and waited for her to be done. But the crew hadn't gone out together in ages, except for racing. And while that was what pumped their blood, he actually liked his garage family.

A man in a red-tailed coat over sweatpants jogged out onto the center track. "Welcome to tonight's bouts," he announced.

The crowd applauded and several people hoisted beers. The skaters began exiting the track, two teams lining up on the benches, while the remaining two took to the sidelines at the edge of the player area.

"For those of you new to derby, we're going to do a quick demonstration. Ladies, volunteers?" Rinkmaster turned toward the benches and bowed, while players took to the track.

The announcer walked the crowd through the demonstration, with the help of the players. It seemed pretty easy. Four players from each team beat the crap out of each other, and the remaining two scored points for passing opposing players—legally. There was something special about helmet covers, but he was too distracted by Madison—Helena Destroyer—coasting around as part of the demo.

The crowd stomped on the wooden floor and banged cans together, cheering for the demo girls as they wrapped up the explanation. Aiden watched Julian out of the corner of his eye flinch yet again. Damn. Julian needed a break—or else he was going to break. They didn't have the luxury of taking time off to regroup. They were always on the job, but Julian more than most needed to decompress, relax a little.

Rinkmaster led the crowd in a surprisingly good rendition of "The Star Spangled Banner." Aiden noticed Matt edging closer to the player bench. Was this man for real? Aiden hoped Matt got a fucking clue before Aiden had to do something drastic. The last thing he needed was a cop snooping around. When the song ended and the players not involved in the first bout scattered, Matt was shoved into the crowd, out of the players' way. It would have to do for now.

Julian passed him a beer as the first lineup of players took to the track for real. Madison was on the starting line wearing one of the helmet covers with a stripe down the middle. People chanted her name and a few had posters with her moniker painted on them and violent epitaphs like, CRUSH THE COMPETITION or DESTROY THE JAMMER. The only indication she gave of acknowledging the crowd was a little wave, but other than that, she was all business.

"You ready for some derby?" Rinkmaster yelled into the microphone.

The players all hunched over, poised and ready to go. Unlike the demo, he could practically feel the room waiting to exhale.

"Tonight, the Deadly Dames take on the Butchering Beach Babes. Is this going to be a replay of last season? I don't know."

A referee blasted his whistle and the girls shot forward. There was jostling, girl bumping into girl, and the speed—he hadn't expected the pack to shoot out quite so fast. A referee blasted twice on his whistle and the two point-scoring players—jammers—flew off the line. They skated low and fast. He didn't know which to watch, the pack of girls or the jammers.

Aiden glanced at Lily, the Deadly Dames jammer, eyeing her opponent. The other girl seemed focused on motoring past her. Lily swerved, hitting the other jammer hip first and sending the girl wide out of the second turn and over the boundary line.

"Oh man! Did you see that? A'thing'a Beauty just knocked Slamstrong out of bounds. Look at her fly." Rinkmaster kept the audience appraised of the movements from the DJ perch.

Aiden sat forward, beer forgotten. A'thing'a Beauty, or Lily as he knew her, reached the back of the pack. The players in green formed a solid wall, not letting her pass. He didn't see a way around that defensive formation. Every time A'thing'a Beauty dodged, they moved with her until their own jammer was right there with her.

Helena Destroyer—Madison—swooped to the outside, circling around behind the pack and coming alongside her jammer.

How was that supposed to help?

"Slamstrong's making a break for it on the inside—Oh!"

Another pink blocker swerved, crashing into the green jammer and both girls went tumbling onto the inner track.

"Slamstrong is down. Sindercella sacrificed herself and is going to the penalty box for that one. Madam Penal will make her sit in the Cage of Shame."

Aiden glanced at the cage—which was a real, human-sized cage with two chairs inside of it and a woman who looked a bit like a sexy Darth Vader in a black bathing suit, mask, and cape.

Back on the track, Madison pushed her way through the green players. Her fellow pink blockers swarmed, jostling and breaking up the line. A'thing'a Beauty kept low and right behind Madison, who plowed a way through the pack, all the way to the front.

"Oh, and Helena Destroyer whips A'thing'a Beauty out of the pack and you have your first—lead—jammer!"

The crowd went wild as A'thing'a Beauty tapped her hips with both hands. The referees blasted off a couple blows on the whistle and the players relaxed. Quickly, the players on the track exited to the bench and another collection of ten girls took the track—but none of them was Helena Destroyer.

Aiden relaxed back into his chair and lifted his beer to his lips, except it was empty.

"We have a trash bag somewhere?" he asked the girls.

"It's not my job to pick up your shit. Why didn't you bring one?" Roni didn't bother looking at him, her eyes were only for the game. But then again, this was right up her alley. Sexy clothes. Fast action. Little violence. If they didn't have such an all-consuming mission, he'd bet both twins would be the league's next recruits.

"You done with that, mister?" A kid, probably no more than eight or nine years old, had crawled toward him.

"Uh, yeah."

"Can I have it?" The kid stared at the empty can with greed in his eye.

"I'm not sure that's a good idea."

The boy lifted his gaze to Aiden's face and gave him the most pitiful puppy dog stare.

"Please? I have to get the biggest beeramid. I have to! I want to give my girlfriend a season ticket."

Beeramid? Was the kid serious? He couldn't possibly be old enough for a girlfriend, but what the hell?

"Okay." Aiden handed the can over after making sure it was drained of every last drop and watched the kid scurry over to a few adults sitting on the ground, right on the edge of the crash zone.

He placed eight cans up in a line, and began stacking seven across the top, forming the base of a pyramid.

This was a thing? Pyramids of beer cans? Aiden shook his head and settled in to watch the next jam. Madison had explained some of the game, but it had gone right over his head. Now though, he was getting the picture.

Another jam came and went, and yet a third lineup took the track. The hits the girls were doling out were vicious. A couple had gone tumbling or slammed onto the ground so hard that he was surprised when they popped back up as quickly as they did.

He scanned the crowd, but the only face he didn't like was the detective. No sign of the Eleventh or Dustin's thugs.

"Roni, what did you find out about our friend?" Aiden asked over his shoulder.

She sighed and leaned forward. "You want to talk about that now?"

"I want to know what I'm dealing with."

"What's to tell? He's a cop, who does coplike shit. There's nothing dirty about him. He's squeaky clean and he doesn't like me. I tried to pick him up at lunch and you'd have thought I was a whore trying to turn a trick the way he laid into me. Then, when I did finally give up, he pulls me over and the way he was talking, I thought he was going to read me my rights."

"For what?"

"Fuck if I know."

Well great. That's what they needed. A cop jumping at his shadow and in their way. If Roni couldn't distract him the old-fashioned way, Aiden might have to figure something else out.

"Your girlfriend's back on the track," Julian said.

Aiden straightened in his chair and glanced at the kid. He had a full beeramid now, set just inside the crash zone. Smaller beeramids were popping up all along the caution tape.

The players lined up and he ignored the beeramids. Helena Destroyer wasn't the pivot this time. She was positioned at the back of the pack, but to him, she still stuck out. It wasn't just because she was hot. It was the way she held herself. The look in her eye. She had a focused mind-set on this game, and nothing else mattered. Other players eyed her, but Madison ignored them. She was unshakable.

The whistle blared and they were off, the jammers a second behind them. The pack moved slower this time. Helena Destroyer swept back and forth, keeping one eye behind her. Her team's jammer closed the distance and slipped through the pack like a fish through water.

The green jammer was slower. She hit the back of the pack as they completed their first circuit of the track. Helena swerved, and he could see her intent, she was going to hit the jammer hard. The green jammer shifted her whole weight and slammed into Helena first, sending her sailing through the air. She tucked and rolled out of the second turn, almost straight at Aiden, and right into the kid's beeramid.

Madison shook her head, no doubt orienting herself, before extracting her skates from the audience and standing. She shook off a can, stepped through the debris, and powered on, building up speed and racing to catch up to her pack.

Aiden blew out a breath.

Fuck, derby was one hell of a sport.

Chapter Sixteen

Madison was spent. Done. Her body ached. Her lungs were exhausted. Even her eyelashes were calling it quits. Thank goodness the bout was over. Except now all she could think about was everything else.

Derby did that for her. Gave her an escape. On the track it didn't matter who she'd been married to, what was going on, or how much money was in her bank account. All anyone cared about was that she hit hard, skated fast, and stayed out of the Cage of Shame. There was more to it, but so long as she did those three, she was doing okay.

She shouldered her bag and glanced around the curtained-off players' area. She wouldn't put it past Matt to flash his badge and sneak back here. Something was up with him. Flirting with her, being at her game, it was weird and she didn't like it. She stepped outside through a set of side doors into the cool night, hoping to avoid him by taking the back way out. A couple of girls sat on the gravel to one side smoking and a few others sipped beer in a small group a couple yards away, but it was quiet. A sort of haven, where they could come down off the post-game high before joining the party.

On the other side, the lot was lit up like daytime, but over here it was dark. She picked her way over the gravel, her eyes adjusting to the lower light.

"Madison."

She started one second and groaned inwardly the next. Feet crunched over gravel, coming closer. So much for sneaking out.

"Hey, Matt. Enjoy the bout?"

"Yeah, that was something else. You're really great out there." He smiled. At first, that smile had disarmed her. He seemed sweet, but she'd quickly learned it was another tactic of his. "Want me to carry that?" He gestured to her bag.

"No, thanks. I've got it." Now how did she get rid of him?

"Haven't found any more leads on your bike. Did you want to come by the station and see what we found?"

"No, that's okay. I didn't leave anything in it."

"Do you need a ride home?"

"Oh, no."

The pleasant smile faded, and the cop stared back at her, hard and unyielding.

"Is Aiden DeHart giving you a ride?"

She opened and closed her mouth, one second from telling Matt to fuck off, but that wouldn't be very smart.

"I'm sorry, is something wrong?" she asked.

Matt took a step toward her, until they were almost touching. She wanted to back up, to put space between them, but he'd probably follow her.

"I know more than you do about this guy. Madison, he's not good news. Please, let me protect you."

"Protect me?" She suppressed the urge to laugh. The last time he'd tried to protect her, her car became a bonfire.

"Aiden is dangerous."

"I know that. Do you think I'm stupid? Everyone in my life is either dangerous or in danger because of me. You've made that abundantly clear."

Matt stared at her for several moments. She couldn't see his expression in the shadows, and she was glad she couldn't. "I don't want to see you hurt."

Was the flirting fake? Did Detective Smith have some sort of a thing for her? It couldn't be real. Sure, he was a good guy, upstanding, probably with the savings account and 401(k) she so wanted her future significant others to have. But he wasn't for her.

"I'm a tough cookie."

"Even cookies crumble."

"You're cute."

A tall figure with wide shoulders came around the corner and she sucked in a deep breath.

Aiden.

The sight of him turned her insides to goo. The thrill of his nearness set her off, but she knew it couldn't last. Still, being with Aiden made more sense than returning Matt's awkward flirtation. Besides, he made her feel safe, which was something Detective Smith had never managed.

Aiden strode toward them and without asking her, took her sweaty bag of gear and shouldered it.

"You did good, babe." He leaned down and buzzed her cheek with a peck. Quick, harmless, and very public.

Heat rushed to her face and her stomach seemed to be trying to twist itself into a pretzel. Her reaction was silly and Aiden's caveman claim didn't mean anything.

"Ready to go?" Aiden asked.

"Yeah."

"Nice to see you again, man." Aiden shook Matt's hand before urging her forward with a palm against her lower back.

"Lily brought some boxes for me," she said, pitching her voice low. They rounded the corner into the well-lit parking lot. It was beginning to clear as people headed for the after-party, which would undoubtedly be crazy.

"Do you know where she's parked?"

"Yeah, right there, the blue Prius." She pointed at a little car a couple spaces away. The doors were all open and a couple of girls were clustered around while heavy rock music blared.

"I'm over in the grass lot. How about I go get the car and drive it over here. Cool?"

"Perfect. I can take my bag."

"I've got it." He turned, heading toward the overflow parking lot, leaving her at odds for a moment.

She strolled to Lily's car, trying to ignore the curious gazes of her friends.

"Need a ride home?" Lily asked.

"No, Aiden's taking me." Madison and Lily had talked about this, but it was clear her friend was still less than enthusiastic about the arrangement.

Lily turned toward another girl, dismissing Madison. Lily would have to get over it or tell her she wasn't okay with Aiden. If it came down to that before her deal with Aiden was done, well, she didn't know what she'd do. Madison hadn't told her about the deal with Aiden or what Dustin wanted from her, and it was probably for the best. She wanted her friend to be safe.

"Hey." Madison edged closer to Sindercella.

"What's up her cooch?" She nodded toward Lily.

"She doesn't exactly like Aiden."

"Doesn't like him? What's not to like? He's hot, polite, and flirted with *Sobo*."

Madison grinned. Aiden had held his own pretty well. "Yeah, well, she doesn't know him. No big deal."

"It's the best friend thing. He's competition for your time."

Only for right now.

It hurt to admit that now, but it was the truth.

"Hey, do you know what ever happened to Alison Plunderland?" Madison asked.

"Ally? Damn, what makes you ask about her?"

"I saw that guy she used to date the other day at Stoke's."

Sindercella leaned closer and whispered, "She moved. That guy was bad news. Last I heard she's in Atlanta on their alternate roster. I bet she gets on a team within the month, and Lord knows their travel team could use her. They were not good this last season." Sindercella sighed and shook her head.

Madison nodded. That was good to hear, for Alison. Not so good for her. What if Raibel caught her next?

"Damn, that's a sweet ride." Sindercella leaned back, peering around Madison.

She felt the rumble of the car before she heard it. Aiden's Chevelle was really a thing of beauty. He parked it just behind Lily's Prius and popped the trunk.

"Enjoy that one, okay?" Sindercella winked and gave her a quick squeeze. "Don't forget to ice your knee."

Lily unlocked her trunk without another word spoken and Madison grabbed the first box she could.

The white boxes didn't appear any different than the others they'd looked at, but she had a good feeling about these. The drive had to be here.

They loaded eight boxes into the back of Aiden's car.

The hair on Madison's neck rose. She glanced around, and found a red sports car parked at the curb, driver's window rolled down and Raibel Canales staring at them.

"A-Aiden."

"I know." He closed the trunk and pushed her toward the passenger side. "Get in."

She plopped into the seat, the last of her energy leaving her, and buckled in. Aiden slipped a Bluetooth headset over his ear as he started the engine.

"Hey. Eleventh is here. You guys still around?" he asked someone that wasn't her. "Great. He's probably got some friends around here somewhere, so be careful."

"What's going on?" she asked.

"Nothing." Yet he reached under his seat and took out the same gun he'd toted around the night before. He tucked it under his thigh.

"Then why the gun?"

"Just in case."

"I don't like this." Racing was one thing, being followed by someone she knew wasn't afraid to hurt people was another.

Aiden hated the fear in Madison's eyes. It didn't belong there, and he had no idea how to fix it.

Canales was escalating things, and while he might tell Madison to not worry about it, his concerns were very real. Bashing the bike was one step closer to hurting actual people, and according to Madison, that had already taken place. This was his fault for underestimating the Eleventh, and Canales in particular.

Aiden needed to take Canales off the streets. He hadn't had a moment to get CJ up to speed and on the same page about bringing in the DEA yet, but when he could make that call—it was happening. There were already too many threats to Madison's life without the Eleventh involved.

"What are we doing?" Madison's voice had risen and she gripped the edges of her seat.

"Waiting."

"For what? Raibel to come over here?"

"No."

He loved the Chevelle, but it didn't have the modifications to beat Canales's Lancer. The little car didn't have a piece of stock still on it. It was a badass racing machine.

A high-pitched whine split through the night.

"That's what we're waiting for."

A sleek, black GT-R zipped down the street, barely missing people. Its tires squealed as the brakes were applied and it skidded to a stop directly in front of Canales's car. Nose to nose.

Julian had the windows rolled down. Even from this distance, Aiden could see the gruesome smile Julian gave Canales. Aiden needed to come up with a plan fast, or Julian would *take care of it.* Canales might deserve it, but the last thing Julian needed was another drop of blood on his hands.

"Hold on."

Aiden gunned the engine and shifted. The Chevelle shot forward, cutting through the parking lot, headed away from Canales. They jumped the curb and he cut the wheel the same moment he stomped on the accelerator. In the rearview mirror, Canales shifted into reverse. A blue blur shot past Aiden going the opposite direction. The blue Lancer turned ninety degrees in a handbreak turn.

"Roni?" Madison craned her neck to peer back at the quickly fading cars.

"Just giving us a little cover."

"But won't he go after them, too?"

"Probably, but for some reason, he's fixed on me." Which was what he didn't need right now.

He took turns too fast, passed cars by swerving into oncoming traffic and all the while, the one thing he could hear was Madison's panting breath.

Lights lit up his back window. Three—no, four cars turned onto the feeder road maybe a quarter mile behind him. It wasn't much of a lead, but it was something to work with.

This late, the highway wasn't busy, but there were still too many people on the road for his tastes. Especially with Canales and whoever this other driver was.

He shifted into a higher gear and let everything else go. The Chevelle's engine rumbled as they flew forward, passing big rigs, SUVs, and other cars. Though the Chevelle could perform at higher speeds, he was limited to how fast he could push it with this many innocent people around.

The other cars were closing the gap.

Julian and Roni's cars zipped back and forth in front of the other two, slowing them down, but there was only so much they could do. Canales was a man on a mission.

The fourth car he recognized. The silver Scion racer from the trip up to Boca. A careful kid. Aiden pitied him. This was no place for a kid, and yet, he'd made his choice. The red Lancer crept up on Aiden's right, while Julian pulled up dangerously close behind Aiden.

"Don't do it, Jul," Aiden muttered. He eased off the gas and Canales drew up next to them.

His window was down, creating drag, no doubt. He would glance at the road, glare at Aiden, check his mirrors, and repeat. Behind them, Julian and Roni had the silver Scion boxed in against an eighteen-wheeler.

This was too dangerous. Far too many people around.

Aiden eased off the accelerator a bit more. Canales kept pace with him.

What if the man had a gun? Of course he would. Aiden had escalated it by pointing one at Canales. There could be a gun aimed at Madison right now. He was on her side.

Aiden felt the press of his gun under his thigh. If he needed to, he'd use it. To protect her. They continued to keep pace for two miles. Enough distance and time that Aiden was starting to feel on edge. What was Canales planning?

He kept one eye on the red Lancer, and one on the road ahead of him. Which left them blind to the rear.

A flash of headlights in the rearview mirror was all the warning Aiden had that something bad was about to happen. The car lurched forward and the steering wheel was nearly ripped from Aiden's grip.

"Oh my God," Madison screamed.

"Fuck." He held on tighter and accelerated, putting distance between him and the silver Scion that had just fucking bumped them.

Julian's black GT-R swerved toward the Scion. The silver car jerked away and Aiden's view was cut off by a big rig.

The Chevelle vibrated on a new note that set Aiden's teeth on edge. They needed off this crazy ride. Now.

The black GT-R shot forward and cut in front of the big rig and Aiden, until Julian was in front of Canales. Right now, Canales was between Aiden and any exit ramp he might try to take, forcing him back toward the heart of Miami.

Aiden accelerated, pulling up alongside Julian. Canales jerked his car to the right, but Roni shot forward, cutting off that avenue.

"What's going on? What's happening?" Madison's breathing was erratic, scared, and he couldn't blame her.

He cut across in front of Julian, then Roni, and into the far right lane.

"You know how derby girls make a defensive line so the jammer can't get through?" He checked his mirrors, watching for the silver car, but it was gone.

"Y-yeah."

"Julian and Roni are my defensive line." If Madison weren't with him, if they weren't potentially carrying the shit Dustin wanted, sure, he'd be tempted to show Canales a lesson. The Chevelle could take a whole lot more of a beating than the Lancer.

Canales sped up, slowed down, but each time, Julian and Roni kept pace with him.

Aiden exited the highway, and wished his crew well. It was another two miles to the closest exit, and by then, he wanted to be long gone.

"Oh my God." Madison twisted to peer out of the rear window.

"We're okay." He reached for his phone, scrolling quickly through his contacts until he found Gabriel, their most resourceful asset. Anything they needed, any car they wanted to boost, Gabriel was their guy.

The Bluetooth rang and rang. . . .

"What's on fire?" Gabriel asked.

"Not yet. I need a place, though."

"Are you hiding or is this for a name?"

"Need to keep a low profile."

"I got a place. It's mostly empty. It's off Fifth and Twenty-sixth above a lighting store. Loft space. That work?"

"Is there a bed and a microwave?"

"It's got sheets and towels."

"Perfect. How do I get in?"

"There's a key hidden inside of a fake rock that's in a planter for a hibiscus plant that's to the right of the door." Gabriel rattled off a security code and exact address.

"You're a lifesaver, man."

"Yeah, just give me something more interesting to do."

Aiden glanced at Madison, who hadn't lost the dazed look.

"Soon, man. Real soon."

He hung up and turned the car toward South Beach and the Arts District, while keeping an eye on his phone. But it wasn't his that rang, it was Madison's. She dug it out of her pocket and frowned at the screen.

"Who is it?" he asked.

"Matt."

He tightened his grip on the wheel. Another problem that needed handling.

"Hello?"

Aiden felt Madison's gaze on him, but he wouldn't look at her. Not while she was talking to that fucking cop. His reaction was extreme and out of line, and he didn't care. For now, Madison was his. His responsibility. His to care about. His. And the cop needed to learn that lesson quick.

"That's—that's awful. Is everyone okay?" She paused and he could actually hear Matt Smith's voice. "No, we aren't anywhere near there. Actually, we just stopped for some food. I hope everyone's okay. . . . Okay. I will. Bye."

Madison blew out a breath and leaned her head back, slouching down until she could rest her head on the back of the seat.

He refused to ask what that call was about.

"That silver car crashed."

Fuck.

"Was anyone hurt?" he asked.

"The driver. He clipped another car, but the people in that one were okay. Matt thinks we were involved."

They were. But it would take the golden detective a while to figure that out. Aiden didn't like the thought, but he was going to have to lean on CJ to make Matt Smith go away.

"Damn it. I'll get Emery to find out who it was, see if we can't do something for them. Offer them a deal on repairs or something."

"That would be nice of you."

"Fucking Canales."

"Where are we going?"

"Someplace safe. We're going to stay at a friend's place for tonight. Do you need anything? Like . . . a toothbrush or something?"

"No, I keep an overnight bag in with my derby stuff. Usually I stay over at one of the girls' houses after a bout."

"Reliving the game?"

"Taking a bath." She chuckled, some of her good humor recovered. The shock of their short race was wearing off. "One thing that doesn't fit on a boat. A tub."

"I see." Good thing Gabriel was providing towels with the digs. "Hungry?"

"Starved."

"There should be a little place around the corner from the loft. How about you take your bath, clean up, and I'll grab us some food. Then we can go through the boxes." Granted, that meant he'd be hauling them up and down the stairs. Some aspects of this job sucked.

"Sounds amazing."

As they neared the loft, Aiden pulled up a map on his phone until he found the exact building. There was a bright yellow shop advertising the latest fashions, a perfume wholesale store, a couple places he couldn't quite tell what they sold, and on the corner, a two-story white building with red doors. It had an industrial appearance, but he could make out a set of stairs leading up to a landing.

He circled around the building and parked in an alley. It wasn't much to hide the Chevelle, but it would have to do.

"We here?" Madison asked.

"Yup."

He got out, stashing his gun in his waistband, and flipped on the flashlight app. He held his breath and circled around the back of the car.

"Motherfucker." He knelt, pressing his hand into the dinner plate–sized dent.

"Oh no, I'm so sorry, Aiden." Madison bent at the waist and they both took in the destroyed bumper and chipping paint.

"Do you know how hard it is to find a bumper in good enough condition?" Fuck. This was going to take weeks of searching. Again. And a new paint job.

That kid better be glad the cops had him, because Aiden wanted a piece of his hide.

He sighed and unlocked the trunk.

Madison gasped. The boxes were overturned, the contents everywhere. So much for hauling the boxes up to them. By the looks of it, they were going to have to go fishing in the trunk. Tomorrow. One glance at Madison and he knew her energy was fading.

He grabbed her bag out from the mess of his trunk and his overnight kit.

"Is it safe?" Madison asked.

Aiden jostled the trunk and tried to pry his fingers under the hood, but it held fast.

"Yeah. Looks like it's just the bumper and some paint."

"I'm so sorry."

"Why?" He placed his hand on her lower back, urging her toward the street. Once he had her settled, he'd do a sweep of the area then get her food.

"Because . . . I don't know."

"Canales has issues with me. Not you." Though if Aiden hadn't been at the game, would Canales have gone after Madison? It was a possibility he didn't want to contemplate. He was supposed to be getting her out of harm's way, not into it.

They walked toward the street. It was late enough the immediate area was shut up tight for the night. Good for them. Bad for anyone searching them out.

The stairs leading up to the loft were narrow, metal, and open to the street. Not ideal, but again, someone couldn't sneak up on them easily.

A row of hibiscus plants stood against the white plaster building, silent sentinels.

Aiden glanced around, but didn't see anyone watching. He bent and searched the first pot for a stone, but came up empty. The third pot yielded the key.

"Come on."

Madison trudged up the stairs. There was a long, red mark where she'd slid on the floor after being hit, and every now and then she cradled her left arm to her chest. The woman was something else.

He unlocked the loft and did a quick sweep of it. Close to fifteen hundred square feet, there was a kitchenette, a full bath, and a bed big enough for four people. If he had to guess, this was someone's party pad.

"I'm going to go get us some food. Will you be okay here by yourself?"

Madison knelt next to the bathroom wall, near the bed. She had her gear laid out, and another bag in hand.

"Yeah. Is it okay if I clean up?"

"Go ahead. I'll lock the door, but if you hear anything—"

"I'll call you. I know the drill." She stood, one side of her mouth hiked up in a lopsided smile.

"Good." He crossed to her and pressed a quick kiss to her lips, as if it was what he always did.

Madison sucked in air. He turned away from her. Maybe he shouldn't take such liberties with her, but touching her, kissing her, they felt natural. Right. If he had to stop he should just turn over her safety to someone else, because he couldn't stop himself.

Chapter Seventeen

Aiden left the loft, locking it up tight, and put space between himself and Madison. His mind continued to stray back to her.

What was he doing?

Hadn't he told himself in the beginning that Madison didn't need him in her life? At least not romantically. Something had changed yesterday. He couldn't put his finger on what, but there was a point, when they'd stopped for a moment in the parking lot, where he'd accepted that keeping his hands off Madison wasn't going to happen. But even then, he'd thought last night would be enough.

He'd been wrong.

Aiden had spent the day peeking at his phone to see if she'd texted him back, reliving the night before—not to mention that morning.

He was well aware that tense situations breed heightened emotions. Which was why he'd always avoided getting involved with a client beyond what was strictly necessary. But Madison was different. He wanted her and enjoyed the hell out of spending time with her, but the most responsible thing to do would be to shut the door on this relationship. Leave it at scorching-hot sex.

The restaurant a few streets over was doing a healthy amount of business, mostly to locals since the waitstaff barely spoke English. He played it safe and ordered a couple burgers.

Aiden ducked outside while he waited and put in a call to CJ. The phone rang twice.

"Caused enough trouble yet?" CJ asked.

"I didn't start it. We need to stop Canales. I was thinking we could call in the DEA. You know the local field agents, don't you?"

"Let me see what I can do."

"Also, and I know you aren't going to like this one—"

"What?"

"Call the police chief. This detective is breathing down our necks. I don't care what you have to tell him, but he's got to back off."

"Shit. You want some fries with that too?" CJ sighed. "I'll have Kathy get on the horn to the DEA. They like her better than me. The cops, they aren't going to be happy about this. I'm just warning you, the chief is probably going to shoot straight with Matt. That means he'll know."

The fewer people who knew about their operation, the better. But some things couldn't be helped.

"Do it," Aiden said. A waitress stepped out of the restaurant, holding a bag of takeout. "I've got to go. Food's ready."

He tipped the waitress and checked his watch.

Half an hour.

It wasn't long, but with two people now after them, it was longer than he wanted to leave Madison alone.

OMW, he texted. He hit the sidewalk at a brisk pace, juggling food and drinks.

His phone didn't chime once all the way back to the loft. By the time he unlocked the doors and let himself in, he was concerned.

"Madison?"

No answer.

He put the food down on an island that ran the length of the kitchenette.

"Madison, you here?"

Her gear was still spread out, and everything perfectly in place.

Aiden pushed the door to the bathroom open and his heart leapt into his throat.

Madison lay in the tub, head tipped back and face turned away from him. The water was hazy.

"Madison!" He choked out her name, going to his knees, reaching for her. She turned toward him.

She blinked several times, her eyes heavy. He wrapped his hand around her arm and pulled her toward him.

"What's wrong?" She sat up, pulling her knees up to her chest and rubbing her knuckles across her eyes.

"You didn't answer your phone. I was calling your name."

"Oh, sorry. I took a shower and then I must have dozed off."

He glanced down at the rest of her. Yeah, she was naked, and the murky water didn't do much to hide her lush curves and inked adornments from view.

"What's in the water?"

"Epsom salt."

"Oh."

That made . . . perfect sense.

* * *

Madison hugged her knees closer to her chest. She hadn't been able to resist the huge tub after her shower. It was easily big enough for several people to soak at once, and she had it all to herself.

"Are you okay?" Aiden's stare was, in a word, intense. He hadn't taken his eyes off her since rousing her from her unintended nap.

"I'm fine." But she might not have been if it weren't for Aiden's quick driving and his friends. That was a reality she didn't want to think too hard about.

He sat down on the tile next to the tub, leaning against the side.

"What are you doing?" she asked.

"Sitting here."

Why? How was she supposed to respond to that?

"Talk to Matt again?" he asked.

"Uh . . . no." What did Matt have to do with anything?

"Does he call you often?"

Matt was the last thing she wanted to talk about with Aiden. Things with the detective were odd at the best of times.

"He calls me every couple of days, sometimes more. I don't answer half the time."

"When you don't answer, does he call again?"

She stared at Aiden. "Yeah."

"He's stalking you."

"Stalking? What? I wouldn't call it that."

"Then what would you call it?"

Why was he being so aggressive about Matt? What did the cop even matter?

"I don't know. Doing his job? Or at least that's what he thinks he's doing. That's what it was. Now it's . . . I don't know. Odd. It's not always about my ex, it's, 'Let me protect you,' and shit."

"Protect you from what?" Aiden spoke slowly and

there was a note in his tone, a deadly one that made her want to remain perfectly still.

"Dustin, I guess." She shrugged. "Why are you so upset? What is it you call what you're doing, sticking to my ass like glue?"

"We are working together on this." Aiden pressed his lips together and stared at her for a moment. "Did he try to protect you tonight from me?"

Yes . . . but she hadn't felt as though she needed it.

Aiden's lips compressed into a tight line and a fire lit in his gaze.

"He did, didn't he?" Aiden pressed.

"Yeah, okay, so what?"

Aiden glanced away. She stared at his profile, trying to sort out exactly what was going on. She hadn't wanted to tell him about Matt because the detective wasn't in her life by choice. They weren't all that dissimilar, but it was in how they interacted with her that they differed. Matt pressured her. Aiden urged her. It was a slight difference, but if she ever accepted Matt's help she'd be putting her head through a noose. Aiden believed he would actually rescue her from it, though he might break all the rules. On paper, it was Matt she should be turning to for help, but in reality, she needed someone like Aiden. They weren't too dissimilar, good men, good intentions, good-looking. . . .

He was jealous.

Aiden of the panty-dropping smile, sizzling gaze, and tantalizing muscles . . . was jealous.

Was that even possible?

Apparently it was.

"I've never accepted Matt's help," she said.

Aiden didn't reply.

"He's a great detective, and I'm sure he means well, but anything he would do only puts me more at risk. He can't help me if I don't give him something on Dustin, and even then, he can't promise it'll be enough."

"But I can?"

"You said you could."

"Is that why you fucked me?"

Madison blinked at him. Her mind did not work in the same ways his did. The connections he saw, the patterns, they weren't how she saw the world.

"What? No." She hugged her knees tighter to her chest. Did he really think she'd do that? After everything they'd been through and all that she'd told him? His suspicion stung and an ache throbbed deep in her chest. "Last night had nothing to do with anything, except you and me. If you can't accept that's what it was, then maybe I need to leave."

"What happened last night?"

"Uh, I'm pretty sure you were there."

"Yeah, but I'm asking you what happened."

"We had sex. What do you call it? Tactical spy shit?" Pinpricks of pain started behind her eyes. She was going to cry, damn it. She hated crying, but she'd allowed herself to be vulnerable with him, and now he suspected her? "I'm not doing this."

She yanked the stopper out of the tub and hauled herself upright, turning her back on the man she'd thought she was growing to care for. A towel hung ready for her on a hook. She wrapped it around herself and knotted the ends between her breasts. She took deep, calming breaths.

"Madison." His hand wrapped around her arm. Why was he always so warm? It soaked into her skin, down to her bones.

"Don't touch me."

She tried to pull her arm out of his grip, but he was too strong. Aiden tugged her toward him and she sloshed through the bathwater, turning to face him. His brows were drawn down and his lips curled into a frown. He cupped her other shoulder, steadying her.

"I'm sorry," he said. Plain and simple.

The apology caught her off guard. She stared at him, as if she might will him to say more.

"Sorry for what?"

His hold gentled and he slid his hands around to her back.

"Being an ass."

"That's a start."

His lips compressed once more.

"For fuck's sake, Aiden." She pushed at his chest but he wrapped his arms around her, bringing them closer, the side of the square tub hitting her shins.

He didn't speak, didn't refute what he'd said. Instead, he bent his head and rested his forehead against hers. First he was jealous of Dustin, now suspicious of her, what next?

"It's hard to trust," he said quietly.

"I thought we established that already. You have to take a risk."

"I take a lot of risks."

He was a great driver. Former soldier. She could see the nature of risk written all over him. But trusting someone intimately, opening up, that was another kind of risk. One she fell into far too easily, while someone like Aiden struggled with it.

"I'm not going to allow you to accuse me of trading sex for your protection." Or cheapen what had been a beautiful memory.

"That was wrong."

"You think?"

"I said I'm sorry."

"For being an ass."

"Yeah."

"That doesn't quite cover it. I think accusing me of screwing you with ulterior motives is a bit more extreme than being an ass."

"You're right. I was out of line." He sighed and slid a hand higher, above the towel, splaying his fingers over her back. "This isn't how any of this is supposed to go."

"You said that before."

"I know. It's just . . . different. I don't know how to explain it."

He was jealous and unsure of whatever this nameless relationship they'd forged was supposed to be. She got that. When he rolled out of her life, she was scared of what would happen to her. Not physically, but emotionally. She was a serial monogamist who had a problem with falling in love. Always had. And here she was, tipping over the edge, about to fall for the most unavailable man she'd ever met, and there wasn't any stopping her.

Aiden cupped her cheek and she let her eyes drift close. Whatever happened between them was already building momentum. She couldn't stop it, and why would she? Being in his arms made her feel alive. At the very least, he would burn away the touch of any man who came before him. It might be a while before she was able to love after him, but maybe, just maybe, this was what she needed.

He tipped her chin up and in his usual style, gave her every opportunity to turn away. For a few seconds she stood perfectly still, her hands on his chest, eyes closed. She felt his breath on her mouth. She curled her toes on the slippery tub and relished the pitter-patter of her heart. The anticipation, wanting him, it was one of the best things about their attraction.

Finally, his lips brushed hers in a quick graze, a quick peck, but he came back setting his mouth against hers.

She fisted his shirt, pulling him closer and deepening the kiss. He wanted to think this was fake? That the passion they'd shared wasn't real? She'd show him how hot they could burn.

Madison wrapped her arm around his neck and lifted up on tiptoe, trying to get closer. Her foot slipped across the bottom of the wet tub and she hit the edge with her knees. She cried out as pain shot up and down her legs. Aiden's grip around her waist was the only thing keeping her upright.

"Shit." She hissed. Her already abused knees ached. Bruises on top of bruises. Lovely.

"You okay?"

She sat on the edge of the tub and rubbed the angry red mark. So much for passion.

"Yeah."

"This tub is trying to kill you."

Aiden bent and scooped her up in his arms in one easy move. Madison gasped, but held still. He walked sideways through the door with her and took her to the bed. He knelt next to her and ran his hands over the marks. The skin seemed to have split a little, but she wasn't bleeding and she'd suffered far worse injuries simply walking around the boat.

"I'm fine," she said. He made her extend one leg, then the other.

"Will you be quiet and let me make sure?"

She clamped her lips together. He cupped the back of her knee, letting the joint bend. It didn't hurt or twinge, but his touch was pleasant. Warm. He slid his palms down her calves and she stopped breathing.

By all rights, she could still be angry with him. But what was the point? He'd admitted he was wrong, and guys did stupid things when their feelings started up.

Their time together was short. She didn't want to waste it being upset, when they could spend time in much more pleasurable ways.

"Do you think I'm going to live?" she asked.

Aiden rested his hands on her knees, his gaze traveling up her body until their eyes locked. The way he stared at her, it made heat crawl up her neck and cheeks.

"I'd say you'll pull through."

The muscles in her thighs turned to rubber and her knees parted.

Aiden reached around behind him and pulled his gun out from under his shirt. He set it on the nightstand with a heavy *thunk*, never once looking away from her. The weapon scared her, but then again so did he. He couldn't change who or what she was, but that same person made her feel safe. He turned her on. Made her want things.

Oh what the hell?

Madison took his face in her hands. He tipped his chin up, lips parted. She swooped down and kissed him. She shoved her fingers through his short hair and pulled him closer. Aiden leaned in, parting her knees until he knelt between her legs, arms around her waist. Their tongues tangled. She couldn't get close enough to him. Desperation blossomed inside of her, she wanted him. Needed him with a fire she'd never before felt.

Aiden's hand slid up her stomach and between her breasts, forcing the ends of the towel apart. She lifted her head, staring down at his hand splayed across her stomach, the towel on the bed, leaving her naked. For a moment, neither moved. He stared at her, she stared at his hand.

Her nipples tightened, due to either the cool air or her heightened state of arousal, it didn't matter. He leaned in closer and blew a hot breath across her left breast.

"I didn't really get to play with these last night." Aiden cupped her breast and kissed the outer curve, over the top and along the inner swell.

Madison let her head drop back, focusing on the feel of his mouth, his heated skin. He splayed one hand against her back and the other plumped her breast from the bottom. She planted her hands on the mattress to keep herself upright. Warmth pooled low in her stomach and her pussy clenched. He licked her nipple, once, twice, then wrapped his lips around the hardened bud and sucked.

She gasped as sensation shot through her body.

He switched breasts, rubbing the flat of his tongue against her sensitized skin while his fingers plucked the abandoned nipple, rolling it between his fingers.

"Oh. Oh!"

Her arms buckled and she sank down to her elbows. He kissed her stomach and she quivered, almost afraid to breathe.

Aiden lifted his head, staring up her body. She felt the graze of his hand on her inner thigh a second before his fingers slid through her folds. He rumbled something in his throat and thrust a finger into her. She gasped and curled her leg around him while he slid in and out of her.

"Fuck, you're wet."

Words were beyond Madison. She groaned something that might have been interpreted as "Yes."

He kissed her hip and she stopped breathing. She didn't know if she could handle another sensual assault like last night. He pulled his finger from her and straightened.

"If you want to tell me no, this would—"

"No clothes." She sat up and grabbed his shirt. Was the man crazy?

He lifted his arms. She swept his shirt off. She flattened her hands against his chest. He had a crest of some sort tattooed over his left pec, and script that ran across his right side. There were more markings though. In the light, she could see little scars dotting his skin, a few ragged marks. He lived a dangerous life, and he wore the marks on his skin. Would what he did for her leave another? She hoped not.

Aiden planted his hands on either side of her hips and kissed her hard enough to steal her breath.

He stood and toed off his boots, hands working his pants button and zipper open.

They were going to have sex. Again.

The thought—the reality—excited her.

"Don't move," Aiden said.

She froze in the act of scooting farther onto the bed.

"I want you right there. Like that. Spread your legs a little."

Her heart pounded. No man had ever wanted to see all of her. They'd always been more interested in getting to the grand finale. Except Aiden seemed determined to strip her bare, expose every last bit of her and take pleasure in it. Of course he gave better than he got, which only pushed her off-kilter. He was so different, which made her want to obey him, despite the natural urge to cover herself.

She let her legs relax and fall open. The cool air touched the apex of her thighs and she shivered while his gaze ate her up.

He tossed his wallet on the bed and shoved his jeans off.

There was so much of him she hadn't been able to see last night.

Aiden closed the distance between them and leaned down until their faces almost touched. He glanced at his wallet and flipped it open.

"I really hope you're in the habit of restocking condoms."

"Not usually, but I made sure today. Just in case."

"I must be a lucky girl."

"You will be."

She chuckled.

He plucked a condom from the wallet and held it out to her.

"Put it on me."

Madison snatched the packet from his hand and tossed her hair over her shoulder. She might not be so good at accepting attention lavished on her, but giving? That was something she enjoyed.

She kissed his cheek, trailing her fingers along his jaw. "Stand up straight, and I will."

Aiden made that low, growling sound deep in his throat. He stared at her like he wanted to eat her whole. He straightened, his erect cock bobbing toward her.

The attraction still sizzled between them, but it was different tonight. Last night had felt daring. Tonight, they were toeing the knife edge of intensity, and yet, there was humor.

Madison tore the wrapper open; her hands steady for once that night. She wrapped a hand around his cock and pumped the velvety smooth flesh.

"Madison." He said her name as a warning.

"What?"

"I am not in the mood for teasing."

"You're no fun."

She rolled the condom on, glancing up at his stony face.

The moment the latex covered his cock, he pushed her onto her back and kissed her. She wrapped an arm around his neck and slid the other between them. He dug a hand into her hair and wrapped the wet locks around his fingers. He turned her face away from him and kissed down the length of her neck. She grasped his cock and for a moment, he stilled. Even through the thin barrier, his heat nearly seared her.

Aiden nuzzled the ticklish spot just below her ear.

"Put me in you," he said.

Alternating waves of warmth and chill swept her body.

"You're awfully bossy." She meant to sound confident and assured, but instead, her voice was breathy, telegraphing just how much she wanted this. Him.

"I can tell you how to do it, if you'd like."

"I'm pretty sure I know how that goes."

He relaxed his hold on her hair. She turned her face toward him and guided his cock to her entrance. The moment his head touched her folds, they both sucked in a breath, and her insides quivered. He flexed his hips, pressing into her. She relaxed her hold, sliding her fingers along his length. He penetrated her deeper.

Her breathing hitched as he withdrew and thrust in earnest, sinking deep. She cupped his balls and he paused while she sucked at the spot on his neck where it joined his shoulder. She slid her fingers along the seam between his testicles and squeezed her internal muscles around him.

Aiden grabbed her arm, hauling it up to his chest. He turned his face, sealing his mouth over hers. He withdrew and thrust hard enough little sparks of color burst behind her eyelids. She wrapped her arms around his chest, sliding her hands down his back until she could grasp his ass.

He stroked in and out of her while he thrust his tongue into her mouth, invading her body. She arched her back, letting the short, coarse hair on his chest rub against her nipples. His hands held her head, while he supported himself on his forearms. She wrapped a leg around his hip and planted a foot on the bed, trying to move in tandem with him.

They breathed in time, bodies joined. She urged him deeper with each thrust, as if she could merge their spirits.

Aiden pulled her ass slightly off the bed, changing the angle. She gasped, tilting her head back. He continued to piston in and out of her, each thrust rubbing her clit. The gentle build-up became an incredible rush. She dug her fingers into his flexing muscles and held on.

"That's it," he chanted, punctuating each with a kiss to her neck, cheek, anywhere he could reach.

She heard herself moan, but she was powerless, not that she wanted to be in control of this ride. Aiden was the driver.

"A-Aiden!" His name turned into a squeal. Her internal muscles clamped down on him and her orgasm burst forth, washing over her.

He continued to move, fucking her through the turbulent emotions, drawing out her pleasure until she sobbed his name. She lay on the bed, her limbs heavy, body spent, Aiden above and inside of her. She didn't even have the energy to open her eyes and look at him, but she felt his gaze on her. Gently, he kissed her cheek and murmured something she couldn't make out.

She wanted to tell him to hold still, let her savor this moment, but he withdrew, easing her legs to the floor.

He went a step further, scooping her up and laying her more comfortably on the bed. For such a man's man, he was surprisingly gentle. He smoothed her hair off her face and tossed a blanket over her.

Madison could love a man like him. Or just him. It was easy, really. She just opened herself up, and fell.

Chapter Eighteen

Aiden tossed the condom into the trash with more force than was necessary. She was everything he couldn't have, and it ticked him off. He glanced toward the door, but didn't hear Madison stirring from bed. He wanted to return to her, wrap her hair around his fist, and pound into her until he came—but he couldn't. He'd watched her come, and it had broken something in him. He wanted to watch her do that—saying his name—again and again. It was the kind of permanence he didn't have any business wanting.

He stepped into the glass-walled shower and turned the spray on hot. His erection mocked him. By the time he finished, he hoped Madison would be deep asleep. After today, she had every right to pass out, except she hadn't had a chance to eat. He'd let his desire take over, instead of ensuring she got proper food and rest. Selfish, but he wouldn't change anything. And therein lay the problem.

The hot water pelted his back. He leaned his forearm against the glass and rested his head against it.

The team always came first. Before his wants, needs, or family, the team was most important of all. He'd thought he could control his attraction to Madison, keep it separate, but the truth was that he wanted her for himself. He'd given up so much, accepting the estranged arrangement with his family for their protection, pushing people away until he was a well-honed machine, ready to perform. It wasn't healthy. Couldn't last. But then, he'd always told himself there was an end date. When Evers was locked up in jail, he could make amends.

He knew how a relationship in his current state would go. Things would be fine, they would be careful, then someday, Evers would catch on to them. They all knew it was a day coming up fast, and when it did, anyone close to their team would be a target. People like Madison and his grandmother. He didn't want to bury Madison like he had his sister.

Aiden opened his eyes and glared at his persistent dick. Hard as ever. Because what he wanted was so close, and he couldn't have it.

If they didn't close this thing with Evers soon, Aiden was going to lose it. The chance at a normal life, the family he'd always thought he'd have someday. He was sick of the operations, of living like he was in a war zone and letting the FBI yank him around. He was a seasoned enough soldier and operative to know that if he didn't take something for himself, if he didn't carve out a bit of normalcy, he'd end up like Julian.

"Aiden?"

Through the fog on the glass, he could see the shapely figure on the other side.

"I thought you were asleep," he said.

"No." She padded across the floor.

"You should get some rest."

Don't come any closer. I can't be responsible.

The door opened, letting in a blast of cool air. Madison stepped in, still naked, her hair loose. He stood stock-still. She reached for him, placing her hand against his cheek and gently kissing his mouth. As much as he knew he should push her away, create some distance, he couldn't.

"Why didn't you come back to bed?" she asked.

"You need to get some sleep." It was the only refrain he could think of as a plausible reason. He wasn't about to tell her the truth.

"We weren't finished." She glanced down at his erection.

"Don't worry about that." It wouldn't be the first time he'd jacked off in a shower.

"Hm." She wrapped her hand around his cock and he gritted his teeth. She pumped him.

"Madison."

"You don't get to tell me what to do all the time, only when I let you."

"But you follow orders so well."

She laughed, and God he wanted to—record that sound, bottle up her essence—something to keep it with him always. He reached out and traced a heart tattooed on the side of her ribs.

"Hurt like a bitch, didn't it?" he asked.

"Pretty sure I cried."

"I regretted that placement within five seconds."

"What does it say?" She glanced at his side.

"It's Greek."

"Well it doesn't look like English."

"Is that what you came in here to do? Ask me about my tattoo?"

She stared at him a second, then slowly blinked. "No, I came in here to give you a blow job. Hands against the wall, big boy."

It was his turn to stare at her. That . . . was not what

he expected her to say, but then again, he should be used to that by now. Madison was never what he anticipated.

She sank to her knees, hands on his thighs. He stared at her, unable to think or process the moment beyond *Holy fuck.* She ran her nails up and down his inner thighs, peering up at him.

"And just in case you have some stupid idea that the only reason I'd give you head is to get something, think again."

"I didn't—"

"Oh shut up and enjoy it." She grinned and wrapped her hand around his cock.

Whatever hardness he'd lost in the moments between being inside of her until now redoubled. His vision blurred. Her hand slid along his length, her fingers finding every sensitive place along the head of his dick.

He swayed on his feet. Had a woman ever made him weak at the knees like this? Probably not. He leaned back against the cold wall and stared down at her.

Madison had one hand around the base of his erection, the other splayed against his thigh, just over an eight-inch scar. Her expression was one of intent. A woman on a mission. He held his breath. She rose up on her knees and bent her head.

The first lick of her tongue along the underside of his cock drove all rational thought from his mind. She pumped his length while treating the crown like her personal lollipop, swirling her tongue over his head.

He made a guttural noise in the back of his throat. Her mouth closed over him and she sucked lightly. The hand on his thigh rose to his balls, rolling them in her palm. The water pelting them had nothing on the heat of her mouth. She bobbed her head slowly, working more of him into her mouth. He rested his hand on the top of her head. Her mouth and hand worked in tandem, stroking all of him.

Let her go at her own pace. Don't take control.

She peered up at him as she slid his cock into her mouth, all the way until he hit the back of her throat. He sucked in a deep breath when she shifted. It felt so good, so hot and fuck—he was going to come way too soon.

Madison worked him in and out, rubbing her tongue along the underside of his cock and sucking. Her mouth was heaven. Way too good for him.

He dug his hand into her wet hair and thrust lightly. She hummed once more, holding still in his grip. He guided her by her hair, working in and out of her mouth, trying to be gentle. She placed her hands on the backs of his legs and scored his skin with her nails. He thrust, rougher than he intended. She dug her fingers in, treating him just as rough as he had her.

Aiden wrapped her hair around both hands and held her while he thrust into her mouth. She sucked and rubbed her tongue over him, driving his control out of the window. He fucked her mouth, trying to gentle his hold, to be careful, but all he wanted was her, to brand himself on her, never to be forgotten.

He pulled out of her mouth once he felt a prickling sensation at the base of his spine. He rocked up on his toes and cum spurted out of his cock. Her hand wrapped around him, pumping him while the orgasm rolled up from his toes, pleasure cascading through his body while she drew the last drops from him.

Aiden released his hold on her hair and slumped against the wall. She rocked back onto her heels, looking up at him. The shower was already washing the evidence of his orgasm away.

He held out his hand and pulled her to her feet, tugging her against him. She smiled, and it was as if the rest of the world ceased to register. So long as Madison had reason to look at him like that, nothing else mattered. He bent his head and kissed her, wanting to drink her in, soak up all that she was.

There was no knowing what would happen, if he could figure out a way to make them work, or if she'd even be interested. For now, he had this moment. Tonight. And he'd sure as hell enjoy them.

He took the soap and washed her once more before completing his shower. Even his stomach was starting to growl, and he'd done nothing but sit on his ass and have a couple of beers tonight. He guided Madison out of the shower, mindful of the slick floor, and bundled her into another of the fluffy towels. Her sleepy smile made his heart do a little summersault. He couldn't remember the last time someone had looked at him with that much trust in their eyes. It made his responsibility to her that much heavier. He settled her on the sofa while he reheated dinner.

"I didn't know what to get you, so I ordered it all and had it put on the side," he said. The microwave dinged.

"I'm easy to please." Her tone was drowsy, and no surprise. Between the stress, her bout, and now another round of lovemaking, it was amazing she hadn't passed out already.

"I'll keep that in mind." He set the Styrofoam container in her lap before situating himself.

For a few moments, they ate in silence. Madison polished off half her burger, showing just how ravished she'd been. He liked this, just being with her. She didn't push him, didn't expect him to be or do anything. Too many people wanted him to fit their ideas of a shop owner, or a driver, or an operative, or a soldier. He was exhausted by the burden of it all. Couldn't he just be?

"So, the tattoo, what does it say?" she asked between bites.

He picked through the fries before selecting the perfect one to dunk in ketchup. His right side prickled in remembered pain.

"One of the officers on my first deployment was a real brainy kind of guy. Big history buff, always telling us about how history repeats itself. I resented him at the time. I mean, it was post-9/11, we were in the thick of a big push, and he goes off about philosophers and the Crusades. He died during that deployment. Our next CO was a prick, and it taught me how good we'd had it. I never appreciated Benny until then."

For a moment, he chewed his food, rolling the bits of memory around in his head. Most of his unit had died without Benny there. Aiden could name the survivors on one hand. The man had known his shit.

Aiden cleared his throat, Benny's voice echoing in his mind, and he recited the tattooed quote. "*First, have a definite, clear practical ideal; a goal, an objective. Second, have the necessary means to achieve your ends; wisdom, money, materials, and methods. Third, adjust all your means to that end.*"

"Did Benny say that?" Madison asked.

"No, Aristotle. Like I said, Benny was a history and philosophy buff." It was probably because of Benny's leadership that both Julian and Aiden survived the hell of their next deployment. After that, everything changed. They were selected for special operations and the courses of their lives were forever altered.

"He sounds like an amazing person."

"Yeah, he was kind of an ass, but he kept everyone breathing."

"What about the bumper on the Chevelle? Think you'll be able to find a replacement?"

"Yeah, it's just going to take a hell of a long time."

"You can't just order one?"

"I could, but it wouldn't be the real deal. See, a lot of people take these cars and refurbish them, make them plush, update the console a bit." He shook his head. "Not the Chevelle. It's a restoration."

"Meaning?"

"Meaning it's the way it would be if it rolled off the assembly line. It's in perfect condition. Or it was."

"How'd you get into doing old cars?"

"My grandpa. He died a long time ago, but he taught me all about cars and because of him, I grew to appreciate the classics. They don't make cars the way they used to. Those cars? They were made to last. It's why you'll see a car from the fifties still cruising down Ninety-Five. The things they're rolling off the lines now?" He shook his head. "They have a shelf life and they do that intentionally. Keep people always getting a new car."

Aiden glanced at Madison, eating her fries and watching him.

"You don't care about cars. Why am I telling you this?" Truth was he could go on for hours.

"It's interesting, but yeah, I don't really appreciate cars the way you do."

"Then why ask me?"

"Because it's not like I can ask where you grew up or what your family is like or why you have a scar on your leg. You can't risk telling me the normal, personal things, but cars—they're like an extension of you." She shrugged and glanced down at the last bits of her dinner. "I just want to know more about you, and it's the only safe thing I can think about."

The sad reality of it hit him full in the chest. He knew almost her entire life story, inside and out, and she could probably list just a few things about him. He wanted to tell her, to share his life with her, but she was right. It was safer for her if she didn't know. And yet, he couldn't stop himself. What was one little story?

"We were in Sangin, this awful town in southern Afghanistan, on a mission. They grow a lot of opium there. Things weren't going well. We were taking fire and trying to get to our extraction point. Julian and I were pinned down in this alley, so he breaks into this shop and we go out the other side. This woman—she had to be high as fuck—comes out of a back room. I freeze. She stabbed me here." He lifted the towel and pointed at the thicker part of the scar, right up near his groin. "And she yanks it, down. I start bleeding everywhere and Julian knocks her out. I was bleeding badly. She cut my femoral artery and I would have probably lost it right there if it weren't for Julian. He got a tourniquet around my leg, carried me out of there, took a bullet doing it, but we survived."

"Oh my God, that's—that's horrible."

"Yeah. Sometimes I think I should have just curled up and died, because Julian will never let me forget that day." He rolled his eyes, but deep down, he was grateful. Despite all the fucked up shit they went through after that, and even now, at least he had a life worth living.

"That's not funny," Madison said.

"I'm joking. Come here." He put their empty trays on the floor and pulled her into his arms. She settled against his chest, sighing.

"I don't want to joke about you dying."

"Morbid sense of humor. Comes with the job." He stroked her hair, content to just hold her.

The loft was quiet, peaceful. He couldn't have asked for a better place to lie low for the night. He'd need for someone to swing by his place and her boat to ensure the Eleventh hadn't decided to target their property beyond Madison's bike. Speaking of her bike, Julian had sent him a couple listings for decent motorcycles that might suit her needs. Granted, he'd like to see her in an armored transport, but there were some battles he knew he'd lose.

A soft snore interrupted his mental listing of the pros and cons of specific makes of bikes. He peered down at her, amused to find that she'd drifted off.

What was he going to do with her?

Madison deserved better than him. There was no doubt in his mind about that. But he wanted her. Could he figure out how to make it work? Was there a way to keep her safe until they wrapped up this thing with Evers and Dustin?

He didn't know. And there was no one he could talk to.

Julian and Gabriel were jaded. The twins lived for the job. John would tell him no before he finished his question. Emery was the last person he'd go to for romantic advice, considering he was harboring a crush he thought Aiden hadn't noticed. And CJ and Kathy, well, it was in their best interests to keep him focused on the job. Madison was a distraction. Except, he needed her. He needed this sense of normalcy, a reason to keep going that lived and breathed.

What he needed to do was talk to Grandma. He didn't usually call her, but maybe this time he'd make an exception to the rule.

Aiden hooked his arm under her legs and stood,

hoisting Madison up into his arms. She groaned and turned her face to his chest. He held his breath until she sighed and seemed to settle.

He carried her once more to the bed and laid her down, pulling the comforter up under her chin. Tonight he needed space, to think. Could he really be falling for her?

Madison shifted and stretched in her sleep. She moaned and her eyes fluttered open.

"Mm, hey," she mumbled.

"Sorry, didn't mean to wake you."

She glanced around, brows drawn down, no doubt wondering how she came to be in bed. Her gaze returned to him and a slow smile spread across her face.

"I'm cold. Keep me warm?" She scooted over and out came the towel, meaning under the sheets, she was naked. It was not a thought he needed to dwell on.

He should say no, put some distance between them, except he dropped his towel and climbed in next to her. Madison fit so well in his arms, her curves nestled against him and a sense of home wrapped the moment up in such a sense of rightness, he couldn't extract himself if he tried. This was exactly where he wanted to be.

Chapter Nineteen

Madison bobbed her knee while they drove through an older residential neighborhood. The houses were all spaced farther apart, trees lined the properties, creating a little bit of privacy. It was nice. She'd expected Aiden to live somewhere flashy, maybe in a loft like where they'd stayed last night. Instead, it was a bit more rural, with elbow room and trees between the houses, each with a bit of land, maybe an acre or two. Hell, she was pretty sure she'd seen goats down the street. He turned into the gravel drive of a large, white ranch-style house with blue shutters. The hedges needed trimming and it didn't appear as though anyone minded the grass, but other than that it was in good condition.

She'd woken up pleasantly enough, but at some point before they'd left the loft, the weight of her omission settled on her shoulders. In the beginning, she hadn't mentioned that Michael Evers flew in and out of her airport because she hadn't known if she could trust Aiden or not. She'd allowed herself to forget that detail because it was easier that way. Except Evers was flying something into the airport tonight that he didn't want documented by customs.

Aiden pulled the car around behind the house. He clicked a fob on his keys and the doors of a large, wooden barn slowly rolled open. He drove into what had once been a horse barn and parked the Chevelle in the back. The stalls had been opened up for three other cars. The Challenger she'd ridden in, and two other cars she couldn't name.

"Damn, it's getting late," Aiden muttered.

Late was almost eight in the morning. They needed to find the drive. She needed to get to work. Somehow they needed to evade the Eleventh—or something. And hopefully Dustin would continue to stay out of her life. Amidst all of that, she had to figure out how to tell Aiden about Evers.

"Let's dig around for the drive really quick. I'd like to get that to my guy for analysis before I meet with Dustin."

"You're meeting with him today?" Madison scrambled to get out of the car and circled around back to the trunk.

Aiden already had it open and was sifting through the contents that had spilled out of the boxes when his phone rang.

"Yeah, something's up with him. I just don't know what." Aiden glanced at his phone. "Give me a second."

Madison stared at him. What was the chance that the thing Evers was flying in had to do with the drive? It was unlikely, but—what if? Did she keep it to herself?

Aiden stepped away, pressing his phone to his face. "Yeah? . . . Good first . . . Well that's what you expected, now what's the bad?"

Her stomach churned. She was keeping things from Aiden and he'd proven time and time again he was just helping her. She had to tell him.

"What? Are you serious? Why? Any reason at all?" Aiden paced the width of the barn, his frown deepening.

She probably should have told him earlier. . . .

"Damn it. That doesn't make any sense. Fine. We'll figure something out." He listened to whatever the person on the other end of the line was saying for a few more moments before hanging up.

"Something wrong?" she asked.

"Nothing you need to worry about," he said.

Madison bit her lip. She didn't want to rock the boat, but damn it, she had to tell him.

"Aiden?"

"Yeah."

"I . . . uh, need to tell you something."

"What is it?" Aiden glanced up from the trunk, his brows drawn down.

"I've been trying to figure out how to tell you this since yesterday. I just—don't be upset, please?"

He straightened, his face going completely blank. That couldn't be good. She opened and closed her mouth, wishing she could go back in time and just tell him. But she hadn't known him then like she knew him now.

"Michael Evers and another guy arranged for a shipment to come into our airport."

"You just found out?" No emotion. Deadpan. So not like the man she'd come to know who laughed and felt so deeply.

"No."

"And you just remembered that he uses Everglades Air?" The uptick in tone made her cringe. Anger. Well, she'd expected that to some degree.

"Aiden, please." She took a step toward him, and he backed up. She stopped, letting her hands drop to her sides. "When you came to me, I didn't know who you were. I didn't know that I could trust you. Talking about my life was one thing. My boss's clients were a whole other thing. I mean, Lily's parents gave me a chance when no one else would. How could I just tell you stuff about their business like that?"

"Why didn't you tell me yesterday?"

She opened and closed her mouth. In the moment, when she'd come face-to-face with Michael Evers, she'd thought about it, but then she'd been afraid. Afraid of Evers. Afraid of losing Aiden. Fear was one thing she was sick of.

"I didn't tell you because I knew you'd instantly suspect me again." Like he was now. It was written all over him from the narrowing of his gaze to the tick at his jaw. "Aiden, please."

She took a step toward him and he retreated one.

That was how it was going to be?

"I trusted you." His voice was a growl, deep in his chest that made her want to cower. "And this whole time you've been lying to me?"

"I didn't lie. I didn't know how to tell you."

"I'm not going to say anything else. I'm too pissed off." His voice was cold, hard, and unlike anything she'd heard from him. "Stay here. The walls are reinforced and there are cameras on the property. Anyone shows up, call me. Find the drive. I'll be back in a minute."

Aiden turned and walked away from her. No arguments, no accusations, just silence.

"Aiden?"

He clicked his key fob at the Challenger and the car beeped. She watched him climb in the white car, rev the engine, and roll out. The heavy door slid shut after him, the locks engaging. She shivered and glanced around the barn-turned-garage. There was another side entrance, but other than that the place appeared secure. So was she a prisoner? Or locked up for her own safety?

Was this how it would end? She knew this fragile relationship wouldn't last, but was this it?

She sat down on the bent bumper and pulled her phone from her pocket. He could walk away from her, but he couldn't completely ignore her. Could he?

> Please believe me. I didn't want to keep that from you. Evers has a plane coming in this evening. It's going to sit overnight for customs to come in the morning. According to the flight manifest, he's flying in six cars.

She hit send on the messages and hoped he believed her. Could the trust they'd built up be eroded so quickly?

Madison stared at her phone for a minute, and then another one. No reply. No call. He really wasn't going to talk to her about it. She sucked in a deep breath as an invisible pain stabbed her in the chest. Stupidly, she'd given him a piece of her heart, knowing full well he'd carve it out of her flesh when things ended. Was this it?

She pressed a hand between her breasts.

There were a hundred scenarios and what-ifs circling her mind. He could preach trust all he wanted, but Aiden had never given her much to go on. If he wanted to be upset with her, so be it. Their deal was about the drive and Dustin. That was it.

She went back to the Chevelle and began upending the boxes in the trunk. They were mostly Dustin's belongings, not hers.

One box held a couple stacks of discs and CDs, another random bits of paper and a marble pen holder. Odds and ends that weren't worth much. She reached back into the trunk and hauled the last couple of boxes toward her. She tossed the top off one and stilled, looking down at a gray external hard drive nestled in a bunch of cords and charging stations. Dustin had always lost his chargers. It would make sense that an important box to him would contain those, and the drive.

She picked the drive up and turned it over in her hands. She'd never seen it before. But, then again, she hadn't cared so much what she took as long as she stole from Dustin like he stole from her. It was petty and stupid. She'd regretted it at the moment she'd done it, but he'd taken so much from her.

Time was getting away from her. There was no way to make it to work on time, but she'd already preemptively texted her boss after her bike turned up in pieces. If Aiden thought she was going to stay put while he was pissed at her, well, he was wrong.

Lily was going to hate her.

Madison dialed Lily's house phone, which she couldn't put on mute, and held her breath. It rang and rang, easily a dozen times. Was Lily angry with her too? They hadn't exactly had a lot to say to each other last night.

"What?" Lily groaned through the phone.

"Morning, sunshine." Madison's throat constricted and she smiled at nothing. Lily had forgiven her. If she hadn't, she would have simply picked up the phone and waited for Madison to apologize.

"Fuck you."

"Fuck you, too. How was last night?"

"Not as much fun without you, but you aren't calling about that. Need a ride?"

"Yeah, I'm sorry. I promise I'll figure something out."

"I have no doubt about that. Where are you?"

"Uh, give me a second. I'm not sure." Madison put the

call on speaker. There were no message icons waiting for her. She activated the GPS on her phone and pulled up her map app.

"What did you do last night?"

"Showered, ate, slept." *Fucked like bunnies.*

"You're lying. You got some." Lily's voice was smug. The sounds of a coffee machine started up in the background.

"You don't like him, remember?"

"I don't know him." She sighed.

One thing about Lily, she was pretty awesome about admitting when she was wrong. That, and she always looked out for Madison.

"Do you feel better?" Lily asked.

"I don't know." Madison's throat constricted once more and it was hard to breathe. Her eyes instantly filled with tears and the ache in her chest was back again.

"What did he do? I will kill him. I don't care how much of a badass he is, he's dead."

"No, no, we just—had a thing and I screwed up. It was really me, but he's being an ass and not giving me a chance to explain. I just want to throat-punch him."

"Oh, it must be bad if you're going for the throat, but at least you aren't wanting to knee him in the balls. If it was that level, I might not let you talk me down from kicking his ass."

Madison laughed despite the pain.

"Where are you?"

Madison rattled off the address from her phone's GPS. Thank goodness for modern technology.

"Dang, okay, that's going to take me at least twenty to get there. At least. Think you can hold on that long?"

"I can."

"Okay, I'm going to be a few more minutes—oh dang. The cable guy is here. I friggen call him and call him and now he shows up? Let me tell him to come back and I'll head over. I don't have time for his lazy ass right now. Good?"

"Thanks, Lily. You're the best."

"Only for you. *Muwah.*"

Madison hung up and blew out a breath. She couldn't ask for a better friend. Whatever she'd done to get Lily, it was luck.

She closed the trunk and rested the drive on top of it for a quick picture. Even if Aiden wasn't replying to her—probably because he was driving, if she were being honest—she could at least let him know she'd found it. This was the bone of their bargain, after all. She took the picture and sent it to Aiden before deleting it off her phone. The last thing she wanted was to be caught with anything resembling evidence of it on her.

"What to do with you now?" She glanced around the garage.

Madison carried the drive over to the stall reserved for the Challenger. There was a small workstation built into the side and a red rolling set of drawers. She opened one at random and set the drive inside. Anyone who didn't know where to look for it would be stuck performing a very long search.

Did she tell Aiden where it was?

Nah, he'd have to call her if he wanted the location.

Madison tried the side door. It opened easily, but judging from the weird locks, she was betting it was a one-way trip, unless she had the key. She hauled her derby gear and overnight bag with her out of the garage and closed the door behind her. The locking mechanism clicked. She grasped the handle and shook it to be sure, but it was secure.

Whatever Aiden was mixed up in, it was serious and she wished him well.

She sucked down a deep breath and tipped her chin up. Someday, when she got her life together, she'd find someone who would love her—and chances were, he'd be cut from the same cloth as Aiden. She had a type she couldn't shake, so why fight it? Good guys didn't come in one shape. He'd proved that. She'd just have to kiss a few more frogs—but she had a few things to do first. Finish her degree. Get a real place—maybe a small condo. She was going to make something of herself.

The gravel crunched underfoot. She walked out to the roadside to wait. Every couple of minutes she glanced at her phone, but there was still no reply.

Oh well, she didn't have time to cry or pine over him. There were bigger problems to solve. Summer semester was starting soon, and she needed some wheels. But it would be a while before she recovered financially. It was just the facts.

Lily's hatchback zipped around a tight turn a couple houses down. Madison shouldered her back and held out her thumb. The car came to an abrupt stop, kicking up gravel and dust.

"Sheesh, how much coffee did you drink this morning?" she asked. She opened the front door and tossed her bag in.

The person sitting in the driver's seat was not Lily.

Madison froze, staring down the barrel of a gun, held by her ex-husband.

"Get in," Dustin said.

Could she run fast enough? Was Aiden secretly hiding around the corner? Would Dustin shoot her if she got in? What if she died with Aiden still angry with her?

"I said, get in."

Madison dropped into the seat, staring straight ahead. She didn't even bother with the seat belt.

"What the fuck are you doing way out here?" Dustin

tucked the gun under his left leg before spinning the car around.

"What do you want, Dustin?" Coldness swept her body, making her limbs numb.

"I want my fucking property, dumb bitch. Where is it?"

"I don't know," she said automatically. It was an argument they'd had several times, and each time she had the same reply.

"You're going to remember."

"Or what? Kill me?"

"That's not a bad idea."

Damn it all to hell. Why did she have to open her mouth?

She glanced around, no idea where they were. The streets and businesses were unfamiliar. Where was Lily? Did he have her? Why hadn't she told Aiden where the drive was? If he had it, could he trade it for her? Would he?

Madison needed to get away. No one knew she was in trouble except Lily, and she might be worse off than Madison.

She placed her hand over her keys clipped to her hip. The pepper spray.

Dustin eased to a stop at a red light.

The gun was under his left leg. If she sprayed him first, could she get away before he drew it?

She slipped the plastic head of the pepper spray around, holding her breath. She tried to mute the *click* of it settling into place.

"What the fuck are you doing?" Dustin grabbed her hand, pulling it up.

Madison held on to the spray. Her worn belt loop snapped. She pressed the button on the bottle and the *hiss* of aerosol spray filled the car.

"What the—ow, fuck! You bitch!"

She held her breath, squeezed her eyes shut and yanked her arm out of his hold while clawing at the lock. The passenger-side door opened and she tumbled out onto the pavement. Madison rolled, got to her feet and ran, blinking bleary eyes. Her face stung from the spray, and it hadn't even been aimed at her.

Madison dodged into a parking lot and ran between the cars. She glanced back, but Lily's hatchback was gone. Had Dustin left her? Or was he still around? What a time to not have a police shadow!

Her heart hammered against her ribs and fear pumped in her veins.

She crouched between two cars, with a light pole at her back, and squinted at her phone. She wanted to call Lily, but she needed help bigger and badder than she was.

Since she couldn't be certain Aiden would answer her distress call, she clicked on the other number he'd given her. The in-case-of-emergency number.

The line only rang once.

"Hello?" a woman said.

"Hi, this is Madison, Aiden said to call if something was wrong and shit is fucked up." She hated how scared and frantic she sounded, but damn it, what about Lily?

"Madison, it's Roni. Take a deep breath. Where are you? What happened?"

Aiden's backup was . . . his mechanics?

"Lily was going to drive me to work, but my ex-husband had her car. I just sprayed him with pepper spray and jumped out. I'm—I don't know where I'm at. I can't see a fucking thing. I was at Aiden's house, but he left and he's pissed at me." Her eyes were watering now, fat tears rolling down her cheeks uncontrollably.

"You're on your cell phone? Tori, come on. Gabriel, listen for your phone, find out where the fuck Aiden is."

"Yeah." The twin sounded awfully competent for just a mechanic.

"Tori, get Emery to track her." A car's engine revved. "Madison? I'm going to be there in a minute. What's around you?"

Emery? But, Emery was Aiden's tech guy or something. Were these people all connected? What exactly was going on?

"I'm in a parking lot, one of those pay-to-park things." She hissed as her skin started to burn.

"Okay, keep moving. You're out in the open, Dustin might still be around and we don't want him to find you."

"Hurry, please, I don't know what happened to Lily."

"Shit. Tori, find Lily's address and get Julian over there."

Madison peered up over the hood of the car to her right. There was a building, but she couldn't make out what it said.

"I can't see."

"You said you pepper-sprayed him? Dang. In a car the spray probably got you, too. The blurry vision will wear off in a minute or two. Unfortunately you're going to burn anywhere you got the stuff on you, but it's probably a lot worse for Dustin," Roni said. "I'm getting closer, and Emery's given me an approximate location."

"I hope that fucker crashes and dies." Wait . . . Madison hadn't mentioned Dustin's name, had she? How did Roni know it?

"From the sound of it, I do too," Roni replied. There was a deadly edge to her voice.

"I can see better now." Madison straightened, looking around her. "I don't see Dustin."

"Okay, I'm half a mile away. Look for a sky-blue car."

Madison straightened and turned in place, her heart hammering in her throat. Her phone beeped, but she didn't have time to look at it. Instead, she jogged toward the street and started walking north on the sidewalk.

"I see you," Roni said.

"I don't . . ." A blue two-door car zipped down the street. "I see you." Madison dashed across the two lanes as the car pulled up.

Tori popped out and flipped the seat forward. She folded herself into the back faster than it took for Madison to find her balance.

"Get in," Roni said.

Madison collapsed into the seat and Roni accelerated, the passenger door closing from inertia alone.

"We got her, Aiden," Tori said from the backseat.

Madison's heart twisted painfully in her chest. Aiden.

"What about Lily?"

"We don't know anything yet," Tori replied.

"The drive—"

"Here." Tori thrust her phone into Madison's hands.

She stared at the screen for a second before pressing it to her ear.

"The drive is in the garage, over in the red shelves—"

"Are you okay?" Aiden spoke over her, sounding more like a roaring engine than a human.

"I'm fine. I got pepper spray in my eyes and on my arm. It burns like a bitch."

"I'm going to fucking kill him."

Why was it statements of violence warmed her heart? There was clearly something wrong with her. A few too many knocks on the head in practice or something.

"The girls are going to take you to the garage. I'll meet you there. You are not going to work today," Aiden said.

"What about Lily?" They'd talk about him assuming he could order her around later.

"Julian should be getting to her house soon. Let me talk to Tori."

Madison handed the phone back, feeling even more adrift. He couldn't even talk to her? She glanced at her phone. One missed call hovered on the screen with a single name below it.

Aiden.

He had called her back.

Chapter Twenty

Madison scrubbed her hands and arms with soap and water in the garage bathroom, biting her lip to keep the curses inside. Why was it starting to burn worse?

"Shit, shit, shit." She backed away from the sink, holding her hand to her chest.

"What are you doing?" Aiden filled the doorway. She was torn between relief at seeing him and dreading what he might say to her next.

He grabbed her elbow and examined her hand.

"You don't scrub pepper spray off with water. It only activates the oil again. Hold on. Don't do anything."

As quickly as he arrived, Aiden darted out of the door. She heard another door bang against the backdrop of a radio playing the latest hits. Sunshine poured in through the open bay doors. Two men in coveralls were working on a blue convertible, not paying her much mind. She remembered meeting them the night before, but their names escaped her.

Aiden returned in a matter of moments with a towel and a carton of milk.

"Here. Give me your hand. Is this the only place you got it on you?"

"I got some in my eyes, but I think I blinked it out."

"You'll still want to rinse them out." He held her hand over the sink and poured a little of the milk over her skin, frowning so hard she thought it might split his face.

The burning subsided a little. She drew a deep breath and sighed.

"Better?" He ripped the top of the carton open and shoved the end of the towel in what was left of the milk.

"A little."

"Good. This is going to take the burn away." He wrapped the sopping wet towel around her hand and forearm, then doubled it up by using the dry half of the towel around that. He pushed her toward the toilet. "Sit."

She sat on the closed lid, cradling her hand to her chest, and peered up at him. Was he still angry with her? Did he blame her for Dustin's stunt this morning?

"Did he do anything else to you?" Aiden crouched by her side.

"No, just a lot of talk. He had a gun though."

Aiden's brows rose. "And you still pepper-sprayed him?"

"It was under his leg. I figured it might be my only chance to get away."

Aiden closed his eyes and reached for her free hand. "That was my fault. I shouldn't have left."

She let him lace their fingers together. Deep down, she couldn't find it in her to be angry at him still. True, if he hadn't left her, she'd never have called Lily.

"Do we know how Lily is?" she asked.

"Julian has her. Dustin left her tied up at her house. Julian thinks Dustin might have intended to use her as leverage against you if you didn't give him the drive."

"Shit."

"Madison, I'm going to take care of this."

"But—"

"No." He squeezed her hand. "This is going to end. I'm calling Dustin and setting up some time to meet with him. I've got the drive, we'll analyze it and figure out how to use it to make him go away."

It sounded too easy. Was that all there was to it?

"Next time someone has a gun on you, don't get heroic."

Madison stared at him, anger boiling up inside of her. This was her fault? He was the one who'd left her. If it weren't for him, she would never have been in this situation to begin with.

"Heroic? I was scared for my life. You were gone. He could have killed me before you got back."

"I was already on my way back when the twins called me with a bike for you."

She blinked. A bike? For her?

That red-hot anger fizzled out just as fast as it had risen.

"Why would you do that?"

"Because I said I would. When I tell you I'm going to do something, I'll do it. I told you I'd get you a set of wheels. I told you I'd take you to work. Believe me for once."

"But you left."

"Yeah, because I was pissed you didn't trust me enough to tell me about Evers already. I figured I needed to cool the fuck down before I said something stupid."

It all connected back to Michael Evers. Why?

"What did he do that made you hate him so much? I mean, you said he does bad things, but you hate him. Why?"

Aiden stood and turned away from her slightly, staring at the concrete floor. Would he tell her? Or was this another of those things that had to remain a secret?

"He had my sister and her husband killed." Aiden glanced at her. "Her husband was investigating another murder Evers was indirectly responsible for, and got too close or pissed off the wrong person. Whatever the reason, they're dead because of Evers. Someone's protecting him. It's why we can't get anything to stick to him. Problem is, we don't know if it's an outside source pulling strings or not. We should have had him a long time ago but . . ." He shook his head.

He'd told her of his sister's passing, but not the why of it. Aiden's family blamed him for that? Why? How could they?

The idea of carrying around that guilt made her stomach knot up. And he lived with that? Every day? No wonder he hated Evers.

"We know he's responsible because he put out a call for a hit. He wanted people to know it was him. I think that's when the cops realized he wasn't just a South Beach playboy, but now they can't seem to touch him. So yeah, it's personal and obsessive, but it's what I've got to do."

She glanced at the open bathroom door. Tori and the two guys had their heads together, looking under the hood of the convertible.

"What about them? How are they involved?"

"They aren't," he said too fast.

Madison stared at him staring at her. He wanted her to believe that? Or was it another of those things she'd have to accept not knowing the truth?

"Okay, if that's what I'm supposed to believe I'll pretend that's the truth." The twins had treated her rescue like a normal thing. Way too pulled together for people who weren't involved in a vendetta against a bad guy.

She'd believed the easy truth for so long with Dustin, and look where it had gotten her. She was growing to care for Aiden, but she couldn't live that kind of life again. It was a sad realization that left her more than a little numb inside. If he couldn't tell her, she needed to prepare herself to walk away.

"Evers is flying in a big cargo plane tonight. He's got six cars on board. They're landing a little before midnight, and the plane will sit locked up in the main hangar until morning when customs can come check it out. He wanted his people to come unload it, which is unusual for this client."

"Huh." He blinked a few times, brows rising. A lightbulb went on behind his gaze, but he didn't say anything to her. "Let's get you washed up inside."

Aiden guided her into the shop front and to the little kitchenette. He started the tap going before unwrapping her arm.

"You're going to want to soak this a couple times today with regular dish soap and water. Don't scrub it, just soak and rinse. Got it?" He submerged her arm in the sink filled with suds.

"What have you got here?" An older woman with salt-and-pepper shoulder-length hair came out from the back office. She had a pleasant smile, but there was steel in her gaze.

"Oh, nothing, Kathy. Just had a little accident is all," Aiden drawled.

"Julian called, said he's almost here. Wanted to know where you were," Kathy said over her shoulder as she headed back to the office.

"Did he say anything else?" Aiden asked.

"Oh, exterminator came by. No bugs."

Madison stared at Aiden. Julian had Lily, wasn't that what the twins had told her?

"Rinse it and come find me in the garage, okay?"

Aiden ignored her gaze and he pulled the stopper on the sink.

She wanted to shake answers out of him. It was so incredibly frustrating to know just enough for her to glimpse a bigger picture, but still be shut out. He wanted to talk about trust? There were a lot more secrets on his side that weren't being shared. She highly doubted he was doing this on his own. So what did that mean?

Madison washed her arm off and rinsed it a few times. Her skin still felt tight and a little odd, but the burning was gone.

She headed out to the garage, glancing toward the office. Roni and Kathy sat with their heads together, a black tablet between them. They seemed to be deep in conversation about something, and she doubted it was spark plug supplies.

There was something going on at Classic Rides. It wasn't just Aiden doing her a favor or getting even with the man who killed his sister. She couldn't put her finger on it though.

A black car zipped around the parking lot. She'd seen that one at the race night with Aiden. Julian's car? She pushed the door open in time to see the car come to a stop behind the garage. Tori and Aiden were already ahead of her, striding toward the car.

Julian popped out of the driver's side, moving faster than any of them. He opened the passenger-side door and Madison's heart dropped.

"Lily!"

Madison sprinted toward the car, brushing past Aiden and shouldering Julian aside to wrap her best friend in a hug.

"Careful," Julian practically growled at her.

"You're okay," Lily said into her hair, clutching her tight.

"I was worried about you."

"Me?" Lily leaned back, swaying slightly. "What about you?"

Julian stepped behind Lily, clasping her shoulders gently.

"Oh no." Madison glimpsed the goose egg growing on Lily's forehead.

"It's ugly, isn't it? I'm going to have to get bangs to cover this up." Lily pulled her hair to the side, but there was no hiding the bump.

"You're not going to be skating for a couple of days."

"Let's go inside, we've got a lot to figure out." Aiden grabbed her hand and tugged her toward the garage.

Lily followed, sticking close to her side.

"What's going on?" she asked.

"I—don't know." Sure, Madison knew the gist of it, but she wasn't stupid enough to think that was all there was to it. In the beginning she'd seen Aiden as this one-man powerhouse, but now she realized he wasn't alone. For some reason, that made her feel even more alienated.

Aiden leaned against the red service bench in the empty bay. He could feel Madison's stare, but he couldn't look at her. Every minute she spent putting more of the pieces together put her life at greater risk. And he'd thought for a minute they could have something after this? What was he going to do? Disappear for weeks at a time? Tell her not to worry about the smell of gunpowder or a little blood? That was the stupidest thing he'd ever thought. Madison had lived with too many secrets to not be able to figure it out. And he couldn't ask her to put herself at risk like that.

That meant today was good-bye.

Once they knew what was on the drive they'd know how to leverage it against Dustin. Put the prick away for a hell of a long time. It would make life safer for Madison, but only if he put distance between them.

He could already feel the hole in his chest where she'd taken up residence.

The last bay door shut, closing the majority of his team in. They were free to talk here, especially since CJ had swept for bugs.

"What the hell is going on?" Lily glanced at him, then Julian. She seemed to be getting some of her fire back. Figuring out how to explain everything to that one was going to take some tact.

"Lily—" Aiden squeezed Madison's hand.

"Your friend's in trouble. We're helping her. That's what's going on." Julian was hovering around Lily, looking none too pleased about her presence. And yet, he hadn't shoved the derby girl at the twins or anyone else to take charge of. Interesting.

"That tells me nothing. Why did Dustin take my car?"

"Dustin wants something from Madison, he thought he could scare her, or use you to get that." Aiden didn't like telling Lily anything. Hell, Kathy was scowling at him for saying that much, but the girls were going to figure some of it out. Besides, Madison would end up telling her best friend that much at least. Better if he controlled what she knew.

"Lily, why don't you come with me and we can get something for your head? Madison, can you help me?" Kathy stepped forward, a motherly expression painted on her face. She smiled at Lily.

Lily glanced at Madison, who nodded.

The three women exited to the office, no doubt where Kathy would evaluate Lily's concussion and keep Madison occupied while he and the crew made a plan. There were serious upsides to having someone like Kathy around. Not only was she amazing with computers and surveillance, but she had more experience as a combat medic than Aiden had time in the service.

"I think it's best if Lily stays here." Julian thumbed at the cinder-block apartment that was little more than a bed and a couple of lockers. "We can stick a TV in there, take turns making sure she stays awake and out of sight. Dustin won't know where to look for her."

"Good. We can tell Madison she needs to stay here to watch Lily and for her own safety." Aiden nodded.

Truth was, he hadn't spared Lily much thought. His world had seemed to end the moment Julian called to tell him the twins were going to pick Madison up from a botched kidnapping. He'd been calling her name, pacing through his barn looking for her. A bad feeling hadn't helped things, but there you had it.

"We need a plan," Aiden said.

"Let's catch everyone up real quick." CJ wiped his hands off on a rag. "The Miami-Dade PD is giving us some space. There are a few officers who have been informed about our operation, one of them is Detective Smith. I would not expect a lot of help from the boys in blue. They aren't exactly happy with us."

"Was Kathy able to get anywhere with the DEA?"

CJ shook his head. "They dug their heels in. Said they couldn't get involved."

"Damn it." The DEA always asked for favors, but were stingy on paying back their debt. The Eleventh should be a slam-dunk hit for them. Aiden put his hands on his hips. "What about the drive? We have it. Emery's going over it now. In fact, let's see what he says."

Aiden dialed Emery and flipped the phone to speaker.

"I'm working," Emery said.

"Tell me something good," Aiden said.

"Good depends on what you wanted to hear."

"I'd like to know that the drive is full of doctored financial records and details of criminal dealings." It was too much to hope that one job would put both Dustin Ross and Michael Evers away for good.

"No luck then. You want to know what your girl was sitting on?"

"You're going to tell me."

"Bitcoins. Six million dollars in bitcoins."

"Bitcoins. Like the digital currency?"

"Yeah. A lot of the more forward-thinking criminals are starting to do some deals in bitcoins. There's no way to track them and no central bank regulating them, so it's an anonymous currency. Makes sense why Dustin's hurting for it. He bounced some checks yesterday. Guy's desperate for money. From what I can tell, it's his fault. Trying to live the life a little too big."

"So we've got ourselves a bag of money. How do we use it?" Aiden glanced around at the faces surrounding him. All of them were thinking, spinning the situation around to see it from a different side. If he wanted to give Madison the future she deserved, he had to figure out how to leverage the drive to help her. Except he had no idea how to do that yet.

"What do you want to buy?"

"That's not what I wanted to hear. Shit."

"I figured. We still giving this to Dustin?"

"Yeah, if nothing else then to just get him to pipe the fuck down for a minute. Who do you think he's trying to pay off? Who's he owe money to?"

"Right now, Evers and some Colombians. He had a

wire denied earlier this week. What do you want to bet it's for the drugs coming in tonight on those cars?"

"Damn. This is making too much sense." In the end, it all came down to money. Dustin wanted more of it, and when he got it, he spent it. Now, he was in deep with the wrong people, namely Evers and the Colombians. Both had a habit of terminating people.

"I'm going to mirror this drive so we give him one that looks like it has his bitcoin wallet and all the currency on it, but when he goes to use it, the coins will be rejected."

"And I could believably tell him I have no idea what the problem is."

"Exactly. He'd have to know where to look to identify them as real."

"Dustin's not that kind of smart. He's a smooth talker, but he's not all that bright. Probably why Evers likes him."

"I looked up that company flying product into Everglades Air. This is the first time they've used this airport. I'm working on getting the records, but I think this is how he's transporting the drugs into the country. I looked up the last couple of shipments. I think he's packing the cars with drugs, flying them over, and getting them taken out of the cars before they go through customs."

"That's a pretty smart theory. And what do you want to bet it's not coincidence those cars are getting here today and Dustin needs those coins?" Aiden's other phone beeped. He glanced at the screen and grit his teeth. "Mirror that drive. Fast. I've got Dustin calling me."

"On it."

Aiden switched calls, inhaling a deep breath. Not a soul moved. He'd like nothing more than to reach through the phone and punch the asshole.

"Dustin, I was just about to call you."

"I need the fucking drive now, DeHart."

Putting Dustin away would be one of the highlights of the year, for sure.

"Well, I have it."

"What? How did you—? That fucking bitch lied to me."

"Easy. She wasn't actually lying. She didn't know she had it."

"Where was it?"

"She had a storage unit up in Deerfield."

"What? How did I not know about that?"

"Not my problem."

Dustin paused before speaking again. This time, suspicion laced his voice. "How did you get it?"

"I picked her up, played it smooth, she took me back to her place and I found the key in a drawer, so I took it. You use a sledgehammer too often when all you need is a light touch."

"Where are you? I'll come get it."

"Not so fast. I can't do that here. There's also the matter of payment."

"I have cash for you. I need to know that you've kept this between us."

"As far as anyone knows, I picked up a girl at a bar. Your ass is covered." The idea of reducing Madison to a nameless, faceless piece of ass made him want to retch, but Dustin couldn't know the truth.

"Good. Good."

"I've got some errands to run for the garage. I'll meet you at Hallandale Beach in two hours."

"An hour."

"Hour and a half."

"Fuck. Hurry it up, DeHart."

Aiden hung up and blew out a breath.

"Here's what I'm thinking." Aiden turned to face

Julian and CJ. They were the two he had to convince. "We give the drive to Dustin. Have Emery stick a tracker in it. Evers has that shipment coming into Everglades Air tonight. That gives us time to put together the evidence to hand over to the FBI."

"Let the Hoovers do the pickup?" Julian's brows drew down into a line.

"You can go. This could be over." Aiden would be in bed with Madison. She'd still be in danger so long as Evers was alive, but he could figure out something. Maybe it was time for a new start. Sell the garage to Julian or the twins, pack his shit up, and hit the road with his girl.

CJ's frown deepened. "Let me make some calls. Don't plan on anything." He headed toward the back lot and his car.

"Let's get some work done, but be ready to move." Aiden strode toward the office. He needed to see Madison, to touch her. They had a lot to work through, but maybe, if everything worked out, they'd have time to do it.

He headed into the offices, following the low voices until he found the three women. Madison glanced up, catching sight of him immediately. He crooked his finger at her and she nodded. Lily was already looking better. Her color was coming back and she smiled at something Kathy said.

"What's going on?" Madison stepped out of the office, sliding her hands into her pockets.

"I want you to hang around here today."

"I can't."

"Madison, Dustin just tried to kidnap you—"

"If I don't go to work today, you don't know what will happen tonight. Besides, if I don't show up Lily's parents will go to her place looking for me, even if I call in, and we do not want them finding her like this." She spoke quieter now. "I'm going to work. There's security. I'll be safe there."

"I don't like it." He pulled out his phone and texted John. His pickup truck would blend in better on the roads around Everglades Air than any of their cars.

She studied him for a moment. "You guys have a plan."

"I might."

"Then you need to know the latest updates on that shipment. I'm it. Let me help. I don't know what's going on here, but I get the idea this is something you've done before. Please, let me help."

He wrapped his hand around hers and pulled her farther away from the office. "John follows you all the way to the gates. When you leave, you don't leave alone."

"I've still got to get a ride to work. I won't be alone."

"I got you something. Come here." He pulled her toward an exterior door and pushed it open.

"Is it long and hard?"

She startled a laugh out of him.

"No, you've already had that. I got you something else. Come here."

He took her hand and led her around to the spot where he'd parked her Honda Rebel that first fateful night when she went looking for trouble. In its place sat a gray Honda CBR650F.

"Wow." Madison stared at the sport bike, her jaw slightly unhinged.

"It's got a lot more speed and maneuverability than the Rebel. Just watch out for cops, they'll think you're out hot-rodding."

"I can't accept this."

"Consider it on loan then."

"How did you get this so fast?"

"I know a guy."

She glanced over her shoulder, gaze narrowing once more.

Aiden held up his hands. "It's all good, I swear. This guy only works on bikes and every now and then he has something he's looking to sell. Lots of guys buy these things, their wives get pissed or they can't make the payments and if he thinks he can flip it, he'll do them a solid and take it off their hands. I was just lucky enough to hit him up when he had something suitable."

"I'll use it today, but I hope you got a receipt," she said.

He stepped up behind her, wrapping his arms around her waist. He wouldn't tell her he planned on keeping her. Yet. He had to be sure his plan would work.

"Use it for however long you need to." He kissed her cheek. "Text me when you get to work?"

"I will. What about—the shipment?"

"I'm working on it."

"What's wrong with the cars?" Her voice was small, no doubt hurting once more by yet another deception. Dustin had kept her right where he wanted her. He hadn't lied when he'd told Aiden that much.

"It's best if you don't know."

There was the distance. It wasn't a physical one, but in that moment he felt her pull away from him. That wasn't about to happen. When this was over, when she was safe, he'd tell her everything. If she could accept his secrets, she could accept the truth of what his life had been like for the last couple of years.

John's pickup eased around the corner. He had a cap on with large sunglasses to obscure his face. Aiden was willing to bet he'd even changed the plates out.

"I'd better get to work," she said.

"Madison."

Aiden didn't let her go. He grasped her face in his hands and kissed her. She jolted at the first press of their lips, but in a matter of seconds her mouth softened and her hands came up to rest on his chest. He groaned. She kissed him back, throwing herself into it just like she did everything.

God, he was going to miss her, but in a few hours, he would never have to part with her again.

He lifted his head, staring down at her, and swiped his thumb over her cheek.

"Get to work before I lock you up." He let go of her face and patted her bottom as she pivoted.

"You could try." Her smile, it did things to him deep down.

She put the new helmet on and got on the bike. She started the engine and sat there for a moment, studying the console.

He wanted to rip her off that bike, kiss her until she panted, and maybe make use of a large backseat—but there was no time for that right now. Later, they'd have all the time in the world.

Madison glanced back, her face obscured by the tinted shield. She waved then pushed off, easing through the parking lot before turning onto the street.

He leaned against the side of the garage, staring at the last point he'd seen her. The last thing he wanted to do was let her go, but the work she was doing with them was going to stop a criminal. He loved her a little bit more for it.

Chapter Twenty-One

Aiden leaned against the hood of the loaner Shelby Mustang at the main parking area for Hallandale Beach. He knew this was a bit of a drive for Dustin, who preferred to be closer to central Miami and the high-rolling party people. But that was the point. Dustin was desperate if he was going to go after Madison himself. That meant this deal needed to go down in a very public place, with lots of witnesses around.

"Aiden, what's your twenty?" CJ said in his ear.

"I am sipping a chocolate shake about twenty feet south of the Ocean Drive entrance. There's a palm tree on my left."

"I see you. Any sign of Dustin?"

"Nah, but I'm early. Any word from the Hoovers?"

They had an opportunity to wrap this up tight. Between the information Emery was putting together and the impending shipment, they could nail Evers's ass to the wall.

"Yeah. You aren't going to like it. They say it's not enough. Do our thing. If we get more on them, they'll back us up."

"Are you fucking kidding me?"

"No. I just got off the horn with Emery. Looks like the operation is split up Colombian-style. Evers is the warehouse. Ross is the sales hub. The shipment's coming in through someone else, which is why we've never been able to sic the DEA on them. We got a couple of aliases for a guy who is a partner or shareholder in a couple import-export companies. They've been using another airport on the other side of Miami, but it's undergoing expansion. The only other airport with the right runway length is—"

"Everglades Air." Aiden sipped his shake when all he wanted to do was punch something. This was a load of bullshit. Now they had to prove the connection? Their crew was agile, inventive, and very talented, but the scope and size of what CJ was proposing was daunting.

Right then, Aiden hated the FBI. He was angry enough he might walk—except there was Madison. He had to make something stick to Evers for her sake. This wasn't about revenge anymore. It hadn't been for a long time. It was about justice. Doing the right thing, but sometimes that sucked.

A sleek, black BMW rolled into the Hallandale Beach entrance and paused. The windows were tinted so dark Aiden couldn't make out the figure of anyone inside. Which meant it was Dustin.

He waited while the car idled a moment.

Come on, dick-for-brains. I don't have time for this.

The car turned toward him and slid into an empty spot almost next to the entrance. It wouldn't be a fast getaway, if that's what Dustin wanted. Then again, he probably had a goon driving him that didn't know any better.

"Dustin's here. Got him?"

"In my sights," CJ replied. "John?"

"I've got him, too."

They didn't actually think Dustin would be stupid enough to try to kill Aiden here, but the truth was, it was not in Dustin's best interests to allow Aiden to continue breathing. Between the Eleventh deal and now handling the bitcoin drive, which Dustin clearly wanted to keep quiet from his boss, Aiden was a liability to the prick.

The driver's door opened and Dustin got out, large, dark sunglasses perched on his nose.

"Is he wearing women's sunglasses?" CJ asked.

Aiden grunted. If they weren't, someone needed to tell the fancy designers Dustin was buying from to lay off. That look wasn't good for any man.

Dustin strode swiftly toward Aiden, none of the cool composure of a man who'd done a hundred or more drug deals in public.

"Wow." Aiden uncrossed his arms and held his hands up.

Dustin slowed his pace. He must really be shaken if he wasn't even trying to be covert.

"What happened to you, man?" Aiden slanted his gaze toward Dustin. He turned and leaned against the Mustang next to Aiden.

"Nothing."

"You're looking pretty red. Accident at the tanners?"

"Shut it, DeHart."

Aiden shrugged and tossed the shake into a nearby garbage can.

"Where is it?" Dustin stared straight ahead, as if the street were the most fascinating thing.

"It's here. Got my money?"

"I've got one better than that—"

"Before you finish that sentence, you should know one of my army buddies is up on a balcony across the street. Now, he's a mean motherfucker and got a couple of medals for being able to pick guys off."

Dustin stared at him now, mouth slightly ajar.

Aiden smiled, but he didn't feel it. "After this, we're done. I don't care about your secrets. I don't want to know who you've done wrong. Let's forget we ever knew each other, okay? I don't want any trouble." It was a line. All of it. Dustin would agree, and in a day or so, he'd try to kill Aiden. Except, Dustin didn't know they were about to put him in a world of hurt tonight.

"You sneaky son of a bitch."

"Takes one to know one, Ross. My money?"

Dustin flashed an envelope in his jacket pocket. Aiden's stomach rolled at the thought of touching it, but it was part of the ruse. If he didn't act like he wanted it, Dustin would be suspicious.

"My drive?"

Aiden sniffed the air, tilting his head sideways. "Is that—pepper spray?"

He couldn't smell a thing, but he was sure enjoying the way Dustin was fuming right now.

"Fuck you."

"Man, that shit's nasty. I'll give you a tip. Soap or anything else is really only going to activate it. Try scrubbing it with plain water and see if it helps. You must have pissed someone off." Aiden shook his head and bit the inside of his mouth.

"Really?" Dustin turned to face him a little. "I tried soap earlier and it did burn a bit."

Damn, had the man never heard of Google?

"Yeah, it's the soap."

"Huh. Good to know."

"It's in a plastic bag in that trash can." Aiden thumbed at the receptacle he'd just thrown his shake into.

"Really?"

Aiden shrugged. "Seemed like a good idea at the time."

Go on, go dig around in the garbage, you piece of trash.

"Shit."

Dustin sighed and crossed to the garbage can. He glanced over the edge and wrinkled his nose.

"Did you really have to do that?" CJ asked through the headset.

Aiden merely chuckled.

Dustin reached over the edge and snagged the plastic bag. He pulled it out, holding it at arm's length despite nothing being on the plastic, and carried it to his car.

This was the moment of truth.

Any crook worth his salt tested the merchandise first. Emery had worked hard to make this new drive look exactly like the old one, down to stripping the casing and putting it on the new one. The question was, would Dustin know what to look for to verify the bitcoins?

The currency was still so new, Aiden didn't think Dustin would know what he was doing.

Dustin set a laptop on the hood of his car and plugged the drive in.

"Think it'll work?" CJ asked.

Aiden wanted to reach through the headset and smack the FBI agent. Like he could answer a question at a time like this.

Dustin poked at the keyboard with his index fingers and leaned close to the screen. The minutes dragged on until Aiden started shifting his weight from foot to foot.

"DeHart." Dustin put an envelope in the same plastic bag he'd had the drive in. He turned toward a second trash can and tossed it in, a stupid grin on his face. "It's been a pleasure."

Aiden didn't smile or wave, he just watched Dustin Ross pack up his equipment and climb in his car. The idiot had to do a three-point turn to get out of the parking lot, something he clearly hadn't thought about when parking.

"Motherfucker," Aiden muttered.

"We following him?" CJ asked.

"What's the point? We know where he's going. How's the tracker looking?"

"Transmitting bright and clear."

Another upside to having switched out the drives was extra space in the case. Emery had whipped up a nice tracking bug to help them keep tabs on where Dustin took the drive.

"Okay, let's pack up and head out of here."

Aiden fished the bag out of the garbage and shoved the envelope in his pocket. Whatever money they collected from these gigs went to charity. It was one of the sticking points the Hoovers hated, but Aiden didn't care. He didn't technically work for them.

A red car slammed on its brakes along Ocean Boulevard.

"Oh shit, we've got company."

Aiden turned and strode back to the Mustang. He jumped in the driver's seat and started the car as the red racer turned in.

He'd taken the loaner Mustang to try to avoid Raibel, and now, he was stuck in a car that couldn't outrun the thug. Which meant he was going to need to talk his way out of this.

Raibel threw his car into park and got out, sauntering toward Aiden in that odd, swaggering manner only thugs had.

"Where the hell did he come from?" CJ said.

"I don't know. He's got a gun in his waistband."

"Well, I've got him."

"Don't shoot. I'm going to try to talk to him." He couldn't be Julian. Killing people wasn't the answer.

Aiden got out of the car and leaned on the door and roof.

"What's going on, Canales?"

"I want answers." Raibel stopped a few feet away, one hand on the gun under his shirt, the other on his hip.

"What's the question?"

"My cars. My product. You took them."

Maybe there was a way to spin this. Raibel and the Eleventh would always have hard feelings toward Aiden. There was no changing that. But that didn't mean they couldn't have the same goals.

"I didn't take anything." He held his hands up. "I might know something, but I didn't do anything."

"You're lying," Raibel yelled.

He lifted his shirt and Aiden dove into the Mustang, throwing himself sideways. A single gunshot fractured the picturesque afternoon.

Aiden shoved the gearshift into drive and stomped on the accelerator. He peered up over the hood just in time to see Raibel dive out of the way. He clipped the back of the red racer with his front fender, shoving through the narrow opening. The car skidded. He made a hard turn onto Ocean Boulevard.

"Aiden. Aiden!" CJ yelled.

"What?"

"You hit?"

"No."

"He must have shot the car. Backup is on the way, we're going to have cops in a minute. Lose that car."

They couldn't fart around with the cops. CJ could sort

it out later and shove it up the Hoovers' asses that they hadn't stepped in.

There wasn't time to make a nice, neat getaway. Even now, Raibel's car was peeling out of the parking lot. Aiden zipped through traffic, but the radiator gauge was slowly rising and the car just wasn't accelerating properly.

"Where's John?" Aiden asked.

"Heading to you."

He pressed the accelerator to the floor, but the engine didn't roar to life.

"Shit," he chanted.

Raibel wasn't slowing down.

The man was enraged.

Aiden turned onto a smaller street, shifting, asking the car for everything. He needed to split, leave the car, and make a run for it. The red car turned behind him, closing the gap fast. The light at the intersection flickered from yellow to red.

He stomped on the brake just as Raibel bumped him. The momentum sent the back of the car spinning, crashing into the cars parked along the street. The airbag deployed, slamming into his chest harder than the bump. He felt the car tip and his stomach flipped a second before the car tilted at ninety degrees and crashed over on the roof. Aiden hit the top of the car, arms around his head, and rolled to his side.

His vision hazed in and out, sounds were distant and it was hard to grasp his thoughts.

Move.

He needed to move.

"Aiden? Aiden! Talk to me, man, what happened?" That was CJ. What had happened?

Aiden glanced around.

"The car's upside down." He dug in his pocket for

the knife he never went without. A flick of the wrist and he slashed the airbag to pieces.

Glass crunched outside of the car.

"I'm around the corner, hold on." CJ sounded frantic.

Aiden rose shakily to all fours inside the ruined Mustang and peered out of the broken windows. A pair of feet were pointed toward him.

He shook his head, but his thoughts were muddy. How hard had he hit the ground?

Raibel crouched next to the car, gun in hand. He lifted the gun, but never saw the man leap out of a truck in the intersection. John sprinted toward them and at the last second pulled back and kicked Raibel with his cowboy boots. Raibel went to the pavement hard. John grabbed the gun and kicked the window. The cracked glass broke further.

Aiden squeezed out, glass scraping his skin, the heated asphalt burning his hands.

"Come on, come on." John grabbed him under the arm and hauled him up. He had to practically drag Aiden to the waiting pickup truck and threw him in before jumping in the driver's seat.

"I've got him, CJ, but damn man, we need a cleanup. Bad."

"Damn it." Aiden winced as Kathy stitched up a deep gash in his shoulder. He was going to be sore. Hell, his neck already hurt just to turn his head.

"Emery's here." CJ tapped his knuckles on the door.

"Get everyone," Julian said from behind the desk. "Close the garage."

One by one, the rest of the crew filed in, their faces grim. Emery and Tori were the last to enter. Emery didn't come to Classic Rides often. Though he was part of their crew, his value to them was in large part his ability to remain unconnected. Today, though, they needed all hands on deck.

"So everyone is on the same page, the FBI claims we do not have enough evidence for them to arrest Evers. Because this import-export company is not directly tied to Evers and we don't yet have the documentation to prove this is his import guy, they will not back us up. It's operate as usual."

He looked around the room, meeting each person's gaze. No one had said it out loud, but this morning, they'd thought they had it. Deliver the proof to the FBI, let them make a raid, and they were done. But that wasn't the case. This was one more mile in a long-haul operation.

"We treat this like we would any other hit," Julian said, taking over. Unlike the others, his job didn't end with Evers's arrest. "Get in. Get the product. We'll take it back to The Shop and chop it, dead-drop the drugs to the FBI. Keep our street cred, don't blow our cover. If we're lucky, Evers will trip up, do something stupid, and we'll grab him in the next couple of weeks."

Aiden didn't believe that. A year ago they'd thought the cops were going to nab him. What more evidence did they have now?

"Aiden, do you think Madison can tell us the specs on their security? Help us out there?"

"Yeah, I think she can." His heart hurt.

If Evers was still a threat, it meant she had to get out of his life. There was no future for her so long as she was in danger. More than anything else, he needed to know she was out there, breathing, happy and alive. Was this mission worth it? It was hard to see the value of what they did when he had nothing. Just a couple of cars, a business, and a growing collection of scars.

* * *

Madison tapped her pencil on the desk, her knee bouncing. She'd raised the blinds so she could look out at the front gates of the airport and watch the cars coming and going. Since she had access to everything, she'd pulled up the security camera footage from the day before to get the make, model, and license plate of the car Michael Evers had arrived in.

She hadn't heard more from Aiden than a few one-word text messages. She knew Lily was doing "okay," and when she'd asked if he'd given the drive to Dustin his reply was "No." Would it kill the man to give her a whole sentence?

It was nearly impossible to concentrate on work. She'd managed only the most necessary of tasks. Other than that, she was staring at the gate.

Her phone rang and she jumped, placing a hand over her chest. She snatched it off the desk. Her heart rose to her throat when she saw Aiden's name.

"Hello?"

"Hey. I don't have a lot of time, so I need for you to listen to what I need and tell me if it's possible." He sounded—stressed. What was wrong?

"Okay." Hell, at this point she just wanted to hear from him, even if it was a grocery list.

"Can you tell me the security shifts, if the cameras installed two years ago have been moved, and what kind of plane Evers is using?"

"I can tell you all of that. Give me a second to pull up the schedule and then the flight log." She rattled off the information he asked for and waited.

"Perfect. Okay, now, I'm going to have to ask you to do something you might not like."

"What is it?" Did he want an arm or a finger, maybe?

"I'd like for there to be fewer people there tonight. No one will get hurt, but the fewer people around means less chance of anything going wrong. Can you do something about that?"

"Actually . . . I can." Aiden wouldn't like it, but he wasn't exactly asking how it was going to be accomplished.

"Good. Act normal today. Go home like always. I'll call you tomorrow when it's all done."

He ended the call before she could come clean. She stared at the phone for a second before flipping through her recent calls and hitting dial on the third one down.

The line rang three times before a man answered.

"Hey, Dave, it's Madison. I was thinking—why don't I take your shift tonight? My bike got stolen and I could use the extra hours. How's that sound?"

Dave sighed. "That would be awesome. I'll make it up to you, I swear."

"Don't worry about it."

"You're the best, Madison."

"Take care of that arm and get rid of this cold."

"You're telling me."

She chatted with the old security guard a few more minutes before hanging up.

Madison had promised herself things would be different after Dustin. She'd do the right thing. Follow the rules. And now, she was throwing everything out of the window for a man she barely knew and a promise. Her heart said she was doing the right thing, but her head wasn't sure. Trust sucked sometimes.

Chapter Twenty-Two

Aiden rested his head against the side of the van and closed his eyes. They hadn't been shut more than a second when Tori jabbed him in the ribs.

"Wake up," she said.

"I'm not asleep."

"Just making sure."

"Look alive, people," Kathy said from the front seat.

"Where are the lights?" CJ said.

Aiden peered between the seats. He'd sat and watched the airport enough to know that at night, it was lit up.

"What's Emery got on the live feed?" Julian asked.

"Emery?" CJ pressed his cell phone to his ear for a second.

Kathy slowed the van to a near stop.

"She's what? For fuck's sake. Drive." CJ did not sound happy.

"What's going on?" Aiden asked, dreading the answer.

CJ didn't reply, only increasing the dread.

What had Madison done?

The last he'd texted her, she was studying. Like a good girl. Had she lied to him?

The van rolled through the open gates of the airport.

A figure filled the guard-shack door, shapely, hair piled on top of her head.

His heart dropped.

No. No. No.

Kathy was able to pull the van straight up to the hangar. The moment she slowed, the doors slid open and the crew started to spill out. By the time Aiden made it out, Madison was there, pushing the hangar door open. The lights inside were low, the halogens needing considerable time to warm up.

John and Gabriel were already lowering the ramp. The cars were stacked two high on hydraulic lifts. There was almost no room around the cars to squeeze inside.

"Madison." He strode toward her, wanting nothing more than to strangle her in that moment.

"Don't lecture me." She spun to face him and gasped. "What happened?"

"I had a wreck. Why are you here?" He grabbed her arm and hauled her into the office. The last thing he needed was a wrench in their plans, even if it had her curves.

"You said to get as many people away as I could. This is the best plan. You get in and out, no one knows you were here."

"But your boss will know you were here."

Madison drew herself up. "I thought about that. You need to knock me out so I have plausible deniability."

He shook his head. "What about when someone asks who was working when his shit was stolen?"

She blinked at him.

Why couldn't she understand? The fewer connections between them, the safer she was. "You might as well just paint a target on your fucking back."

"Don't yell at me."

They'd have to put her in witness protection. It was

the best bet. This was his fault. Aiden should have known that even the slightest hint of a connection to Madison was a bad idea. Evers would be suspicious. He had to know Dustin used to be married to her. It was probably some sick joke between the two how clueless she was.

"Okay, when we're gone, call nine-one-one. Tell them what happened. Be truthful."

"But—"

"No arguments, Madison. I need you to trust me on this."

She glared at him, but didn't utter another word.

"When you get off shift, go home. Text me. I'll swing by in a different car and pick you up." He wouldn't give her the choice to stay or go. Anyone else, he'd leave it up to them, but not her. She had to live. She had to be out there somewhere, safe and happy. Which meant she needed to enter witness protection.

"Okay. Fine."

"Good." He closed the distance between them, crushing her to him and kissing her. She clung to his shoulders, and the little surprised moan she made only heated his blood.

He stepped back. Engines revved. Someone yelled.

Aiden jerked the office door open.

"Got somewhere to drive," John yelled. He jogged around to a second car.

Aiden glanced over his shoulder. He had to be the first to The Shop. They each drove out in the order they were needed, and because Aiden had the most experience flipping cars, he had to be there to call the shots, when what he really wanted to do was stay here with Madison.

"I have to go. Text me," he said.

Madison nodded, her eyes large.

He wanted to bundle her up, put her in the car, and drive off with her. Leaving her here killed him a little. But he'd see her again soon, for the last time.

Aiden climbed in the Bugatti and put the concerns out of his mind. One thing at a time.

"Guys, the other guard is going to be back any second." Madison glanced at her watch.

"We're going as fast as we can," Tori said. She slithered between the cars.

They were packed in so tight, the only ones who could get into the cars and drive them out were the twins. It was a slow process, one she gathered from the nervous glances was supposed to have gone faster. The only ones left were Tori, Roni, and Julian.

Tori eased a car out while Roni slid into the open space and into the next to last car.

"Go," Julian said, waving the mechanic on.

Tori waved. A second later her taillights were a distant speck on the horizon.

A clang and a grunt brought Julian and Madison jogging to the edge of the ramp.

"Roni, you okay?" he yelled.

"Yeah, someone spilled something back here." Roni perched with one foot on the tire track and the other on the curved wall of the plane, avoiding the flat bottom.

It appeared that a two-level hydraulic system simply slid into the plane, allowing for the cars to be packed in, making the most use of the space.

"Come on, pick that lock faster," Julian chanted.

"I'd be a lot faster if you got off my ass."

Roni had an electronic box with a key she stuck into the lock. Some sort of code breaker? The cars were a lot more high-tech than anything Madison had ever driven before.

"Got it." Roni slid into the driver's seat and the car hummed to life.

She eased the car down the tracks, stopping as the wheels came off the ramp. Julian stalked around the car and met her.

"Take this one. You aren't any help here. I'll be right behind you."

"Hurry," he said.

"Really?" Roni rolled her eyes and glanced at Madison.

Madison looked away, trying to not laugh. This was not an appropriate time for that. Besides, Julian kind of scared her.

"Madison, as soon as she gets that car out, call nine-one-one." Julian leaned out of the window, pointing at the plane. His battered face gave him a decidedly scary look, especially with the shadows casting most of his face in relief.

Roni jogged up the ramp.

"I got it." Madison didn't like this plan, but she'd go along with it.

Julian was gone in a puff of exhaust. She'd never seen a Bugatti in person, but she could understand the appeal.

"Shit." Roni's voice echoed in the plane.

"Need help?" Madison peered inside.

The last car was on the second level. Roni was shimmying her way up a support pole, one arm hooked over the top track. Why they'd left that one for the last car, Madison would never know, but it looked like a bad idea to her.

"What can I do?" Madison asked.

"Nothing," Roni grunted between breaths.

Roni grabbed hold of the netting that had been strung tight over the cars and hoisted herself up. But she only went so far. The netting ripped. Madison gasped. She couldn't move fast enough. Roni's eyes widened and her mouth opened on a yelp. She dropped, except her upper body fell faster than her lower body. Her head thunked against the metal tracks on her way down. She flipped a hundred and eighty degrees before hitting the floor of the plane, one foot still suspended in the air by the netting.

"Oh my God." Madison climbed up in the plane.

There was blood. So much blood.

Roni groaned and rolled to her side, clutching her arm.

Madison stood stock-still, frozen to the spot. She was pretty sure shoulders weren't supposed to be down by a girl's boobs.

Think, damn it. If this was derby, what would I do?

Get her flat on her back.

Madison stood on the track, staring at Roni's foot. She didn't want to hurt the girl, but damn, black boots, black netting, and almost no light was a piss-poor combination.

"Knife," Roni gritted out through her teeth, pointing with her good hand.

Madison spied the end of the blade sticking out of the boot on her extended leg. She slid the stainless steel knife out of the sheath and in two swipes, cut the netting.

Roni slowly lowered her leg to the plane floor.

"God, what do I do?" Madison asked.

Normally, this is where she'd call the medic over and take a knee.

"Bleach." Roni's breathing was coming in gasps and pants. She appeared to have a nasty gash on her forehead that was the source of the blood.

"But—"

"Bleach," Roni said with more force.

Madison turned and jogged to the hangar control panel, hit the big red button to close the doors, and flipped the lights off. If her other security person came back, she didn't want to give him a reason to look in here. She turned on the workstation lights along the wall of the hangar to give her light to work by and unlocked the maintenance closet. She wanted bleach? Madison could do one better.

She rolled out the pressure washer and a couple bottles of bleach. By the time she had everything to the plane Roni had limped her way out and was using grease rags to stem the bleeding.

"Pour the bleach over the blood. All of it." She sat down on a metal folding chair, looking worse by the minute.

"Shouldn't we call someone?"

"Everyone's gone. They've got shit to do. Fuck."

Madison uncapped two bottles of bleach and walked up into the plane. She was about to obscure the crime even further. Not only was she helping, she was now covering up evidence. She paused, holding those bottles. Was this the right thing to do?

Her heart said yes.

Her brain said fuck no.

She was already involved. There was no getting out of it if she were ever caught. Might as well make it as hard as possible to do that.

The bleach chugged out, splashing on her shoes, her legs, and all over the plane. She sloshed some on the wall and netting and saved the last bit for the top track. Instead of crawling up the support pipe, she lowered the hydraulic lift at the end and rode it up until she could walk back to the spot and pour bleach on.

"Unlock the door while you're up there."

Madison gasped and put a hand against the car, staring down at Roni below her.

"Sorry. Here. Stick the key end in and press the button. It's easy." She held the device out with her good arm.

"You can't drive. Not with your arm out of the socket like that."

"I'll need you to help me put it back in."

"Roni, I can't do that."

"You're about to hot-wire one of the most sophisticated cars on the earth. You can put a joint back in place. Go on. I'm going to ralph. Trash can?"

"Over there by the silver locker."

Roni wasn't steady on her feet. There was no way Roni could drive in that kind of condition. But she couldn't stay here. The others would be expecting the cops any minute now.

Would anyone believe her if they saw the criminals had had time to pressure-wash the scene? No.

So she'd have to be a hostage.

That was the plan. Madison could drive Roni out of here and they could stage a fake hostage situation or dump her somewhere. It would give her deniability.

Oh my God, I'm making up ways to lie to the police.

This was everything she'd wanted to avoid. It was worse than what Dustin did because now she was an active participant in doing bad things. Breaking the law. With Dustin, she hadn't done anything. She'd been stupidly unaware and completely uninvolved. Here, she'd made the choice to help. That was all her.

Madison's hands shook. She slid the fake key into the

lock. The runner next to the tire track was narrow and didn't provide much to stand on, but she was used to balancing on a metal plate three inches wide bolted to four wheels. That was a piece of cake.

She waited for a moment, watching the screen scroll numbers and slash marks. It beeped once, then the locks disengaged and the headlights flipped on.

Roni hadn't told her to get the car out of the plane, but it had to be done, especially for this plan to work. She climbed in and stared at the console for a moment. Where did she put the key?

"It's a keyless start. There's a button," Roni yelled.

Where the ignition key would have gone was a black button. Madison pressed it and the car revved to life, but there was no full-body vibration like Aiden's Chevelle gave her.

She eased the car into neutral and let it roll forward onto the hydraulic lift. There was a convenient button mounted near enough to her window. She pressed it and held her breath. The car lowered and tilted. Her stomach did odd flip-flops and she pressed the brake harder.

Madison's phone rang, breaking up the near silence. She gasped and came off the break a bit. The lift hit the tracks with a jarring jolt and the car rolled forward. She ignored the ringing in favor of guiding the car safely out of the plane of death. As soon as she had wheels on the ground she pulled her phone out.

"Shit."

It was her other security guard, no doubt wanting to know where she was. If she didn't answer, would he go looking for her? Or just assume she was doing a round?

She didn't answer it.

Madison killed the engine and got out. Roni was

shuffled toward her. The girl was pale and a bit green around the gills. Not good.

"I think I should drive you," Madison said.

"What? Hell no."

"You've got a concussion and your arm's out of socket at the very least. If something's not broken I'd be shocked. You're about to pass out or hurl. Maybe both. You'd crash. Just hear me out. I drive you wherever you guys are going. Tomorrow morning, after someone's for sure found this, kick me out on some back road in the Everglades. I can claim I was kidnapped, but you guys let me go since I never saw any faces. Plausible deniability, right? That's what Aiden was stressing." God, she'd really thought this all through.

"Fuck," Roni spat.

Madison blew out a breath and grabbed the pressure washer.

"I need to hurry. My other guard is back," she said.

"That's just great."

Madison ignored her grumblings and flipped the washer on. It began to chug away, far too loud, but there was no other option.

She began with the top track, spraying it from the bottom up, then the floor of the plane. This was a job she hadn't done in ages. Over time, she'd worn every hat at the airport. It took much longer than she'd have liked to wash the plane out and get rid of the run-off. By then, every sound, even the scuff of her shoes on concrete had her jumping.

"That's going to have to be good enough. We've got to go," Roni said.

"I was thinking the same thing." She hastily wiped down the power washer, but between the bleach bottles, the plane, and the rest of the hangar, her fingerprints were everywhere. She could only hope that working at the airport gave her an excuse.

Madison sighed, wanting nothing more than to crawl into her office chair for a nap. But she couldn't do that. She had to kidnap herself first.

They had to use the key once more to not only unlock the car, but fool it into thinking they had the real key. Madison gripped the wheel, waiting for the automatic doors to open enough to drive out of the hangar. At least it wouldn't be up to her to call the cops.

"Shit. The gate's closed," Roni said.

"What does that mean? What do I do?" Madison stared at Roni.

"Drive through it and hope the airbags don't deploy."

"Are you serious?"

"Dead serious. Drive!"

Madison shifted into gear and accelerated. A figure was coming out of the guard shack, removing his hat. They were halfway to the gates before he seemed to realize there was a car driving at him. He jumped aside, hands waving. They'd all been taught that merchandise wasn't worth a life, good to see that lesson was firmly in place.

"Oh shit." Madison screamed. They hit the gate.

There was a moment of resistance. They were pushing the gate the wrong direction. But the Bugatti had more power and strength. Sparks flew from where metal scraped metal. They burst through the gate with a *pop* and the car flew forward, eating up the road.

"Oh my God. Oh my God," Madison chanted.

"Woohoo, you did it." Roni grinned weakly. "And thank God we didn't have to eat airbag."

"Uh, where am I going?"

Roni sighed. "I'm so fucked."

* * *

Madison steered the car into a deserted yard, surrounded by a chain-link fence. The gate was open and a light slashed out from under a rolling door.

"Honk twice, fast," Roni said. She wasn't looking good. She listed to one side and any time Madison hit a bump, Roni would gasp and groan.

Madison honked twice and a second later the door rose.

"Go," Roni snapped.

Madison rolled the car into a warehouse. The other five cars were up on lifts, missing pieces—if she didn't know these were the same vehicles that had come off the plane she wouldn't have known what she was looking at.

"This is going to be fun," Roni muttered, and pushed her door open.

Madison killed the engine and glanced around. Tori bolted around the car, fussing over her sister. Everyone else paused in what they were doing, staring at them.

John walked up from the fender, mouth hanging open.

"What did you do? What did you do?" He laid a hand on the hood of the car.

Madison opened the door and stood, a little shaky after the drive, and winced at the damage. She hadn't realized how bad it was.

"We aren't going to be able to fix this or smooth the scratches out." John knelt next to the headlight, which was also cracked. He turned toward her. "What the hell did you do?"

"She told me to go through the gate." Madison waved at Roni, trying to ignore the way Aiden was staring at her.

"We give it to the FBI as evidence. Come on." Julian

shouldered her aside and moved the Bugatti into a bay. The other two men followed.

"Kathy, come take care of Roni, I need Tori on that third car." Aiden walked toward the twins, and bent his head to speak to Roni for a second.

Madison didn't know where to look or what to think. A loud *pop* startled her and she glanced at the car she'd driven. Gabriel and John had removed the rear panel and a . . . container of some kind. They handed it over to a man she hadn't seen before. The other two removed several of the containers, lining them up.

Could this be Emery? The person Aiden always seemed to be talking to? The man opened the first container, wearing bright blue gloves, and dumped out several smaller, white bags of—something. Drugs. Was that what was in there?

"Madison."

She inhaled sharply and pressed her hand to her chest. The way this night was going, she'd die from a heart attack.

"Holy shit."

Aiden grabbed her shoulders and gave her a little shake, bending just enough so she couldn't look around him.

"Why couldn't you just do what you were supposed to?" He spoke low, his voice pitched for her ears alone, with rage in his eyes.

"Why don't you tell me the truth about what you're doing? You made me think you were doing this on your own—for some reason. Is anything you told me the truth? Did you even have a sister?"

He glanced over his shoulder. There was a decided lack of chatter coming from the others, which felt wrong. The short time Madison had spent around his friends, they'd never shut up.

"Shit. Come here." He took her hand and led her through a set of swinging doors into a room lined with metal shelves and things that looked vaguely like car parts.

Aiden dropped her hand and paced the length of the room.

"What lie are you going to tell me this time?" she asked.

Aiden stopped a couple of feet away. His arms were streaked with grease and his black shirt looked pretty beat up.

"I work with the FBI."

She stared at him. Was he serious? Did he expect her to believe the government would sanction people stealing cars?

"Prove it," she said.

"What happened to trusting what I say?"

"This is a lot to take in, Aiden." She shook her head. "I just covered up a crime and stole for you. I need more."

"I can't tell you more than that. Hell, you shouldn't even be here." He pushed his hand through his hair, and for once, he appeared genuinely worried.

Was that because she'd found him out? Or was he concerned about her? She wanted to believe it was for her benefit, but could she trust herself? Her gut said to take Aiden at his word—which was crazy. And stupid. But it would ease her conscience about what she'd just done.

"Aiden, done yet? Kind of need some help."

Madison could tell them apart by their voices. She'd spent time around these people over the last week. They were real people to her. And though they were rough around the edges, some of them badly damaged, they were good people. Weren't they?

"Should I catch a cab home or something?" she asked. He might not be FBI, but she couldn't see Aiden doing anything bad.

"Hell no. Just—stick around. I'll take care of everything, but I've got to go." He crossed to stand in front of her. His gaze was hard, and yet she felt as though she saw more of him now. The weight that he seemed to shoulder made more sense now.

Aiden touched his fingertips to her cheeks, lifting her face slightly before brushing his lips across hers.

She was in over her head, and she knew it. Was she letting her feelings for him blind her to the truth?

Chapter Twenty-Three

"She has to go into witness protection."

Aiden turned toward Kathy. Of course the others would have sent her.

The Shop was quiet, the last of the five salvageable cars were gone and the product bagged and tagged for the FBI drop CJ would do in another couple of hours. It was time to get home and rest before they all pretended it was another normal day at Classic Rides.

Kathy leaned against the door and peeked in.

Madison sat curled up, her head resting on a desk that had been in the warehouse when they'd taken it over after an FBI raid and seizure. He pulled the door shut and turned to face Kathy.

She lifted her hand and rested it against his cheek, giving him a sad smile. *Motherly* wasn't a term he'd use to describe Kathy often, but she had her moments.

"She got to you. There's nothing wrong with that. Truth be told? I'm glad to see you still have it in you, but think about her future."

Aiden turned and took two strides away—but to where? There was nowhere to go that this wouldn't follow him. Kathy didn't make any sound, but he felt her presence.

"She needs to go away. Maybe just for a little while, Aiden."

He got it. He hated it, but given the options, he'd rather see Madison alive instead of dead. Except he couldn't speak around the lump in his throat. Couldn't tell Kathy to shut it and stop beating him over the head with the truth he already knew.

"It isn't fair." She sighed and rested her elbows on the workbench, chin resting in her palm, gazing up at him. "Did you know when CJ and I got married our boss tried to bully us into getting it annulled?"

Aiden swallowed his pain down, focusing on this rare glimpse into CJ's and Kathy's lives. They might play the role of being one of the crew, but they also held themselves a bit apart.

"I thought the FBI didn't have rules on employees dating or being married?"

"Someone's done their homework. They don't, but it's not exactly smiled upon. By then CJ and I had worked in the field and been a couple for, damn, five or six years. Getting married was just me being old-fashioned. Some things we do for the job, and some things we do for ourselves. You need more for yourself, Aiden, and I'm sorry it has to be this way, but maybe when all this is cleared up she can come back."

"I hope she doesn't." He lifted his gaze to the ceiling. "I hope she goes somewhere and finds a new life she doesn't want to leave behind."

Aiden didn't know how long this thing with Evers would take or where it would go, but he didn't want Madison to wait for him. Today's false hope was hard enough to swallow. She had a life to live, and he'd chosen his path, regardless that he liked to blame the FBI for backing him into a corner.

"Think you can talk her into lying low until we can get the paperwork rolling for her?" Kathy asked.

"Yeah."

"Why don't you take the morning off? I can open the shop." She squeezed his arm. "Say good-bye. Make it count."

"I'll do that." He scrubbed a hand across his face. The lump was back. Good-byes sucked.

Kathy turned and headed for the bunker, a long room they'd outfitted with cots and some emergency medical equipment. They'd set Roni up after Kathy's initial checkup. The twins would have to keep a low profile for a while until they knew if the cops connected them to the theft at the airport or not. It was doubtful, since the FBI had scrubbed the national databases of their existence, but there was always a chance something could go wrong. And it usually did to some degree.

He stood once more, facing the office door. Once he woke her up, there would be questions he couldn't answer. For a few, brief seconds, she'd looked at him with suspicion and distrust, and though he'd deserved it, he hated it too.

Kathy was right about one thing, he needed something for himself. There was more to life than taking Evers down, and he'd lost sight of that. Madison had made him realize there was more than the job. He couldn't replace her. No woman would touch his soul as she had, but life rolled on.

Aiden pushed the office door open and winced when it squeaked. Madison inhaled sharply and sat up straight, swaying in the chair and blinking.

"Hey, it's just me," he said quietly.

"Hey." She rubbed her face, smearing a bit of the makeup on her cheek.

"Come on, let's get some sleep." He took her hand and tugged her to her feet.

"Where we going?"

"My house. Canales got picked up on a minor charge and is spending the night in jail, so we're good." For tonight, at least. Very soon, they'd have to do something about the crew leader.

"Oh, good."

He guided her out to the street where he'd parked one of their many secondary vehicles. Once he got Madison situated and buckled, he checked in with Emery one last time to make sure the coast was clear.

It took three car changes and nearly forty-five minutes to make the trek home, but on nights like these, it paid to be cautious. They'd never before been able to make a grab at Evers so directly. Usually they were catching chatter that a shipment had arrived and snatching it from his lackeys or even his buyers. Things were about to get a lot more interesting now that they made a direct hit. Not to mention Dustin was going to get a new asshole when the bitcoins turned up fake.

Tomorrow was going to suck. The waiting was the worst, and they'd be stuck sitting on their hands to see what Evers's next move would be. The most telling thing would be where the blame fell. Right now, the easiest scapegoat would be Madison. She had too many ties to Evers and working at the airport was too convenient.

If he'd stuck to the plan and had little to do with her, would things have turned out differently?

Aiden pulled the Challenger into the barn and cut the engine. Madison was still out cold. No surprise there. He leaned against his door and watched her for a moment. Though the interior was dark, he knew the shape of her face well enough to trace it in by memory.

How was it she'd wormed her way into his heart in such a short amount of time?

"Hey. Wake up." He gently shook her.

Madison groaned and sat up, blinking around her.

"We're at my place. Come on."

He got out and made it to her side of the car before she'd even unfastened her seat belt. He took her hand and helped her out of the car. Chances were it would be the last time. Tomorrow he'd turn her over to FBI agents who would make her into a new person.

They left the barn behind and entered his house through the kitchen. He couldn't remember the last time anyone had been to his place, save Julian.

"Wow, nice kitchen." Madison strolled around the square kitchen with its island.

"And I barely cook. Irony is that the sellers redid it just before I bought it."

"That's a shame." She opened the fridge.

"Shit. Are you hungry?" There wasn't anything in his fridge or freezer considering he barely had time to sleep here as of late.

"Not really, just being nosy."

"You should probably get some sleep. Why don't you take my bed?" He'd reinforced the exterior wall and window. The door also had a sturdy lock and kickplate, which made it the safest room in the house, because again—he mostly just slept here.

Madison merely blinked at him, still half asleep on her feet. He took her hand and led her through the living room and into his bedroom. How he wished this were under different circumstances. He'd like nothing better than to lock the door and spend the next couple

g to bed?" she asked.
. I'm—working on a few things." He
ed laptop.
g away from her. That was what he
e right thing to do. For her and him.
ver, hadn't gotten that memo. She
, and instead of telling her to go away
n't be privy to his work, he stared at
his moment to memory. Her odd, half
r hair was messy, how her nipples peb-
e cloth and the flex of her thighs as she
ever particularly admired a woman's
ot until her bout in that skirt.
d his lap, one hand on his shoulder while
tern on his cheek with the other.
that tired anymore," she said.
e groaned. This couldn't happen. In a
rs, she'd hate him. Wouldn't she?
we should talk."
at do you want to talk about?" She didn't
wer. She kissed him, her warm, soft body
r arms wrapping around him.
ow," he managed to get out between kisses.
morrow." She buzzed his lips then chuckled.
fuck me instead."
empting. His body was already reacting, his
ening, his blood pumping, but he couldn't.
?
issed his lips, his face. Her touch was tender,
him down in the one way he couldn't defend
If she wanted to hit him, he knew what to do.
en she treated him with care, when she made
ile and laugh, he had no defense for that. None

morrow, he'd regret this, but right now, he
d her.

of hours getting lost between the sheets, except he couldn't do that. Tomorrow, she'd hate him for taking her life away.

"Bathroom's through there. If you need anything, holler, okay?"

She glanced at the big, king bed then at him.

"Where are you going?" she asked.

"I've got a few things to do." Like, make the couch into a bed, where he'd lie awake all night.

"Are you going to tell me anything?" She walked to his side of the bed and sat down on the edge, arms wrapped around herself.

"I can't. It's safer the less you know."

"But you work for the FBI?"

"I didn't say I worked for them." Not that they hadn't offered, but that was one noose he'd like to keep his neck out of.

"But, why couldn't the FBI just raid the airport?" She toed off her shoes and turned toward him.

He bit his lip to keep from saying more. God, wouldn't he like to know the answer to that?

"Can you just tell me if I did the right thing? If helping you was worth it?" She pulled her knees up to her chest and wrapped her arms around her legs, looking so small and lost.

Aiden went to her, sitting next to her and reaching out to grab her hand.

"Our methods aren't exactly normal, but we're fighting the good fight, I promise you. What we're doing—it's keeping drugs off the street. And we're working on the source. That's what I can tell you."

Madison blew out a breath. "Okay."

"Get into bed." He got up and pulled the covers

down, holding them for her while she slid between his sheets and snuggled his pillow.

Aiden kissed her cheek, unable to just leave her.

"Finish up your stuff and come back to me, okay?" she said.

He didn't answer, because he wouldn't be joining her. It was past time to cut the string binding them together. Severing this connection was going to suck, but it had to be done.

Aiden tiptoed out of the room and closed the door behind him. Despite the weariness wearing him down, he needed to do something. He grabbed his laptop from his hall closet hiding spot and settled in on the couch. Though electronic surveillance was mostly Emery's gig, there were a few things anyone could do.

He brought up a couple popular social media sites and the profiles of several of the Eleventh's key players. The chatter could sometimes be a tip-off. Most of the pertinent posts he could see on the public profiles were trash talk to the effect of getting even.

Another time, and Aiden could have spun this, figured out a way to deflect the Eleventh's attention, except they couldn't afford to take an eye off Evers. Whatever his next move was going to be would change the game.

He fired off a message to Emery, CJ, and Julian.

Looks like 11th will make bail 2morrow.

They'd have to figure out something to keep them busy. Maybe set them up, though Aiden didn't like it. The crew was getting crooked enough they'd make their own bed, but it would be highly convenient to shove them in the pen now.

Evers's people were silent online, which seemed to be

Aiden breat
touch, they were
disposal of evide
was poised to stra
people who bough
a used car special.
little, no one was the
were doing. And the
people with enough ca
be rich boys and peop
world. The drugs would
their crew's only other o
uct and that could get me
handle the stuff for eviden

If their operation were
would sit in evidence. But h
deep cover, flipping the cars ga
might figure out a way to pin t
had to play their role true to th

He set the laptop on the coffee
staring at the ceiling. If anything
now than before. Which sucked.

The bedroom door swung o
shouldn't look, but he couldn't stop
had stripped down to her tank top and
was drawn over one shoulder and she l
door slightly. It was a visual he didn't ne
he'd want to see that every morning.

Aiden cupped the back of her head and pressed close, scooting to the edge of the sofa until their bodies fit together like puzzle pieces. She moaned and moved her hips. He broke the kiss, resting his forehead against hers. A wave of pleasure rolled over him.

He wrapped his arm around her hips and stood, swaying slightly as he found his center of balance. Madison gasped and clung to him, kissing his neck and the sensitive place just behind his ear. He carried her into his bedroom, shoving aside tomorrow and what would come next in favor of being in the moment.

If this was the last time he got to be with her, why shouldn't he enjoy it?

He set her down on the edge of the bed and stepped back, admiring her. She smiled and it felt as though an invisible fist gripped his heart. Losing her was going to suck. A piece of him would go with her, wherever she went. Even if she hated him. He'd always love her, even when she left.

She slid off the bed and reached for his shirt. He shook off her hands, but she pushed them away.

"Let me, for once?" She grasped the hem of his shirt and tugged the dirty, grease-stained garment up and off.

He tossed it toward the hamper, not caring if it made it in or not. She grasped his waistband and loosened the belt, leaving it in the loops while she tabbed his jeans open. There was nothing hurried about her movements. She paused to kiss his chest, just over the tattoo. Her fingers smoothed over his side, trailing over a scar and following the line of muscles along his abdomen. She unzipped his pants and he toed out of his boots.

Madison's knees buckled, but he caught her by the elbows and walked her backward until she hit the edge of the bed.

"I'm not that patient tonight," he said.

She sat back on the mattress, her eyes a little larger.

He pushed the rest of his clothing off and stepped toward her. Madison's gaze slid down his body. She wanted him. He could see it in the way she stared at him. In time, if they had it, maybe he could win her heart, but they had hours left. He wouldn't tell her how he felt, but he'd show her, and maybe in a year or more when she didn't hate him anymore, she'd remember tonight and realize that he loved her.

Aiden splayed his palms over her thighs and ran his hands up, under her tank top. Madison lifted her arms, arching her back. He continued his journey across her stomach and to her ribs. Her breasts filled his hands, and for a moment he paused, squeezing them. She grinned up at him, that impish glint in her gaze. She was trouble, through and through.

He needed her. Now.

He kissed her, pushing her back onto the bed. She wiggled her tank top up and off, seemingly just as hungry for him as he was for her. He kissed down her neck, worshipping her body. Every inch of her had to be committed to his memory. He pushed the thoughts of why away, and focused on her. This moment.

He plumped her breasts, pushing them together and gently rolling the peaks between his fingers. She arched her back and groaned. He loved that sound, how she seemed to lose herself in what they did, completely surrendering herself to the passion between them. He kissed one nipple, then the other, taking his time with each.

"I thought you said you weren't patient." Madison's voice was low, husky.

"I'm not. I'm busy."

Aiden hooked his fingers into the waistband of her panties. Hadn't he put these very panties on her this morning? It seemed like ages ago. He tugged them down, running his palms along her thighs and down her calves. She had fantastic legs.

It didn't elude him that in helping him she was giving up everything. He couldn't ask that she love him, he hoped she never felt the way he did about her, because it would break him. This woman, this innocent and infuriating woman, could break him.

"We're doing this right," he muttered. He pulled the blankets and sheets down to the foot of the bed.

Madison rose to her knees, kneeling in the middle of the bed, and fuck if he didn't wish he could take a picture of just how damn sexy she was. Her hair tumbled over her shoulders, long enough to barely cover her areolas, yet she gave no mind to her nudity. All she wore was a smile. He couldn't risk a picture or even a memento of what they had. Only memories.

He grabbed a condom from the box he'd left on the nightstand. The receipt was still stuck under it from when he'd stopped at a drugstore a couple of days ago—just in case. He crawled into the bed and she snagged the foil packet before he could stop her.

Madison ripped it open, plucking the latex and tossing the wrapper over the side of the bed. He reached for it, but she held it away.

"I'm doing it," she said.

He opened his mouth to tell her exactly what was going to happen but . . .

How could he deny her?

"Go on then," he said.

He sat back on his heels and waited for her to scoot closer.

Madison's smile widened. She edged closer, wrapped her hand around his cock, and leaned in.

"Oh hell no. I'm coming inside you tonight." He dug his fingers into her hair and brought her face to his, kissing her deeply. She groaned and her grip tightened on his erection. He broke the kiss, sucking in a deep breath. Her hand slid up his length.

"Is that so?" Her smile couldn't get any bigger. Just looking at her like this was the best thing in the world.

"You wouldn't have come to me if that wasn't what you wanted."

"You got me." She lifted her shoulders. "I want you. All of you."

He released his hold on her hair, not trusting himself to say anything more.

She rolled the condom while holding his gaze, and if he weren't mistaken, her cheeks tinged just the palest pink. What they had was special. He liked that she felt free enough with him to be bold, even if it was at times damn inconvenient.

Madison placed her knees on either side of his. Her hands went to his shoulders before he caught on. He might not agree with all her decisions, but this one he could get behind. Aiden cupped her ass, steadying her. She straddled his lap, her breasts pressed against his chest, and their faces perfectly aligned. When she came, he'd see it play out on her face.

She chuckled and moved her hips, grinding against him.

"That's going to feel a lot better when I'm inside you. Trust me," he said.

"I do."

He plunged into her depths with his fingers. She sucked in a deep breath and dug her nails into his shoulders.

"Oh." Her fingers flexed and she leaned on him more. He curled his fingers, stroking her inner walls.

"I do love how wet you get," he murmured against her cheek.

of hours getting lost between the sheets, except he couldn't do that. Tomorrow, she'd hate him for taking her life away.

"Bathroom's through there. If you need anything, holler, okay?"

She glanced at the big, king bed then at him.

"Where are you going?" she asked.

"I've got a few things to do." Like, make the couch into a bed, where he'd lie awake all night.

"Are you going to tell me anything?" She walked to his side of the bed and sat down on the edge, arms wrapped around herself.

"I can't. It's safer the less you know."

"But you work for the FBI?"

"I didn't say I worked for them." Not that they hadn't offered, but that was one noose he'd like to keep his neck out of.

"But, why couldn't the FBI just raid the airport?" She toed off her shoes and turned toward him.

He bit his lip to keep from saying more. God, wouldn't he like to know the answer to that?

"Can you just tell me if I did the right thing? If helping you was worth it?" She pulled her knees up to her chest and wrapped her arms around her legs, looking so small and lost.

Aiden went to her, sitting next to her and reaching out to grab her hand.

"Our methods aren't exactly normal, but we're fighting the good fight, I promise you. What we're doing—it's keeping drugs off the street. And we're working on the source. That's what I can tell you."

Madison blew out a breath. "Okay."

"Get into bed." He got up and pulled the covers

down, holding them for her while she slid between his sheets and snuggled his pillow.

Aiden kissed her cheek, unable to just leave her.

"Finish up your stuff and come back to me, okay?" she said.

He didn't answer, because he wouldn't be joining her. It was past time to cut the string binding them together. Severing this connection was going to suck, but it had to be done.

Aiden tiptoed out of the room and closed the door behind him. Despite the weariness wearing him down, he needed to do something. He grabbed his laptop from his hall closet hiding spot and settled in on the couch. Though electronic surveillance was mostly Emery's gig, there were a few things anyone could do.

He brought up a couple popular social media sites and the profiles of several of the Eleventh's key players. The chatter could sometimes be a tip-off. Most of the pertinent posts he could see on the public profiles were trash talk to the effect of getting even.

Another time, and Aiden could have spun this, figured out a way to deflect the Eleventh's attention, except they couldn't afford to take an eye off Evers. Whatever his next move was going to be would change the game.

He fired off a message to Emery, CJ, and Julian.

Looks like 11th will make bail 2morrow.

They'd have to figure out something to keep them busy. Maybe set them up, though Aiden didn't like it. The crew was getting crooked enough they'd make their own bed, but it would be highly convenient to shove them in the pen now.

Evers's people were silent online, which seemed to be

protocol when shipments were due to arrive. It would be impressive if it weren't a criminal organization.

Aiden's phone beeped with an incoming text from Emery.

Go to bed. Just made delivery.

Aiden breathed a sigh of relief. With Emery's magic touch, they were able to move the cars. It wasn't a legal disposal of evidence, but considering their operation was poised to straddle the law, it worked. Besides, the people who bought the cars thought they were getting a used car special. Once the odometer was tweaked a little, no one was the wiser, unless they knew what they were doing. And they usually didn't. About the only people with enough cash to buy the flipped cars would be rich boys and people who wanted to play in their world. The drugs would go to the FBI, simply because their crew's only other option was to destroy the product and that could get messy. Easier to let the Hoovers handle the stuff for evidence.

If their operation were a normal FBI gig, the cars would sit in evidence. But because their mission was deep cover, flipping the cars gave them street cred. They might figure out a way to pin this on Evers yet, but they had to play their role true to the very end.

He set the laptop on the coffee table and leaned back, staring at the ceiling. If anything, he was more awake now than before. Which sucked.

The bedroom door swung open. He knew he shouldn't look, but he couldn't stop himself. Madison had stripped down to her tank top and panties. Her hair was drawn over one shoulder and she leaned against the door slightly. It was a visual he didn't need, because now he'd want to see that every morning.

"When you coming to bed?" she asked.

"Go back to sleep. I'm—working on a few things." He gestured to the closed laptop.

Distance. Staying away from her. That was what he was doing. It was the right thing to do. For her and him.

Madison, however, hadn't gotten that memo. She walked toward him, and instead of telling her to go away or that she couldn't be privy to his work, he stared at her, committing this moment to memory. Her odd, half smile, the way her hair was messy, how her nipples pebbled beneath the cloth and the flex of her thighs as she moved. He'd never particularly admired a woman's thighs, at least not until her bout in that skirt.

She straddled his lap, one hand on his shoulder while she drew a pattern on his cheek with the other.

"I'm not all that tired anymore," she said.

Inwardly he groaned. This couldn't happen. In a couple of hours, she'd hate him. Wouldn't she?

"Madison, we should talk."

"Why? What do you want to talk about?" She didn't let him answer. She kissed him, her warm, soft body melting, her arms wrapping around him.

"Tomorrow," he managed to get out between kisses.

"Fuck tomorrow." She buzzed his lips then chuckled. "Actually, fuck me instead."

It was tempting. His body was already reacting, his cock stiffening, his blood pumping, but he couldn't. Could he?

She kissed his lips, his face. Her touch was tender, wearing him down in the one way he couldn't defend against. If she wanted to hit him, he knew what to do. But when she treated him with care, when she made him smile and laugh, he had no defense for that. None at all.

Tomorrow, he'd regret this, but right now, he wanted her.

kissing her deeply. She groaned and her grip tightened on his erection. He broke the kiss, sucking in a deep breath. Her hand slid up his length.

"Is that so?" Her smile couldn't get any bigger. Just looking at her like this was the best thing in the world.

"You wouldn't have come to me if that wasn't what you wanted."

"You got me." She lifted her shoulders. "I want you. All of you."

He released his hold on her hair, not trusting himself to say anything more.

She rolled the condom while holding his gaze, and if he weren't mistaken, her cheeks tinged just the palest pink. What they had was special. He liked that she felt free enough with him to be bold, even if it was at times damn inconvenient.

Madison placed her knees on either side of his. Her hands went to his shoulders before he caught on. He might not agree with all her decisions, but this one he could get behind. Aiden cupped her ass, steadying her. She straddled his lap, her breasts pressed against his chest, and their faces perfectly aligned. When she came, he'd see it play out on her face.

She chuckled and moved her hips, grinding against him.

"That's going to feel a lot better when I'm inside you. Trust me," he said.

"I do."

He plunged into her depths with his fingers. She sucked in a deep breath and dug her nails into his shoulders.

"Oh." Her fingers flexed and she leaned on him more. He curled his fingers, stroking her inner walls.

"I do love how wet you get," he murmured against her cheek.

down, running his palms along her thighs and down her calves. She had fantastic legs.

It didn't elude him that in helping him she was giving up everything. He couldn't ask that she love him, he hoped she never felt the way he did about her, because it would break him. This woman, this innocent and infuriating woman, could break him.

"We're doing this right," he muttered. He pulled the blankets and sheets down to the foot of the bed.

Madison rose to her knees, kneeling in the middle of the bed, and fuck if he didn't wish he could take a picture of just how damn sexy she was. Her hair tumbled over her shoulders, long enough to barely cover her areolas, yet she gave no mind to her nudity. All she wore was a smile. He couldn't risk a picture or even a memento of what they had. Only memories.

He grabbed a condom from the box he'd left on the nightstand. The receipt was still stuck under it from when he'd stopped at a drugstore a couple of days ago—just in case. He crawled into the bed and she snagged the foil packet before he could stop her.

Madison ripped it open, plucking the latex and tossing the wrapper over the side of the bed. He reached for it, but she held it away.

"I'm doing it," she said.

He opened his mouth to tell her exactly what was going to happen but . . .

How could he deny her?

"Go on then," he said.

He sat back on his heels and waited for her to scoot closer.

Madison's smile widened. She edged closer, wrapped her hand around his cock, and leaned in.

"Oh hell no. I'm coming inside you tonight." He dug his fingers into her hair and brought her face to his,

He pushed the rest of his clothing off and stepped toward her. Madison's gaze slid down his body. She wanted him. He could see it in the way she stared at him. In time, if they had it, maybe he could win her heart, but they had hours left. He wouldn't tell her how he felt, but he'd show her, and maybe in a year or more when she didn't hate him anymore, she'd remember tonight and realize that he loved her.

Aiden splayed his palms over her thighs and ran his hands up, under her tank top. Madison lifted her arms, arching her back. He continued his journey across her stomach and to her ribs. Her breasts filled his hands, and for a moment he paused, squeezing them. She grinned up at him, that impish glint in her gaze. She was trouble, through and through.

He needed her. Now.

He kissed her, pushing her back onto the bed. She wiggled her tank top up and off, seemingly just as hungry for him as he was for her. He kissed down her neck, worshipping her body. Every inch of her had to be committed to his memory. He pushed the thoughts of why away, and focused on her. This moment.

He plumped her breasts, pushing them together and gently rolling the peaks between his fingers. She arched her back and groaned. He loved that sound, how she seemed to lose herself in what they did, completely surrendering herself to the passion between them. He kissed one nipple, then the other, taking his time with each.

"I thought you said you weren't patient." Madison's voice was low, husky.

"I'm not. I'm busy."

Aiden hooked his fingers into the waistband of her panties. Hadn't he put these very panties on her this morning? It seemed like ages ago. He tugged them

Aiden cupped the back of her head and pressed close, scooting to the edge of the sofa until their bodies fit together like puzzle pieces. She moaned and moved her hips. He broke the kiss, resting his forehead against hers. A wave of pleasure rolled over him.

He wrapped his arm around her hips and stood, swaying slightly as he found his center of balance. Madison gasped and clung to him, kissing his neck and the sensitive place just behind his ear. He carried her into his bedroom, shoving aside tomorrow and what would come next in favor of being in the moment.

If this was the last time he got to be with her, why shouldn't he enjoy it?

He set her down on the edge of the bed and stepped back, admiring her. She smiled and it felt as though an invisible fist gripped his heart. Losing her was going to suck. A piece of him would go with her, wherever she went. Even if she hated him. He'd always love her, even when she left.

She slid off the bed and reached for his shirt. He shook off her hands, but she pushed them away.

"Let me, for once?" She grasped the hem of his shirt and tugged the dirty, grease-stained garment up and off.

He tossed it toward the hamper, not caring if it made it in or not. She grasped his waistband and loosened the belt, leaving it in the loops while she tabbed his jeans open. There was nothing hurried about her movements. She paused to kiss his chest, just over the tattoo. Her fingers smoothed over his side, trailing over a scar and following the line of muscles along his abdomen. She unzipped his pants and he toed out of his boots.

Madison's knees buckled, but he caught her by the elbows and walked her backward until she hit the edge of the bed.

"I'm not that patient tonight," he said.

She sat back on the mattress, her eyes a little larger.

Chapter Twenty-Four

Madison groaned. The bed pitched and rolled. Morning storms were the worst.

"What? There now?" Aiden's voice sliced through her sleepy fog.

She picked her head up and cracked one eye open.

The white room with the dark wood furniture was not her boat. Aiden shimmied into his jeans, his head tilted to the side with his phone pressed to his ear.

"I'll be there. Keep him busy." Aiden turned toward the bed and paused when he saw her.

She smiled and one side of his mouth hitched up and that dimple, man, she'd stroked his face and he'd smiled at her so big last night. When she saw the dimple, she knew she touched his heart. The world was a crazy, messed-up place, and yet they'd found each other. She didn't know what was going to happen today or tomorrow, but she trusted him. And yeah, she was more than a little in love with him.

He slid his phone into his back pocket and zipped up his jeans.

"Hey, sorry I woke you. It's a lot earlier than I'd have liked to get up." He circled the bed to sit on the edge.

"It's okay. I'm surprised your phone didn't wake me." She threaded her fingers through his, unable to keep the warm fuzzies at bay. Was it insane to think that she'd found someone amidst the hell Dustin tried to create?

"It was on vibrate. I've got to run over to the garage for a bit."

"Is this a Classic Rides thing or a . . . ?" Was she allowed to say "FBI" out loud?

"Neither, really, just an appointment I forgot about. Why don't you go back to sleep and I'll bring you back some breakfast?" He ducked his head and kissed her, quick and hard. "Then I can wake you up the right way."

Her toes curled. Exactly what way was the right way? She couldn't wait to find out.

"I like the sound of that."

"Me too." He stood and walked toward the closet.

She'd like nothing more than to spend all night in bed with Aiden, but what about Everglades Air? Her job? Her friend? What if the cops had tried to find her?

"Hey."

"Hm?" Aiden stepped out of the closet and pulled a shirt on.

"What are we going to do about last night and me?" Last night she'd done what had felt right in the moment. Today, she was beginning to realize just how far the ramifications went. Not only had she stolen from a criminal—she'd stolen from her boss. Someone who treated her like family.

"We're working on it. I just need you to hang here. Lie low. Don't answer the door for anyone. Lock this door and sleep until I get back." He pointed at the doorframe. "This is reinforced steel. This whole room has been outfitted as a safe room."

"Oh. Like the garage?" She tucked the blankets around her and sat up.

"Exactly like the garage." Aiden pulled on his socks and shoved his feet in his shoes. He seemed to be in an awful hurry for just an appointment.

"Have you seen my phone?" She glanced around.

"No. It's probably for the best if you turn it off. Don't call anyone. I've got to go." He crawled up from the foot of the bed and kissed her once more. "I'll be back."

"Can't wait."

She smiled and watched his ass while he slipped out of the bedroom. Why did she have the sinking suspicion Aiden was keeping something from her? Because he probably was under some guise of protecting her. She didn't like it, but then again, she was in deep now. At least she didn't have to worry if what Aiden was doing was the right thing or not.

Except, she'd done the bad thing last night. Lily and her family were going to be worried about her. And she'd betrayed them, for the sake of doing a good thing. It was such a messed up situation to be in. But Aiden was working with the FBI. They were the good guys. Weren't they? She flopped back on the bed and blew out a breath.

For her sanity, she needed to believe Aiden would do the right thing by her. That in the end, the bad guys would get what they deserved and the victims—like Lily's family—would be compensated for their loss. Besides, Aiden had to be the good guy in all of this. If not, she'd just fallen for another con man criminal.

Madison placed her hand over her heart and stared up at the ceiling. It had been so long since she'd cared for a man. The anxious uncertainty swirling in her breast was enough to drive her nuts. When all of this was over, she had to wonder what her future would be. Could something work between Aiden and her? She was reasonably certain the man cared for her. The sex was great, but it was more than that. When he was in her and staring at her, it was as if for those few brief seconds their souls meshed and they were one person.

The digital clock on the dresser ticked away the minutes, but Madison couldn't seem to fall back to sleep. With as little rest as she'd had over the last couple of nights, it was a wonder she hadn't just passed out when her head hit the pillow. Aiden had been gone for over half an hour. At this rate, she wasn't going back to sleep. Between her obsession with Aiden and worry over Lily and work, she was up for the day.

She sighed and slipped out of bed, arms wrapped around herself, and tiptoed around the room. Aiden said she shouldn't contact anyone, but what if Lily was trying to find her? Or, maybe they didn't realize she was gone? But that would be silly. There were two other people who knew she'd been there last night. She could look at the messages, maybe check her voice mails, couldn't she? The last thing she wanted was for Lily and her family to be worried about her.

Madison frowned and turned in a circle, taking in the room. Her jeans were folded on top of the dresser with her bra. Wouldn't she have left her phone there? Maybe she'd dropped it in the barn or in the car?

There was no way she'd go back to bed now. Between the albatross of guilt weighing her down and Aiden's promise of return—she was awake, like it or not. She got dressed and scraped her hair back into a messy bun. Aiden had said to stay put. It wouldn't hurt to take a quick look around in case she'd dropped it.

She flipped the lock and peeked out, but the house was empty.

One quick look around.

Madison wiggled her feet into her shoes and wandered out into the living room. Aiden's home was a little on the plain side—lots of white walls and tile floor—but the furniture was all bachelor. Large, overstuffed pieces that were black, brown, or solid wood. It was a change from the flamboyant norm that was a typical Florida home. No color or decoration. There was little to no personality here. It was as if he'd saved that entirely for the cars, leaving a blank slate here.

He worked with the FBI, whatever that meant.

There were so many questions. Could she be satisfied leaving them unanswered?

If she wanted to keep Aiden in her life, she might have to.

She let herself out through the back door and crossed to the garage. She tried the side door, but the knob didn't twist. It was locked up tight.

Madison sighed and stepped back. She should have known better. There was no way Aiden would leave his precious cars vulnerable. She wasn't sure where he lived, but petty crime was everywhere in Miami.

Just to satisfy her curiosity, she circled the barn and tried the sliding door, but the locking system was secure. She'd just have to hope Aiden got back soon. The only other place her phone could be was in his car. Making Lily and her family worry was low on her list of things to do.

She retraced her steps back to the house. Maybe there was a landline she could use, but it wasn't like she knew anyone's number these days. She stopped at the edge of the patio slab, her lungs refusing to draw breath.

The kitchen door was open.

She distinctly remembered shutting it.

If Aiden had returned she'd have heard the *purr* of his car.

Her heart pounded. She shouldn't have left the bedroom.

Madison turned—and ran straight into her rat-bastard ex-husband.

Aiden turned into Classic Rides, cursing under his breath. An unmarked SUV and a police cruiser sat out front in the shade of the palm trees that lined the side of the lot, the two uniformed cops staring at Detective Smith gesturing at Gabriel, who merely nodded. Good luck getting the mechanic to talk. Gabriel was about as silent as they came.

Aiden pulled the Challenger around behind the garage. The last thing he wanted right now was for the cops to look too closely at his street-modified ride. He doubted they'd give him the professional courtesy and turn a blind eye. He'd skirted the boundaries of legal.

He parked haphazardly and got out of the car. Kathy was waiting for him in the first open bay, little lines bracketing her mouth. It was the only indication today was not a normal day. The twins were nowhere to be seen and Julian would no doubt have made himself scarce. CJ was rolled under an old Ford pickup truck banging around. The man did not know cars—he knew tech—but he was learning.

Aiden handed Kathy Madison's cell phone. He'd hated taking it, but they couldn't risk her making contact with anyone right now. The world needed to think she'd been kidnapped. They'd have to find a body at a morgue that they could outfit with enough DNA to be a match and roll it into the Everglades, maybe with the last Bugatti. After that she could go into witness protection with no one the wiser she wasn't alive. Whatever the solution would be, first, they had to deflect the heat.

"Detective Smith." Aiden strolled out to join Gabriel.

"Wondering where you were." Matt had his hands on his hips and a pair of aviators perched on his nose.

"It's Monday. We usually give everyone a little leniency. What can I do for you?" They'd been pretty lucky to stay under the Miami-Dade Police Department's radar until now. They might be an FBI operation, but their methods weren't always legal. So long as they produced the desired results, the people in charge didn't ask any questions. It'd only been a matter of time. Too bad they had to take notice of their little operation now.

"Where were you yesterday around one o' clock?" Matt wasn't beating around the bush. At least he was only interested in the wreck and not last night. But, Everglades Air fell under a different jurisdiction. It would take time to connect anything to them—if they ever did.

"Yesterday?" Aiden stared over the detective's shoulder. "Hm, Gabriel, didn't I run up to Boca for those parts for the Jag?"

"Yes, sir."

"Anyone confirm you were there?"

"Uh, sure, I've got a guy who picks up parts for me. He knew I was coming, but left them on the porch." Aiden dug out his wallet and handed over his junk dealer's business card. So often, people rolled the old cars into the junkyard and left them. The bodies might be weak, but the parts were still good.

"But he didn't see you?" Matt took the card and turned it over.

"Nope, but he's got a security camera. I bet I'm on it." Crap. He'd swung by the junkyard an hour before he'd met Dustin for the trade. They'd have to do some quick work to get the time stamps altered, but there was always the chance the junk dealer wouldn't work with the cops unless a warrant was involved.

"Anyone else confirm you were there? What route did you take?"

Sweat rolled down Aiden's spine. Security and traffic cameras were too risky to doctor. If Matt wanted to track him down that bad, the only thing stopping him would be an FBI order.

"What's going on, man? Bitter I took your date?"

Matt frowned and glanced at Gabriel, then back to Aiden.

"Gabriel, why don't you go help with that pickup truck? I promised we'd have that transmission ready by Wednesday." Aiden spoke without glancing away from Matt.

"Sure thing, boss." Gabriel turned and strolled back into the garage.

Matt took a step toward Aiden. The detective was a couple inches shorter, with the build of a runner. The sport coat was too tight on his shoulders. A little digging into the detective proved he liked to be hands-on working a case. Aiden figured the coat and glasses were for show, to appear more official.

"I know you have a beef with the Eleventh Street Gang. One of their guys caused a wreck yesterday, shot up a few cars before we picked him up, but strange thing is, there's no driver for the other car. A couple people said a man with light-colored hair was pulled out of a Mustang by a guy driving a pickup truck and left the scene. Wouldn't know anything about that, would you? Don't you have another guy, a redneck, that works for you?"

The ache in Aiden's shoulder, neck, and back knew all about that, but he'd have to power through it. He resisted the urge to glance behind him to see if John's truck was there.

"Sorry, man, like I said, I had a busy day yesterday here." He thumbed over his shoulder.

"I don't believe for an instant you work for the FBI," Matt said quietly.

"We both know the truth, Detective."

"I don't believe it. Guy with your record? Not likely. Where'd you get the scratches from?" Matt gestured to Aiden's forearms.

When the window broke, the flying glass had cut him, but not much. Aiden held out his arms.

"Huh. I guess that happened last night."

"And last night you were . . . ?"

Aiden cocked a brow at Matt. "None of your business."

The phone in Aiden's back pocket began to vibrate, except he couldn't remember which phone was in what pocket. Was that his phone? Or the burner he'd been using?

"Look, DeHart, I don't know what you're doing, but I don't trust you. What were you doing yesterday?"

Aiden glanced over Matt's shoulder. The other two cops were too far away to hear what they were saying. "I had a face-to-face meet with an asset. There was FBI coverage. I bet part of it was recorded. Unfortunately, I can't share the details of our operation, but I can remind you that you've been asked to give us some space, so, Detective? Back the fuck off."

"I could arrest you for fleeing the scene. FBI won't look too kindly on you doing that."

Aiden forced his hands to relax. Punching Detective Smith wouldn't solve any of their problems.

The other pocket began to vibrate. Who the hell was trying to get ahold of him at close to eight in the morning? Something was happening. And good things rarely happened this early.

Aiden took a step toward Matt, staring him down. "I don't want to start a pissing match with Miami-Dade PD. I just want to do my job. Now, unless you've got some evidence to charge me with, get off my property."

"I'm sure our guys will swab the interior and find something. I'll pin this to your ass yet, FBI or no." Matt turned and stalked toward his SUV.

Aiden waited, watching the detective and two officers load up and roll out. Why did they have to get the detective with a vendetta?

He turned and strode into the garage, pulling both phones out.

"Aiden." Kathy hurried to his side and grabbed his forearm. "Emery just called, said someone's tripped the alarm at your house."

"Anything on the cameras?" While Aiden didn't stand for cameras inside the house, he had a couple outside, just in case.

"He's pulling those up."

Aiden unlocked his burner phone and pulled up the missed calls.

Dustin Ross.

"I've got to get back to my house. Something's not right." Damn it. Why hadn't he left Madison's phone? Maybe she'd have ignored it?

He jogged back to his car, Kathy behind him.

"I'll get Tori over there too, just in case."

"What about the paperwork?" The sooner Madison was gone, the safer she'd be.

"It's started, but that takes time."

Fucking FBI, with their red tape and a hundred forms. They were dealing with a life here, a very precious life.

Chapter Twenty-Five

Madison sucked air in through her nose. The fabric tied around her face cut into the corners of her mouth and wound round her eyes. Her head and shoulder throbbed from where she'd bounced off the metal floor of a van. Her wrists were bound together by what felt like a zip tie.

"Get her out of there." That was Dustin. She knew his sleazy voice anywhere.

Hands grabbed her by the shoulders and hauled her onto her bottom before dragging her across the van. Her feet dropped onto gravel and she was yanked upright, but she couldn't quite tell which way was up or down. She started to tilt, and a hand wrapped around her arm, jerking her in the other direction. She could smell tropical flowers and salt, while the sound of the ocean was so close she almost expected to be on the sand.

"Inside, now. She better have my money, Ross," someone else said. The voice was familiar, but she couldn't place it.

She whimpered. Another hand squeezed one of her many bruises in a tight grip. Her heart pounded and she was pretty sure she was going to be sick. Bile coated the back of her throat and she found it hard to breathe the thick, humid air.

Madison was hustled across gravel, dragged up some stairs and into a building. The cool air hit her and she shivered, chill bumps breaking out over her skin. She nearly tripped over her own feet as she was shoved to the side and forcibly turned. The feel of sunlight faded and everything behind her blindfold grew dark.

Fighting back was useless. She was still light-headed from the smack to her face when she'd tried to kick someone after they'd bound her wrists. Why had she left the bedroom?

"Put her there," the familiar voice said.

She was shoved onto a hard bench or seat. Someone jerked at the knot holding her blindfold and gag combination together and the fabric fell away. She spat out the taste of the material and blinked around her. It was a dark, interior room that could have been in any building. She was in a metal chair, and a few others lined the walls. A matching desk was shoved in the corner behind the three men staring at her.

Some goon she didn't recognize. Dustin Ross. And Michael Evers.

"W-what's going on?" Fear curdled her stomach. This was oh so very bad. She was fucked. Royally so. There was no coming back from this.

"I'm hurt." Michael Evers spoke without emotion or even the semblance of feeling. "Hello, Madison."

"What the hell?" Her voice trembled when she spoke. She twisted her wrists, but the plastic refused to give.

I'm dead. This is it.

"Did you know I've been protecting you? Dustin here wanted to kill you when you filed for divorce." He gestured at her ex-husband. "I told him no, because then people would ask questions and make a mess. It was far easier to let you live. Go on about your sad, miserable life. I did that. And this is how you repay me?"

She glanced at Evers, then Dustin. Dustin glared at her, the open hatred hot enough she flinched away from him. It wasn't a surprise he wanted her dead, she'd heard it herself a couple of times, but Evers had played a role in it?

"What are you talking about?" There was no way they were going to just let her go. She sucked in a deep breath and yelled, "Help!"

Dustin crossed the floor in three strides and backhanded her so hard she twisted and fell off the chair. Her head throbbed and firelike pain licked her skull. She curled up, bracing for a kick, something. Her head swam once more. It hurt so bad.

"Ross," Evers snapped. "Touch her again and I'll give her a baseball bat and a go at you just to watch you scream like a little girl."

"She's the reason we lost the drugs." Dustin thrust his finger at her, gaping at his boss.

"Would she have if you had left her alone like I told you to? And you're the reason the money is gone." Michael stared Dustin down, his expression cold. He gestured to the third man. "Pasha, help her up."

Pasha wasn't gentle, but he hoisted her back onto the chair before backing away and taking up a place at the door. Her face stung and she could taste blood now.

Michael grabbed another chair along the wall. The room was plain, light gray walls, polished concrete floors. Easy to clean up. He dragged the chair over to her and sat, face-to-face.

"I understand wanting to get back at Dustin. He hasn't been fair. I tried to stress to him that an amicable parting would make things go smoother in the future, but for some reason he seems intent on making things difficult. I propose a trade. You tell me where my shipment is and where my money has gone, and I make sure he leaves you alone." Michael nodded toward Dustin, who'd taken a few steps back.

"Then where were you when he burned my car? Or when he sent one of his idiots after me to scare me?" Fear turned into anger. He wanted to pretend like he gave a fuck? That he'd actually leash Dustin?

"Those were unfortunate instances." Evers glanced at his nails. Liars could rarely look someone in the eye.

"Bullshit."

He sighed and lifted his gaze to her face. Now she felt the power of his cold, calculated stare. She sucked in a deep breath and forced herself to stare right back at him. He took one step toward her, wrapped his fingers around her jaw, and forced her to look up at him.

"Where's my shipment and my money, Madison? I know you copied the drive, and I'm betting you were involved in last night's theft. I'm giving you options when I don't have to. I could let Pasha question you. He was in the Russian version of the Special Forces. They train anything human out of their men." Evers leaned forward, elbows on his knees. "I'd suggest he start with your fingers."

She was going to be sick.

She couldn't give up Aiden and his crew. She wouldn't. No matter what Michael Evers or her low-life ex-husband did, she'd take the knowledge to the grave if she had to, just to spite them.

Aiden pushed the front door of his house open, his heart hammering against his ribs.

"Madison? Madison, you here?" he called out.

"I told you—"

"Shut the fuck up, Emery." Aiden ducked into the bedroom—but the comforter was thrown back and she wasn't there. The living room was as he'd left it, even the laptop on the coffee table, but the back door was open.

"She's gone. They grabbed her behind the house," Emery said quietly. He'd called as soon as he'd gotten the feed up, but Aiden couldn't believe it. Not without seeing it with his own eyes.

He paced out back to the barn and punched in his entry code. Maybe—just maybe Emery had gotten it wrong? He stepped into the makeshift garage, but it was silent. The cars sat in their stalls, the workbenches untouched.

Madison was really gone.

This was his fault. He should have never brought her back to his place, not after Dustin had picked her up. He'd thought Dustin would be too busy to worry about Madison, but he'd been wrong when he couldn't afford to be. This was all on him. What had he done?

"Talk to me," Emery said.

Aiden couldn't reply. He covered his mouth with his hand and left the barn.

He stood in the space between the house and the barn. He'd had the slab poured to serve as a patio area, and Kathy had fussed at him about adding some color, so she'd put in some flowering plants along one side. The gravel ran right up to the concrete. This was where they'd grabbed her. And he hadn't been there to protect her.

"Julian's almost there. We're going to put together a plan. I've got some ideas."

"Shut up, Emery." He jabbed his Bluetooth, ending the call.

Michael Evers wouldn't hesitate to kill her. Sure, he might not pull the trigger, but he had no qualms about ordering it done. They didn't have enough solid evidence to charge Evers, but they knew he was responsible.

Aiden's phone began to vibrate, but the Bluetooth remained silent.

He jerked his burner phone out of his pocket and stared at Dustin's name floating on the screen. A ransom call?

"What?" Aiden didn't try to hide his frustration. Couldn't if he wanted to.

"Hey, Aiden."

"I thought we weren't going to do this anymore, Dustin? You know, after you wanted to kill me?" Aiden paced the length of the patio.

"It was nothing personal." Dustin's tone was far too . . . nice.

"What do you want?"

"While you were working Madison over, did you get any information about who she's hanging out with? Talking to? Maybe someone offering her a job?"

"What?" The shock was real. Dustin hadn't figured it out? It wasn't obvious?

"She's more of a bitch than I thought she was. She pulled one over on me and I need to know who helped her."

Julian's black GT-R pulled around the house, spraying gravel with the speed of his stop. Aiden stepped back, staring at Julian as he jumped from the car.

"Let me call you back. I might know something, but I have to look into it." Aiden needed off the phone. He had to gather his wits, come up with a story, something

Dustin would believe long enough for them to figure out how to save Madison.

"Great. Good."

"Dustin?"

"Yeah?"

"It's going to cost you."

"Whatever it takes. Just bring them to me. Today. Understand?"

Dustin was desperate. He must also be in a panic if he were being this straight with Aiden. The job he'd done for Dustin before had taken a considerable amount of vetting and scrutiny.

He ended the call and turned to face Julian, who stood at the edge of the slab.

"What are his demands?" Julian asked.

"They don't fucking realize it was us."

Julian's gaze widened. "The hell?"

"I'm serious. He wants to know who Madison's been hanging out with. Who I think might have helped her." Aiden paced up and down the slab.

Who did they know that was in town? There were plenty of guys running this or that scam. Miami was a hotbed of criminal activity.

"You aren't going to like this suggestion, but I need to at least put it out there." Julian crossed his arms over his chest.

Aiden stopped, staring at his friend. The job and war had changed Julian into someone Aiden barely recognized at times, but when it came down to a rock and a hard place, Julian was the only person Aiden wanted at his back.

"We could let Madison take the fall for us. She knew the minute she got involved with the job last night—"

"No. Hell no. Don't even say it. Don't you fucking say

it." Aiden crossed the distance between them before he realized what he was doing, fists balled up.

Julian took a step back and brought up his hands, palms out.

"Wow, right then—I told you I had to say it, not that we're going to do it."

"That's not an option."

"Okay, then we come clean to Dustin."

"If we do that, it's all over. We need a plan. Something else." Aiden glanced at Julian's car. Who was the only other group that had a beef with Dustin and Evers? It was stupid. Kind of crazy. And destined to fail. But they only needed it to be believable long enough to snatch Madison.

"What are you thinking, man?" Julian shifted from foot to foot.

True, Aiden sometimes had crazy plans that didn't always work, but right now, they needed crazy. That extra shot of nitrous oxide just before the finish line.

"Call Emery," he said.

The Bluetooth chirped once before ringing.

"Yes?"

"I need Raibel Canales's cell phone number and hopefully his location. Also, tell Tori and John I'll need them as backup."

"Is this a MacGyver plan?" In the background, Aiden could hear Emery typing.

"Maybe."

"I'll warn Kathy."

"We might not want to tell CJ and Kathy."

"Why?"

"Because they probably won't like my plan."

"This should be fun then."

"The number, Emery."

Emery rattled off Raibel's phone number. Aiden punched it into his contacts and saved it, just in case.

". . . Aiden?"

"Yeah?"

"Try to not get Tori hurt?"

"I'll do what I can." He ended the call and pressed dial on Raibel's contact. The Bluetooth rang and rang.

"Hola?"

"Raibel."

"Who is this?" Raibel's voice was unmistakable. Cold. The voice of a killer devoid of emotion.

"Heard you made bail this morning."

"Aiden DeHart. How the fuck did you get this number?"

"I paid someone."

"I'm going to nail your ass."

"Before you try to do that—want to know who boosted your cars and stole your product?"

Silence.

Technically, Aiden wasn't lying. He'd just worked as the extended arm for Dustin, taking care of the gig. Right now, whatever it took to get Madison out safe, he'd do it.

"If you aren't interested—"

"How do I know you're telling me the truth?"

"Because when I tell you who it is—it'll all make sense."

"I'll be the judge of that."

"Dustin Ross did it on Michael Evers's orders. He was asking me about you and your operation a few months ago, but I told him to go to hell. I want no part in what you guys are doing."

Raibel started cursing over Aiden in rapid-fire Spanish, some of the combinations he'd never heard before. Julian stared at him, shaking his head and pulling out his phone, no doubt to relay marching orders to their crew. Their window of opportunity would be small.

"I can show you—"

"Stay out of my way, DeHart."

"But—" Shit. Aiden needed to get Raibel to Dustin.

"I mean it." Raibel ended the call.

"Fuck." Aiden spun around, but stopped himself from throwing the phone. He didn't have time to replace it, not now. "We're going to have to grab Raibel."

"What are you planning?" Julian asked.

"Set Raibel up as Madison's accomplice. While they're busy with him, they won't notice us."

"Now, how exactly do you plan on grabbing Raibel?"

"No clue." Aiden shrugged. It wasn't a good plan, but it was better than giving a piece of his heart up for dead. Madison was his heartbeat. How could he live without her?

Chapter Twenty-Six

Madison twisted her hands, but the plastic only cut into her wrists further. They'd left her alone, but for how long? She had no idea what was going on, but she didn't think Michael's polite routine would last long. She'd seen TV. Her father had told a few war stories about men getting captured. Soon they'd turn Pasha loose on her to torture the information out of her. Would she be able to keep her mouth shut? Derby made her tough, but this was something so far beyond that.

What if she couldn't take the pain and told them?

She stood and paced the room. There hadn't been an opportunity to tell Aiden she loved him. Would he know? Maybe it was better if he didn't. The death of his sister hurt him, and she didn't want whatever happened to her to weigh on his soul.

The door banged open, bouncing off the wall. She whirled and froze. Dustin held out his hand, slamming the door back once more. He'd shed the suit jacket and now only wore slacks and a button-down shirt. How had she ever been attracted to him? Why hadn't she been able to see that he was a loser?

"I'm going to enjoy this," he said.

Fear almost paralyzed her.

Madison backed into the corner farthest from the door, pressing herself against the wall. Dustin strode across the room. She hunched her shoulders, unable to keep from cringing. The hell she'd let him hurt her without giving as good as she got. Madison focused on her rage, all the hardship he'd put her through. Dustin reached for her and at the last second she drew her leg up and kicked, aiming for his knee. She felt the impact on the ball of her foot and pushed harder, putting her shoulder against the wall and shoving him with everything she had.

Dustin cried out, pitching backward.

This might be her only chance at freedom.

Madison dodged his flailing arm and darted around him. If she could get out of the room, maybe she could get away. Hope spurred her on, but Pasha filled the doorway. She ran full tilt into him, almost bouncing off his bulk. He grabbed her by the arm. Dustin screamed profanities at her.

"No," she wailed. She couldn't even be satisfied about kicking Dustin because in the end, she was still at his mercy.

"Get her out of here," Dustin spat right behind her.

Pasha propelled her ahead of him down a hallway. They passed a utility room with a side entry. That must be where they'd brought her in. She was led into what must be the main part of the house—or mansion. It could have been any number of wealthy Miami homes. Windows, gleaming wood surfaces, polished marble floors, and light fabrics. A couple of green, fanlike plants sat near the windows, a bit of the outdoors brought inside. It was a contemporary beach theme. Michael Evers stood at a bar set into the corner of the room pouring a drink. Several other men with guns tucked in their waistbands sat or stood around the room.

Michael glanced up at her, swirling his drink. "Good. We're going to have a little chat with your friend soon. Make yourself comfortable."

Her heart leapt into her throat. She couldn't breathe. This wasn't happening.

Aiden was coming here? Why? He couldn't.

"Oh, scared now? Want to tell us the story of how you decided to steal from me?" Michael smirked.

"Fuck you," she said. Pasha shoved her into an armchair.

Dustin followed them, a dark scowl on his face.

"You shouldn't have gotten rid of this one, Dustin. She's got spunk. Probably manages money better than you do. Maybe she's the one I should have hired." Michael turned and strolled toward a white table strewn with papers.

This was bad. Very, very bad.

Aiden pulled the Challenger into the driveway of Michael Evers's mansion and cut the engine.

He was alone, but that was the way it would have to be. Raibel had disappeared into the wind and with no leads or time to spend finding him, Aiden had to do something. Making this meet with Dustin—and maybe Evers—was necessary. If nothing else, he wanted to get a glimpse of Madison and know she was okay. It was hard to think beyond that, but he had to. Given enough time, he could haul Raibel in to take the fall, but he wasn't ready to risk Madison's neck for him.

The two-story mansion was in one of the more modest, older money neighborhoods of Miami. Well respected and private, it was a hard place to purchase property. Emery's initial search told them the house had been renovated following Evers's buy. The end designs were well documented on both the architect and interior designer's portfolios. Thank goodness for the Internet. The house's beachfront location played a large part in the difficulty of maintaining it. The first level let out onto a stone patio with a pool that appeared to be an extension of the ocean. There was even a dock with a couple boats moored to one side, so they wouldn't disturb the view.

Two men approached from either side of the car, hands on their barely concealed guns. Aiden placed his hands on the steering wheel and waited for the one on his side to open the door. There was a big difference between the guys Dustin employed for flash, and those Evers had guarding his home. These were professionals who knew how to operate. Aiden needed to pull off appearing as nothing more than a guy with a thing for speed and grease under his nails.

His door opened and the man gestured for him to exit. Aiden stood and glanced around, taking stock of his surroundings. It was another beautiful Florida day. Too bad Evers was ruining it. There were men posted at intervals around the fence, discreet but probably armed. Something had Evers spooked. Was it them? Had they stepped into something they didn't understand?

"Should I do something?" he asked, playing dumb.

"Hands on your head. You packing?"

"No." Aiden laced his fingers behind his head and waited for the guy to pat him down. He had a knife in his boot, but anything else he'd never be able to sneak past these guys, so why bother? Neither checked the car.

"This way." The other led the way into Michael Evers's house.

Aiden had been outside of the mansion once casing

the joint, while it was being fumigated and empty, but never inside. He followed the guard in through a set of frosted glass doors that let into a foyer with a curved staircase. Julian had a long-range scope on the place, so he'd warned him of the layout and that he wouldn't like it.

Madison sat in direct view, in an armchair. One eye was slightly swollen and she sported a busted lip. She sucked in a breath when she saw him, but other than that, she gave up nothing.

Good girl.

It took everything in him to not rush to her side. God, she was amazing. Any other woman would have cracked and given them up already, but not Madison. She stuck by what she thought was right—even when it hurt her. If they lived through this, he'd make sure nothing ever hurt her again.

"This is your guy?" Michael Evers stood up from where he sat and walked toward Aiden. Evers sized him up as if he were livestock, his gaze calculating.

It was the closest Aiden had ever been to the man, and it was damn hard to not haul back and punch his lights out.

"Yeah, this is DeHart." Dustin sat on a bar stool, a bag of ice perched on his knee while he leaned on the bar. "He's a good guy."

"Then where is Raibel Canales?" Evers walked a slow circle around Aiden.

"Hell if I know. I only told Dustin what I heard, that it was Canales who hit you last night." Aiden couldn't look at Madison. He kept Evers in his sights, watching him in a mirror or by the reflection of the glass windows.

"How do you know it was Canales?" Evers asked.

"I don't know for sure, that's why I said—*it's what I've heard.* Everyone knows the Eleventh has been up in arms since their shit went missing. You're the big operation in town." Aiden shrugged and glanced at Evers, more interested in the placement of the others in the room.

"That's pretty convenient." Evers glanced at Madison. "How does she fit in?"

Aiden followed Evers's gaze to Madison. She was staring at him, her skin so pale and her hair sticking to her face despite the coolness of the room. "Canales used to date one of the derby girls. He's friends with Madison. Saw them hanging out at her bout." He shrugged, hoping she was following. "Sorry, babe, nothing personal."

"H-how could you?" Her words were barely above a whisper. Fear, no doubt, was crippling her.

"Like I said, nothing personal."

She sucked in a deep breath, something flashing in her gaze as she gathered herself. "You asshole, I trusted you!"

Ah, there she was, and that mouth.

"Shut her up." Evers waved at Madison.

A bulked-up guy with a shaved head stalked toward her, something that looked like a bandanna in hand.

Evers pivoted toward him, head tilted to the side. "It's too neat. You're lying, or there's something else going on. I don't know what it is, but I want to get to the bottom of this."

"Lying? Excuse me? I'm doing him a favor just showing up here." This wasn't good. Aiden had hoped to at least bluff his way through this meet and get out. There wasn't a realistic hope of extracting Madison, not without more of a plan in place. But if Evers pegged him as part of the hit, that would make the rescue a bit . . . problematic.

"You. Over there." Evers pointed at Aiden, then the sofa adjacent to Madison.

The guard who had escorted him inside stepped toward Aiden, gun in hand. Now that they were inside there was no need for pretenses. The MP-446 Viking handgun was pretty much a calling card. The guy was no joke. A Russian Spetsnaz soldier was a killing machine, pure and simple. The Russian government liked to pretend the Spetsnaz didn't exist anymore. If so, then where had this guy come from and how were the Russians involved with Evers?

"There's no need to point a gun at me." Aiden held up his hands and walked toward the sofa. Since he hadn't been able to wear a wire into this, Emery had hacked his phone, making it capable of transmitting audio from Aiden's location.

He sat on the sofa, leaning back and forcing himself to pretend he was at ease. Madison stared at him, wide-eyed and innocent. He just kept not looking at her, at least not directly. He could see her in the reflection of the glass easily enough. God, he hated what they'd done to her.

Dustin seemed content to nurse a drink and grimace at his knee, while the guards stared at Aiden. At least six sets of eyes were trained on him, one of which was a Spetsnaz, two carried themselves like Special Forces. The other three might pass for Cuban at a glance, but Aiden was willing to bet if he got his hands on their passports, they'd be Colombian nationals. Americans, Russians, and Colombians. Interesting and potentially volatile. They didn't all play well together, so what were they doing working for Evers?

From the little surveillance they'd been able to do, they knew there were close to twenty people in the mansion. The staff was nowhere to be seen, so eight laypeople were unaccounted for somewhere. Which left—what? Four guards outside? Where was Evers's accountant? His lackey? The other people who helped in his day-to-day operations?

"Here's the problem." Evers reached behind him and pulled out a pistol. "You're lying. I know it. You know it. But he doesn't."

"What?" Dustin blinked, looking for all the world like the idiot he was.

"We don't clean up messes, Ross." Evers pivoted toward him, lifted the pistol, and shot, hitting Dustin square in the chest. The report of the gun was enough to make ears ring.

His arms flung out and he toppled backward on the stool, hitting the rug.

Evers stalked toward Dustin, lying on the floor in a growing pool of his own blood, gasping for air. Madison hunched over, whimpering on the sofa.

"I warned you about causing a mess, and now look what you've done. Years of working with the Colombians, possibly ruined because of you and your greed." Evers glanced up. "Call Juan. Clean this up."

Aiden caught a flash of light out of the corner of his eye. It was beyond the house, at the fence line. He didn't know what that signal was supposed to entail, but suffice to say—there was a plan forming. He just needed to bide his time. Either his crew would get them out of here, or he'd have to use his distraction card and make a run for it. God, he didn't want to have to use the distraction, but Madison was worth it. He'd once said he'd bet his Challenger that she was innocent, well, it was time to pay up.

He wished he could communicate it to Madison, give her at least a little reason to relax. She might have hated Dustin, but seeing him killed in front of her was traumatic. She must be frightened. He hated that she was here, that he'd put her in danger. This was all supposed to be easy. Where had it gotten off the rails?

They descended into an uneasy silence, punctuated by Dustin's wheezing breath.

One side of Evers's mouth hitched up and a sinking feeling plunged through Aiden. "Pasha, I'd like for you to make our female guest less comfortable while I have a chat with Aiden, here. I think we have a lot to discuss, don't you?"

Madison tried to speak around the gag, but it was tied too tight. Aiden didn't dare move to help her. Had he already made a wrong move? Or was Evers bluffing? What were they really going to do to Madison?

Pasha crossed to them. He grabbed Madison by the shoulders and hauled her to her feet. Aiden didn't look at her, didn't glance, lest he make this worse by appearing to care, though on the inside he was ready to bash in the heads of every piece of shit in this place.

"Where's my product, DeHart?" Evers asked.

Whatever his crew was going to do, they needed to get on with it, before Madison paid for their crimes.

A phone chimed across the room. One of the guards glanced at it. Though Aiden's focus was on Evers, he saw the man jerk.

"Boss," he said.

"Not interested," Evers replied, never taking his gaze off Aiden.

Another series of flashes made him tense. Whatever was going to happen was about to go down. Something moved on the other side of the frosted front doors.

"No, boss, look—"

A utility truck slammed through the front doors, shattering the glass. Aiden threw himself onto the ground, taking cover behind another sofa. The two Special Forces guards moved toward the danger, while Evers and the Colombians took cover out of line from the front door. The rear fenders of the truck were too wide to make it through the doorframe. It lurched to a stop, engine chugging, but no one in the driver's seat.

For a second, no one moved, not even Aiden. What the hell was that?

A red car streaked through the yard, a man hanging out of the passenger window with an automatic rifle. Gunfire broke the stillness as bullets peppered the glass. Little white circles spread where the bullets hit the glass—but did not break.

The Eleventh.

His crew knew the house was outfitted with bulletproof glass.

More cars drove across the lawn. People yelled from elsewhere in the house. Maybe the staff? The truck bobbed and moved a moment before two men stood up in the back of the bed, guns in hand.

The two Special Forces guards picked them off before the Eleventh guys got off a single shot.

Aiden glanced in the direction Pasha had taken Madison then to Michael Evers. This could be his chance to get Evers, but doing so would put Madison at risk.

Evers strode to the desk and unhooked his laptop. "Shoot anyone who comes through that door. Understand me?"

The Special Forces guards didn't move or acknowledge their order. Evers made a disgusted sound in the back of his throat. His gaze fell on the two Colombians.

"Come on," he said. His lip curled in contempt.

The Colombians drew their weapons, shoulders hunched, and followed their boss.

Any minute now the Eleventh would find an unlocked door, or another way in. The Special Forces guys were worth ten goons, but even they could be overwhelmed. This could turn into a bloodbath—and Aiden had no gun.

Chapter Twenty-Seven

Evers strode down the same hall where Madison had gone earlier.

More shouting from the truck and bullets pelting the house drew the attention of Evers's security. They weren't paying attention to Aiden.

He army-crawled across the living room toward Dustin. A quick check of his pulse revealed he'd died, probably choking on his own blood. Aiden patted the man's pockets until he found a gun. The other guards were too busy to pay him any mind, so he rose to his feet and lunged down the hall.

From the sound of it, someone had moved up to take the place of the fallen street racer. The Eleventh was either about to establish themselves as a major player in the Miami drug scene, or be massacred. Either way, Aiden didn't want to be caught up in it.

That's why Raibel had been willing to take him at his word. It wasn't so much a belief in Aiden's bullshit, but more just an excuse to storm the old guard, as it were.

Only one winner would emerge from this kind of standoff. It'd be better if Raibel emerged the victor—and how fucked up was that thought?

Aiden rolled toward the hall, throwing his weight into the momentum. He pushed to his feet, keeping low, and grabbed the knife from his boot. He ducked down the hall. Bullets hit the side of the house, sounding almost like popcorn popping as it hit the reinforced walls.

Shutting out the sounds of gunfire and yelling was a difficult task, but Aiden needed to listen for Madison or Evers. Evers's men would kill Madison, given the opportunity. He clearly didn't care what his boss said in regard to her. All he saw was rage. Aiden's focus had to be getting her out alive, no matter that this was the closest he'd ever been to the criminal.

Aiden pushed the first door open, gun at the ready. The office was empty. The second was a cleaning closet. The third door was open. He could hear whimpering inside. When he caught Evers, it would take an act of God to keep from killing the son of a bitch.

He stepped into the doorway.

Madison sat in a corner, arms contorted behind her, knees drawn up to her chest. Hair had come loose from her bun and hung limp around her face. The Spetsnaz was nowhere to be seen. He rushed to her side, but pulled back from crushing her to him. They weren't out of the clear yet.

"You okay?" Aiden slashed the bonds holding Madison's ankles together and the makeshift gag.

"What are you doing here?" she demanded the moment it was out.

"Getting ice cream."

"You aren't fucking funny."

"Did you see which way Evers went?"

He yanked his phone out and hit dial.

"You alive?" Julian asked through the Bluetooth headset.

"Barely. What the hell is going on?" Aiden asked.

"He went that way." Madison pointed down the hall.

"Eleventh showed up. They've got the place fucking surrounded. I wasn't aware they had assault rifles or anything like this gear. This is looking bad, man. How many people does Evers have in there?" Julian had that tone in his voice, the one that said he was ready for a fight.

"I'm not sure. There're four guards up front and one I can't account for." Aiden crossed to the door and glanced back toward the living room.

"The four outside are dead. What about Dustin and Evers?"

"Dustin is dead. Evers, I'm going to find, but he's got a Russian super soldier with him."

"Those aren't good odds. You need to get out of there now, man. We pulled back to the property line on the east side. Tori said to tell you sorry, but the Challenger's a goner."

"Do I have an exit open?" Aiden could hear yelling from the front of the house, but no gunfire. He put his back against the wall and peered out of the door, glancing toward the front and the back.

"Not really. I mean, you could get out through the back—"

"I bet that's where they went. There's house staff I haven't seen."

"Damn. If you could find a way out, I'd get you. Don't know how, but I'd get you."

Aiden grabbed a set of zip ties from the desk and shoved them into his pocket.

"I'm going to find Evers. If there's a way out of here, he'll be using it. It was about money all along. Tell Emery he was right. Dustin drained Evers and they were in the hole. That's why the bitcoins were so important. Tell him." In case Aiden couldn't.

He ended the call, his gaze on Madison.

She seemed to be on the verge of tears. "God, I hated him, but I'd never wish him dead."

"I know, baby, I know. I need you to hold it together, okay?

"What are we looking for?" she asked.

"Evers. We follow him out of here, catch him if we can."

Madison nodded, but she was still so pale and she swayed a bit.

"Come on. Stay close. Keep your head down." He wanted to take care of Madison and look after her injuries—there wasn't time. If they didn't get out soon, they could be killed.

"What's going on?" She flinched as gunfire hit the house.

"I told the Eleventh that Dustin hit them, and now they're retaliating or maybe just hitting the old guard. It's a power-play move, regardless." He peered down the hallway back toward the living room. There were a few bodies slumped over the top of the truck now.

"Why would you do that?"

"Diversion. Come on." He took her hand and led her farther into the house.

A large kitchen spread out to their right, the dining room overlooking the ocean. The back doors were open. The cars couldn't drive over this part of the property because of the large rocks placed around the pool to shield it from neighbors. The gang's heavily modified cars simply didn't have enough lift to access this part of the property.

"Aiden!" Madison pointed at the beach, barely in their line of sight. Evers and three of his guards were making the jump from a dock to a small speedboat.

"Damn it." Aiden strode toward the door, snatching his phone up. "Evers is getting in a boat. The speedboat, white, red stripe." He didn't know if Emery had a way to track the boat, but if there was one, the Walking Brain would have his back.

"Watch out." Madison tugged him sideways. Two men crouched on the rocks, their attention on the house—not the boat and Evers's getaway.

They crouched behind the kitchen bar. Bullets hit the back windows.

It appeared he needed to use his distraction card—again. Aiden punched in the number he'd committed to memory that morning.

"There's going to be an explosion. I need you to run with me. Can you do that?" They'd have a narrow window of confusion while the remaining Evers security and the Eleventh sorted themselves out.

"Okay. Where are we going?"

"The docks." If they could get into one of the boats, they could likely follow Evers wherever he was going. "Ready?"

He pressed dial and braced himself.

A breath later, a blast shook the house so hard even the bulletproof glass seemed to vibrate with the explosion.

Good-bye, Challenger.

"Come on." Aiden grabbed Madison's hand, pulling her after him.

The two men who were on the rocks were nowhere to be seen.

It was a thirty-yard dash to the docks down a flagstone path bordered by shrubs and flowers. Tire tread showed where at least one vehicle had swerved this far back.

An engine revved, coming closer.

"Faster," he shouted over his shoulder.

They reached the dock, bullets hitting the ground

where their feet had been. Aiden vaulted over the metal railing onto a small yacht. Madison jumped aboard and he pushed her ahead of him up into the cockpit.

"Keys!" Madison patted the dash and glanced around.

"Forget it." Aiden stared at the fuel levels. "It's not going anywhere."

"What do you mean?" She whirled to face him, her gaze a little wild, knife still in her hand.

"There's no fuel." He ducked his head and peered out of the tinted windows at the two men getting out of their cars. First, he had to get them out of there. Then, he could worry about what came next. This was a clusterfuck of epic proportions. "Stay here."

"What are you doing?"

"Getting us out of here."

It wasn't going to be a fair fight. The Eleventh was a gang. Guys who had no training, no knowledge of what they were doing and probably hadn't considered that their actions meant they could die. In comparison, Aiden couldn't count the number of people whose blood stained his hands. When it came down to Madison's life or theirs, Aiden would choose Madison.

The stairs to the deck were vulnerable, but once he hit the deck there was a bar that could provide cover from the land. It was a matter of how fast he could act.

"When I tell you, follow me, okay?" Aiden inhaled and drew upon the years spent as a soldier. It might not be a dusty Middle East village, but it was a war.

He bent, reaching as far down the rails as he could before swinging forward and letting himself drop to the deck in a crouch. The sound of men yelling in Spanish reached him. Footsteps hit the wooden dock.

Aiden rose slightly, keeping low, and aimed at the nearest gang member.

Them. Or Madison.

He squeezed the trigger and swung his gun toward the second before the first hit the ground. The second man held an assault rifle, his arms thrown out, center mass exposed. Aiden squeezed off two shots.

Killing never got easier. Especially when it was something this stupid. Drugs weren't worth dying over.

"Madison, come on," he shouted over his shoulder.

Would she come? Would she follow a man she now knew beyond a shadow of a doubt killed?

He jogged to the first body, but didn't pause to check for a pulse. The bullet through the cranial cavity made that unnecessary. The second had already drawn his last breath.

Aiden glanced back, dreading the prospect of having to force Madison from the boat. Instead, she edged past the first body, hand over her mouth. Of course he'd shocked her. He hated it, but it was the reality of his life.

He jogged to the Mazda Miata SSM two-seater idling closest to the docks and got in. The driver wouldn't be needing it anymore. Madison was only a few seconds behind him.

"Uh." She stared at the passenger side. The seat had been removed to make room for more NOS tanks.

"Get in." He shifted into drive.

"Okay, okay." She plopped down on top of the tanks, one hand braced on the dash, the other on his seat.

He pressed the accelerator, hating the high-pitched whine of the muffler as they built up speed. Madison bounced as they went over the uneven turf. They sailed past the other cars, who took them for their crew member. The debris of the Challenger was spread out in front of the house, one palm tree was pretty damaged and so was the front of the house. But, it had bought them time.

"Call Emery," Aiden said. They hit the street and he straightened the car out.

Madison almost slid into his lap, but held on tight to her handholds. There was only one way out of the community, and he needed to get there fast. The cops would be here any minute, and once they were on the scene there wouldn't be any getting out.

"I've got him," Emery said without preamble.

"Where?"

"I think he's headed to his accountant's house. The guy has water access and is only two miles away by water. He should be there any minute."

"What about the others?"

"Julian is behind you. Tori and John should be halfway there by now."

"Any chance Evers is going somewhere else?"

"There's no guarantee. It's just a guess."

"Address?" Aiden took a right out of the community and didn't slow his acceleration. The back of the car whipped around and the tires skidded. Madison almost slid straight into his lap.

"Texting now."

Aiden jabbed his Bluetooth, ending the call.

"Madison, get my phone. Right pocket. Call Detective Smith."

"What?"

"Just do it. And turn the navigation on."

She gripped the side of his seat. He lifted his ass enough for her to wiggle her hand into his pocket and pull out the slim phone. Without prompting, she tapped at the screen.

"Got it. Navigation?" She slid to the right and he swerved around a minivan.

"Yeah."

The disembodied voice of the navigation spoke into his ear, guiding him to their potential destination. If Evers went to the accountant, it wouldn't be for long. Maybe to pick up some crucial information and get a ride out of town. They'd have a short window.

"There. That should be Matt."

"Detective Smith," Matt drawled into the line.

"Smith, it's Aiden DeHart. If you want to arrest Michael Evers, do not hang up." If the FBI wasn't going to back them up, he'd at least use the police to do what they wouldn't. Legally, only Julian, Emery, CJ, and Kathy could make arrests since they were FBI agents.

"What? I'm heading to Evers's house now. What are you talking about, DeHart?"

"He's not there. I'm texting you an address. Be there. With backup."

"How do I know you're telling me the truth?"

"We've both been screwed over. I'm trying to make it right." He nodded at the phone. "Text him."

Silence met him on the line.

"Smith?"

"I'll be there. If you're lying to me—"

"I'm not."

The call ended. He'd have to trust the detective would show up or they'd be cruising with their asses out the window.

Aiden glanced at Madison. She held on to the handhold above her head, her feet were braced on the floorboard, and she gripped the back of his seat.

"You okay?" he asked.

"Can we talk about me later?" He hit a bump and she winced.

He could let her out somewhere to hide or let Kathy or CJ pick her up. They had to know what was going on by now. Except he didn't want to entrust Madison to anyone else, and neither did he want her out of his sight.

"Do you want me to stop?" He glanced at her. "I can stop and let the others go."

His sister was dead. Catching Evers might make him feel as though he'd done something to avenge her, but it wouldn't be enough. Nothing would ever be enough to bring her back.

"What? No. Go." Madison stared at him like she didn't recognize him. Well, that was two of them.

God, he loved her so much.

He should probably tell her before they drove into enemy fire, but the words stuck in the back of his throat. Even if they arrested Evers, she'd still have to go into hiding. She would be a key witness and her life in jeopardy. Forever. No matter what happened today, she still had to be safe.

Aiden checked his rearview. A cherry-red car swerved lanes, followed closely by two other cars he recognized and a couple he didn't.

Raibel Canales.

"Shit." Aiden shifted and flew through a light as it switched to red.

"Call Tori," he said.

The line only rang once.

"What?" Tori had none of her sister's calm behind the wheel.

"I need to lose them. Think you guys can keep Raibel busy?"

"What do you think we're doing? Go already," Tori snapped.

Aiden grinned and ended the call, swerving down a side street. He wove his way through smaller lanes, getting away from the road the others were taking. Shaking a tail was easy stuff, he just had to hope Raibel didn't tag his crew's cars like Aiden did.

"It's ringing," Madison said.

Aiden glanced at the screen.

Raibel Canales. The guy was a parasite Aiden couldn't shake.

He jabbed his headset. "What?"

"Where are you? I'm gonna kill you, DeHart." Raibel yelled into the line, any shred of humanity gone.

"Not today, Canales."

Aiden ended the call. Evers first, then Canales, if the cops didn't get him first.

The minutes ticked by. They took the least direct route to the accountant's house. By the time they turned into the subdivision with its palm tree–lined street, Aiden's teeth were on edge.

A black sports car caught his eye.

Aiden leaned forward and waited for the next cross street.

Sure enough, Julian kept pace with them one street over.

It was just the two of them. They'd done a dozen missions or so just like that.

"When we get here, stay in the car, keep the doors locked. If anyone comes out, especially if they're armed, drive off. Go to Classic Rides. Understand?"

"You're going in there by yourself? You can't do that. What about the cops?" Madison's gaze weighed on him.

"Julian will be there. I have no idea how long it'll take

the cops to get here." Chances were, they wouldn't be allowed to run with the sirens, just the lights, and law-abiding cops wouldn't drive like he did.

"Against how many? Four? Five? I don't like this, Aiden."

They weren't great odds, but there'd been worse.

The street was a dead end. The accountant's house was there, backed up to the water.

Aiden inhaled and shifted, pulling the parking brake and letting the car come to an abrupt halt. Julian was a beat behind him, and flew out of his car, gun up. Aiden's focus narrowed to the man frozen in the act of descending the stairs.

"Stop right there," Aiden yelled.

Michael Evers stood poised with a briefcase under one arm, his laptop in hand and a set of keys dangling from his fingers.

"On the ground, now," Julian bellowed.

Another figure filled the doorway. A thin man dressed in a tan suit and blue shirt held a six-shooter to the back of Evers's skull.

"Guns down." The accountant. "I'm more interested in my likelihood of getting out of here than preserving his life. I will shoot."

"Where're your guards?" Aiden asked.

Julian sidestepped to the left. The pristine yard was not the place anyone wanted to have a standoff with guns in hand, but here they were.

"I shot them," Evers said calmly.

There was no way to back that statement up, but it wasn't out of the realm of possibility.

"Guns down now, gentlemen. You want him alive more than I do." The accountant was a shark.

"You'd do us a favor killing him," Aiden said. Anything to draw the bean counter's attention to him. He might appear cool as a cucumber, but chances were, it was a bluff.

Tires squealed and the hair on the back of Aiden's neck rose. He dropped to a knee and quarter-turned, just enough to glimpse behind him. A red fucking car turned, following the same path Julian had. Raibel's arm extended out of his car.

Pop. Pop. Pop.

A man screamed.

The accountant went down and Evers tumbled into the bushes.

Julian stood and fired at the red car. One blast and another scream. The red car zipped around the cul-de-sac and sped away. Aiden didn't hesitate. He bolted forward, snatching Evers and rolling the man onto his back, holding him at gunpoint. Julian joined him, going to a knee next to the wounded accountant.

He could end this right now. Right here. For Madison. For Andrea. For Julian. For himself.

Chapter Twenty-Eight

"Aiden?" That voice sliced through the red haze that pushed him to squeeze the trigger. How hard would it be? Not that damn hard. "If you have to do it, I understand."

He needed to know Evers was gone. That he was out of all of their lives, but this wasn't his way.

Aiden knelt, pressing the muzzle of the gun against Evers's forehead. Evers didn't flinch, didn't show a drop of emotion. Aiden whispered for his ears alone, "If I were anything like you, you'd be a dead motherfucker, but I want to see you pay worse than I want you dead."

The sound of several engines heading in their direction put him more on edge. Friends? Or enemies?

"Madison, get back in the car."

Three cop cars and Smith's unmarked SUV screeched to a stop.

"You think the cops will make me pay?" Evers smirked. "You're an idiot. And I'm going to kill you."

"Yeah, just try it." Aiden shoved the gun in his waistband and glanced at Julian. The accountant was whimpering and whining. Clearly not dead. "Smith, come get your man."

"I'm going to kill her last," Evers whispered. "She'll know it was your fault."

Aiden hauled back and punched Evers, just like he'd wanted to a thousand times. The jackass flopped on the grass, groaning.

One of the cops pushed him aside, hand on his gun.

"Leave him," Smith barked. He planted a knee in Evers's back, spouting his Miranda rights, charging him with kidnapping. It was the most obvious charge to level at him first, since they had a living, breathing witness in Madison.

Aiden backed up and glanced inside the house. He could see two bodies lying in the living room, just like they'd been told. Madison came to his side and wrapped her arms around him.

"I thought I told you to get in the car," he said.

"I don't follow orders well." She squeezed him tight.

Together, they watched the cops load Evers into the back of a cruiser while the others administered first aid to the accountant. He'd live, but he wouldn't like it.

The whole moment was surreal.

The cops would take Evers into custody. From there, he'd be transferred to federal custody and if justice were served—spend the rest of his miserable life in prison.

It was over.

There was no joy, no sense of satisfaction. All it was, was another task scratched off the list. What he really wanted was to wrap his arms around the woman he loved and start a new day. But she was still in danger. More so now. As long as Evers breathed, he'd be a danger to her, to him, to everyone they loved.

Aiden wouldn't have another day with Madison.

* * *

Madison sat in the passenger seat of Julian's car. She wanted to ride with Aiden, but the cops gave him enough crap about the stolen car he was driving, they hadn't wanted her to chance riding in it.

Julian glanced at her. "You did good."

"I didn't do anything." Madison shrank against the door. He was Aiden's friend, but there was a coldness to Julian she didn't understand. "Where are we going?"

"The Shop."

Their private garage where all sorts of secret things happened.

"What happens now?" Madison asked.

"Depends."

"On . . . ?"

"On what the cops do. This is going to change everything." Despite what Madison would have assumed was a good thing, Julian didn't appear thrilled by the outcome. "You better lie low for a while. Cops are probably going to link you to this."

"W-what?" Madison stared at him. She should have figured, but for some reason it was still a shock.

"It's okay, we'll cover that sweet ass." Julian glanced her way and flashed a quick smile.

Madison slumped in her seat. Dustin was dead. It was too surreal. She'd wanted to be free of him, she'd never expected this. The drive to the warehouse was a blur of sharp turns, revving engine, and burned rubber. Madison couldn't focus her thoughts beyond shock.

Was she dreaming?

Before she knew it, Julian pulled into the warehouse. People were clustered inside, just out of sight. The car barely stopped before her door opened and Aiden was there, kneeling next to her.

She stared at him, maybe really seeing him for the first time.

He'd wanted to kill Evers today. Not that she blamed him. There'd been a thirst for blood in his eye, and for a moment—he hadn't been her Aiden. But he'd come back. In the blink of an eye, he was there.

Aiden rested his hand on her knee, squeezing it gently. The others huddled together. There was no sign of the cars they'd stolen from her airport, but the whole crew was there.

"Hey," Aiden said.

She leaned toward him and wrapped her arms around his neck, breathing easy for the first time in hours. His arms circled her, squeezing as he rested his head in the crook of her neck. Her chest shuddered and for a moment she thought she might cry.

She could have died today. They all could have died. And somehow, they were fine.

"Aiden—I'm so sorry," Madison said.

He pulled back a little, frowning at her. "For what?"

"For today. Everything."

"We survived. Come on." He took her hand and pulled her out of the car. "We're gone, guys," he said to his crew.

A few nodded, but most simply watched them leave.

Aiden led her out into the yard and unlocked a rather plain-looking sedan. He even held the door for her.

"Where are we going?" she asked, staring at the seat.

"Somewhere safe. You have to get out of Miami, right now. Please get in."

She couldn't argue with that. Madison sank into the seat, not too comforted by Aiden's statement. He closed the door, climbed into the driver's seat, and started the engine without another word. Madison stared at him, but there was nothing, no sign of the man she'd grown to love. Just a solid wall between them as he drove out onto the street.

"Aiden—where are you taking me?"

"Somewhere safe."

For some reason, she didn't trust him this time.

Aiden pulled onto the long, gravel lane that led to his grandmother's cabin. Though he made the trip only once a month, he knew every bit of the land like the back of his hand. Madison snoozed in her seat. Either she'd gotten the drift he wasn't answering questions or exhaustion had won over. He preferred the company of her sleeping form to the way she stared at him, as if she already knew he was about to betray her even further.

He turned into the drive of the cabin. The windows were all dark and nothing moved besides the wind in the trees. It would be nice to stay like this, quiet, peaceful, but he needed to roll out Madison's future, get her adjusted to the idea of never being Madison Haughton again.

Madison groaned in her sleep and sat up, blinking around them.

"Where are we?" she asked.

"My grandma's cabin."

"What are we doing here?" She perked up at that, peering around with more interest.

He opened and closed his mouth, the words sticking in his throat.

"Aiden?" She turned toward him.

"We're going to meet some FBI officials here tomorrow morning. They're going to take you into protective custody. Witness protection. At least until Evers's trial, but it might be permanent."

"What? Why?"

"It's too dangerous for you to be in Miami."

"No." She shook her head. "No way."

"Madison, just—listen to me."

She stared at him, but defiance was written all over her face.

"This is the only way," he said.

"No it isn't. It's the only way you want to see things." She popped her seat belt and pushed the door open.

Aiden ground his teeth together and climbed out of the car. Madison was halfway to the dock before he followed her. How could he send her away when he just wanted to keep her for himself? But he couldn't. She was a person. Not a car he could lock up in his barn. For her protection, he needed to stay away from her. There was something going on within the FBI, some reason why they'd been shut out like they had.

He approached her slowly, struggling for the right words to make her understand how much he needed her to go. To stay alive. To be happy somewhere else.

"You don't get it," she said before he'd spoken. "I just got my feet under me. I can't start over again, not on my own."

He had no argument for that. The FBI would set her up, but they weren't going to hold her hand through it.

"What about me?" he asked.

She turned toward him, her gaze slicing bone deep, but he didn't let it deter him.

"Just because Evers is behind bars doesn't mean it's over. There are still guys like Dustin out there who will be following his orders. Just 'cause your ex is dead, it doesn't mean some other lowlife won't crawl out to take his place. They'll be after me, you, all of us. The hardest part might be over, but we're not done yet. I can't focus on picking apart his organization if I don't know that you're safe. Madison, I need to know you're alive and breathing. I need you." He reached for her, wrapping his hands around hers. "I need you to be safe. Because . . . because I'm in love with you."

Madison's eyes widened.

That was not what he'd meant to say. . . .

"I'm not leaving." She shook her head. "Evers is in jail. It's over. You can try, you can send me away. I'm just coming back. I love you, Aiden. You can't get rid of me."

"You don't understand—"

"No, you don't get it."

"Madison, listen to me." He squeezed her hands. "Just because he's in jail doesn't mean you're safe. There's still people who will answer to him—"

"And you want to trust someone else to keep me safe?"

That was plain dirty.

Madison pulled her hands from his and looped her arms around his neck. He shouldn't let her twist him around like this, but he didn't want to send her away. He wanted to be near her, always.

"Aiden, you can't tell me you're in love with me and expect me to walk away," she said.

It was what he wanted to hear. Of course he wanted her with him. He wanted to think beyond the job, about a life and a future. There wasn't a way to make that happen, was there?

"I can't put you at risk like that."

"I'm not asking you to. Aiden, I'm willing to figure out a way to make this work, but only if you're going to fight to make it work too."

He couldn't let her go. He knew he should, but now that it was time—he pulled her closer. It wouldn't be an easy future, Madison was choosing a life where the future was uncertain.

"You move in with me. The boat isn't safe. Work at Classic Rides. Kathy hates pretending to do administrative work. Finish school." Those were his terms. If she wanted to be part of his life he had to be able to protect her.

"We can give the living together a trial," she countered.

"I have to know you're safe."

"I know." She slid her hands around to cup his face. "You've pushed your family away so they'd be safe. I have a pretty good idea what the risks are. I'm saying—let's give this thing a try. I've done everything wrong. I want to do this right."

"I'm a control freak, I get too many speeding tickets so my insurance is ridiculous, and I won't always be able to tell you where I've been."

"As long as I know you're one of the good guys, I can trust you. I . . . I love you, too."

Those words . . . He grinned as joy wrapped around them.

"I don't know how good I am." His thoughts where she was concerned weren't good at all. The things he wanted to do to her might just be illegal.

"I don't know about that. You're pretty good at some things." Her lips curled up into a sensual smile and his heart throbbed. He loved this woman, and he'd fight to keep her safe, to keep her in his life.

This was a pretty good week.

Epilogue

Two months later . . .

Madison fidgeted with the strap on her purse. Aiden pulled down the street, muttering numbers to himself. He stopped in front of a green bungalow, but it was the next-door house that had her attention.

105 Pickett Street.

Madison blew out a breath and turned toward Aiden.

"Is this a good idea?" she asked.

He shifted into park and faced her. "Did you change your mind?"

Aiden took her hand and lifted it to his lips. He kissed her knuckles and her heart melted. For all that she'd lost since meeting him, she'd gained even more.

"What if they're still mad at me?" she asked.

"Madison, it's your mom. She said she wanted to see you and that your sisters would be here."

"I know, but—what should we talk about?" Her life had changed in the last two months. She no longer lived on the boat or worked at the airport. Her relationship with Lily was broken. It would take a long time to fix. She'd left the airport and started working at Classic

Rides, under the watchful eye of the FBI. So really, her life had played right into Aiden's plans, not that she minded much.

"Roller derby and school are safe topics. Work—maybe mention you're taking over the books, but leave the Hoovers out of it. They're hard to explain."

"I wouldn't tell them that."

"Just—talk to them. Ask them what they've been doing."

"What are you going to do?" She squeezed his hands.

"I'll hang around."

"I know—say as little as possible, don't mention you, less I say the safer it is. Right?"

"You got it, babe." He leaned across and kissed her.

"Okay. I'm doing this." She looped her purse over her shoulder and pushed the door open.

"They're going to love you. Just like I do."

She paused, glancing over her shoulder, smiling at Aiden.

"I love you," she said, relishing the rush she got every time she said it.

"I love you, too. Now, get out of my car." He swatted her bottom as she got out.

Madison pushed her shoulders back and strode down the walk, turning through the gate. The house was cute, with flower beds and toys strewn in the yard. Did one of her sisters have children? She'd missed so much, but she wouldn't change anything. Without Dustin and their divorce, she'd never have met Aiden. Their lives would never be normal, but they wouldn't lack for excitement.

The front door opened before she'd made it halfway to the door. Her mother had aged, there was silver in her shoulder-length brown hair, and she'd lost some weight. Her mother paused, mouth open, eyes wide.

Tears sprang to Madison's eyes and all she wanted was to hug her mother.

"Madison?"

"Hi, Mom."

"Oh, Madison!" Her mother rushed down the stairs. Madison met her at the bottom, wrapping her in a tight hug.

"Is she here?" someone said from inside.

"Come here, girls," her mother yelled.

Madison's sisters and two toddlers spilled out of the house, enveloping her in hugs and tears. The only thing missing from the perfect picture was Aiden. But there was a price to pay for their love. Someday, she'd be able to bring him home, but today was her homecoming.

Aiden watched Madison's joyful reunion with one eye, and his rearview mirror with the other. There wasn't a threat—yet. Between his crew's vigilance and the good will of the police department, they'd been looked after, but that would change someday. The Haughtons slowly wandered inside, Madison weighted down with two kids before she'd hit the front door. She had a good family, and someday, he hoped to make amends with his the way she was, but for now, he'd live vicariously through her.

He pulled out his cell phone and dialed the one number he only called once a month. It rang several times before an older woman said, "Hello?"

"Hey, Grandma." Aiden smiled.

"Hey, I haven't heard from you in a while. Missed you the last few months."

"I know, things have been busy."

"You mean dangerous." His grandmother didn't

know the scope of what he did, but she knew enough, and she knew him.

"A little."

"You doing okay?"

"Yeah. I was wondering what you were doing next weekend."

"Fishing, probably."

"Think you could do with some company? There's someone I'd like for you to meet." Madison was his future. She'd filled a hole inside of him.

"I could be talked into that. Do I need to make up a bed?"

"No, ma'am. We'll be fine in the guest room."

"It's that kind of someone, now is it? Shoot. Must be someone special."

"She is, Grandma."

"Oh hell, the plumber is here. I've got to go. Bring another fishing pole."

He didn't think Madison would catch much. She talked too loud, but he wouldn't have her any other way.

Aiden hung up the phone and laced his hands together behind his head, settling in for a long wait. But it wasn't anything compared to how long he'd waited to have her in his life. What was an hour or so to forever with her?

Keep reading for a special sneak peek
at the next Hot Rides novel,

SHIFT,

coming in August 2016!

*Nothing shines like classic cars under the Miami heat.
With engines revving hot and emotions running high,
sparks are sure to fly. . . .*

Tori Chazov isn't exactly the girl next door. For one, if the neighbors found out she's an FBI asset and the daughter of a KGB defector, she'd have to grab her go bag and run. Then there's her day job: making magic happen under the hood of big beautiful muscle cars. She's more likely to be wearing engine grease than mascara, and most guys don't fantasize about their mechanics.

But then most girls don't fantasize about FBI tech geniuses, either, and Tori has it bad for Emery Martin. Emery has a past. She can see it in the way he keeps his body honed like a weapon, in the mysterious scars under his snap-button shirts. She can see it in the way his eyes follow her around the room, even though he never says a word.

He's going to have to start talking now, though. A vicious Russian hit squad is on the way to Miami to take Tori out for good. And without Emery's help, she might not make her last great escape. . . .

Some operations he could see unfold before the first move ever happened.

Emery Martin watched the little drama unfold across the street where two Iranian jewel thieves were no doubt pissing their pants, surrounded by six federal agents. Emery sipped his martini, but he couldn't enjoy the taste. He hadn't been able to think about anything since his last conversation with the frightened thieves.

The Russians are sending someone to Miami for a hit. It's not us. Word is it's some old grudge, but we don't want to be anywhere nearby when that goes down.

There were only two people in Miami the Russian mob might want to take out badly enough to send a hit team after them instead of hiring some dime-bag thug.

The Chazov twins.

Tori.

Emery fired off a quick text to the arresting agent. He'd struck a deal when the case agent came to him with a gig outside of Emery's current operation. Emery would work his regular, high-end document forgery angle, keeping the thieves stateside long enough to get a warrant, and the Feds would allow Emery first crack at them. It was time for the suit to live up to his part of the bargain.

Though Emery was employed by the FBI as an agent and field tech, his role was much more elaborate. Deep cover. He leveraged his ruined reputation and embellished criminal past to create a persona that fit the FBI's needs, while he got to work for the good guys and pull in a paycheck that didn't leave him hating the air he breathed. It was a deal that worked.

His phone buzzed with an incoming text.

Alley.

It wasn't an ideal location, but he needed to know for sure why an assassin team was coming to Miami.

Emery kept his head down, slipping out the back door of the club and into the alley. No one would comment about him making a clandestine exit. After all, everyone knew Emery was a money launderer and go-to guy when the needs were high-tech. Too bad the majority of his customers wound up in jail or passing on merchandise that was bugged by Uncle Sam.

An unmarked van idled at the end of the alleyway. He kept close to the brick wall, eyeing the van. A man stepped out of it, closing the door quickly behind him. The yellow FBI letters were emblazoned across the back of his bulletproof vest.

"Seriously? Are you trying to make me?" Emery glanced from the vest to the arresting agent. The last thing he needed was for someone to link him to the FBI.

The agent ignored his protest. "They said someone's coming to do a hit on some girls. That's all they know."

"They—who? He mentioned a hit team." Emery

jerked his head toward the van. He'd learned a few things while stalling the thieves. Like all the lowlifes in Miami were suddenly finding somewhere else to be for the foreseeable future.

"Doesn't know who. Just that it's the Russians sending them. Got to get them to lockup." The agent thumbed toward the van with one hand and held out the other.

Emery shook it, trying not to grimace.

"Thanks again."

"Don't mention it," Emery replied. He stepped back, keeping to the shadows, and put as much distance between him and the van as he could.

Assassins in Miami.

That was the last thing he needed.

He paused at the end of the alley and watched the van pull out onto the street. It merged with the evening traffic, blending in seamlessly. He was already mentally sorting the who's who of the Russian mafia in the States. He'd made it a private study to know each and every face, their record and family vendettas. The FBI wouldn't appreciate his recreational uses of their intelligence, but he couldn't find it in him to care. Not where she was concerned.

Tori Chazov.

She was his every temptation. The one bright spot in dark days strung together in a blur of surveillance and counterintelligence. Emery's life was a twisted mess, but hers made his appear to have been a cakewalk. Tori and her twin, Roni, were the daughters of a KGB spy turned American informant almost thirty years ago. Their old man was dead, but the girls were still kicking. They were also part of his undercover FBI team, pretending to be nothing more than talented mechanics at Classic Rides, a garage that specialized in muscle car restoration.

Though Emery had never been tasked to keep an eye out for those who still had a beef with the Chazov family, he did it for Tori. Not that she knew, or would even appreciate his vigilance, but it made it easier for him to sleep—when he could manage to close his eyes, which wasn't very often lately.

He turned the corner and strode through the alley, heading toward the valet lot where he'd left his ride. If something bad of the Russian variety was coming to town, it couldn't be good for Tori or her twin sister, even if they weren't the intended targets, which he found unlikely. There was no connection between the mob and the criminal organization they were stalking. None at all. There wasn't even a Russian presence in Miami to speak of. So why now? What were they after?

He needed to set scans to run all TSA screenings against his database, which was on top of his current mammoth workload.

Three months ago, he'd thought they were finally in the clear, that their primary objective was completed and the job done. The whole purpose of their team setting up in Miami was to take down the kingpin of the biggest drug ring in south Florida, which they'd done without harming a single civilian. Except their target, Michael Evers, was still in police custody. Not rotting in a federal penitentiary. And there were no new marching orders. Add to it a rival car gang who wanted to see Emery's crew dead, and he'd spent more time lately watching his rearview mirror than the road ahead of him.

"Shit," he muttered.

He hovered in the alley as two patrol officers and a man in a polo shirt and slacks walked around Emery's Tesla Roadster. The hundred-thousand-dollar car was a hand-me-down from a government bust meant to bolster his street cred. Too bad it also made him stick out at the least opportune times.

Emery sucked in a deep breath. He wasn't a people person, preferring his bank of computer monitors to actually dealing with the living. The last person he wanted to interface with was Detective Matt Smith. The cop had kept his distance after Aiden brought him in to make the arrest on Michael Evers. What was more, Matt Smith knew their secret and hadn't shared it to Emery's knowledge. At least Matt hadn't e-mailed, texted, or chatted about it. To cover their asses, Emery had hacked the good detective's accounts and set up a program to record every keystroke. Matt Smith hadn't so much as run a search on any of them.

That was a lie.

Matt had looked up Roni's record once, but nothing came of it. Emery had ensured the girls had nothing out of the ordinary in their public files. Still, it was curious.

Emery pulled out his phone and activated the app that connected to the car. The electric vehicle had almost a full charge and it didn't appear that the good detective had attempted to tamper with the vehicle. Good for both of them. Emery had somewhere to be. Too bad it didn't appear as though Matt was going anywhere.

"Can I help you, officers?" Emery strolled toward the trio and one nervous valet, hands at his side.

Detective Smith stood at the front of the car, hands on his hips. He'd pushed his sunglasses up on his brow, messing up his perfectly gelled blond hair. Aiden had nicknamed the cop Golden Boy, which was fitting. To Emery's knowledge, Matt colored inside the lines.

"You wear something besides your grandpa's clothes?" Detective Smith smirked.

Emery stared at the officer. He'd heard every variety of insult in his life. Picking on his clothes was about as boring as it got. Besides, the clothes were designer—some name brand all the South Beach hotshots were wearing. Yeah, it looked ridiculous, but it also helped his high-rolling, go-to-guy image.

"What do you want?" he asked.

"Checking on a stolen car report. Running serial numbers, is all."

Was this some kind of code? Did Smith want to talk? Then why bring the uniforms? Only an idiot would think the Tesla was stolen.

"Where's DeHart?" Smith asked.

"I believe he has a date tonight, so you'll have to get in line for your good-night kiss." For a couple months, before their crew got involved, Matt had tried to shield a woman named Madison Haughton from her ex-husband, one of Michael Evers's fall guys. Emery, like many others, had suspected the detective of being sweet on Madison, but Smith wasn't her type. She'd moved in with Aiden DeHart and had all but taken his last name in the intervening three months.

Matt stalked around the car and got up in Emery's face. The detective was about the same height, but Emery was willing to bet the good ol' cop would go down easy. That was the problem. Cops had to fight fair, while Emery fought to survive. He'd had plenty of practice and had managed to keep most of his skin, while he was willing to bet Matt had only ever suffered scraped knuckles and a black eye.

"I need to talk to DeHart," Matt said, pitching his voice low.

That was it?

Something had to be up if the detective couldn't just ring the garage, but this wasn't the place to talk about it. First the Feds, now the cops, there was far too much brass in this part of Miami tonight for Emery's tastes.

"We'll be in touch." Emery pitched his voice louder, so the uniforms heard. "Unless you have something of worth to the public of Miami to say to me, get away from my car."

Matt glanced down. "That knee of yours is looking a little tight. Bothering you?"

Fuck you.

Emery didn't say it, but he sure as hell tightened his right hand into a fist. Matt had to be digging on a device that Emery hadn't hacked yet if he knew about Emery's knee injury. Instead, he gestured to the valet who produced his key fob.

"Don't let me catch you sniffing around my car again, Detective. You won't like the consequences." Emery would have to dig around on the detective a bit more. Truth was, they could use him. Especially if Smith could tell them why Evers wasn't in federal custody.

Something wasn't right, and Emery had to get to the bottom of it all before shit hit the fan. His team relied on him to head off or warn them about possible threats.

He dropped into the Tesla and slid his phone onto the cradle. The engine hummed to life, barely noticeable compared to the noise other cars made. The suit jacket and button-up shirt were stifling, but he didn't have time to shed them. The cruiser backed off, giving Emery enough room to burn a little rubber as he left the lot. The cops didn't make any move to tail him, but he still kept an eye on his six.

Unlike the rest of Emery's crew, he worked away from the garage and cars in a fortress of solitude and servers.

Not many knew he was connected to the mechanics at Classic Rides, and he liked it that way. It gave him the freedom to perform tasks the others couldn't. Which meant it was probably easiest for Matt to approach him rather than the others without drawing notice.

The on-board computer muted the music as the clatter of an old-timey phone rang through the speakers.

"Incoming call from, Tori," the mechanical voice announced.

His pulse jumped. Were the Russians here already?

"Answer," Emery said.

The car's system beeped, activating the call. He tapped the steering wheel and consciously decreased the pressure on the accelerator.

"Tori?"

"Hey, are you at home?" Grease. Laughter. Mint gum. Torn coveralls. A hundred little details about her he'd catalogued flitted through his brain. There was a new one to add to his list. Strain. Her voice didn't contain any of the sunshine it usually did.

"No. I'm headed there. What's up?" Screw it. He accelerated, cutting in front of an eighteen-wheeler and turning onto a side street, then onto another two-lane road, zigzagging his way through the heart of Miami.

"I just . . ." She sighed. "Roni's going to the Orlando Race Battle with the others."

"Oh."

He scrambled to recall the discussion they'd had about the merits of the trip in their last get-together at The Shop, a warehouse they'd outfitted for their less-than-legal operations. On one hand, the crew had a lot of targets on their back and dividing the team for an upstate race was leaving them handicapped in Miami. On the other, the rogue Eleventh Street crew's leader might not be able to help showing up and burning rubber, giving them an excellent opportunity to bust his ass.

A serious point of contention was Roni, Tori's sister. Not only did the Eleventh and Evers want her dead, but she'd bled all over a crime scene. The cops hadn't connected her to it—yet—but they would eventually. Having Smith in their corner would be handy to know what was rolling down the hill at them, but until tonight they'd kept their distance. Add to it there might be some extra heat from the Russians and he wasn't sure the race was a good place for Tori's sister.

"What do you want me to do?" Short of murder, there wasn't much he wouldn't do for Tori. It was a new, sad state of his obsession that he realized just how far he was willing to go.

"Can you keep a tracker on her?"

"I already track everyone through cell phones and the GPS in your cars." Did Tori know? His other sad, sick fascination was pulling up her location on an auxiliary screen while he worked and watching her red dot blink, teasing him with all the things she might be doing.

"No, I mean, something she wouldn't take off or intentionally disengage."

So Tori knew. Had she given him the shake before?

Emery checked his rearview mirror. He'd hit a quieter side street and the only lights behind him were overhead. Coast was clear. He pressed the accelerator, kicking up his speed.

"What do you have in mind?" Tori had a way of leading people into her plans. Smart, because she wasn't seen as the instigator. The others never noticed, and truth was, Tori had a sharp mind for strategy, but she wouldn't play those tricks on him.

"Roni broke the clasp on her necklace. I picked it up and was thinking . . . could you do something with it?"

"Not sure. I'd need to see it." He could picture the necklace in detail—both twins wore them. Gold chain, nothing too fancy, with a locket smaller than a dime and a charm featuring one of her saints. He'd never figured out which one of the Orthodox figures it was because he rarely allowed himself to get that close.

It was one thing to admire Tori, to be conscious of her movements, but he'd drawn the line at seeking her nearness. Girls like her didn't exactly date the resident geek.

"Well . . . that's what I called about. I was kind of hoping you were home, but I guess you're out tonight."

"Where are you, Tori?"

"Your house."

He glanced at the phone, itching to pull up her location via the tracking app he'd created for their team. She was at his house? Tori knew where he lived? The only team members who'd been inside his house were CJ, Kathy, Julian, and Aiden. The rest more or less ignored him unless something was broken or they needed a bit of tech.

"I'll be there in fifteen. There's a gate to the left of the house, go through it and wait on the patio."

"Yes, sir." She chuckled and he could hear the squeak of the gate. "I knew you lived in a nice area, but I don't think I realized how fancy it was."

The house was another government seizure they'd handed down to him. From the paint to the knick-knacks, even some of the photographs, it wasn't his. He might sleep and eat there, but the house would never bare his thumbprint.

"Man, we need to have pool parties at your place."

"Anytime." The pool and the converted shed were the only features he made regular use of. What would it be like to take a break from work, go out by the pool, and find Tori sunbathing?

It was temptation. The likes of which he didn't need.